Leif Enger is thirty-nine ~~and lives~~ with his wife and two yo~~ung children~~ in Minnesota. *Peace like a Ri~~ver~~* is his first novel.

11/10

PEACE LIKE A RIVER

Leif Enger

BLACK SWAN

PEACE LIKE A RIVER
A BLACK SWAN BOOK : 0 552 99935 0

Originally published in Great Britain by Doubleday,
a division of Transworld Publishers

PRINTING HISTORY
Doubleday edition published 2001
Black Swan edition published 2002

1 3 5 7 9 10 8 6 4 2

Set in 11/12pt Melior by
Falcon Oast Graphic Art Ltd.

Black Swan Books are published by Transworld Publishers,
61–63 Uxbridge Road, London W5 5SA,
a division of The Random House Group Ltd,
in Australia by Random House Australia (Pty) Ltd,
20 Alfred Street, Milsons Point, Sydney, NSW 2061, Australia,
in New Zealand by Random House New Zealand Ltd,
18 Poland Road, Glenfield, Auckland 10, New Zealand
and in South Africa by Random House (Pty) Ltd,
Endulini, 5a Jubilee Road, Parktown 2193, South Africa.

Printed and bound in Great Britain by
Clays Ltd, St Ives plc.

To Robin

The country ahead is as wild a spread
As ever we're likely to see

The horses are dancing to start the advance –
Won't you ride on with me?

Clay

From my first breath in this world, all I wanted was a good set of lungs and the air to fill them with – given circumstances, you might presume, for an American baby of the twentieth century. Think about your own first gasp: a shocking wind roweling so easily down your throat, and you still slipping around in the doctor's hands. How you yowled! Not a thing on your mind but breakfast, and that was on the way.

When I was born to Helen and Jeremiah Land, in 1951, my lungs refused to kick in.

My father wasn't in the delivery room or even in the building; the halls of Wilson Hospital were close and short, and Dad had gone out to pace in the damp September wind. He was praying, rounding the block for the fifth time, when the air quickened. He opened his eyes and discovered he was running – sprinting across the grass toward the door.

'How'd you know?' I adored this story, made him tell it all the time.

'God told me you were in trouble.'

'Out loud? Did you hear Him?'

'Nope, not out loud. But He made me run, Reuben. I guess I figured it out on the way.'

I had, in fact, been delivered some minutes before.

My mother was dazed, propped against soggy pillows, unable to comprehend what Dr Animas Nokes was telling her.

'He still isn't breathing, Mrs Land.'

'Give him to me!'

To this day I'm glad Dr Nokes did not hand me over on demand. Tired as my mother was, who knows when she would've noticed? Instead he laid me down and rubbed me hard with a towel. He pounded my back; he rolled me over and massaged my chest. He breathed air into my mouth and nose – my chest rose, fell with a raspy whine, stayed fallen. Years later Dr Nokes would tell my brother Davy that my delivery still disturbed his sleep. He'd never seen a child with such swampy lungs.

When Dad skidded into the room, Dr Nokes was sitting on the side of the bed holding my mother's hand. She was wailing – I picture her as an old woman here, which is funny, since I was never to see her as one – and old Nokes was attempting to ease her grief. It was unavoidable, he was saying; nothing could be done; perhaps it was for the best.

I was lying uncovered on a metal table across the room.

Dad lifted me gently. I was very clean from all that rubbing, and I was gray and beginning to cool. A little clay boy is what I was.

'Breathe,' Dad said.

I lay in his arms.

Dr Nokes said, 'Jeremiah, it has been twelve minutes.'

'Breathe!' The picture I see is of Dad, brown hair short and wild, giving this order as if he expected nothing but obedience.

Dr Nokes approached him. 'Jeremiah. There would be brain damage now. His lungs can't fill.'

Dad leaned down, laid me back on the table, took off his jacket and wrapped me in it – a black canvas jacket

8

with a quilted lining, I have it still. He left my face uncovered.

'Sometimes,' said Dr Nokes, 'there is something unworkable in one of the organs. A ventricle that won't pump correctly. A liver that poisons the blood.' Dr Nokes was a kindly and reasonable man. 'Lungs that can't expand to take in air. In these cases,' said Dr Nokes, 'we must trust in the Almighty to do what is best.' At which Dad stepped across and smote Dr Nokes with a right hand, so that the doctor went down and lay on his side with his pupils unfocused. As Mother cried out, Dad turned back to me, a clay child wrapped in a canvas coat, and said in a normal voice, 'Reuben Land, in the name of the living God I am telling you to breathe.'

The truth is, I didn't think much on this until a dozen years later – beyond, of course, savoring the fact that I'd begun life in a dangerous and thus romantic manner. When you are seven years old there's nothing as lovely and tragic as telling your friends you were just about dead once. It made Dad my hero, as you might expect, won him my forgiveness for anything that he might do forever; but until later events it didn't occur to me to wonder just why I was allowed, after all, to breathe and keep breathing.

The answer, it seems to me now, lies in the miracles.

Let me say something about that word: miracle. For too long it's been used to characterize things or events that, though pleasant, are entirely normal. Peeping chicks at Easter time, spring generally, a clear sunrise after an overcast week – a *miracle*, people say, as if they've been educated from greeting cards. I'm sorry, but nope. Such things are worth our notice every day of the week, but to call them miracles evaporates the strength of the word.

Real miracles bother people, like strange sudden pains unknown in medical literature. It's true: they

9

rebut every rule all we good citizens take comfort in. Lazarus obeying orders and climbing up out of the grave – now there's a miracle, and you can bet it upset a lot of folks who were standing around at the time. When a person dies, the earth is generally unwilling to cough him back up. A miracle contradicts the will of earth.

My sister, Swede, who often sees to the nub, offered this: people fear miracles because they fear being changed – though ignoring them will change you also. Swede said another thing, too, and it rang in me like a bell: no miracle happens without a witness. Someone to declare, Here's what I saw. Here's how it went. Make of it what you will.

The fact is, the miracles that sometimes flowed from my father's fingertips had few witnesses but me. Yes, enough people saw enough strange things that Dad became the subject of a kind of misspoken folklore in our town, but most ignored the miracles as they ignored Dad himself.

I believe I was preserved, through those twelve airless minutes, in order to be a witness, and as a witness, let me say that a miracle is no cute thing but more like the swing of a sword.

If he were here to begin the account, I believe Dad would say what he said to Swede and me on the worst night of all our lives:

We and the world, my children, will always be at war.

Retreat is impossible.

Arm yourselves.

His Separate Shadow

I now think of my survival as my father's first miracle. Dr Nokes himself named the event miraculous once he woke up and washed his face and remembered who he was.

The second, I suppose, is that the doctor turned out wrong about the brain damage. I'm happy to say none surfaced until I entered tenth grade and signed up for Plane Geometry; but since I can still feed myself and grind out a sentence in English, you won't hear me complain.

Dad's third miracle – and one of the most startling, if not consequential – happened in the middle of the night, in the middle of North Dakota, just after I turned eleven.

It was the trip I shot my first goose, a medium-sized snow. We were staying at August Shultz's place, four hours west onto the Great Plains, hunting near the homestead Dad grew up on and still quietly longed for. The goose was a joyous occasion, and for a while we could all speak to each other again. That is, Dad and Davy could speak again – Swede and I rarely quarreled, for I never held opinions in those days, and hers were never wrong.

I do remember that the tension in the car, going out,

was so potent I fell asleep as soon as I was able. A veteran bystander to hard moments, I knew they went by quicker when you were unconscious. Davy was sixteen then, a man as far as I was concerned, with a driver's license and a knockout four-inch scar down his right forearm and Dad's own iron in his spine. That night they sat in the front seat of the Plymouth, green-gilled from the dashlights, not speaking at all.

We were late getting started, as happened often, because Dad had to lock up the school after the football game. Swede and I yawned in the back seat, boxes of shotgun shells stacked at our feet. The sky spat ice and water. It rode up on the windshield, and from time to time Dad pulled over so Davy could jump out and scrape it off. That Plymouth had a worthless heater. Swede and I rode cocooned in gray army blankets and stocking caps, the two of us scratchy as horsehair. Twenty miles into the trip she slipped off her rubber boots; then I felt her toes creep up against my hip. Oh, but they were cold. I pulled them into my lap and rubbed them while up front Davy opened a thermos, poured coffee into the lid, and without looking at Dad handed it over.

Still not a word between them. The road beat backward under us. In a few minutes Swede's toes felt warm and she was breathing evenly through her nose. I kept my hands tented over her feet, pigeon-toed there in my lap, laid my head back against the seat, and slipped away as well.

Before dawn we settled among decoys in one of August's barley fields. Dad and Swede lay on their elbows side by side, the two of them whispering under a swath. Davy and I took the opposite flank, he with his clawed-up Winchester goose gun. I was too young to shoot, of course, and so was Swede; we were there purely, as she said, 'for seasoning.' In all the years since I don't remember a colder morning afield. Rain can outfreeze snow. We lay between soaked ground and soaked swaths with a December-smelling wind coming over our backs. As the sky lightened we heard geese chuckling on the refuge away to the east. The rag decoys puffed and fluttered. I yawned once, then again so hard my ears crackled.

Davy said, 'Don't go to sleep on me now, buddy.'

He could say it; he wasn't cold. Though his gloves were nothing but yellow cotton, he could handle an icy shotgun in evident comfort. I had on his outgrown leather mitts with two pair of wool liners, yet my fingers were clenched and bloodless. It seemed to get colder as the day came on. When Davy said, softly, 'Old Rube, I could live out here, couldn't you?' I was too frozen to tell him yes.

Minutes later I woke: Davy was poking me in the side. Finger to his lips, he nodded east. A lone snow goose was approaching, fighting the wind, making low questioning honks at our flock of rags. I put my face against the ground, trying not to move – a goose is an easy bird to spook. The loner's honks got louder and more confident as it decided to land for breakfast. It was utterly fooled. I'd actually started feeling sorry for the doomed bird when Davy grabbed my shoulder and spun me so I lay on my back. He jammed the Winchester into my hands.

'Take him, Rube.'

The goose was straight overhead. Not twenty feet high! I flung off a mitten and tried to aim. The gun was way too big but I balanced it out there and yanked the trigger. Nothing happened – something was stuck – then Davy's hand zipped out and clicked the safety off. The goose was just beyond us but still so close I could hear its panting wings. I yanked again, shot wild, and the recoil slammed my shoulder into the mud. My ears rang high and clear, and the goose finally understood and tilted off to the left while I pumped another shell into the chamber and fired again. The goose still didn't fold but caught the wind and sailed over the barley like a kite. Tears were in my eyes – I'd missed two easy shots and wasted Davy's present to me. Blind with despair I fired again. The goose had to be out of range; yet somehow it shuddered, went graceless, and made a controlled fall to the ground some eighty yards away. 'You did it,' Davy said. 'Good shot – you took him the hard way, buddy. Better go finish him.'

But as I handed him the gun, almost sobbing with relief, Swede streaked past in her corduroy coat yelling, 'I'll get 'im, I'll get 'im!' and Davy said, 'Aw, let her chase the old bird down,' so I watched her go, yellow hair bouncing behind her stocking cap.

Downfield, though, the goose seemed to have recovered its wits. It stood upright, taking stock, its head so high and perky I feared it might take off and fly after all. When it saw Swede coming it turned and sprinted away.

I'm telling you that goose could run.

Seeing this Swede lowered her head and went full steam, mud and chaff raining off her bootsoles. Dad started laughing, whipping off his cap and whacking it on his leg, while the goose stretched out its neck and bolted across the barley. Reaching the end of the field it encountered a barbwire fence. It stopped and turned as Swede closed in.

Did you ever see an angry goose up close? It's a different bird from those you've watched flying south or waddling in city parks. An adult goose in a wrathful mood can stand up and look a third-grader right in the eye, and that's what this fellow did to Swede. She got within a yard and stopped cold. She'd seen Dad wring a few goose necks and understood the technique, but those had been badly wounded, pathetic creatures – they'd seemed almost grateful to get it done with. This goose still owned its spirit. Later Swede told me she felt numb, standing there with her hand out; the goose had one blind, clouded eye, plenty eerie in itself, but Swede said the good eye was worse. She looked into that good eye and saw a decision being reached.

'It decided to kill me,' she said.

From where we stood, though, all we saw was the goose raise its wings and poke its beak at Swede. She spun, slipped to one knee, then was up and shutting the distance between us. The terrifying part, for her, must've been glancing back and seeing that goose coming after her just as hard as it could, wings spread, its black beak pointed at her rump. Dad was laughing so hard he was bent clear over and finally had to sit down on a gunnysack wiping his eyes. Swede led the bird straight toward us, and when she pounded past, Davy leaned over and snagged it just behind the head. A quick twist and he handed it to me, wings quivering. He grinned. 'All yours, Natty' – after Natty Bumppo, Mr Fenimore's matchless hunter. It was a heavy goose. I realized I was warm, standing there with my mitts off, even hot. I held my goose with one hand and Davy's Winchester in the other, smelling gunpowder and warm bird, feeling something brand-new and liking it quite a bit. Swede, though, was crying, her face in Dad's belly, even while he laughed helplessly on.

Swede felt bad about that goose for a long time. For an eight-year-old girl she put enormous stock in courage. To be routed across a barley field by an incensed goose gave her doubts about her character.

'He's really a big one, look at him,' I said, once we were back at August's farm doing the job you might expect; behind the barn was a hand pump and an old door set across a stock tank for a cleaning table.

Davy was whetting the blade of his hunting knife, a bone-handled Schrade. He said, 'You want me to show you how?'

'I shot him, I'll clean him.' I had no urge to actually

gut the bird, but I was eleven and a hunter now – a man just beginning his span of pride.

He gave me the knife, handle first. 'Don't forget to thumb out the gizzard. We don't want sandy gravy, uh?'

As he strode away I noticed how the clouds had racked up, thick and low, and how the light was going though it wasn't yet noon. Maybe this affected me, or maybe it was just the thought of cleaning that goose by myself, but I sure wanted Davy to stay.

'I'll save out the heart for you,' I called after him, and he turned and smiled, then climbed a low ridge of cottonwood and willow brush and disappeared.

I had, of all things, a lump in my throat. Luckily Swede was standing at my elbow and said, 'First thing, you have to cut his head off.'

'Well, I know that.'

She prodded the goose with her finger; plucked, it looked pimply and regretful.

'Then the wings,' she said.

'You want to clean him?'

Swede let it go and stepped over to the ruins of a grain truck that had been parked behind the barn to rot. She shinnied up the big rumplike fender and sat there with the wind tugging her hair. It was a cutting wind; the light was leaking from a mottled yellow sky. Imagine a sick child all jaundiced and dirty about the cheeks – that's how the sky looked. I picked up Davy's knife and tried it against my thumb, then beheaded the snow.

Watching, Swede said, 'Forgive me running, Rube?'

'What?'

'I ran away.'

'From the goose? Swede, it wasn't any big deal.' I tossed the head into a cardboard box we'd found in the barn and went to work on the wings. They came off a lot harder than the head; I had to saw the knife blade back and forth.

'Come on, forgive me,' she insisted.

I nodded, but said nothing. Those wings were gristly fellows.

'Out loud,' she said.

She was the most resolute penitent I ever saw. 'Swede, I forgive you. Is it all right now?'

She hugged her elbows. 'Thanks, Reuben – can I have the feet?'

I whacked them off at a chop apiece and tossed them up to the truck. Swede caught them and scrambled over to the grainbed. My hands were freezing and I dreaded the next part – I ought to've taken Davy's offer to clean the goose. Aiming at a spot under the breastbone, I plunged in.

'Swede,' I said – just talking so she'd stay with me – 'I don't get what's wrong with Davy.'

She didn't answer right away. She sat on the flatbed toying with the goose feet. She took so long to speak I got involved in a tangle of guts and forgot I'd said anything.

Finally she said, 'He's mad about Dolly.'

'Oh.' Davy's girlfriend. 'How come?'

She looked at me. 'You heard,' she said. 'Last night, driving over.'

We'd gotten a late start, as I mentioned. The football team had been busy getting whomped; it was almost eleven before we got on the road.

'I was sleeping.'

'You were faking, I could tell. Just like me.'

We heard the screen door open, up at the house. 'Pancakes in five minutes!' Dad hollered. The screen slapped shut.

'Really, I was asleep – I swear it, Swede.'

'Israel Finch and Tommy Basca had Dolly in the girls' locker room.'

'What – how come?' Two boys had gone into the girls' locker room? You wouldn't have caught me in any girls' locker room. I might even have snickered, if it weren't for the look on Swede's face.

17

'They beat her up, Reuben. During the football game. Dad caught 'em.'

It was only then that the names sunk in: *Israel Finch*, *Tommy Basca*. I shrunk up inside my coat. 'How bad, Swede?'

'She's okay, I guess. I heard Dad say he got there *in time*.'

'What, did he chase 'em off? Did he fight 'em?'

'I don't know. He wouldn't talk about it to Davy.'

'Dolly's all right, though?'

'I guess so.' Swede, a goose foot in each hand, made them walk daintily along the edge of the flatbed.

'Then why's Davy mad? Wasn't he happy Dad caught those guys?' I didn't even want to say their names aloud.

'I don't know. Ask Davy if you want.'

I wasn't sure I could do that. Though there were only five years between Davy and me, lately they'd seemed a weighty five. At times it felt like he was Dad's brother instead of mine.

Finishing the goose I held it under the pump until water surged clean from the cavity, then went up to the house with Swede. On the way she showed me how by pulling a tendon she could make a goose foot contract and relax. She made the foot into a tight goose fist and said, 'Youuuu dirty raaaaat!' For a kid sister she did a very adequate Cagney.

We hunted again that afternoon, under skies so cold frost paisleyed the gunbarrels. Davy had missed the pancakes, but Dad had served them up merrily to Swede and me and not commented on Davy's absence; then he stoked the woodstove and the three of us went to our rooms to snooze. That's how goose-hunting is – you rise early and do the cold, thrilling work; then come in and eat; then fatigue sneaks up and knocks you flat. I pulled up the quilt and slept like a desperado. I woke to Davy sitting on the bed across

18

from me, wiping down his shotgun with an oiled rag.

'Hey, Natty,' he said, seeing me stir.

'Hey, Davy. We going back out?'

'A little bunch went down on the west quarter. Canadas.' He hiked his eyebrows at me. 'We're gonna crawl up.'

'Okay!' I threw the covers back, stretched, and tried to shake out the murky dream I'd been having – there was a reptile of some sort in it. Davy laid the shotgun across his knees and leaned forward. A warm tobacco smell clung to him.

'Listen, Rube. You heard us talking about Dolly last night, didn't you?'

'I was asleep. Swede heard, though.'

'Well, she didn't hear everything. Dad kept shut, to keep from scaring you guys, but you should know this. Finch and Basca made some pretty vicious threats. To Dad, I mean.' Getting me by the eyes, Davy said, 'They talked about hurting his family.'

It took me a second to realize he meant us. Dread landed flopping in my stomach. We'd never had an enemy before, unless you counted Russia. I watched my brother closely.

'They're basically loudmouths,' he said. 'Cowards, windbags; they won't do anything. I don't want you to worry. Just keep an eye out, that's all.' He was entirely relaxed, saying this, as though it was nothing we couldn't handle. It reassured me but was unsettling too. The way he mentioned Dolly, for example – breezing past her name as though she were somebody else, an aunt or something. He said, 'Okay?'

'Okay.'

'And let's not mention it to Swede, Natty. All right?'

'Nope. We don't need to scare her, I guess.'

'Good.' He reached down and picked up my boots and set them in my lap. 'Now let's crawl up on those Canadas.'

*   *   *

19

A crawlup, if you're not familiar, is a different kind of hunt from waiting among decoys. I stuck with Davy again, Swede with Dad, and we squirmed on our bellies up a shallow rise beyond which a few dozen honkers were feeding on stubbled wheat. This time there was no whispering among us; the light was almost gone and though we supposed the geese were close we couldn't hear them and had to crawl on faith that they were there at all. It was a very serious crawl, even though Swede on my left was pretending to be a wild Sioux brave creeping up on some heedless cow-poke – a game I'd happily played also, when hunting, until that morning when Davy handed me his gun. Now suddenly I found it quaint, and when she sneaked a look at me I grinned and winked, instead of keeping my Sioux composure, and she frowned at me savagely and went bellying forward.

At the crest of the rise lay a small rockpile. We wiggled up to it and Dad peered over. 'They're pretty far,' he whispered. Now we could hear them, uttering occasional harsh honks. They sounded uneasy, and when Davy had a look he said, 'They're walking away from us, look at 'em waddle.'

There wasn't a thing we could do; the geese were out of range. I was disappointed all out of proportion. I'd been hoping – expecting – that the Canadas would be right there for the taking. Also that Davy would again give me the shot. (It's strange – that morning I hadn't expected to fire at a live goose for two, three years, and it hadn't troubled me a bit. Now I wasn't going to get a shot at these present Canadas, and the fact had me ready to cry.) Then came a great racket of honks and the geese rose up in a panicked layer and beat westward into the wind, away from us. Dad got up on his knees and took aim but didn't fire. Davy didn't even raise his gun.

The voices of the Canadas faded to a dim disorganized music, and we rested against the rocks.

'Well,' Dad said.

The cold seeped through clothes toward bone. Joyless and bushed, I sat pouting over having crawled so far for nothing. Dad was just getting up when Davy said, 'Wait.'

He watched the dirty western sky. When he said, 'Down,' Dad knelt slowly back among the stones.

A honk came seeking us out of the distance.

'One of 'em's broke off from the group,' Davy said quietly. 'There.' He pointed at something none of the rest of us could see.

We huddled into what little cover we had. Half a minute later we saw the goose coming toward us. My, it was high. Dad relaxed. A bird that far up is all but beyond the reach of lead shot. Swede soughed in defeat.

'Stay down,' Davy said.

The goose now commenced a wide swing round the field, while Davy melted into that rockpile as if to join it forever. I remember the low angle at which he held the shotgun; I remember his shadowed, patient eyes – he looked ready to burst from cover and chase down an antelope. The odd thought came to me that Davy was hunting alone – that Dad and Swede and I weren't even there, really; that we existed with him as memories, or fond ghosts watching his progress.

The goose circled the field once, saw nothing interesting, and gained altitude; it might've been considering Mexico, it was that high. It flew over the rockpile on its way south, and when it did Davy rose to one knee and shot it out of the sky.

That night Swede and I lay somewhat breathless under a hill of quilts. For drafts there was noplace like August's farmhouse; you could roast under such strata and your nose still cold as a glass knob.

'What do you think Davy'll do – about those guys?' Swede whispered, eyes alight. Though I'd promised not to scare her with any Finch and Basca talk, she kept coming back to them.

'What do you mean, do? They're just cowards, windbags.' An unsatisfactory answer to a warrior like Swede. She jounced a little under the quilts, which let in some cold, and we listened to talk from the kitchen: August and his wife, Birdie, larking through the old stories with Dad. Davy was in there too, drinking coffee with the grownups, keeping his silence.

'You think he'll fight 'em?'

'Why would he? Dad took care of those guys already, didn't he? In the locker room.'

Swede said, 'Davy thinks they got off easy, can't you tell? He's being such a grouch. Boy, I'd hate to be those guys when Davy gets hold of 'em.'

I thought that was awfully bold of Swede on Davy's behalf – you understand, I would never bet against my brother, but these two fellows were as serious a kind of trouble as you could purchase in Roofing back then. To call Finch and Basca the town bullies doesn't touch it, as you will see.

'Maybe,' I said, 'we just ought to wait. All right?'

We settled, yawned, and listened to August Shultz talk about Doot, his fleet quarter horse in days of yore. We knew about Doot. As kids, Dad and August had been neighbors, only a few miles from here. August would ride over in the mornings and pick up Dad, who'd be saddling his paint Henry in front of the barn, and they'd race the last half-mile to school. Though Henry was a dozen years older than Doot, Dad was by nature a flat-out rider whereas August had inherited the cautious temperament of his German forebears. On calm autumn days the dust raised by Dad and Henry would hang above the road for hours; to August's great credit, he never exhibited resentment about the constant losing. In fact, though August's judiciousness cost him transient glory, it probably saved his farm any number of times; it probably accounted for his now owning three farms, including the one he loaned us to hunt on every fall. Dad's family, the Lands, had not only lost their farm toward the end of the Dust Bowl years, they'd never again owned anything like the ancestral namesake. We'd become renters – which was, in our case, about all that the family of a small-town school janitor could expect.

Swede murmured, 'I'm sleeping, Reuben.'

'Back to your room, then.' She'd slipped in with me because the room I shared with Davy was nearer the kitchen, the better to eavesdrop on the grownups.

She got up, kissed me, and stood by the bed in her cowboy-print pajamas. 'Rube, you're almost like Davy now, aren't you? I mean, you shot a goose this morning.'

She meant to compliment me, but the fact was I'd been thinking this over. By the time we left to steal up on that little bunch of Canadas, I'd almost begun to believe I'd taken that goose on account of my own skill – as if I hadn't blown two easy shots before lucking out on a long one. But Davy's work on the lone Canada had slapped me awake. I had in my mind, that night, the image of Davy I'll carry with me always, a picture that is my brother more than any other I might recall. It's Davy at the very top of his motion – risen to one knee, Winchester at his shoulder, barrel pointing a few degrees from straight up. His hat's fallen to the rocks behind him and his short blond hair stands stiff as a wolf's. His right index finger is just whitening on the trigger, and on his face is nothing at all but the knowledge that the goose is his.

Not confidence – I understand confidence. What Davy had was knowledge.

I reached out and squeezed Swede's arm. 'Sure I am,' I said. 'Good night.'

Waking past midnight I departed this dream: I was crossing a shallow river that smelled of dying plants,

23

my bare feet sinking in muck, the far shore concealed by fog. Not a sound but the swirl round my shins. Then a breeze touched me. The mist corkscrewed away and I saw the shore. A dead horse lay swollen there, tail in the river. I stopped midstream, my breath gone, and woke gasping to the windowful of moonlight and Davy in his bed snoring, arm thrown across his eyes.

I was scared to go back to sleep. There'd been something worse on that riverbank than just a dead horse, I was sure of it. I'd barely awakened in time! Sitting up I realized, with some relief, that I had to go to the outhouse. Normally I'd have dreaded this, for the usual dark and scary reasons, but this time the idea seemed outright friendly – a chance to walk that vision off. I slipped from bed and pulled on my pants and carried my boots into the kitchen. A kerosene lantern was lit on the table. I took my coat from its hook and went out.

The privy stood next to a leaning corncrib downhill from the barn. I felt better, standing under the big clean moon, and even considered going back inside and trying to hold it till morning. But you know how it is – you might barely have to go at all, but just step out in the cold. Suddenly I had no choice, so I hunched my shoulders and headed for the outhouse, the moon bouncing my shadow off the grass.

Then, nearing the barn, I heard footsteps.

Nothing stealthy about them, just shoeleather on wood. It sounded like a man strolling a boardwalk. Still, the noise raised my short hairs, in the middle of the night like that, until I figured it must be Dad, pacing the flatbed of the old grain truck parked behind the barn.

The steps stopped abruptly – which prickled my skin some more – then continued as before.

By now, understand, I *knew* it was Dad. You know the meter of your father's walk. Still, it was the dead of night; the smell of the dream hung around me; all sorts of lunar imaginings had hold of my brain. So I crept up quiet next to the barn and catwalked in its shadow until I could peek round the corner at the grain truck.

Dad, sure enough, was pacing the flatbed. He was praying – nothing unusual for Dad; he liked to walk as he prayed.

Did I say earlier that the flatbed sat up off the ground about three feet? Because I should have; it matters here.

Dad's hands were clenched and pressed to his eyes; he wouldn't have seen me had I flapped my arms and flown. His lips were moving. Though he often comforted Swede and me by quoting from the gospel of John, *Let not your hearts be troubled*, it was plain Dad himself was suffering the labors of a troubled heart; over the business of Finch and Basca, I figured, or over Davy, who clearly saw the matter as unfinished. I indulged in a black thought or two about my brother – snoring back in the house, the bum.

And then, as I stood watching, Dad walked right off the edge of the truck.

I saw it coming – his knuckles jammed to his face, his steps not slowing at all as the edge approached – I meant to rush out and warn him, but something froze me tight. I stood there with my knees locked and my heart gone to water, while Dad paced over the edge.

And did not fall.

He went on pacing – God my witness – walking on air, praying relentlessly, a good yard of absolutely nothing between the soles of his boots and the thistles below. As he went, the moon threw his strangely separate shadow to the earth; a sleepy pigeon cooed from the barn; Dad's boots touched the tops of a thatch of tall grama growing up among the thistles, and they waved as if stroked by wind. I will forget none of this. Nor the comfortable, fluttery feeling it gave me, as though someone had blown warm smoke through a

25

hole in my center. Dad went perhaps thirty feet, paused, and started back. His eyes were still clenched shut; I don't know whether he ever recognized how buoyant was his faith that night. But in the sudden quiet – his feet noiseless, hitting nothing – I could hear his supplications. Straining my ears, I was surprised to catch not Davy's name but mine. Then his bootsole struck the flatbed again and he was pacing as any man does, connected to the solid and the natural.

It might seem odd to you that at this point I remembered why I'd come outside in the first place. In growing discomfort I looked at the outhouse. Getting there meant clutching my pants and lurching straight past Dad – and him walking on the hand of God! I knew what *heretic* meant, for Swede had read me more than a few bits of gruesome history. A person didn't like to take chances; there was a willow thicket across the yard, and I took myself there in a hurry.

Beauteous Are My Cakes Indeed

We arrived home to find our front door tarred black, top to bottom. It was late, a cloudy night, and none of us saw anything amiss at first – for my part, I was too preoccupied with the task of breathing. All the long drive I'd felt the air changing, turning warmer, thicker, filling with invisible mites that colluded against my lungs. By the time we got home it was all I could do to totter up the steps with the two newswrapped geese in a sack. Dad was right behind me, his arms full of unconscious Swede – who, by the way, was whistling through her nose in an unflattering fashion, proof that this was no faked snooze. Then Davy, who had the house key, said, 'What's this junk all over the door?'

What it was was most of the contents of a one-gallon can of Gamble's roofing tar, spread thick over our sturdy portal by means of a putty knife. Next morning we were to find both can and knife tossed among the junipers flanking the house; for the present, Davy simply turned silent and Dad businesslike. He carried Swede across the violated threshold and put her, still dressed, into bed; then, noticing my shallow gasps, ordered me to sit in his own stuffed chair and not move until he could attend to me.

A word here about this business of taking a breath.

If you're someone who's never had to think about it, never had to exert muscular effort to do it – never lain awake through endless dark hours knowing you'd *stop doing it forever* if you happened to fall asleep – then indulge me. Think of a bellows, such as you use to rouse a fire. Really moves the air, doesn't it? Now imagine a tiny, malignant, wind-carried seed entering that bellows on the inhale and sticking inside. Slowly – slowly! – a sponge begins to grow. You don't even notice, early on; you just have to work a little harder to get a flame. But as time passes you see that the bellows won't close all the way; it's taking shallower gulps. And down inside the sponge keeps growing. You shut your eyes and concentrate, hoping to head this off. Air in. Air out. You imagine the Arctic, its clean snow-scape where no pollens lie. You imagine a great white bear trotting on the ice pack under a cold blue sky; he's been trotting that way for days – air in, air out – his bellows a happy machine; look at him cover the ground. You think, I am the bear. It works for a short while, or seems to. The snow creaks, your nostrils steam, you trot, you breathe – but soon you give it up. Despite all stratagems, your bellows is spongebound. Your breaths are sips, couldn't blow out the candle on a baby's cake. And now the air gets close and sticky all around; and working those filled and paralytic lungs you understand, in a frozen sweat, that morning is miles and miles away, and the house is quiet with the smooth respirations of your family, and if you fall asleep from pure exhaustion the sponge will win and you will be singing hymns by sunrise, at the feet of the Lord, in a body glorified.

I do not exaggerate.

I sat on Dad's chair with my bellows full of sponge while he lit the kitchen stove and laid a pan of water over the flame. He shook some salt into the water, then soda, then disappeared downstairs and returned with a quart canning jar.

'Kerosene,' he explained. 'Let's see if it strips the tar.' He winked at me in such easy form I recalled the sheltered feeling I'd had witnessing his walk off the grain truck. It was comforting, but I'll have to say it didn't make breathing any easier. For the first time the thought ingressed that if this man, my father, beloved by God, could work miracles – if he could *walk on air* – then fixing my defective lungs ought to be a picnic. Yes, indeed, a day at the old beach.

When the water boiled, Dad set the pan on a cutting-board and that on my lap in the chair. He draped a blanket over my head for a steam tent. Immediately it was so hot under there I imagined my face darkening and rising like a loaf of yeast bread, but my chest did start to loosen.

'All right?' he asked.

I nodded under the blanket. He opened the door and cold poured in. I could hear him unscrewing the jar of kerosene, tearing up rags, working at the tar. The door had been a lovely dark green – hunter's green, Dad called it – the single adornment to a clapboard house as white and midwestern as any you've seen. Come December that green door gave the place a Christmasy look that atoned for our want of pretty lights. I felt awful for Swede, who was by now the chief deliverer of Christmas spirit in the family – she'd learned to make sugar cookies the year before and, in fact, made them about three times a week from Thanksgiving on. We did our best to eat them. Unorthodox with embellishments, Swede had once used frozen peas instead of raisins because of the color; she'd made Santa's curly beard from pieces of uncooked elbow macaroni. I remember Davy crunching heavily through one of these, Swede eyeing him closely; I remember Davy's flawless display of gladness and enjoyment, eating Santa quickly and entirely and pro-ducing afterward a happy burp that convinced even me he had liked it.

Dad said, 'Well, I've got the sill fairly clean – the door is a goner, I guess.'

I shrugged under the blanket.

Dad said, 'I think I better tell you how this came about.'

But I didn't want to hear anything further about Israel Finch and Tommy Basca. It's true I'd been curious enough earlier, but we hadn't been home then; we'd been four hours' drive distant, which made the whole problem, while troubling, also abstract. Now we'd come home to a house defiled. When Dad had switched on the porch light, revealing the door, my stomach jumped. I wanted to puke. I'd been standing by Davy and felt waves of something spooky come off him; I felt straight off that a piece of our lives had changed, as certainly as our cheerful green door had gone to black.

'I know about Dolly and those guys,' I told Dad.

He took his time with this information; he'd not wanted Swede and me to know. I was grateful for the blanket over my head. Finally I heard a low chuckle.

'Well, then, here is your chance to learn about the principle of escalation,' he said.

I'd heard the word before, spoken by teachers when asked to explain about the school fallout shelter. 'Like in wars?'

'Yes, exactly like in wars.' I heard him pull up a kitchen chair. 'How's the steam, working good?'

I nodded.

'Fine. Now. Let's say a war begins. One nation wants what another has: property, gold mines—'

'Helen of Troy,' I contributed. Swede had told me all about her and the thousand ships. It was hard to believe.

'Sure, Helen of Troy. Wonderful comprehension, Reuben. Now. This fortunate nation has no intention of giving over its bounty, so the aggressor decides to take it by force.'

'Okay.'

30

'Good. Let's say the defending nation is also the weaker; however, it has good strong allies.'

'Friends?'

'Yes, friends. So, after the first engagement, the defender's allies step in and take a hand . . .'

Well, so it went. At one in the morning, smelling of tar and petroleum, Dad framed his locker-room skirmish as a composition on wartime ethics. Absorbing as it was, such interpretations do have a way of muffling the shouts of those who were there – namely, Israel Finch and Tommy Basca.

And they shouted, all right.

Here is what I learned later, from Davy, after he'd pried details from Dolly herself: a bouncy clarinetist whose talent was greatly exceeded by pure goodwill, she'd been playing in the pep band during the football game. After halftime she and a few others ran up from the field to the school band room to put away their instruments. Dolly meant to accompany friends to the bowling alley, since our team was getting whomped as usual – the Plainsmen never generated much suspense. As they were leaving, Dolly remembered a pair of shoes she'd left down in her athletic locker. She told the others to go on ahead, she'd catch up.

About this time, Dad was in the *boys'* locker room, which had just been vacated by the Plainsmen themselves. The score so far placed our team at a 21-to-3 deficit, and halftime had gone hard for the lads. Coach Heintz was a man who took defeat personally and so made it as personal as he could for his players – especially for his son, Robert, a pale, artistic sophomore who looked grotesque in shoulder pads. Unfortunately, Robert had botched a pass in the end zone with moments left in the half. If he'd ever in his life hoped for benevolence it must have been on the queasy trot up to the locker room for the midgame pep talk, but his hopes had a hideous end. Dad later said he could hear Coach Heintz's popeyed invective all the way to the cafeteria. Arriving at the locker room minutes later, pushing his wide broom, he found the players gone back to the field and a puddle of vomit on the floor in front of Robert's locker.

He was shaking sawdust from a five-gallon bucket when he heard a rowdy laugh just beyond the cinder-block wall – in the girls' locker room. By then, no one else ought to've been in the building, certainly not in the girls' locker room, and *certainly* not if they weren't even girls.

Dad listened just long enough to hear a second laugh, this alongside a scared yelp; then he took his long broom and unscrewed the head from the hardwood handle.

Dolly was kneeling at her locker when she heard the wheeze of the locker-room door. She thought it might be her friend Christine, who'd been bound for the bowling alley along with the others. Christine was her confidante – the one she talked to most, I suppose, about the crush she had on Davy. Then the lights went out, and nobody answered her nervous call, and Dolly saw the jumpy beam of a flashlight appear on the wall beside her.

I have to credit Dolly. No screamer by nature, she clutched the hardest thing she could get her hands on in the dark – the Master padlock hanging from its hasp. *Simple! Nothing to it!* those boys must've thought, seeing Dolly crouched with her sweet chin set hard; imagine the crazed gladness in their hearts! Israel laughed once; then Dolly up and fired that pad-lock at a place above the flashlight, God bless her all her life, and it struck Israel Finch to the left of his Adam's apple, so that he dropped the light and seized his neck. For a moment Dolly expected to escape – 'I'm all bloody,' Israel yelled, 'I'm bleedin', Tommy!' – but unhappily the padlock had only nicked some capillaries and missed the all-important jugular. Slipping past Israel she bumped straight into Tommy Basca, who hadn't a flashlight to give him away, and he clutched on to her with a snort.

Then Israel Finch got to his feet and pointed the light at Dolly. He told Tommy to hold her arms, and Tommy roared as if they were the funniest words in his reduced language. Realizing his cut wasn't mortal, Israel slapped Dolly across the mouth, told her she was in for deep regret now, boy, and reaching forth his strong smelly hands rent open the front of her sweater. That, Dolly said, is when she would've started to give up inside, had she not looked over Israel's shoulder and seen Dad coming. Keep in mind he ought not've been visible at all; there were no lights on but the flashlight, which was aimed at Dolly. She said Dad's face coming toward them was luminous of itself, glowing and serene, the way you'd suppose an angel's would be, that it rose up behind Israel Finch like a sudden moon, and when Tommy Basca saw it he was so startled he dropped her right down on her bottom. She said Dad was as silent, those next moments, as he was incandescent; he made no sound except a strange whistling, which turned out, of course, to be the broom handle, en route to any number of painful destinations. What was odd, she said, was how the boys weren't even up to the job of running away – Tommy went screeching to his knees before the first blow landed, and Israel prostrated himself and moaned as though the devil had hold of his liver. The two of them just lost their minds, Dolly said, while her own reaction was nearly as insensible; she suddenly could not stop laughing. Here was Dad, his face still lit though now even the flashlight had gone out, smiling (Dolly said) though his eyes looked terribly melancholy, whacking Finch and Basca every second or two while the pair of them shrieked in no English you'd recognize – Dolly said the laughter just flooded through her and came not only from relief, as you might surmise, but from a reckless and holy sort of joy she had never felt before, not even while cheerleading.

I'd have given much to have seen all this myself – or,

better, to have let Davy see it. It was Davy's contention, when he learned what those fellows had meant toward Dolly, that no mere thrashing was sufficient punishment. He may have been right. And yet, unhappy as he was with Dad for not killing the boys outright, I wish Davy had witnessed the incident. It may not have 'put the fear of God in 'em,' as Dolly hopefully supposed, but it surely did insert the fear of Jeremiah Land.

So Dad gave Dolly a ride home, talked briefly with her father, and returned to the school to lock up. The football game was over – 56 to 6 – and when Dad finished up and stepped outside in his overcoat, there stood Israel. His posture was peculiar and appeared to hurt him. He said, nasally, 'Something you should know, janitor.'

Dad remarked later, to Davy, how swollen and discolored Israel's face looked, like a big winter squash.

'Tommy and me are watching your family,' said Israel Finch. 'All of 'em. You understand?'

'Escalation,' Dad said.

The water had cooled under the steam tent. 'Well,' I mused, 'what should we do back?' It was our turn, after all, and though I couldn't picture Dad carrying the battle back to Finch and Basca over a wrecked door, the very word – *escalation* – sounded like something bound to carry you up and forward, regardless of your wishes or ordinary sense.

But Dad chuckled and swept the blanket off my head. 'Nothing; of course, nothing! What those fellows don't realize is, we've already won. The victory is ours.'

I blinked up at him. He said, gently, 'You don't understand either, do you, son?'

'No, sir.'

And he swung me up and carried me off and tossed me on my bunk, just as if I hadn't done a whole lot of growing up in the past few days alone.

* * *

I succeeded in worrying about this escalation business for a good day and a half before worry died, as usual, at the hands of routine. Swede and I rose muddy-eyed each morning at six – Davy being already up and out, running his line of muskrat traps. Dad would be sitting at the kitchen table when we went in, his King James open before him, coffee on the stove making its wondrous smell. We fixed oatmeal with bowls of condiments set alongside: white sugar, currants, flaked coconut. As the oatmeal puffed and steamed, Dad would lean back at the table, shut his eyes and his Bible simultaneously, remain in such attitude a minute or two, then pop up declaring what gifted chefs we were, dipping a spoon into the pot as if it contained something exorbitant and full of clams.

And then to school, where I swam upstream through geography and grammar and where Swede, who disliked long division, tried to win her teacher's favor by composing heroic verse. What was Miss Nelson supposed to think when Swede, dimpled and blond, coming up on nine years old, handed in a poem like 'Sunny Sundown Delivers the Payroll'?

> The men who worked the Redtail Mine were fed up
>   with the boss.
> They swarmed around his office door like
>   blackflies round a hoss.
> 'No wages these three months!' one cried. 'Let's
>   hang the lousy rat!
> He'll starve our very children, boys, while he
>   himself gets fat!'
> And true enough, behind the door, a fat man
>   shook and wept;
> The wobbling bags beneath his eyes said this
>   man hadn't slept.
> A messenger had brought him word that made
>   him feel his age:
> Valdez, last night – the third straight month! – had
>   robbed the payroll stage.

Swede had lost her heart to the West early on, something that gave Dad no end of delight. He supplied her with frayed Zane Grey paperbacks thrown out by the school library, *Wilderness Trek* and *Robber's Roost* and of necessity *Riders of the Purple Sage*. Swede popped them down like Raisinets. You have to admit she learned the language.

> *And now the mob broke down the door, and now*
> *they found a rope,*
> *And now the boss was on his knees, a prayer was*
> *his last hope.*
> *'Oh, God, I'm not an evil man, though everybody says*
> *It's all my fault that we ain't caught the devil*
> *called Valdez.*
> *Oh, God, if you would ransom me from those*
> *who'd have me swing,*
> *Please find the man and send him who can plug*
> *the bandit king—'*

I have to tell you I like this one quite a bit. There's nothing like good strong meter to make a poem mind its manners. Show me free verse that nails a moment like this does:

> *Then each man felt the air go still; each felt a stab*
> *of dread;*
> *Each heard the sound of danger in a dancing*
> *mustang's tread.*
> *They watched the horse come down the street; they*
> *watched the rider halt;*
> *They watched him size them man by man, as if he*
> *knew each fault.*
> *His clothes and hat were black as ink, his dancing*
> *mustang pale,*
> *His eyes were blue and hard enough to make the sun*
> *turn tail.*

He said, 'You want to hang this man, I'll give you
   each the same.
I don't much like a mob,' said he, 'and Sundown
   is my name.'

And it goes on: Sundown takes the payroll job, as
you might expect, and gets bushwhacked by Valdez,
who, it turns out, is smarter than anyone gave him
credit for, and the ensuing chase leads into country
where the sun is hot as madness and the ground
crunches like cinders, there meeting 'many a snake,
and many a skull, and many a parched ravine.' I've
kept a lot of Swede's old verse. This one carries a note
on the back from Miss Nelson, in her tranquil,
feminine hand: *Excellent! Next time you see your Mr
Sundown, tell him you know a schoolmarm who'd like
to meet him.*

Yes, yes sir – routine is worry's sly assassin. It only
took us till Wednesday night to get a little careless.

It was church night, of course. We went to a
Methodist church, though not yet members; we'd
switched from Roofing Lutheran the previous year, a
move I didn't wholly understand. The new minister
wasn't half the exciting preacher our old one was.
Pastor Reach was slight, with a limp and a speech
problem that altered some of his consonants. Swede
and I had been used to oratory; our former pastor
could exhort like everything and owned what Dad said
must be a special edition of the Holy Bible, for it contained things omitted from our own – references to
card-playing, for example, and rock and roll, and the
Russian people. Our former minister had so much
energy that simply pastoring wasn't enough; he also
wrote regular editorials for the paper in the county
seat of Montrose, which riled up readers and made
him a star. Pastor Reach had no such ambitions. He
had a wife, Eunice, who played the piano and whom

I'd once overheard praying aloud that the 'fig tree might blossom.' He had a plain Bible, like ours, and preached right out of it. Always regretful of his sinful nature, Pastor Reach was a great advocate of forgiveness, in which he put a lot of stock. Thrilling he was not.

Yet this Wednesday night I was especially keen to be at church, for two reasons. A revival crusade was setting up in Montrose, and Pastor Reach had prevailed on the esteemed Reverend Johnny Latt to come over and preach; also, I suspected the blackhaired and winsome Bethany Orchard would be at the service.

I wonder yet what might've happened had Dad and I stayed home that night or had Davy and Swede gone with us to church. Wars escalate in mysterious ways, unforeseen by good men and prophets. The fact is, Swede didn't come – the only time I remember being in church without her – which happened to be fine with me, on account I was hoping to talk to Bethany without my sister for an audience. Swede's absence seemed, actually, pretty convenient.

So thoughtlessly we sling on our destinies.

In the car Dad said, 'I suppose you've heard things about the Reverend Johnny.'

'Jeff Swanson called him a Bible-thumper,' I ventured. Actually, Jeff had started with Bible-thumper and warmed expansively from there.

Dad considered this. 'Everybody thumps something, Reuben.'

'Do things happen, when he preaches?' Other things I'd heard: how at a word from Johnny people fainted down to the floor to twitch, while others spoke in strange babylike languages and prophecies flew through the air like bats. If you came on the right night, atrophied cripples were said to heave up out of wheelchairs and stagger forward in gratitude.

'I hope so, Rube,' Dad said. We pulled up to the church, which appeared crowded already. I opened my door but he put a hand on my knee. 'Reuben. Do you know why Swede stayed home with Davy?'

'No, sir.'

'Because I'm not sure Swede is ready for this. In fact, I'm not sure you are.'

'I am,' I said, a little abruptly; Bethany Orchard had just traipsed into the church and, a moment before the door closed behind her, had poked her head out and smiled at me. Dad said, 'Goodness, what a cutie,' my ears heated up, and in we went.

I won't spend too much time on Reverend Johnny because what happened there isn't half as important as what was happening at home. But did you ever go to church and see the minister rise first thing with a trumpet in his hand? That's what the Reverend Johnny did – oh, yes. Our mild Roofing Methodists were unused to musical instruments, except organs and pianos, but they took to this trumpet right away, and the reverend played like Gabriel, by which I mean loud and with the authority that comes of a good ear and large lungs. A great big fellow, Reverend Johnny Latt, had to be in his seventies, yet still so upright and wide in the shoulders and with such dark swept-back hair he could've walked without fear down your choice of mid-night alleys. He had with him a saxophonist younger brother, an organist wife with a soft voice and a sweet shipwrecked expression at the eyes, and a heavy, weak-looking son who played of all things the flute and who you knew straight off wouldn't be the one to carry the Latt crusades far into the future.

The music alone lasted as long as our normal Wednesday night service – fine music, I believe to this day, and well tuned, and performed to the glory of God, but all the same uncommonly loud. My head throbbed after half an hour. For relief I looked side-ways, where through the rising heat Bethany looked cool as a May morning. On we bore through 'He Leadeth Me' and 'The Old Rugged Cross' and, shock-ingly, 'When the Saints Go Marching In,' at which I felt (rather than heard) Dad chuckle. On through a trumpeted rendition of 'Shall We Gather at the River?' at once so beautiful and so calamitously loud I could've wept for either reason. Peeking sideways, Bethany glimpsed my eye on her. 'Onward, Christian Soldiers.' Nearing the hour mark I closed my eyes and saw a picture of myself, from the side, a runnel of blood sliding out of my ear.

This, followed by a glance to find Bethany gone, and I rose from my seat and slouched from the sanctuary. Feeling Dad's gaze I turned and sought his approval. Reverend Johnny was well into a bold rendering of 'Amazing Grace,' standing tall, not leaning back as jazz trumpeters do but straight and wide as a Roman pillar, the sound growing out of him with no hint of approaching abatement. The reverend had chops not a jazzman in the world would have argued with. And as I pushed open the swinging door, still looking back, Dad rendered some grace of his own, winking at me to go ahead, take a break, understanding that the trumpet in its glorious proximity was hero enough for any mortal ears.

I found Bethany downstairs in the kitchen, peeling an orange from the Westinghouse drawer. When I put my head in at the door she said, 'Reuben, are you hungry?'

'Sure.'

'Come on, I'll share it with you.'

Bethany Orchard was twelve – only a year ahead of me at school, but in the universal race children run toward the doubtful prize of maturity she was leagues out front, a realization that arrived as I stood with her in the basement of Roofing Methodist and she fed me orange slices with her fingers. (Not my fault; I'd reached for the orange; she said, 'No, let me. Here.') As she peeled the sections away one by one, a locustlike buzz entered the back of my brain. I'd been pleased at first to realize I was slightly taller than Bethany, but her fingers – approaching with an orange slice – reaffirmed the gulf between us. Her fingers were long, capable, conversant: a woman's fingers, slightly reddened from some recent scrubbing. Her fingers were the oldest part of her. I couldn't think of a thing to do with this information. I couldn't think of anything at all. The locusts neared. The bits of orange her fingers placed in my mouth were so ripe I barely chewed. Overhead the music changed and slowed. When the orange was gone I dared look at Bethany, who showed nothing but a businesslike attitude, sweeping the cupped peelings into a palm and lobbing them into a wastebasket. She was without shame. Afraid she'd go back upstairs I said, 'I cook meals at our house, sometimes.'

She looked at me, and I was like Kipling's jungle beasts who couldn't meet the eye of man. I commenced hunting about the kitchen, opening cupboards as if with a purpose, coming up at last with a box of Bisquick and a pound of butter from the Westinghouse.

Bethany said, 'I think there's some syrup over the stove.'

I am afraid we missed the Reverend Johnny's sermon. Though I recognized full well when the music stopped and the preaching began, by then Bethany and I had moved on to whisks and bowls and eggs of ambiguous purity, and the gladness of being alone with this girl was stronger than the unease I felt at putting one over on Dad, who was expecting me back upstairs.

What brought us up at last was a case of alarm – a hard thump from overhead, as if the Reverend Johnny had received some coronary visitation. A light fixture wobbled. We froze and heard the reverend's voice, jagged and intermittent. A second thump rattled the fixture. Somebody shouted, '*Amen*,' and then it was as if Armageddon opened out above us, such salvos of thumps and whacks shook the church. Imagine a storm hailing whole arms and legs! Did we zip! Up the steps and a sliding stop at the sanctuary door, where I heard an urgent voice say, approximately, *bahm, toballah, sacoombaraffay*; straight off a different voice raised up to translate: 'I am among you tonight, my children,' it said, amid blooming amens. Cracking the door we saw the Reverend Johnny Latt reach out to touch a man on the forehead. It was Mr Layton, who'd stood behind his dimestore counter these endless years, an egregious miser and congenital grouch. The reverend's eyes were shut, and as his fingers touched Mr. Layton's bright scalp, Mr Layton fell backward without utterance, slipping between the ineffectual arms of the younger Latt brother, who'd crept up behind to make the catch. The impact had no visible effect on Mr Layton, who lay at peace in a room littered with supine Methodists. Reverend Johnny opened his eyes and peered around for others in range.

There was a pressure on my arm that I recognized as Bethany's hand. I looked into her face – her close, scared face. She asked in a whisper if they were all right, these folks lying about. It's true the place raised neckhairs. 'They're fine,' I said, looking for Dad, who'd know.

Therianus-dequayas-remorey-gungunnas, a man called out, plus a paragraph or so more. I'm not making fun; the language was complicated and musical, an expression outside human usefulness. Expectant silence followed. The Reverend Johnny surveyed the room. At this moment I noticed that the smell of our pancakes – Bethany's and mine, and they'd been good ones – had floated upstairs, a fabulous smell. It occurred to me we might get into some small trouble for using the kitchen during service.

Then Reverend Johnny spoke up. 'Does someone have the interpretation? Who's hearing the word of the

Lord tonight?'

Nobody said a thing.

Johnny Latt persisted. 'Someone's fighting obedience tonight! Speak up, for no prophecy goes untold. Joe, is it you?'

And Joe, a bull-shouldered patriarch whose shirt stretched wet across his back and who looked to be in deep communication with the Almighty, rose without hesitation and gave it a shot. 'O my sons and my daughters, how I love thee! How I wish to provide for thee! Yea, I long to surround thee with delicious smells, heavenly smells! How gladly will I sit thee down in my banquet hall, for beauteous are the cakes therein! Oh, golden is my syrup! And unto me shall gather the hungry from every nation . . .'

What a shame Swede wasn't there. She'd have adored that prophecy; who knows what commentary she'd have whispered in my ear? But my wheels turn a beat or two slower than Swede's, and anyhow Bethany's hold had whitened on my arm. 'Oh, Reuben,' she said, 'your dad's down!'

He was stretched on his back right up by the pulpit, as if he'd been first to go. I had a fleeting sense of forsakenness. I was marooned; though I knew most everyone here, the sight of Dad out cold on the floor momentarily tipped bedrock. I pushed open the door and went to him, stepping, I'm afraid, on some innocent hands. It was like walking out of a plane crash. Dad looked comfortable, though: arms above his head, feet pointed inward. Some of the others' eyes were twitching beneath the lids. Not Dad's. He looked exactly like he did on the odd sleep-late Saturday morning when he'd worked long at school the night before: appreciative, vaguely surprised, and above all unconscious. I knelt at his side.

But how do you wake a man knocked cold by love? Because, as he told me later, that's what it was: the electric unearned love of the great Creator, traveling like light down the nerves of the Reverend Johnny's arm, crackling out the tips of his fingers. I looked at Dad's face – at creases I'd never noticed, the nap of loosening skin at his throat. In that instant it seemed to me he deserved to rest this way for days and days. Then a jolt hit my shoulder and I felt hands shaking me as if jarring something loose. Lights snapped in my eyes, my ears plugged and opened, and there was a sudden easing in my lungs that showed me how hard I'd been working to breathe. Charged with fear and oxygen I turned to see who had hold of me. No one did. No one in fact was near me except the Reverend Johnny, now talking casually with his younger brother. He wasn't even looking at me.

But his hand, his right hand, was brushing my shoulder.

I can feel it still, that sizzling jump inside my organs. It didn't feel good, not as I would've suspected the touch of the Lord might feel, but I wouldn't say it felt bad either. It only felt powerful, like truth unhusked.

Once torched by truth, Swede wrote years later, *a little thing like faith is easy*.

Had I her gift for getting to the core, I'd be tempted to chew on this awhile – on truth and its odd conduits. But a witness must obey his strengths, and mine, forgive me, lie in keeping the story moving. So here is where my father wakes. He sits upright, and his eyes are wide and troubled, and, 'Son,' he says, 'we have to leave.'

Because he knows, somehow, what we have done: we've stayed too long at church.

So let us leave. Let us get to the Plymouth with an impolite quickness – let us *fly*, as witnesses of eras past might say. Because at home, the hard and escalating war has paid a visit. And it's Swede, my darling sister, who has met it at the door.

Your Toughened Heart

A canyon dim and deep and cool was where he'd
  made his lair,
A labyrinthine cavern strewn with bits of bone and hair.
It smelled within of smoke and sin and blasphemy
  and dread,
And none would choose to walk that way who were not
  walking dead.
Yet down the quiet canyon wall a weary rider came –
A rider bent with grief yet bent on justice all the same.
And while the stormclouds rise on high, and ruin
  moans and grates,
The rider Sundown draws his Colt, and Valdez grins
  and waits.

Swede was alone in the house. Dad and I were at
church, of course, and Davy was in the garage loft,
working on a secret, Swede's ninth birthday being two
days off.

Who could imagine someone would come to the
door, in plain sight, such a lovely October evening,
with evil in his heart? Who understands such hatred
as bedeviled that doomed visitor? Who would believe
his boldness as he knocked?

But Dad had spoken correctly: they did not know

they'd already lost. Israel Finch didn't know it as he heard Swede running to answer the door; Davy didn't know it as he worked in the garage, soaping years off a stretch of braintanned leather. Swede certainly didn't know it as she scuffed and lurched across the yard toward a smoking Chevy with Tommy Basca at the wheel and Israel's hand against her mouth. Oh, no: Swede didn't know it at all. What Swede knew was that seconds ago she'd been writing down rhymes to describe the bandit king Valdez, *daring eagle-hearted thief and he who of these hills is chief* – growing a soft spot for the bad guy, like every other writer since Milton. Well, no more. The bitter taste of Israel Finch's palm, his unwashed smell, her own terror at the proximate unknown – all this took the sheen off villainy.

Thus does a romantic canyon hideout, *an outlaw palace built of rock*, become a smelly sinhole *strewn with bits of bone and hair*.

No more sympathy for Valdez, boy.

Now Sundown's wound is seeping and he's tilting
  as he rides;
His eyes are red and gritty as he scans the canyon's
  sides.
He hadn't known the nature of the man whose
  track he sought,
And it sickened him to death to see the things
  Valdez had wrought.
One day an upturned stagecoach and its driver's
  ghastly hue,
The next a blackened farmhouse and its family
  blackened too.
So many graves had Sundown dug, his hands
  were chapped and sore,
And now he prayed to God for strength to live and
  dig one more.

Israel made her sit on his lap in the Chevy. Tommy pulled away from the house, dumb as any good chauffeur, and when they'd gone a few blocks Israel took his hand from her mouth and said, 'Now, you see how easy that was?'

I won't give a detailed account of the ensuing twenty minutes. I wasn't there. Later Swede would characterize the interlude as 'a small and dirty time,' and though in these days of abductions and mayhem and bodies turning up in ditches Swede's ordeal might seem almost innocuous, to think of it still hurts me, physically. I feel it churning yet.

A nine-year-old shouldn't be dragged from her house by someone who hates her.

Nor be forced to hear the language of the unloved.

Nor be jiggled in the laps of perverts.

A nine-year-old shouldn't be told, 'We'll take you home now, but we'll be back. We're right outside your window.'

And now, because a story is told for all, an admonition to the mindsick:

Be careful whom you choose to hate.

The small and the vulnerable own a protection great enough, if you could but see it, to melt you into jelly.

Beware those who reside beneath the shadow of the Wings.

The first Davy knew of Swede's capture was her return. Finishing his work in the garage he cleaned his hands on a rag and came in the house to make coffee, entering at the back door just as Swede slammed in the front. Her shoulders were bent forward and she cross-cupped her elbows in her palms. She was not crying. Her face was white. Davy saw her looking thus and swept her up and smelled at that moment the oilsmoke rush of the departing Chevrolet.

That night I eavesdropped on the grownups again: Dad and Davy and Ted Pullet, the town cop, drinking coffee in the kitchen. Swede was asleep for real, which somehow made me fearful – that and Pullet's manner. He sat there talking to Dad in tones so reasonable I suspected he wasn't even on our side.

'I'll talk to those boys in the morning, Jeremiah. I swung over there after you called, on my way here. They aren't home, either of them.'

You see what I mean? *Those boys. I swung over there.* I didn't understand how Pullet could be so casual. I slipped out of bed and peeked in the kitchen.

Dad said, 'You can do better than talk, Ted. You know Finch.'

'You said yourself they didn't hurt your girl.'

Davy hadn't wanted to call Pullet at all. This was Finch and Basca's third offense, and as far as Davy was concerned their woeful moon had risen. He had his jacket on and car keys in hand when Dad pulled rank and called the law.

Waiting, Davy asked, 'How many times does a dog have to bite before you put him down?'

And now here came Pullet with his timid logic. 'You gave them a pretty bad scare that night in the locker room, Jeremiah. They're just kicking back a little. Basca's aunt wanted you arrested, you know.' Pullet smiled, but his fingers shook on the rim of his cup.

Davy got up from the table at this, set his coffee down, and left the house.

Pullet watched him go. 'Jeremiah,' he said, 'you of all people should understand young men who might get overheated.'

'They pulled her out of the house, Ted. Her own home. Threatened her, put their hands on her.' A pause, then again: 'You know Finch.'

This referred to Israel Finch's departure from school the previous year. One day he'd got up to leave in the middle of Remedial Math. The teacher, young and uncertain of his authority, moved cautiously to block the door. Israel seized the teacher by the hair and bent him toward the floor. Wordless, on his knees, the teacher closed his eyes and Israel Finch let go the hair and stepped back and delivered a kick to the stomach that took the teacher's wind and ruptured something inside. The class went numb; the teacher slumped; the noise his head made hitting the floor started three girls crying at once. Israel left Roofing and went briefly to a reformatory, which failed to prove up to the name. By the time he returned Tommy Basca had quit school also, his options there seeming limited.

'I'll talk to them in the morning,' Pullet said. But by now I recognized the fear inside his voice.

He was no good to us.

This he would verify the very next day, returning after visits with Finch and Basca to tell Dad that those boys were just playing – kicking around – had meant no harm. I remember the clear contempt in Davy's eyes and the set of his mouth as he listened to this folly. I remember hoping Ted Pullet wouldn't look up at his expression and take offense, though now I understand poor Ted must've known it was there, must've felt it. Must've chosen against seeing it.

Swede for her part said nothing to me about Finch and Basca. The day after it happened we went to school as always, and getting home she somewhat forcefully pulled out her little hardheaded doll with eyes that closed when you laid it down, a toy that hadn't seen daylight in months. She carried it about, changed its clothes impatiently, ran a brush over its stiff hair. But the doll had a grievous, unmothered expression, as if it knew its time was short. Once as Swede was rocking it her blouse rode up and I saw two black thumblike marks down low on her side. That night I went into her room and found her working fiercely at her tablet and the doll nowhere in sight.

'Just writing,' Swede told me, but I knew she was doing more than that.

She was killing off Valdez.

And in the morning she turned nine years old, in a reckless celebration defying all dread. We sneaked early to her bedroom, where she lay awake pretending otherwise according to tradition. In the gray light I discerned her lips in a tight smile and her eyes fluttering behind the lids. Then Dad softly sang 'Happy Birthday' and she sat up in bed, rubbing her eyes like some storybook child, a beautiful sight; I can't tell you how relieved I was to see her look so glad.

She wanted my present first, probably because it was smallest; the most I'd been able to come up with was a paperback western by one Frank O'Rourke. It was secondhand, which bothered none of us; I'd gotten it from the literate bachelor a block over, Mr Haplin, who'd feigned haggling and accepted an Indian-head penny in trade.

'I'm sorry it's not a Zane Grey,' I said. The fact was that Mr Haplin, while an awfully good sport, collected Zane Greys; the Zane Greys stayed put.

'It's all right,' said Swede, smoothing the cover. The book was called *The Big Fifty*.

'It's about a buffalo hunter.' I'd paged through.

'It looks swell,' she said, then, 'Daddy!' because he'd laid on her bed an awkwardly wrapped package that came untaped with no help at all and revealed a great solemn typewriter, black as a Franklin stove, its round keys agleam.

'Daddy!' Swede said again, in disbelief.

Grinning, he handed her another package: a ribboned ream of 20-pound bond. 'Now put those cowpokes of yours in print.'

She touched the keys, ratcheted the carriage, pinched the curling ribbon and waved inked fingers. I never saw Swede look happier than she did with that monstrous machine sinking in her bedclothes; as if her world were nothing but huge blue-skied future. But the smudges on her fingers made me think of the bruises I'd seen when her blouse rode up, and I wondered how much they hurt and how much she thought about them.

'Thanks so much,' she said, and may we all be paid one day with looks such as she gave Dad.

Then Davy, who'd smiled silently through everything so far, knocked us all flat by stepping out of the room and back in with a Texas stock saddle fragrant and lustrous on his shoulder. He said, 'Someday you're going to need this,' and laid it on the floor beside her bed.

Swede opened her mouth and couldn't find a word in it. While loving all things Western, I doubt the facts of horse and saddle had ever occurred to her as real; they were simply poetry, though of the very best kind. *Hammerhead roan* and *dancing bay pony* and, now I mention it, *Texas stock saddle* – to Swede such phrases just loped along, champing and snorting and kicking up clover. And rightly so: take away such locutions and who's Sunny Sundown? Just a guy out walking.

So the spell of the West, cast already by Mr Grey, settled about Swede like a thrown loop. There's magic in tack, as anyone knows who has been to horse sales, and a rubbed saddle, unexpected and pulled from nowhere, owns an allure only dolts resist. Swede's was a double-rigged Texan with red mohair cinches, tooled Mexican patterns on fender and skirt, and a hemp-worn pommel. It was well used, which I believe gave all our imaginations a pleasing slap, and it had also arrived quixotically. Davy had bought it off a farmer who'd bought it off a migrant laborer who'd traded his horse for a windbroke Dodge truck on a dirt road north of Austin; the migrant had said good-bye to his loyal beast but kept the saddle out of sentiment. Days later under northern skies he understood that its presence in the pickup only made him heartsick and he unloaded it cheap to the farmer, who, though confused by Spanish, understood burdens and the need to escape them.

All this Davy told us with Swede astride the saddle on her bedroom floor. Davy's work had brought the thing back to near perfection; the smell of soaped leather, which is like that of good health, rose around us. It was flawed only in the cantle, where the leather had split and pulled apart. Davy acknowledged with frustration that this must've happened years ago and he was unable to mend it. 'But it doesn't matter for riding,' he said.

'That's true,' Swede said practically, just as if there were a pony out waiting in the yard.

Well, the day defined extravagance. Though wisdom councils against yanking out all stops, Swede did seem joyously forgetful of recent evils, and we kept the momentum as long as we could: waffles for breakfast, sugar lumps dipped in saucers of coffee. I remember it as October days are always remembered, cloudless, maple-flavored, the air gold and so clean it quivers. After lunch (toasted cheese sandwiches), Dad opened the coat closet and with great care unfolded something scarlet, crinkled, shroudlike. When he called it a balloon I was confused at first, thinking of the rubber kind. This one was of tissue paper and at least ten feet high. It had an open bottom weighted with a circle of wire. In the backyard Swede and I held the bottom of the bag while Dad lit a coffee-can mixture of gas and number-two fuel oil. Heat-fattened in minutes, the balloon commenced to tug. When it was pulling hard enough to lift a good-sized cat, Dad set a hubcap atop the can to quench the fire, and we let it go. It went up quickly – a light wind slipped in from the east and the balloon caught it, tilted a little, then righted into a smooth, angled ascent. When the balloon was a dark bug on a pale blue wall Dad jogged Swede with his elbow. 'Ah, Swede,' he said, 'nine years!'

A car horn sounded out front. Davy trotted round and came back looking like he'd burped sour. He said, 'Dad, it's Lurvy.'

Swede looked aggrieved. She said nothing aloud, to her credit.

'All right,' Dad said. His carriage drooped an inch or so, I won't say it didn't, but you couldn't have guessed a thing from his face. The horn honked again, and Dad went around front and laughed boldly once and told Tin Lurvy to come in for coffee.

Picture a fat man, suit full of sweatspots, knees pointing inward for support. Imagine the voice of a much picked-on yet somehow hopeful child. If John Calvin was right, destiny had a serious grudge against Tin Lurvy, a purple-faced, futile, tragically sociable traveling salesman. Had he only been pushy he wouldn't have been a problem; Dad never minded hurrying Fuller Brush men along. But Lurvy didn't push – in fact, he never mentioned what he was selling unless you asked. I suspect few people did. Merchandise didn't seem to matter much to Lurvy, except as conversation – garrulous conversation, too, because Lurvy preferred to run about one-quarter drunk. Along American turnpikes he had failed to peddle vacuum cleaners, saucepans, patent medicines, candy, cufflinks, hairpieces. (I didn't know all this at the time, but would learn it soon, gracefully worded, in his obituary.) Though he probably came through Roofing but once or twice yearly, it was more than enough to establish him as a kind of mean joke among us clannish kids. One Christmas Eve (the dishes done, the gospel of Luke read aloud, presents imminent), Davy looked out the window and said, 'Oh, no, Tin Lurvy's driving up!' The bluff dropped my organs into my shoes. Worse, it turned prophetic: Lurvy really was driving up, except he was only as far as Michigan at the time. Come New Year's Eve (10 p.m., popcorn rattling in the pan, Swede and I looking ahead to the one time all year we'd see midnight), Lurvy drove up for real. Atop the stove were four glossy carameled apples, one for each of us to eat at the stroke of twelve. Lurvy ate Dad's.

The arrival of Tin always turned your day in unexpected directions. Here we'd been trying to give Swede a birthday to make her troubles flee; now we wanted to flee as well. It had to be done quickly if at all; otherwise protocol took hold, like the death rigor, requiring a person to respect company and sit and listen, in the case of Lurvy, to pointless recitations about people you didn't know, most of them Democrats. Illinois Democrats, Delaware Democrats, Ohio Democrats – gracious, how Lurvy admired them all. 'The Democratic Party is the best family I got,' Lurvy liked to declare, a truer statement than any of us knew.

So while Dad started a pot of coffee and hunted around for cookies, Swede gathered Davy and me behind the house. 'It's *my* birthday,' she said. 'I didn't invite Mr Lurvy!'

She never would've pouted so in Dad's presence; it was unacceptable form – and anyhow there was something about the fat salesman that brought out the Samaritan in Dad. We all recognized this, including Lurvy. The advantage was all his.

'Maybe if Dad bought something from him he'd go away,' I suggested.

Swede was suspicious. 'What's he selling?'

'Encyclopedias,' Davy said. '*World Book* encyclopedias. They cost a couple hundred dollars.'

From inside we could hear Dad setting out cups and opening cupboards, and also the cheerful insensibility of Lurvy's opening monologue – the sounds of hope landing facedown.

Swede said, 'I'll just go in and help Dad find the cookies.' Poor duty-wracked girl, she was almost crying.

'No. Let's go to the timber,' Davy said. 'Let him find the cookies, Swede. He knows where they are.' The timber was a hundred-acre woodlot at the edge of Roofing wherein lay solace for the hard-hit.

'No, he doesn't,' Swede said bitterly. 'He doesn't.'

'They don't need cookies anyway,' Davy said; then, grinning, 'Let 'em eat cake,' which brought a giggle from Swede. There was a joke here I didn't get. But she shook her head and replied sagely, 'The cake's what I'm trying to save.' It was her birthday, after all – I suppose she'd baked that cake herself. Gathering all possible drama she said, 'If I'm not back in two minutes, you guys go on without me.'

And do you know, she wasn't back – not in two minutes, or five, or ten. Then Davy said, 'Let's pull out, Rube,' and peeking through the window I saw poor Swede installed at the kitchen table, tall glass of milk in front of her, a single desolate cookie lying untouched on a saucer and lament in her eyes. Dad by now looked not just patient but downright indulgent with Lurvy, whom I could hear talking through the glass: *I tell you I ordered me an Airstream trailer? Twenty foot. Got a bathroom in it with running water. Even a pot! Ha-ha!*

It grieved us, leaving Swede that way, but she'd volunteered, so off we tramped down county blacktop. The afternoon was still bright and smelled of wheat stubble and warm dust. Sometimes we stepped down into the high killed grass to spook hares out of the ditch – Davy had snagged his little carbine out of the garage – but we weren't really hunting and he didn't pull on any of the hares, just sighted down the barrel at them zigzagging away.

The timber, I should tell you, was one of the best places God ever made. The trees were mostly burroaks, wide knuckly giants whose leaves in autumn turned deep brown and beetleback shiny. Dried, those leaves were so stiff you could feel them through the soles of your shoes. A fellow named Draper owned the land then, a happy old crank, and he ran a few independent Jersey cows on it to keep the grass down. In the timber we'd seen badgers, mink, fox, an overconfident fisher stretched out smiling on a limb; these beyond the usual million gray squirrels and woodchucks. Also in spring and fall were crows by the dozens, shiny-eyed bellicose buggers swaying in the high branches, cawing and losing their balance and flapping languidly.

Abruptly Davy asked, 'Did you see Swede's bruises?'

I nodded. 'She didn't say anything. I just saw by accident.'

'You think Dad knows?'

I didn't, really. 'Maybe.'

We kicked on toward the deepest part of the timber; the deader oak leaves get, the more noise they make. My lungs were getting a little stiff on the intake, and Davy was keeping a quick, frustrated pace.

'You think,' he said, 'that Dad is afraid?'

I stopped – had to – crouched for breath. 'Afraid of what?' I'll admit my mind was occupied. Sometimes when the breathing goes it goes like *that* – like smoke filling a closet.

'Finch and Basca. Are you okay, Rube?'

I nodded, shut my eyes, took in as much air as I could and let it out slow, all the way out, down to the bottom. I said, 'He's not afraid of those guys. He beat 'em up in the locker room that night.'

Davy said nothing. Maybe that was what had him so irritable: he thought Dad was scared. Maybe it scared him in turn, or maybe he just thought it was weakness. Finally he said, 'Are you scared, Rube?'

'Naw.'

He watched me breathe awhile. 'You think God looks out for us?'

'Well, yeah,' I said.

And Davy asked, 'You want Him to?'

I nodded, thinking, What an oddball question.

We had a strange encounter in the timber that day – we came across a tramp, curled up houndlike beside a ruined fire. We heard him snoring, is how it happened, sawing away like Sunday afternoon. Pushing through

56

undergrowth we crept forward till we saw two shiny black things lying one atop the other; they turned out to be the soles of two shoes, which became attached to a set of ragged stockings, then the gray pants of some throwaway business suit. At last we stood in a tiny clearing amid dead brush, looking down at a small red-haired redbearded fellow, sleeping away most desperately, his back propped against an army duffel. He hadn't a single gray hair that I could see – I suppose he was in his thirties, at most – but his legs were so thin the socks bagged, and the grit of decades seemed settled in his face. I remember the smells of cold fire, and old sandwich meat, and another that was new to me then – a sorrowful taint as of long disuse. The smell of a room not opened in years.

We left the tramp lying there, us boys a little stunned at such need for sleep; we backed away, and didn't speak, and moved a bit more quietly through the timber going home. We never saw the man again. I'm not even sure why I mention him here – it's not as if he pops up later, holding a clue or moral or other momentous piece of story. (It's tempting, certainly, to assign him the duty of harbinger. He'd make a good one, so worn and dessicated beside his sorry coals. But I doubt he was. A tramp can be just a plain tramp, you know; he can build a fire in someone's favorite woods, even ours. It was a strange moment, is all.)

But when we stepped out from the trees – stepped out into a peevish wind, the sky telling of winter, evening-colored at four in the afternoon – shouldn't I have felt something then? As we walked toward home, toward lighted windows, shouldn't I have sensed the Lands adrift, pushed off course, gone wayward?

Supper that night was Swede's favorite, a red-potato chowder Dad mixed up with hunks of northern pike. Seasoned with vinegar and pepper this was our king of soups; a person didn't even want to put crackers in it.

My heart sank when I entered the kitchen and saw Dad standing at the stove, nodding and stirring while Lurvy talked on. His senses roused by the aroma of creamed pike and reds, Lurvy was expounding on his most cherished road meal of all time, a bowl of Fisherman's Stew he'd ordered in Seattle at a place called Iver's Acres of Clams. Yes, Iver knew his mollusks. Proficient biologist as well as canny gourmet, Iver knew where the best clams resided – stalked the beaches himself, daily, to shovel them up fresh, and so on. I felt we were being set up; that no matter how delicious Dad's batch of chowder, we would all be subjected, during its consumption, to a comparison with Iver's wondrous clams, in which our king of soups would be reduced to something along the lines of a jack. I saw this coming and perhaps Davy did too, because he said, with mild impertinence, 'Where's your next stop, Mr Lurvy? Do you have a long way to go?'

But Lurvy only smiled. 'No scheduled stops, son. It's thoughtful of you to ask. Interested in traveling, are you? Let me tell you about a little seafood place I found up in the Cascades . . .'

Meantime I peeked into the pan Dad was stirring and became alarmed; why, he'd only made a regular batch. With Lurvy at the table he ought to've tripled it, even I knew that. Lurvy could eat this much all by himself, without noticing! Inside my mind we all sat down, Lurvy to our prized soup and the rest of us to bread and butter; I imagined Lurvy slurping joyously, pausing only to denigrate the broth; I saw the final spoonful vanish; I heard his belch of conquest.

'Something wrong, Reuben?' Dad said. I looked stricken, I guess.

'Is this all the soup?'

Dad grinned, saying, 'Well, of course,' and for a moment I understood Davy's chronic impatience. Sometimes it really was as if Dad had no clue at all.

Lurvy said, 'Better wash your hands, kids. No dirty

fingers at this table,' and then, without rising to wash his own, reached for the napkins Dad had laid out and tucked two of them into the top of his shirt.

The soup, I must tell you, was peerless. The beloved Iver himself must have authored no such broth, for Lurvy said nothing of clams, or Seattle, or anything that might detract from the present delectation. He ate a bowl in owlish silence, confounded I guess by excellence, and seeing this we kids all ate the faster, comparing the man's appetite with the humble size of the soup pot.

'More, Tin?' Dad offered, and Lurvy held up his bowl.

With that second helping, the silence broke. Lurvy had found joy at our table and settled in as though home from the wars. Spooning up soup, he looked benevolently around at the four of us. He said, 'I had my appendix out last month; they showed it to me when I come to; it was yellow as paint and six inches long. Your normal appendix goes about three and a half. Did you know that?'

Well, none of us had known it until that moment. Perhaps if we'd owned *World Book* we would've, but there commenced an education on appendixes and their ailments and removal, Lurvy's in particular, that speaking for myself I'd rather have heard after supper. Between spoonfuls Lurvy told us how your appendix is shaped like a worm and hangs leechlike on to your large intestine; how it can go bad with no warning whatever and land a normal happy person in a world of hurt. He told how his own appendix had grown beyond its intended duty (the nature of which eludes doctors to this day) until it almost did him in. He was sitting in a tavern in Pennsylvania, talking to a purveyor of dark German ales – a good Democrat, incidentally – when he felt faint and stood to clear his head. Next thing he was on his back, conscious only of a fertile nausea and an awful groaning, such as sick cats make, and of the ale man kneeling above, pinching Lurvy's nose shut and kissing him like the world would end. ('Did you kiss him back?' Swede said, aghast; Lurvy held up his bowl; Dad ladled in soup.) Resuscitating cloudily, his mind befogged, Lurvy could only assume that the ale man had lost his wits, and also that the prolonged and strangely pneumatic smooch was the source of the nausea. What would *you* do? Lurvy asked us. Wouldn't you lurch upward, trying to get away? And if your forehead happened to crack the ale man's nose and knock him colder than a Catholic mackerel, was that your fault? He told how, when the ambulance arrived, it was obliged to cart them *both* off, the pending appendectomy and the sleeping ale man, whose nose, Lurvy said, lay dead flat against his face. ('Who'd like more chowder?' Dad asked. 'Me,' Lurvy answered.) The operation had gone well enough, except the anesthetic hadn't been applied appropriate to Lurvy's great size, and he'd remained frowzy throughout, asking the surgeon what *that thing* was, and whether he'd washed his hands, and once believing he was eight years old again, having his tonsils out.

During this discourse Lurvy ate at least five bowls of soup. Could've been six; things run together under the spell of epics. I myself had only one bowl, the last spoonful of which had just entered my mouth when Lurvy took off describing his diseased appendix, all yellow and foul, like some pusworm dropped in a doctor's pan. The image stopped my supper then and there but had no effect on Swede, who ate, I believe, three bowls, probably out of principle, it being her birthday. Later, after cake, when Lurvy had gone, Dad admitted he'd had two bowls of soup despite the morbid narrative. He was a little wide-eyed at the integrity of his own broth, asking Swede, 'What did I put in it? Did we fix this batch differently? My goodness.'

All this from a pot of soup meant to feed the four of us

and no more. A *small* pot of soup. Was I the only one who noticed how many bowls were served, how the pot was replenished as though from a well, how there was somehow enough again and again to fill the ladle? Cleaning up the dishes after supper I felt a surprising weight in the faithful vessel and, lifting the lid, beheld a pot still more than half full of our king of soups.

Make of it what you will.

But onward. Between supper and what came later I remember a cold rain dripping off the eaves as Lurvy's taillights eased away. I remember Swede's head against my shoulder and her saying, 'You think it'll turn to snow, Reuben? Oh, I hope it turns to snow!' I remember Dad moving slowly in the house, a terrible headache having taken him almost the moment Lurvy departed. Walking stooped, reaching to turn off lights that hurt his eyes, Dad tripped over Swede's saddle, which she'd dragged into the living room. When she ran to him he said, 'Don't worry – don't worry,' and picked up the saddle and carried it to her bedside. But his head was ringing with a pain visible at the edges of eyes and mouth.

Swede and I went to bed early. Davy slung on a coat and left the darkened house. I lay wakeful, conscious of breathing, discomforted at Dad's stumble, at the pain that blinded him. And I wondered again about Swede's bruises, how much they'd cost her in fear alone. Rising I looked out the window: Davy's lit tobacco was an orange dot in the rain. I crossed the hall, whispering, 'Swede, are you awake?' But she was already far gone into night, mouth open, her breathing faintly snotty. I was pleased to see *The Big Fifty* turned on outspread pages beside her bed; she'd gotten a ways in before the day overtook her. Beneath the rainshot window the saddle camped in a pearly glow. It drew me. I knelt and touched the leather: the soft polish of long miles, the gentle orderly smell of horse and paste soap. There is magic in tack, as I said before, and it's

61

no embellishment to say that saddle seemed almost to breathe and sigh in some easy creaking dream of the West, just as Swede was likely doing. I ran my hand down the slope of the horn, down the slick sitting place and up the swept cantle, and that's when I noticed that the flaw – the pulled-apart leather Davy had been unable to fix, that he'd apologized for – was gone. I felt with both hands, though the saddle in its luminosity showed me well enough that the breach in the leather had closed. The wound had simply *healed up*. I felt a comfortable strangeness, as if smiled upon by someone behind my back; I sat on my haunches there in Swede's cool room and remembered how Dad, after stumbling over the saddle, had picked it up in his patient hands and carried it here and set it down again. I touched the cantle: just smooth leather, not even a seam.

Make of *that* what you will.

Sometime past midnight the rain turned to snow. I could tell by the difference in the sound against the window: a less sharp, wetter sound. At first I thought that was what wakened me.

Then the door handle turned – the back door, off the kitchen. I knew that little squeal. How I wanted it to be Davy coming in, smoky and quiet and shaking off water, but Davy was inside already, sleeping not five feet from me, breathing through his nose in satisfied draughts. Nor was it Dad, for I could hear him too, rolling to and fro in sleep, wrestling his headache.

I heard the dry complaint of the kitchen floor, of the place beside the broom closet where joists groaned underfoot, and if I'd had any doubt that someone had got inside the house it vanished when a damp current of air came in and touched my ears and forehead.

Davy smacked, swallowed, sank to yet more earnest sleep. My lungs shrank with expectation; my whole surface hurt; I ached to creep across and wake him but felt benumbed, crippled. Now for the first time I heard real footsteps. They crossed the living room. A shoulder bumped the mantelpiece. My windowpane filled with a burst of driven snow and I abandoned myself to the knowledge that I'd waited too long to wake Davy. What would happen now would happen.

The steps came forward. They stopped at my door. I felt, more than heard, someone's hand upon the knob.

Then Davy spoke from beside me – 'Switch on the light' – his voice so soft he might've been talking in his sleep. But he wasn't. He was talking to whomever stood incorporeal in the doorway. 'Switch it *on*,' he commanded, and next thing we were all of us bright-soaked and blinking: me beneath my quilt, and Israel Finch standing in the door with a baseball bat in one hand and the other still on the switch, and poor stupid Tommy all asquint behind his shoulder. Davy was sitting up in bed in his T-shirt, hair askew. Somehow he was holding the little Winchester he'd carried in the timber that afternoon. And holding it comfortably: elbows at rest on his knees, his cheek against the stock, as if to plink tin cans off fenceposts.

It is fair to say that Israel had no chance. I'm not saying he deserved one. He stood in the door with his pathetic club like primal man squinting at extinction. How confused he looked, how pinkeyed and sweaty! Then he lifted the bat, the knothead, and Davy fired, and Israel went backward into Tommy Basca, and Davy levered up a second round and fired again.

Did you ever hear a rifle shot inside a house? Inside a plastered room? You may imagine how the place came alive, even while the opposite was happening for Israel Finch. (He had no last murmur that I could detect; the round made a bright black raindrop above and between his two eyebrows so that Swede, much later, would write that his corpse *lay painted like a Brahmin maid*.) He was on his back in the hallway with that dot on his forehead and no exit wound behind (a good argument, Dr Nokes would bluntly note, for small calibers) when Swede came flying from her room. She saw, besides Finch, Tommy Basca on his stomach with hands aquiver toward the door, and Davy stepping up behind him. And she saw me, I suppose: me watching the end of all our lives as we had lived them heretofore. I remember the sound of Swede's gasping voice and her exhaled *huff* as Dad yanked her into the bathroom and slapped the door shut. I looked at Tommy Basca, who was shot too, though not cleanly as was Finch. Tommy clawed the floor, bawling incomprehensibly, and his eyes rolled, and there was genuine terror inside his voice, and I knew with certainty he was seeing all the devils waiting for him, whetting their long knives, that he could hear their gabbling shrieks, that the smell of sulfur so quick in the room issued from some dim mouthlike chamber panting after his soul. Standing above him, Davy levered up a third cartridge.

I ought've looked away but couldn't.

He lowered the barrel to the base of Tommy Basca's skull. For an instant my brother seemed very small – like a stranger seen at a clear distance. He showed no tremor. He fired. Tommy relaxed. The house went quiet except for Swede, sobbing behind the bathroom door. The sulfur smell hung a moment, then faded. Davy straightened, not looking at me or at Dad, who emerged with arms scratched red from restraining Swede. Davy wiped his face, said, 'Well . . .' then stepped over Tommy and out the door.

And when did he know just what he'd done? We've wondered that, Swede and I. When did it come to Davy Land that exile is a country of shifting borders, hard to quit yet hard to endure, no matter your wide shoulders, no matter your toughened heart?

Peeking at Eternity

No one would be more annoyed than Davy if I tried to recast the predicament under some redemptive glow. Two boys were dead in our house and there was no bright side to the matter. I recall Davy sitting on the basement stairs under a yellow bulb, jacket dragged on over his T-shirt, his face oily with rain. He wouldn't speak and his eyes showed a narcosis that was fearful to me. We waited together for Ted Pullet to arrive. Dad, far gone in prayer, held Swede in one arm and gripped Davy's shoulder with the other. I recall a sensation of splitting in two, of becoming smaller. I babbled to Davy that it would be all right, that he had not meant to do it.

Which woke him from wherever he'd been, for he turned and snared my wrist. 'Don't say it's all right, Rube, don't say it. I meant to do it. I meant to. You hear me?' I could only nod frantically. Cars had driven up while he spoke, and we heard doors thumping and voices and saw red lights bouncing off the windows.

Davy said, 'Here we go then.'

He was always impatient with our family's general insistence that things turn out for the best.

* * *

True story: in the spring of Dad's twenty-eighth year, he was raised up by a tornado, along with most of the roof above him and a few loose boards he was setting into the floor.

This was when he was married to my mother, attending a little school in Iowa under the GI Bill. In those days Dad's love of books and scholarly quest kept him happily consumed – he was one of those honorably ambitious self-educated men loved by American folklorists, a Lincoln-hearted reader who might walk ten miles to borrow a volume of poetry by John Donne or a novel by Melville or, to be particularly honest about it, Owen Wister. Loving to study and possessed of unusual compassion he leaned naturally toward medicine, and I imagine my mother falling easily for this generous and handsome and obviously rising young man. (To this day, in fact, it is easy for me to conjure the look our lives might've had, if Dad had but held course: an unassuming farmhouse with a wide-swept porch, surrounded, I'm guessing, by a few head of Angus beef on a pastoral acreage, because a doctor needs his recreation, a couple good quarter horses in a painted corral, Mom coming out the back door slapping flour off her apron, calling us kids for supper, looking pleased and content. Surprising, isn't it, how close such pictures lie beneath the surface?)

From what I heard those were fine times. Davy was a year old and tottered roguishly around the glad-hearted poverty of married-student housing; Mother fed him and wore thin from the chase and read him to sleep from Robert Louis Stevenson. Dad studied the bones of the science department's hanging skeleton, name of Yorick, a short scurvied fellow gone the color of weak tea. A professor of Dad's told him Yorick was no conscientious volunteer but was instead a hard-luck Calcuttan who'd been dredged from the Ganges River and been boiled clean and had ridden the black market to the American Midwest. It made a person think. When not studying, Dad worked, sweeping and painting in the athletic building twenty hours a week, unknowingly getting all the education he was going to need right there in his coveralls. It was the athletic building, Dewey Hall, that the tornado struck, just past eleven one heatsoaked night in September. This, by the way, is the only story Dad ever told us *in whispers*: how the tornado came cruising up out of the south, birthed from a yellow cloud; how it touched earth at the fringe of town, a pale umbilical rope, to corkscrew almost shyly up College Drive, gathering dirt but little else. Next morning the first thing emergent residents noticed was their street, swept like never before, and all streetside grass combed and pointed as if in praise to some passing magnificence.

Dad was working late, installing new floorboards on the basketball court where a light fixture had fallen the previous winter – it just worked loose and fell, interrupting a home game, injuring no one but thrilling the crowd with its descent and powdery detonation. Dewey Hall was the only building on campus not made of brick, and the tornado came for it in absolute maturity, no umbilical growth now but a strong slender lady hip-walking through campus – past the science hall, past English, jumping Old Main and the library with deliberate grace and lighting on the shallow roof of Dewey, where Dad toiled alone. He said it didn't sound like a train, as the wisdom goes, but like a whole mountain breaking loose and skidding sideways over the ground, and looking up he saw shingles in the air, and bits of sky-light glass hovering in slow circles; he saw incandescent fixtures likewise floating, torn from their sockets yet their filaments whole and gloriously charged by some storm-bent physics; and as he sprang for the basement steps – not fifty feet away – he heard the great slab of ceiling tear loose and felt himself move upward, ascending in bodily confusion out of the range of gravity and earth and earthly help.

Meantime my mother, awakened in their third-floor garret by the hissing wind, leapt up in time to see the rotating head of the funnel coast overhead, lit municipally from below. Gusts of sand raked the panes. No accumulation of hard feelings can diminish my admiration for what she did then, which was to fly nightgowned into Davy's tiny room, seize a folded quilt, and brace it against his window. Thus she stood while the noise rose from a hiss to a many-noted baying; thus she stood as all lights failed and glass burst elsewhere in the building and the noise became everything a mind could hold.

As Dad told the story this was always the moment of triumph, the turn of the war toward winning: Mother is leaning against the window, standing between the gale and little Davy, and at the storm's very crest, when it is like a war come seeking what it might devour, she feels the slightest easing in the glass. At the same time Davy stirs and smacks, he rolls to his stomach, the glass goes still beneath her hands, and by the time Davy's settled back into sleep, the war's moved on, to the north.

(But do you think the worst is over? Remember, Dad is only now on the ascent — hammer in hand, he's peeking at eternity — Mom's tears of relief are just standing at the corners of her eyes. Nope, the worst, for Mom at least, is still to come.)

First thing she did, Dad told us, after the storm moved on, was to run out groping for the hall telephone they shared with the third floor. To ring up Dewey, of course — to check on Dad. The line was dead, no surprise, but a strange thing; the handset was hot. Not warm as if from someone's hand but *hot*, charged, voltage-goosed. Mother had it to her ear before her palm registered pain. Later she would say the scorched phone scared her more than the storm. It seemed outside of nature. It foretold evil. Dropping it, she felt her way back and pulled Davy from his crib and held him for comfort. I imagine them at the window she'd stood braced against, looking across campus, but you couldn't see Dewey Hall from there, the lights were still out, and anyhow Old Main stood up between them.

Within the hour, someone knocked. In the dark, wrapped in a robe, Mother opened the door to a small committee of men, their lanternlit faces the color of burning paper. The man in front said, 'Mrs Land, Dewey Hall is down.'

And there it was: the worst. She heard them out, their descriptions of the torn building, the void where the roof had been, the twists of painted siding and electrical wire and ruinous plankage spread north-ward in a long littered swath. They'd taken lanterns and hoisted wreckage and found no sign of Mr Land. Others were searching even now. They needn't have told my mother she should prepare for still harder tidings, but they were clumsy fellows and no doubt completely at sea. Was there a right way to deliver the sort of news they carried?

As to my mother's state of mind in those next hours, I can only guess. Once in my life I knew a grief so hard I could actually hear it inside, scraping at the lining of my stomach, an audible ache, dredging with hooks as rivers are dredged when someone's been missing too long. I have to think my mother felt something like that. Maybe Davy woke and distracted her; maybe she was numb; maybe she had the reserves to begin planning even then how best to make her way in a world that had been so friendly only the night before. All I know for sure, from Dad's telling, is this: she was at the kitchen table late that morning, having dressed and fed Davy and set him to riding his reined footstool, when the hall phone, restored to service, began to ring. She sat a long while, wanting someone else to get it, but the whole floor had emptied, gone to class and to work and to walk blinking round the former Dewey Hall. At last she got up and answered. A woman asked for Mrs Jeremiah Land.

'Speaking,' said my mother.

'Did your car survive the storm, Mrs Land?' the woman asked.

My mother said, sharply, 'What are you talking about?' Be patient with her, now; think of her long night.'

'Mrs. Land' the woman said, 'I'm Marianne Evans. Our farm is four miles north of town. I got a man here drinking coffee on my porch. He says he's your husband.'

Well, we all hold history differently inside us. For Swede such episodes retold themselves into a seamless and momentous narrative; she had a Homeric grasp on the significance of events, and still does; one of her recent letters asks, *Is it hubris to believe we all live epics?* (Perhaps it is, but I suspect she's not actually counting on me for an answer.) Dad, he himself would say, was baptized by that tornado into a life of new ambitions – interpreted by many, including my mother, as a life of no ambitions. Finishing out that semester, he moved his family off campus and found work as a plumber's assistant. This was the anticlimactic denouement to his whispered tornado story: having been whisked through four miles of debris-cluttered sky, having been swallowed by the wrath of God and been kept not just safe but unbruised inside it, having been awakened midmorning in a fallow field by a face-licking retriever – Dad's response was to leave his prosperous track and plunge his hands joyfully into the sewer. An explanation is beyond me other than to repeat what he would often say, the story ended, his hands tucking up the blankets, 'I was treated so *gently* up there, kids.'

But the whole thing bothered Davy, and with Dad

out of earshot he'd say so. You couldn't get blown around in a tornado, he said, and not get banged up. It didn't make sense. It wasn't right.

Swede challenged him. 'Are you calling Dad a liar?'

'Of course not. I know it happened. It just *shouldn't* have. Don't you see that?'

'No,' Swede replied.

But I saw what he meant, or I would eventually. Davy wanted life to be something you did on your own; the whole idea of a protective, fatherly God annoyed him. I would understand this better in years to come but never subscribe to it, for I was weak and knew it. I hadn't the strength or the instincts of my immigrant forebears. The weak must bank on mercy – without which, after all, I wouldn't have lasted fifteen minutes. History simply hadn't equipped me as it had Davy. You had only to look at his hands to see it: his hands were hard as any man's, and quick – quick as eyesight. They moved always as with a purpose long known. History was built into Davy so thoroughly he could never see how it owned him.

And Mom? I can only believe she sat down and wept, after that phone call, as any loving wife might do. How she must have rejoiced, how frantically she must've driven to the Evans farm – and the clasping and shuddering of that reunion must've been a thing Marianne Evans would tell her neighbors about and remember in her heart on rainy evenings while her husband worked in the barn. Happily for Marianne, she would not see the changes that tornado wrought. She wouldn't see my mother's puzzlement as Dad surrendered his studies and his prosperous future; nor my mother's attempts to make the best of it. These attempts lasted quite awhile, really – long enough to bear Swede and me – but she must've felt Dad had violated some part of the covenant between them. She departed without explanation or epilogue. We heard, later, that she married a doctor after all, in Chicago, an

71

older gentleman whose first wife had died; we heard they patronized the symphony and the theater and enjoyed choice memberships. But none of this did we hear from Mother, for no letter or call did we once receive; nor did we ever meet the gentleman on whose behalf we'd been erased.

They put Davy in cuffs and drove him to the Montrose jail and the rest of us to a motel for the night. Easing away through the rain we saw an ambulance backed onto the lawn, a deputy stooped smoking on the porch, and the freeze and fade of windows struck with camera flash.

The whole thing was no less a tornado than the other.

Next day when we went to see Davy, Swede tried to kick him. She was crying and incensed and he reached to comfort her, and she gave it a stout try between the bars, only to clank her shin.

'Good grief, it's lucky I'm in *here*,' Davy remarked, as Swede hopped about, biting her lip. Grim as it was, I could see Dad was glad for the joke. Davy'd shaken off the concussed glaze of the night before. He was in a little cell with tan lighting and squashed flies on the wall, but he'd not grown fangs or become a creature changed beyond knowing. When Swede had got the mad out and hugged Davy through the bars, Dad told us to say goodbye and wait for him in the hall.

That was the hardest thing – going out that door. It was so thick and closed so heavily we couldn't eavesdrop through it, not even with the paper cup Swede swiped from the watercooler.

Dad was quiet when he joined us. We walked out to the car, the wind flapping staleness off our clothes.

'He seems all right, doesn't he?' I said.

'Sure he does,' Dad replied.

It seemed a long ride home. We got there at supper-time, and Swede and I looked around in the cupboards. Normally Dad would've taken over and worked up some meal or other, or at least suggested that Swede and I do it, but instead he just sat in a kitchen chair and leaned back shuteyed.

Thinking of supper, I asked, 'You want us to do anything, Dad?'

'Persevere,' he said.

It was a better answer than we wanted. What else to do when the landscape changes? When all mirrors tilt? That first week Swede rose as usual and demanded that I help her cook Dad's oatmeal, but he could no more eat it than he could wave and run for Congress

Suddenly, lots of people we didn't know were calling and dropping by. Reporters, yes: an apologetic writer from the county weekly in Montrose, a sad-mouthed fellow from the *Star* in Minneapolis, two different radio men, slumpshouldered from their big reel-to-reels, and the first TV correspondent ever sighted locally, which merited an article and photo of its own in the *Montrose Observer*. We also heard from certain bold and ambitious lawyers who'd read the early accounts and, for some reason, from a slew of young women who'd seen Davy's tragic mug in the news and imagined him misunderstood.

Meantime, a lot of people we did know, and whose cheerful encouragement I'll bet Dad could've used, were staying away. A few examples? How about Harold Barkus, the gas and oil man who did all the repairs on our aging Plymouth, who once came to Dad drunk and weeping after his wife had left, and drooled a quart into our couch that night as he slept, and left next morning sober and galvanized, with a hot breakfast in him? Harold Barkus wouldn't even fill our gas tank anymore, instead sending his gangly boy out to do it. Through plate glass we could see Harold, sitting in his office, not looking out.

How about Leroy Biersten, the principal of the

school, who'd hired Dad and who'd sat grieving at our table when his daughter turned up pregnant by a fled serviceman? Do you suppose Leroy could think of a word of comfort?

Maybe it was fear, I don't know; maybe embarrassment. Maybe these people put themselves in Dad's place, figuring they'd wish for no one to say a word if their son had shot down two boys; if it were their son sitting all day all night in that courthouse cell.

Or maybe – could this be? – they just reasoned Dad was due some grief. That a man like him couldn't be exactly what he seemed. Perhaps it relieved their anxious souls that the clock ran against Jeremiah Land as it ran against them all.

I think of Oscar Larson, who liked to take Dad fishing because it seemed the walleyes always gathered round when Dad was in the boat. And of Gary Sweet, the butcher, whose walk-in freezer Dad had fixed during the July hot spell the previous summer, saving the integrity of uncounted beeves. I think of Ron Simonson, the odd-jobs man, who could count on Dad for occasional work – sharpening mower blades, shingling the garage, doing such tasks as Dad would've been delighted to do himself had Ron not needed employment. And I think, can't help it, of those friends of Job's in the Old Testament, the men who came to Job as he lay there in his bed of ashes, all twisted with boils and the loss of his children, and said to him, *Now what did you go and do?*

Of course vindictiveness is an ugly trait and, yes, I do mean to forgive all these nice deserters; I mean, eventually, to say, to their ghosts if not their living faces, *It's all right. I understand. I might've done the same.*

Not yet, though. Let me bear witness first.

Two men I remember who did not desert – no, three. They were the Methodist preacher James Reach, and Dr Animas Nokes, and also Mr Layton, first name of

Gerard, the dimestore man who'd been struck of the spirit at the hand of Reverend Johnny Latt. Reach and Layton and Nokes: these three.

Strangely, it was Dad who seemed to suffer most, and Dad whom these few rallied round, while Davy – who had aimed and fired, aimed and fired, aimed and fired – Davy sat suspended on a county bench and seemed on the whole the same boy who'd always been my favored brother. Though some thinner; he didn't eat much in there. I remember a moment when he rose from his seat against the cinderblock and put his arms around me through the bars, and I put mine around his narrow waist. Then I saw how dark he was beneath his chin, and how his skin looked rough and loose like a much older man's. He grinned and wouldn't let me cry. 'Say, Natty' – his hands strong upon my shoulders – 'don't you eat those geese yet. You keep those in the deepfreeze till I get out. Just a little while.' At this I recall a stirring of the jailer who stood close by, a fleeting chuckle of his keys as if at Davy's words, *till I get out; a little while.* But I held my eyes on Davy's and saw a thing that jailer couldn't: I saw the shine of certainty, of faith, of some knowledge inside my brother; and I knew in whom I could believe.

But if Davy didn't get much reassurance in person – and you know, even Dolly didn't go see him, not right away – he surely did get it through the mail. Especially those first days, when the newspapers leaned graciously in his direction. Not the *Montrose Observer*, which still had the Finch and Basca families to live beside and so took an almost ludicrous care with the story; but the Minneapolis daily's first few headlines were the stuff of scrapbooks. TEENAGE SON DEFENDS HOME AND FAMILY. HELD WITHOUT BAIL AT SIXTEEN — DAVY LAND JAILED FOR SHOOTING ASSAILANTS. DAVY'S SISTER: 'HE SAVED MY LIFE.' (This last was a triumph for the solemn fellow from the *Star*, who sat at a distance watching our house until Dad went into the backyard to rake;

the reporter then sprinted to a phone booth, Clark Kentlike, dialed our number, and by pure good manners got a sentence or two out of Swede before Dad, hearing her voice through the screened windows, returned, rightfully suspicious.)

These stories lit fuses under an astonishing number of folks. They wrote letters as if impelled by nature; as if Davy embodied whatever it was they'd thought long-lost and wanted back.

Dear Davy Land,

In this Godless day of corrupt youth and permissiveness toward criminals it is reassuring to see a young man stand up in defense of hearth and home. That you are reading this in jail is no surprise to me but instead a sorrowful commentary on the way we treat those who dare to do what is right. Lest you begin to doubt yourself let me reassure you. Those fellows who broke into your house were cast from evil molds, they had in mind to hurt and kill, and they reaped what they had thought to sow. Your bravery gives us all new hearts,

Sincerely

Dear Davy,

I'm a widow (young) whose good husband died two months before our house was broke into by a bad boy from the neighborhood. Often I have wondered what my husband would of done had he been here and now I think I know. He was a strong man. He had eyes remindful of your own, as struck me when I saw your picture. I am sorry for you to be where you are right now but am praying for you daily. Will there be a trial? I am enclosing a recent photograph of myself.

Warm regards

So many letters came those first two weeks that one of the deputies, Walt Stockard, who'd managed to father four restive daughters before his twenty-seventh birthday, brought in a shoe box to hold them all. The shoe box was festooned with pink ribbons and all manner of brocade and peppermint swirls laid on with crayons, so that it looked like it ought to hold valentines; every day Stockard would replenish the box from that morning's post and in slow hours would pull up a chair and prop his boots on the bars, dipping into the mail and reading aloud. 'Here's one from a Maggie in St Paul.

Dear Davy,
   I am in the ninth grade at Washington School, we have just begun to read William Shakespeare, our teacher Mr Willis demands we read *Julius Caesar* even though he *knows* it is *Romeo and Juliet* we all desire. I hope you will write back, I would like to have a pen pal, maybe we could tell each other our thoughts, I am only fourteen but everyone says I am mature for my age.

'And say, Davy – it's got perfume on it.'
None of this was comforting to Dad, however. There arrived a day when the phone budged into our dinner-table quietude, informing us that Davy would be charged with two counts of manslaughter – that charge instead of murder because of Davy's age and because the victims had entered the house bent on mischief. 'Mischief?' Swede said. '*Mischief?*'
   I knew what she meant. *Mischief* was the word Dad used when we ventured into the timber with a hatful of firecrackers, meaning to explode cowpies. In fact we were now beset with a whole lexicon of legal apple-sauce; Swede and I eavesdropped on a man in a beard and a tan baggy suit who sat at the table drinking the coffee Dad so tiredly poured, the two of them talking in quiet voices about *jury selection* and *presumption of innocence* and *change of venue*, this plea and that plea, bail reductions, and judicial prejudices against

violent youth. Salient to me in the visit of the bearded man was not so much his language as his expression, which was wise, guarded, and unencouraged by encountered fact. 'Judge Raster lost his wife last summer,' he told Dad. 'It has not made him soft.' And from this grave disclosure I drew my picture of Judge Raster; a blackrobed hulk, face like a shark's, noose clutched behind his back.

The bearded man, Dad told us next day, was Thomas DeCuellar. He was Davy's defense attorney, appointed by the state. We knew he was a good man because he was on our side and had twenty years' experience in various courts of law, and because he'd brought with him, from his wife, a quart jar of dill pickles she had put up herself, with cloves of bluish garlic and, DeCuellar said, somewhere in there, a jalapeño pepper.

Days came, went. Davy sat; reporters left town in search of new misfortunes; the strange mail dropped off. One morning Swede didn't come out of her room and foiled my snoopish concern by propping a chair beneath her doorknob. 'I'm working,' she declared. 'Don't bother me.'

Her tight-throated resolve gave me new wells of unease to plumb. 'Working on what?'

'Isn't your business.'

She was writing, of course; I could hear the whir of the typewriter carriage as she rolled in a sheet. The fact made me nervous in some abstruse way. What I wanted was for Swede to be Swede: that is, glad and funny and belonging to me, as usual. We'd always been an exclusive pair, she being smart enough for the two of us and never begrudging me her secrets.

'Is it Sunny Sundown?' I asked – sounding, I know, like some dumb jealous boyfriend, but all the same you should've heard the passion she was pouring on those keys.

She didn't answer, so I moped away to the kitchen to eat cornflakes in solitude. Dad was back at work by now, having taken leave after the shootings, and by rights we ought to've been back in school; but Dad, though a believer in education, had never respected the glowing objective of perfect attendance (a goal set for kids, he said, 'by adults with ruined imaginations'). Before returning to his job, he'd sat down with Swede and me and asked if we felt ready to undertake classes and sociability again, or whether we'd like another week at home.

What do you think we were, idiots?

Besides, I suspect Dad didn't want us back in school yet. He was weathering quite a gale there himself, though we didn't know it; Superintendent Holden, first name of Chester, a man whose face was a mine-field of red boils, had decided to scour that janitor's teeth' (his precise words, as told to me later by the daughter of a school board member who'd invited heinous old Chester over for rolls and gossip). I will give you an example of such scouring. Remember how, the night Finch and Basca broke in, the rain changed to snow? Well, it snowed two inches before changing back to rain the next morning, and the rain came cold and steady for some days thereafter, so that the gutters of Roofing ran with brown water, and runoff from the railroad grade sated the yards of trackside residents, and the boulevard maples and elms grew rank and black, their limbs swooning. Had the city been more carefully engineered – had the storm sewers been of greater capacity or the school been built on higher ground – this would've been harmless enough. And yet on Saturday afternoon, two days before Dad returned to work, the sewer system came full. It was stuffed! Squatting on its low plot the school became a living illustration of the properties of water, which, as you know, seeks its own level. How much detail do you need? How much can you stand? I'll spare you beyond saying that when Dad got to school Monday morning he encountered a basement shin deep in evil, a swamp of soft terrors afloat and submerged, a furnace choked and dead, a smell to poise your wits for flight.

Superintendent Holden called off school, of course. But do you think he called a plumber?

The first two days, Dad didn't even come home. He telephoned to ask that I bring him a sandwich and a clean shirt; his voice betrayed the headache that had been riding him all week. When we reached the school Dad met us at the top of the basement steps. His hands were clean but you ought've seen his clothes. He tried leading us away but we looked past him and beheld what he was up against. Did you know that air can have a taste?

'Where's Mr Ringman?' Swede asked suspiciously. Mr Ringman was 'second janitor,' meaning he didn't have as many keys as Dad.

'Well, he left.'

'Couldn't you come home?' I asked. 'Mr Ringman gets to go home.'

Dad said, 'Mr Ringman quit.' Boy, his expression was hard to read. Then, 'Swede, it's all right. Don't, now,' because she'd teared up and was leaning toward him, about to fling her arms round his waist. He glanced at me, alarmed; did I mention his clothes? So up I stepped and Swede laid her head against my chest to cry while I held ungracefully onto her, and Dad's washed hands smoothed her hair and shielded her face and blessed her, it seemed to me, against all coming trouble.

Of note, I think, is that Roofing Elementary actually had a contract with a pipe-and-furnace man in Montrose in order to deal with just such catastrophes. His name was Jack Benedict and he was accompanied always by a big and fractionally tamed raccoon, Roach, who would tangle his leash around

80

your ankles and then bite you when you tried to unwrap him. Jack Benedict had paid many a slippery visit to Roofing Elementary, including the time Roger Capps, who would later join the army and die falling out of a helicopter, snagged his teacher's wig off her head in a fire drill and zigzagged with it through the crowded hall, finding sanctuary in the boys' washroom, whence was heard the inevitable flush. Not to lose my point here: the school had no compunction about calling on Jack Benedict until Superintendent Holden decided Dad's teeth needed scouring.

As far as I was concerned, Mr. Ringman had the right idea. But Dad just bent to work, firing up a widemouth pump that sucked with a repellent sound and coughed organic matter through a window into a parked truck. He dismantled the furnace, cleaned it piece by piece; he mopped and disinfected, his fingers and lungs corroding from borax. His lack of complaint must have provoked Superintendent Holden, who came to our house after Dad finished up. It was eight in the evening; Dad was in the tub with his head on a rolled towel. Holden clomped up the porch and knocked, hard.

I opened the door and stood there. He wasn't coming in short of pushing me physically.

'Evening, Mr Holden.' I hated him, I'll admit, and would soon hate him more, but a person had to feel sorry about his face. I don't know if you've ever tried a dish called tomato pudding. It's cooked soft and is ever so red and lumpy.

He said, 'Your dad here?'

'He's taking a bath.' I stayed put. Seeing Holden come up the steps, Swede had run to her room; now, faintly, I heard her call, 'Did a skunk walk through our yard? Pee-yew.'

'Well, tell him something for me.' Holden was angry but thought I couldn't discern it; he was one of those people who believes all kids have blunted senses. 'I bet he's forgot the parent-teacher meetings tomorrow night. He spent so much time cleaning up his base-ment mess, he never swept the classrooms for two days now. He'll have to get to it before school tomorrow. Tell him I said to come in early.'

'Good night, Mr Holden,' I said. From her room Swede hollered, 'Oh, it's getting worse! Awful, awful!' But Holden didn't get it. There was nothing in his eyes but spite.

So home we stayed, Swede and I, for one more week. The lawyer, Thomas DeCuellar, came by several times. He said little to us about his hours spent with Davy, though he later remarked he had never represented anyone so unconcerned with his own defense. Patient enough in telling the facts, Davy balked at attempts to place him in too kind a light. Mr DeCuellar saw the shootings as a clear and winnable self-defense in which Davy's hand was forced to violence, a rhetoric that displeased my brother. He was not forced, he told Mr DeCuellar; if he hadn't wanted to shoot those fellows, he wouldn't have done it. To say otherwise suggested that he, Davy, was not in control of his actions. Mr DeCuellar suggested we are all forced at times; we are none of us wholly our own masters; other-wise, why couldn't Davy simply leave his cell, walk out a free man? And Davy, who could be contrary, replied, Well, maybe I will. Nor could Mr DeCuellar raise in Davy a suitably dramatic remorse. Though Davy allowed he felt bad, about Tommy especially, he couldn't see what this had to do with his defense. Mr. DeCuellar said the court was sometimes inclined to mercy toward the contrite, to which Davy replied if contrition meant a soulfelt repentance born of wrong-doing, then it had yet to kick in. Poor Mr DeCuellar! Even his petition to have Davy tried as a juvenile was slapped down, a decision that brought a few more calls from reporters who wanted reaction from the family. Speaking for myself, the notion of Davy as a juvenile never made sense anyway. Sixteen or not, Davy was an adult, and had been for a long time.

Swede meantime sat in her room, whacking at the typewriter and occasionally banging her palm on the wall in frustration. This went on for hours. It was unnerving. One afternoon I went out to shoot baskets at the wire hoop we'd bolted to the garage and was startled to see Dr Animas Nokes standing at attention outside Swede's bedroom window. He was carrying a sack that I knew by now would contain a loaf of Mrs Nokes's onion bread and, with luck, also a pie; seeing me he motioned for quiet and I went and stood with him. Swede's windowshade was pulled and strange noises issued from behind it: typewriter keys, yes, but also a sort of desperate chant, Swede's own voice rendered distant and tribal, searching for meter. Dr Nokes looked a question at me.

'Doggone poem is giving her trouble,' I said. I felt pretty resentful about it. We weren't at school, after all; a lot of good free time was going down the drain.

'Ah,' said Dr Nokes, as if some great mist had parted; then, 'Reuben, you look like a boy who understands how to treat a pecan pie.'

That same night – I remember because the pie was still very much with me – Swede showed up in my room dragging her sleeping bag. It was one of those cheapies with a vinyl shell and I heard it crinkling all the way from the hall closet. She opened the door and pulled it in after her, vinyl and mold smell entering too, and she spread it on Davy's bed and snaked down into it and thumped Davy's pillow until it was comfortable and she was sure I was awake. I whispered, 'Hi, Swede!' not caring a bit that I sounded overjoyed to see her. I *was* overjoyed; she'd been grousing in her room for days, and I'd started to wonder had I made some grave mistake.

83

'Reuben, can I sleep in here?'

'Sure.' There wasn't much moon. All I could see of her looked like a white kitten crouched on the pillow.'

'From now on?' she said

'Till Davy gets back.'

The white kitten leapt and hovered – Swede had sat up. 'Reuben, you really think he'll come back at all?'

Now that was one of the worst questions I'd ever been asked. Out of nowhere my throat lumped; I kept still, to stop anything else happening.

'Reuben?'

But I couldn't talk about Davy right then, and it made me cross how close I was to crying. A grouchiness emerged, which was no small relief. 'How come you been in your room so much anyhow? Don't you know others of us live here?'

She was quiet a moment, during which I regretted being harsh; then she said, 'Well, I'll tell you about it if you want – you grump.'

I sure had missed my sister.

What happened to Swede, which I'll admit didn't make a lot of sense to me at the time, was that she couldn't kill Valdez. That is, Sunny Sundown couldn't kill him. Bear with me. After Finch and Basca grabbed Swede that day, you might recall, old Sunny's adventures turned a little grim. Remember how he kept trailing along after Valdez, finding worse and worse?

> One day an upturned stagecoach and its driver's
>   ghastly hue,
> The next a blackened farmhouse and its family
>   blackened too –

The day Swede sat me down and read me those lines I began to understand how truly scared she'd been. Till then I'd been picturing Valdez as one of those banditos in *Zorro*: sitting a scrawny horse, sneaky grin and eyebrows, the kind of villain who'd dig for earwax to groom his mustache. And you know, I'd liked him that way: sly, nasty, but certainly no match for any hero worth the name. Now, overnight, Valdez had come unbound. He'd grown personally. He was a monster. I worried that real damage had been done to Swede, something that might plague her not for weeks but years. I imagined her at twenty-five, hair gone white, skinny and ulcerated, a fearsome picture. Also, it bothered me that the poem now seemed likely to turn out wrong. One thing had to happen, and soon: that pig Valdez had to die, and Sunny Sundown had to kill him. Honorably and inevitably. With one shot. And Valdez had to fall down on his back and lie out-stretched on the scorched earth, his eyes wide open in the noonday sun, so that we knew he was dead and not faking it.

I said to Swede, 'What do you mean, you can't kill him?'

'It doesn't work. I've been trying and it doesn't *work*. What can I do?'

She sounded a little panicked. I thought something might be happening to her mind. I said, cautiously, 'Can't you think of a word to rhyme with *dead*?'

She didn't answer.

'I'll help you, Swede. Let me help you – how about *head*? Like he got shot in the head, and fell down dead. Or *spread* – he fell down dead, with his arms outspread. Or *lead* – say, *lead* is a natural—'

'Reuben, that's not what I mean.' How quietly she interrupted – out of respect, I judged, for the literary roll I was on. 'It's not that I can't write it. I've written it already ten ways. More than ten.'

If she could write it, what was the problem? I sat confounded. Mistaking my silence for doubt, Swede recited:

*'And as the gunshots echo back against the canyon
     walls,*
*Valdez begins to totter – now he staggers – now he
     falls.'*

'Yeah,' I said,'yeah!'

*'And later, Sundown finds a match and lights it
     with a stroke;*
*'Cause graves in sunbaked ground come hard – a
     man can use a smoke.'*

'Swede, that's great! He buries him and everything –
now what's the matter?' She'd flopped back on the
pillow. So much weight my praise carried.

'Just because I write it doesn't mean it really
happened.'

I had to hold that in my head awhile. I knew she
knew what she meant, and I hoped she'd assume I did
too.

She said, 'It doesn't matter if it sounds good. I can't
write it so he's really dead.'

You see what I mean. I said, 'It's just a poem, Swede.
Here, tell me another ending.'

Heavy sigh.

*'When judgment came as gunfire to determine bad
     from good,*
*And Valdez lay all soaked in blood, and weary
     Sundown stood.'*

'What's wrong with that?' I demanded – though
honestly I wasn't crazy about it either. I preferred the
other one, where Sunny lit the cigarette after putting
Valdez in the ground.

'It doesn't work,' she declared.

Well, you can't bargain with someone who won't
sell. If she was miserable and intractable about staying

so, what could I do about it? This would've been a good time for me to shut up and go to sleep, but the slow fever of jealousy had been lit in my veins. Swede was talking some language to which I knew the words but not the meanings. It scratched my pride. I tried making my voice gruff, like Davy's. 'Listen, Swede, who's running this story anyway?'

She didn't answer. She was right not to. It was a dumb old question.

When Sorrows Like Sea Billows Roll

Ten days before the start of Davy's trial, this article appeared in the Minneapolis *Star*:

A VICTIM'S STORY

His aunt called him Bubby because as a child nothing made him happier than sitting on her back step, blowing soap bubbles that rose and drifted across the yards of this small middle-American town.

'I was a second mother to him,' Margery Basca said. 'Bubby lived with me when his parents had difficulties. He was easy to have. Oh, he was sweet.'

Last month, on a night that brought the first bitter snow of autumn, Bubby – Thomas Basca, age seventeen – was shot dead in a house across town. His parents, Stanley and Karen Basca, have been unwilling to talk with the press about the loss of their only child. Now, that child's favorite aunt has agreed to tell her story to the *Star*.

I won't belabor you with the rest of the *Star* piece, beyond revealing that it vexes Swede to this day. ('It's hackneyed,' she pronounced recently, poking through decaying clippings at my kitchen table. 'Maudlin. Asinine.' Swede grew up unforgiving of journalistic convention.) Yet the story had sway; it can't be denied. Looking back at how the Finch and Basca families shunned the papers at first – cussing over chain locks at forward reporters – the timing of their turnaround seems predestined, as all history does when you think about it. By the time Margery Basca decided to talk ('By the time she sobered up and got her house cleaned,' said Swede), the reporters had pretty well run the string out on Davy Land's heroics and seemed cheerful at the prospect of laying him low. The Associated Press strewed the Bubby story all over Christendom, and I mean to tell you it got results. Do you think poor Mrs Basca could've guessed at the power of tragedy? Could she have expected the letters of warmth and sorrow that suddenly bloomed in her post-office box? ('Could she,' Swede asked cruelly, 'even *read* those letters?') My sister's resentments notwithstanding, Margery's pitiful recital contained a certain truth that I, at least, eventually had to face. Tommy Basca was an idiot, but he wasn't purebred evil. You could see looking at him that he might be somebody's Bubby. He tagged after Israel Finch because Israel Finch liked having a disciple and no one else was witless enough to want the job. I suspect even Swede could be brought around to the truth of this, but remember, Tommy was an accomplice the night of her horrible ride. He grinned during it. Swede comes by her blind spot honestly.

But the *Star* piece, for all its mawkishness, dropped a tasty new ingredient in the stew. Observing the public response, even Tommy's bereaved folks, Stan and Karen, patched things up long enough to pose pathetically for an AP photographer. (I've got that clipping too, by the way; as a picture of American underprivilege it could've won awards. You never saw people of more threadbare hopes, their eyes dustbowl-flat. Remember those photographs they used to take out West, of dead outlaws propped frowning in their coffins?)

I have a number of letters here that arrived for Davy in the days just before his trial. I'm guessing Walt Stockard didn't read *these* out loud.

Dear butcher,

This is to let you know what I think of a person who shoots somebody that way. That Basca kid never even owned a gun. Because, he didn't like killing things. Not like some who will shoot anything that moves for the fun of slaughter. You're like the nasty kid who waits in shadow for the little harmless twerp to walk by on his way to school, then you grab the twerp and whack him around awhile because you like to see him scared. Well you listen to me, butcher. The Bible says the meek are going to inherit the earth. And when they do every last harmless twerp will rise up emboldened, and they will join together, and they will hunt down all butchers and cast them off cliffs and into rivers until the earth is cleansed. In the meantime I hope your trial is a great success and that the judge gives you the electric chair, you butcher, or however it is done in this present day. Hang you by the neck until dead.

Very sincerely

The sentiments here are representative of the new surge of mail; people love an underdog, especially a dead one, and poor Tommy made a dandy, so blank and trusting. How hideous my brother suddenly appeared to patrons of printed news, how base and small-souled! You'd have thought poor Bubby broke into our house still wearing short pants. (Though I'll admit the letter has some panache; this fellow really found his voice once he hit on the *harmless twerp* idea. That's a good phrase, *rise up emboldened*; it sounds like something Swede might've written, and besides it's hard to argue against the meek turning the tables at long last. I don't blame the writer, who, from his remark about Tommy not owning a gun, betrays the earnest influence of the Margery story. How could he know how wrongheaded it was?)

Even Davy's fellow inmate, Mighty Stinson, took delight in the sudden downturn of public opinion, lifting his head to say, 'Pretty much of a hotshot – great big Davy Land.' Mighty, who got no mail, was housed two cells down; a perplexed fry cook of twenty, he'd hooked a lady's checkbook left behind at the cash register. The lady realized her mistake in minutes and was back to claim it, but by then Mighty was trotting down to the First National, where he produced the checkbook and wrote one out to cash for $35. That First National was the lady's own bank, and that all three tellers on duty knew the fry cook on sight meant little or nothing to Mighty. 'You're such a hotshot, let's see you bust outa here. Bust me out too while you're at it,' he said.

All of this troubled Thomas DeCuellar. The trial, which would start Wednesday at the courthouse in Montrose, was our small world's favorite conversation by now; on Sunday night Mr DeCuellar sat down tiredly at our kitchen table and told us how it was.

'People are placing their sympathies with the dead boys,' he said. There was bread and cheese on the table, and he built a sandwich. 'You wouldn't have any of those pickles left?'

'They're all gone; our compliments to Mrs DeCuellar,' Dad said. 'I don't understand why it matters. The jury is supposed to be impartial.'

Mr DeCuellar looked at Dad, a careful look. 'Oh, they are. They'll do their best. Jeremiah, have you been reading the papers this week?'

I remember how long it took Dad to answer that question. Mr DeCuellar chewed his bread and cheese. Swede and I sat quietly. I had a feeling the adults didn't know we were in the room – a feeling we were getting away with something, and a sadness that it was nothing to be prized.

'I've read them,' Dad said.

'You have to assume the jury has also. Of course they'll be sequestered once the trial starts. Until then, they're quite free. Quite at liberty.' You know, Mr DeCuellar did speak like a lawyer, but he didn't mind doing it with his mouth full of bread and cheese. He turned, unexpectedly, to us. 'You know, compadres' – using that word because Swede liked it – 'the situation could be much worse. Do you know how they conducted trials back in Saxon England?'

Swede shook her head. She liked most everything about Mr DeCuellar: his black-coffee eyes that seemed, in poor light, all pupil; his pipe, a small neat meerschaum he extracted now from a baggy pocket; and his way of speaking to us, which, Dad said, was in the manner of men who had wanted children for decades and never had them.

'Do you remember the Battle of Hastings?' he inquired.

'1066,' Swede replied. 'King Harold took that arrow – right in the eye!'

'Exactly.' Mr DeCuellar beamed. 'Well, before that, England was in Saxon hands. The Saxons invented jury trials, but they also tested for guilt *by ordeal*.' He said this last in a portentous whisper while pressing sweet shredded tobacco into the bowl of his pipe.

Swede hunched up. 'That sounds awful.'

'Yes, it was. A man might point to his poor neighbor and say, before the judge, "He stole my grain." Henceforth the accused would be bound securely. "Stoke up the fire," the judge would cry out, and the poor man, having no argument spoken in his favor, would have a red-hot iron laid across his palm. Or his hand would be pushed into boiling water – *tssssssssssss*!'

'But if he was innocent!' Swede protested. Mr DeCuellar could be ruthless on an audience; my goodness, but he loved history.

'If innocent, he would pass the test. His flesh would be unharmed.' He struck a match and drew a gob of flame down into the bowl. The tobacco glowed and settled. He said pleasantly, 'So people believed.'

'Then no one ever passed,' Swede observed darkly.

And Mr DeCuellar replied, 'It's recorded some did pass; some men accused of murder and theft were tried this way and left unscarred.' He looked at Dad. 'Probably not many, hm, Jeremiah?'

Dad said, 'Maybe, Tom, you ought to tell us what we can expect of the trial – how it all works.'

'Yes, of course. It's quite simple.' And Mr DeCuellar spoke a brief clear paragraph about the properties of justice, about the efforts the prosecution would surely make to discredit our brother and portray him as a brutish reprobate, and finally, as if to cancel budding doubts, about Davy's brave defense of us his family. A most heroic act, he said, as anyone could see. When Mr DeCuellar stood to go, Swede rose also and hugged him hard around the waist.

I recall that, before leaving, Mr DeCuellar offered Dad two counts of advice for the coming days. First, maintain a happy composure at work; second, answer no questions, especially from reporters. We were to stay out of the newspapers, which, he said, had never really seen the problem with Saxon justice.

Good advice is a wise man's friend, of course; but sometimes it just flies on past, and all you can do is wave. Because the next day, speaking of ordeals, Dad went and got fired by his boss Mr Holden, with half the school looking. Honestly, I hate to even tell you this part. Who wants to hear a story that's nothing but misfortune? All the same, there's a detail or two it'd be improper to leave out, and anyway Dad didn't have a whole lot of himself invested in the janitorial field. You don't have to worry about his self-respect, is what I'm saying, though you might light a candle for Mr Holden's, if you are that sort of person.

It transpired in the cafeteria of Roofing Elementary. Several classes, mine included, were assembled for the morning milk break. Because of impending Thanksgiving we all had on pilgrim hats cut from stiff black paper, and Mrs Bushka downtown at the bakery had sent over some gingerbread turkeys, bedecked with orange and yellow frosting. You can imagine what a treat these were, especially juxtaposed against our general feelings toward the cafeteria. Even as we sat, prying lids off milk bottles, we could hear the persecuted cooks banging around back in the kitchen, grandmas barking at each other, preparing the daily grotesque. I remember Peter Emerson predicting meat loaf for that day's lunch – Peter, looking uncharacteristically solemn because of his pilgrim hat, explaining his logic: 'The butcher's truck goes to the dump every Thursday. This smells like the dump Fridays.'

It was, nonetheless, a glad-hearted gathering there in the cafeteria, at least until Mr Holden came down to make some brooding remarks about Thanksgiving, probably having to do with privation and death. He'd certainly picked the right career, had Mr Holden; his every feature spoke of resentment and annoyance and, to people under five feet tall, of physical danger. His poor face looked always festering with some imminent parasitical hatch. Nothing could quiet a happy crowd of kids like Mr Holden's unannounced appearance – he loved superintending; he was made for it. So when he marched in that morning with a determined grin on his face, we froze. Boys and girls recognize sinister as handily as dogs do. Here it was. My best guess now is he'd got it in his head to try 'relating' to us – but when he produced a paper pilgrim's hat from behind his back and put it on his own head, I think we all nearly bolted. I had a nightmare once in which the Devil entered my room and opened my closet and started trying on my clothes. This was similar. Mr

Holden stood there with his mouth grinning and his eyes in some sort of torment and the pilgrim hat – well, I'd actually thought those handmade hats were pretty neat until the superintendent donned his. Suddenly they seemed repulsive, and I reached up and took mine off.

Then Mr Holden said his few words. I've forgotten them – doesn't matter – no doubt he thought we were all spellbound and that he was giving Miss Karlen and the other teachers present a fine lesson in captivating schoolchildren. What had my attention, though, was something I hadn't noticed before. I'd been so transfixed by Mr Holden's strange manner, I hadn't seen the neatly scripted letters near the squared-off top of his hat. Very small capitals in white chalk, easy to miss but really quite readable: SHOOT ME! they said, in letters so smoothly drafted Miss Karlen herself might've written them.

Well, I saw that and wanted to laugh. Not just wanted to – I tell you that laugh was down in my stomach, like bad beef; it meant to come out. Desperately I strove for placid thoughts; which meant, of course, not looking at Mr Holden's hat. Not thinking those words. And yet they called, like a summons, like a hissed invitation, SHOOT ME!, calling to the laugh inside my belly. You want torture? A giggle crept up the old esophagus; I swallowed it down. My eyeballs watered. The worst of it was I seemed to be the only kid who'd noticed. Either that or everyone else had iron control, a terrible thought. I looked around; glazed faces everywhere. No one else had seen! Oh, but that moment was a lonesome place. Mr Holden talked on; I molared the inside of my cheek; the laugh stayed put but I felt it down there, accruing strength. Goodness, it made me nervous. I chanced a look at Mr Holden. SHOOT ME!, plain as day! I swallowed about twelve times. Then Peter Emerson leaned over to my ear. 'Bang,' he whispered. I knew defeat. Through mouthplastered hands the laugh ripped forth – *hoo-hoo-ha-ha-wha-wha-wha* – a ruddy bray that condemned me to the stares of aghast pilgrims and who knew what violent repercussions at the hands of Mr Holden. I laughed so hard my sight went dark. I laid my forehead down on the table to sob. Did anyone laugh with me? Who knows? I do remember it felt solitary, as the wave rolled off, and I remember looking up through tears to see the glaring superintendent, death in a hat, SHOOT ME! still writ upon his mighty crown, and I remember wishing *I* could arrange to be shot at that moment and have it done with.

It occurs to me now that I have no idea what became of Superintendent Holden. Is he somewhere alive yet, a distressed old man in suspendered baggies, fixing his nightly suppers from tin cans, fearing his own reflection? Or did his conscience take pity and kill him early on, as Swede suggested might be just?

Well. He didn't kill me, though I don't doubt his intention; it was his very eagerness to reach me that wrecked his day, because he started for me, all right, but was so anxious about it he clipped his thigh rounding the table. Do you remember how tippy those milk bottles were? Struck by more than a sidelong glance they'd whirl and spill. Mr Holden took that corner in the meat of the thigh, and half a dozen of the little soldiers leapt from the tabletop and burst wondrously at our feet. That froze Mr Holden, and just as he was about to do some real superintending, too. The cafeteria was silent except for the contents of one tipped bottle streaming off the table to the floor – a lonely bathroom sound. Beside me Peter Emerson, feeling left out because his bottle had stopped just short of the edge, moved his elbow furtively. The bottle tipped, sailed out, exploded. 'Aww,' Peter said aloud. He was the happiest kid I ever knew.

And then, as would happen, Dad appeared. Instinctively I feared for him, for a curse seemed hovering in that room. And I'll admit I feared for myself as well. I owned a bit of rotten pride in those days that recoiled at the sight of Dad in coveralls. It didn't seem fair, you understand. I knew Dad was the smartest, best-hearted, most capable man in any room he occupied, knew too that he was beloved by God, that whatever he touched was apt to prosper, sometimes in mighty and inexplicable style. To see him therefore in janitor clothes seemed to me the result of a strange and discomforting arithmetic. How could it be that his boss was a man like Mr Holden – whom Swede called Chester the Fester on account of his face – a man who treated Dad with feudal contempt? Who talked about scouring Dad's teeth?

And this bothered me, too: Dad would come into a room, pushing his broom, and always some dumb kid would turn to me and smirk. *Janitor's kid. Mop jockey. Cleaned up any good puke lately?* I'm sorry if you thought better of me, but the fact is I spent whole hours imagining alarming humiliations for those kids – big dumb kids, always, with effortless all-star lungs. Oh, yes, and hours spent thus were not bitter but passed like joyous dreams, in which Bethany Orchard always chanced along to see the dumb kids at their most abject. It's true. No grudge ever had a better nurse.

But Dad was in his usual fine humor that day in the cafeteria, diagnosing the breakage, catching my eye and Peter's as we watched from our benches and sending us a wink. His face betrayed delight, for he'd entered at the moment of Chester's fabulous lurch. It took him perhaps twenty seconds to gauge the damage, unlock a supply closet, and set to work with a ragmop and bucket, and in that time Mr Holden saw before him an opportunity to set an example. To superintend. To *scour*. As Dad knelt for broken glass Holden stepped up next to him so that Dad was working around his knees. He looked slavelike down there, bending for bits of bottle as Holden stood, hands on hips, dissatisfied as Legree. I could barely watch. Behind me Miss Karlen encouraged the class to finish our gingerbread, but the kids sat bewitched. Something horrible was happening. I looked at Mr Holden, whose hat was now off. He was looking back at me, holding my eye, for I'd done him an outrage. At his feet Dad worked patiently, tossing shards onto a tray, finally standing and finishing up with the mop, using the rinse bucket so the whole stretch of floor was a continent of shine and good health.

Mr Holden said, 'Land, we have to talk.'

Dad looked at his boss, surprised by some alteration in his voice.

'There've been complaints,' the superintendent said.

Miss Karlen said softly, 'Children, we must go now—' and guess what Holden did. He held up one hand for silence, not taking his eyes off Dad. He wanted everyone there.

'All right,' Dad said.

'Last week, when you were cleaning up your little mess down the basement, two people reported you stumbling around down there. Talking out loud to yourself. Two different people came to me and said so.'

Dad said nothing. I didn't know what Holden was getting at, saying next, 'This isn't the first time. I've seen it myself. Come down to the boiler room and I hear you chattering away.' He spoke with quiet reason, as if Dad were some disturbed child – oh, how I wanted to kill Holden! I wanted him dead and his grave unkept! 'Jeremiah,' he said, his voice a disapproving murmur, 'I'm aware you passed clean out a couple of weeks ago. In public,' Holden said. 'In *church*,' he added most sadly, deeply concerned for the ruined dignity of the employee before him. 'Don't you think your problem is getting out of hand?' he said.

I entered here into some sort of shock, for I understood three things at once: first, that Superintendent Holden was accusing my father of drunkenness, a charge so preposterous that God would surely flatten him before our waiting eyes. I also understood that word of the sensational Johnny Latt service had spread, and how people will apply the unkindest parts of themselves to any heard intelligence. And I understood, with my soul turning sour, that Dad would not defend himself within our hearing. I do not doubt that Holden understood this also.

Miss Karlen began quietly rallying us children to leave, in spite of the fine example being set by the administrator; Miss Karlen's slender face was a dark displeased red, for which I ever after gave her the devotion of an ally. As we clattered up our trays I heard Holden demand Dad's explanation; I saw Dad lean down and voice a soft reply. At this the superintendent made the most fitful transformation – his neck compressed into his shoulders, his hands clawed and shrunk upward into his sleeves, he stamped his foot like the maladjusted. He was Mr Hyde! He roared a few words, and Dad became a former janitor.

Most boys, I am guessing, have never watched outright as their father was stripped of his livelihood, and I don't want to pound it too hard, but the cruelty of that moment still impresses me. I left my milling classmates and headed for Dad, where he stood in rapt surprise facing Holden. I hadn't in mind to say anything, and indeed I didn't; for as I approached Dad lifted his hand, sudden as a windshift, touched Holden's face and pulled away. It was the oddest little slap you ever saw. Holden quailed back a step, hunching defensively, but Dad turned and walked off; and the superintendent stood with his fingers strangely awonder over his chin, cheeks, and forehead. Then I saw that his bedeviled complexion – that face set always at a rolling boil – had changed. I saw instead skin of a healthy tan, a hale blush spread over cheek-bones that suddenly held definition; above his eyes the shine of constant seepage had vanished, and light lay at rest upon his brow.

Listen: there are easier things than witnessing a miracle of God. For his part, Mr Holden didn't know what to make of it; he looked horrified; the new peace in his hide didn't sink deep; he covered his face from view and slunk from the cafeteria.

I knew what had happened, though. I knew exactly what to make of it, and it made me mad enough to spit.

What business had Dad in healing that man?

What right had Holden to cross paths with the Great God Almighty?

The injustice took my breath away, truly it did. I felt a great hand close against my lungs and Miss Karlen escorted me gasping to the nurse's office, where Mrs Buelah plugged in her teapot and made a steam tent from a bolt of tan canvas.

When Dad came to take me home – having boxed up the contents of his single drawer in the boiler room – I wouldn't go with him. I stayed on Mrs Buelah's couch. Dad lifted a corner of the canvas and peeked under.

'Looks like I'm getting a little vacation,' he said.

I nodded.

'I'm sorry you saw that.'

His getting fired, he meant, not the other thing.

'How about we go home?'

But I shook my head. I just couldn't go with him. Nor could I tell him it wasn't his public mistreatment that stole my breath and blocked my tongue; it was something too mean to explain. It was the fact that Chester the Fester, the worst man I'd ever seen, even worse in his way than Israel Finch, got a whole new face to look out of and didn't even know to be grateful; while I, my father's son, had to be still and resolute and breathe steam to stay alive.

Late in the Night When the Fires Are Out

Early Wednesday, under red skies, we drove to
Montrose for Davy's trial. We'd been told to be at the
courthouse at 9 a.m., but the DeCuellars insisted we
breakfast at their house at 7:30. There's no way a
person can really prepare for someone like Mrs
DeCuellar. Buxom and businesslike on her doorstep,
once she had you inside she became the woman you
wish had lived next door all the days of your child-
hood. She was short, round, bright. At the age when
most women begin putting up their hair, she wore hers
long, for beauty, and it *was* beautiful – black and
woolly, her very own buffalo robe. She had turquoise
earrings and crisp metallic perfume; helping Swede
off with her coat, she knelt and put her cheek to
Swede's and held it there a moment before getting up;
then she said, 'Breakfast's ready, sweet ones,' and
marched us to the kitchen. It was fitting, that march;
there was something about Mrs DeCuellar that
reminded you of a bass drum.

And breakfast? What would you say to butter-
crumbed eggs that trembled at the touch of your fork?
To buttermilk biscuits under tumbling steam? To
orange sides of salmon lying creamed upon blue
saucers? What would you say to fresh peach pie, baked

not the night before but that very morning? For *breakfast*? And through everything Mrs DeCuellar, like a small sun beside her proud and outshone husband, beamed down on Swede and me. It seemed, honestly, like a mistake. I couldn't remember ever being so easily liked.

Thus braced against the evil of the day, we went to the courthouse. We'd thought to visit Davy before it all started but were informed this was impossible and advised to wait on benches in the hall until the jury was seated and given instructions. ('What instructions?' Swede wanted to know. '"Listen carefully"?')

In fact, I've learned, trials are mostly a succession of waits. When the benches became restrictive, we up and bushwhacked around the big hall. We waited all morning. When others began to arrive, including some newspaper men of our aquaintance, a clerk came and asked if we'd like to wait in a separate office, the three of us. We were glad to. A whiskery yellow-eyed old man was sitting on the neighboring bench; a reporter sat with him, calling him M. Finch. The old man didn't answer; his hands shook; he had those thirsty fingers. Stan and Karen Basca stood in uneasy conference by the water fountain; Stan's sister Margery, the famous aunt, had just hove into view down the hall. We followed the clerk to a barren office with a long table acrawl with cigarette burns, and a few minutes later in stepped Mr DeCuellar to say it would be a bit longer – the prosecuting attorney, whom I remember only by his first name, Elvis, had detected an attitude problem in one of the jurors.

'Will it be a long time?' Swede asked, not a hint of whine in the question, she liked Mr DeCuellar that much.

He looked at her, brought out his meerschaum, and squatted comfortably. Lighting the pipe, he said, 'Tell me, Swede, who in your family is champion in War at Sea?'

Swede blinked, and Mr DeCuellar slipped a notebook from his pocket saying, 'You've grown up so big not knowing how to play War at Sea? I don't believe it. Here.' It is thus I most often remember that good lawyer – he sitting slouched on a folding chair, notebook on his knee, Swede leaning into him as he pointed and strategized, the pants of his brown suit bagging at the ankles.

We played War at Sea right up through noon, Swede and I, and then, just when I'd hit on a pattern for locating and destroying her fleet, the door opened and it was Mr DeCuellar again and the trial was about to commence.

You've seen courtrooms; this one had dark wainscoting all around and a raised jury box fenced by a brass rail, and after we'd all stood up and sat again it had Judge Raster, whom I'd pictured as some predatory deep-sea critter, sitting behind his high desk. In the flesh the judge had the kind of wavy white hair I associated with benevolence, the hair of soft-touch aunts who keep mints in candy dishes within your reach; though his eyes, behind half-glasses, evoked no such hopeful impressions. Surprisingly, my first sense of Judge Raster was of a man who clung to small vanities. He had a preening look. You don't like to think it of a judge.

Davy was in the front pew beside Mr DeCuellar. I was surprised what a short and unrakish figure he cut. You play these things in your mind beforehand, you know, and somehow Davy's entrance into that crowded courtroom – this boy so much interpreted, the silent and notorious Davy Land – was always accompanied in my thoughts by an awed hush and perhaps a thud or two, as young women, glimpsing him, fainted away.

In real life nobody seemed to be looking at him. He had on khaki pants, a chambray shirt. He needed a shave and looked to have dropped some pounds. I wanted to run forward and make him look in my eyes.

After certain formalities Elvis, the prosecutor, rose to get things started. He cleared his throat and preached an eloquent and transparent sermon on violence, a five-minute redaction in which Davy ceased being any human being's brother and became an icy double murderer who forefigured not only his crimes but how those crimes would be read by a common populace starved for heroics. The confidence with which Elvis knifed my brother's honor left my mouth dry. Israel Finch grew into a lost boy of great promise, who despite his broken home and juvenile record showed natural talent in the areas of negotiations and auto mechanics. And Tommy Basca – Elvis's ace – Tommy was just some forlorn kitten, out mewing in the dark and the cold and the rain. Through all this I gaped occasionally at Swede, who appeared snakebit and vengeful.

Then up stood Mr DeCuellar to respond. I don't remember his words, but in general feeling – well, remember how the great Daniel Webster argued against the Devil for the soul of Jabez Stone? The Devil had him beat, you recall, as long as Webster stood on logic. You can't argue with a signed contract, and Jabez, the dolt, had signed. But Webster saw victory in the Devil's face and in the faces of that hellish jury, the whole lot of them leaning forward licking their lips, and he calmed himself and began to speak instead about what makes a man a man, and the nature of the soul, and its very Creator whence comes all freedom, and so on. And the Devil himself did wither in the face of this bigger logic – and so, it seemed to me, must Elvis wither, and judge and jury also, when Mr DeCuellar had finished his wise and simple statement.

They didn't seem impressed, though.

In fact, there came some fairly bad moments after that.

One came when Elvis called Stanley Basca to testify.

Till now I'd thought I had the facts by the tail – wasn't I an eyewitness? – but Stanley had been treasuring up a zinger to impart to the court.

'Davy came around to Finch's place that night. Rotten night out. Nine o'clock or thereabouts,' Stanley said.

Elvis: 'Did you see him yourself?'

Stanley: 'Yes, sir. It was Davy Land. I was over to the Finches' looking for Tommy; he was all the time over there.'

Elvis: 'They were best friends, your Tommy and Israel Finch.'

Stanley nodded. Swede later suggested this was because he didn't want to admit it out loud.

Elvis: 'And what did you see Davy do?'

Stanley: 'Well, he had something in his hand. A tire iron, I guess, or pry bar. Hard to tell in that rain. Anyway, he whacked every window out of the Finch boy's car.'

Elvis: 'You're saying Davy Land came to the Finch residence. With a tire iron—'

Stanley: 'Or pry bar, it could of been—'

Elvis: '—and smashed out the windows of Israel's car, in which the boy took inordinate pride.'

Stanley: 'Well, yes, sir. And the taillights – he got those too.'

Now don't worry, I'm not going to make a practice of this transcription business, but as I said there were salient moments. Those gathered stirred audibly – a surprise revelation! Here was what they'd come for, all right! For me, of course, the surprise quickly deadened into a recognition that it was perfectly true. Swede and I had gone to bed early; so had Dad, on account of his headache. Davy'd gone out into that freezing rain. And later, when I'd thought him asleep? When the footsteps entered our house? Wasn't I amazed when the lights came on and there he was sitting upright, holding his Winchester as if he'd taken it to bed?

Of course he'd taken it to bed. I saw it now. He knew they were coming. He'd issued them an invitation.

I looked at Davy's face, couldn't read it, and looked at Dad's, seeing not shock but sorrow and austerity. Evidently he knew about this. I checked Mr DeCuellar – he knew it too. At that moment a wall inside me shifted. Gravity took hold, and I knew my brother had no chance inside that courtroom. Piece by piece our defensive architecture failed. Margery Basca testified, the tears standing in her eyes, how poor Bubby had gone to the store for her twice a week, getting the bread and milk and on occasion a dozen eggs, doing his uncomplaining best. Yellow-eyed old Mr Finch – Israel's grandfather, it turned out – told in quiet convulsive tones how Israel was without doubt the most maligned and abominated young man in Roofing: 'He didn't make friends that well,' et cetera. His voice left him after just a few moments. Elvis graciously articulated the old man's powerful if obscure emotions, then released him to go wrestle the tormenting ague. Davy's erstwhile girl Dolly was sworn in, throwing tragic looks at him, and recounted her experience in the locker room. It clearly troubled her to do so, for she understood the use Elvis was making of her: establishing for the jury the extant hate between Israel Finch and Davy. (Coming to Dad's part in it, though, she may have eased the damage. How was a court of law to take her description of his luminous appearance? Peeking at the jury here, I saw most of them were studying Dad, possibly for radiance, or a look in his eye, or other unnatural credentials.)

All this time I was fighting a magnificent swarm of butterflies. Mr DeCuellar had told me I'd have to testify, as the single eyewitness of the shootings. He didn't tell me the prosecution was saving me for last – my story being useful in throwing away the key – but Swede had figured it out and didn't spare me the knowledge. In craven dread I sought Swede's help in rewriting events to Davy's advantage, but Mr DeCuellar reassured me, saying to be honest and forth-right, though frugal in detail. 'Answer only the question,' he said. 'Short declarative sentences. No big prose.' Well, he didn't have to worry about that. Who did he think I was, Swede? Anyway, I hadn't a lot of choice, and Mr DeCuellar promised to fix my mistakes in his cross-examination. I remember wondering, with a whole day still between me and the stand, whether the whirl in my stomach might be a blossoming case of flu. Surely they would excuse a witness who was busy throwing up. I worked at it awhile, remembering something Peter Emerson had told me: that if he thought hard about puking, or better yet remembered instances of his older brother puking, he could just about bring on the real thing himself. I shut my eyes. Once in school, going down to lunch from our third-floor classroom, Valentino Vail had leaned over the banister without warning and loosed a cataract of orange vomit. The stairway was the usual open stack and Valentino's breakfast just dropped forever, three stories down, touching a good number of lives as it rocketed past and hitting the basement tile with a sound zoo-keepers must hear sometimes, around the elephants. I was right behind Valentino and saw it all – an astonishing puke that was discussed for days. Yet even this, vividly invoked, could not move my stomach to violence. I envied Peter's mental potency.

'We're going to lose, Reuben,' Swede told me that night.

We were socked into sleeping bags on the floor of Mr DeCuellar's study. Though the day had been troublesome and the night was black with a racketous wind, still I found this small library a reassuring place. How could anyone who'd read so many books lose a case in court? Then I remembered Stanley Basca, and the way Elvis had turned righteously toward the jury during his testimony, and I agreed with Swede, though not aloud.

She then said, 'We've got to break him out.'

I should've known it was coming. 'Oh, Swede, don't now.'

She sat up in her sleeping bag. 'We could do it – bust him out of there. Really. Tonight!' She had hold of my shoulder. 'I'm not kidding.'

'I know it.'

She was up, padding around. 'They're gonna convict him, Reuben – you see it same as I do. You want Davy in prison?'

A gust gnashed at the window. I said, 'We can't even drive, Swede,' but it carried no water. She paced in the gloom, full of deadly schemes.

'We'll wait till they're asleep – take some of Mrs DeCuellar's cookies – offer 'em to the guard, tell him we've got to see Davy – when he turns to me you grab his gun,' and so on. It was one of those rare moments when I actually felt older than Swede. Seizing it, I told her to grow up. She went silent and fell to studying bookcases. Mr DeCuellar had left a reading lamp on in a corner as a night-light – had he children of his own he'd have known better – and it so illumined the room I could read the spines from where I lay. C. S. Lewis. Graham Greene. Charles Dickens – lots of Dickens. She returned to bed at last with a book of poems by Robert Louis Stevenson.

I said, 'Read me a couple, Swede.' Few writers can match Stevenson; both danger and peace inhabit his verse; it throws a very wide net. So Swede lay beside me reading 'Land of Nod,' 'My Ship and I,' 'North-West Passage,' and 'The Lamplighter,' with its wistful narrator:

> But I when I am stronger and can choose what I'm
>   to do,

> O Leerie, I'll go round at night and light the lamps
>   with you!

My heart still breaks with that poem, I love it so.

Then Swede was quiet some little time – I wasn't asleep yet but was on the doorstep, a dream just opening up.

'Listen to this one, Reuben.'

I opened my eyes. She was propped on an elbow. Sleep already had me in the legs and arms, but Swede looked bright and scared. She read:

> 'Whenever the moon and stars are set,
> Whenever the wind is high,
> All night long in the dark and wet,
> A man goes riding by.'

Gooseflesh rose. Outside the wind thumped around; the reading lamp flickered but stayed on. She whispered:

> 'Late in the night when the fires are out,
> Why does he gallop and gallop about?'

I said, 'Let's sleep, Swede.' Though I couldn't have – not anymore. There was a prescient chill in those lines, in her voice.

> 'Whenever the trees are crying aloud,
> And ships are tossed at sea,
> By, on the highway, low and loud,
> By at the gallop goes he:
> By at the gallop he goes, and then
> By he comes back at the gallop again.'

Had I not been eleven I'd have squirreled down and drawn the sleeping bag up over my head. Maybe you're thinking there's nothing creepy about this

109

particular poem. I'm telling you, that night there was.

But Swede was watching me for reaction so I just yawned, a big fake one, and asked was that the end.

'It's a sign,' she said.

Which of course put a keen point on the vague dread I was feeling. You don't like to say *It's a sign* at such times, or hear it, or even think it, for fear the words themselves will bear it out.

'What does it mean?' I asked.

'I don't know.' She shut the book and turned out the light and waited awhile and then said, 'I think it means we ought to break him out.'

Next afternoon they put me on the stand. I felt like a parakeet up there: new chinos, a green wool sweater that itched at the neck, my hair slicked to pudding. I looked at Dad, who smiled back; at Dr Nokes, who winked; at Swede, who was leaning forward pestering Mr DeCuellar in the moments before swearing-in. I laid my hand on the Bible, and when finished looked at Davy, who was straight across the floor. He was making faces, trying to bust me up, just like back in church.

Now, be warned. I must witness here against myself, and so, as a human brimful of vainglory, may attempt excuse. If so, pay me no mind. The fit will pass.

Elvis came up in his bow tie. He asked some chatty questions about school, friends, bullies, stuff I liked to do. It irritated me, for I knew what he was up to – getting me comfortable, warming the clay. Also showing the jury how concerned and thorough he was by getting on good terms with Davy's kid brother. 'Patronizing' was the word Swede used later, though by then I was too mortified to ask anyone exactly what it meant. But I was properly terse. I looked him in the eye and answered him straight. And when he came to the end of his getting-to-know-you questions, what he and the court mostly knew was that he hadn't got to me with his smiles and joshing; this was one eleven-year-old who'd never take sides against his brother. I gave him nothing at first, I promise you.

But gradually – oh, it hurts! – something began to work on me. I began to have, of all things, self-confidence. It crept up like an oily friend. It seemed to me that Elvis began to look less certain of himself, walking to and fro. Clearly he'd expected I'd be putty by this time. And my own voice sounded particularly grown-up, I thought, saying, 'No, sir, that's not so,' or 'Sir, he's my brother, and I ought to know.' I sirred him to death; I sirred him with a disrespect he had to comprehend. And hearing these things from my own mouth I thought, *Not bad.* Pride is the rope God allows us all. When Elvis asked if I'd had scary dreams since the night 'these things transpired,' I replied, 'Certainly not, sir,' with what I imagined was the hauteur of a condemned legionnaire. Of course hauteur is an odd adornment on a boy that age – but oh, that gallery of faces, all watching me. Faces of friends and erstwhile friends, of interested strangers, of newspapermen. They were my sun, my water. I remember hoping, unreasonably, that Bethany Orchard was there watching, and in fact I did look for her with such concentration that Elvis had to beg my pardon to bring me back. At some point I looked at Mr DeCuellar and saw alarm in his eyes. I actually wondered what was wrong, which tells you how far gone I was.

Then Elvis, who'd been working his way forward from the locker-room incident, said, 'Reuben, the night the boys came by and took your sister for a ride' – a *ride*; how do you like that? – 'what happened that night? Before the sheriff arrived? Do you remember?'

As if I might have forgotten. As if the chill of Israel Finch's intrusion wouldn't be forever as close as air to skin. Memory chasing pretense for a moment, I said, 'Well, Swede was white. And she looked real small.'

'Small?'

'Yes, sir. Usually she's as big as me.' In retrospect it was as telling a statement as I ever made. It also produced an audible ripple of goodwill for this youngster on the stand. Immediately I felt reduced, from budding hero to guileless moppet. Elvis turned to the gallery and made the most of it, and I'm ashamed to say how his doing so tweaked my attitude. Having lost ground here I ought've simply dug in, humbled, and held my new position, but I'd become a proud twerp over the preceding fifteen minutes.

Turning back to me, Elvis smiled. 'Reuben, was Davy angry that night?'

He thought I was hesitating out of fear to answer the question. I confess to you now I was only looking for the right voice – something legionnaireish. Oh, I still wanted to do my best by Davy, I hadn't forgotten him; but I wanted to sound smooth doing it, you see. Like a hotshot, Mighty Stinson would've said.

Elvis prompted. 'Something like that happening to his little sister – say, *I* would've been upset, a thing like that.'

Reaching down for a good low register I replied, 'No, sir, Davy was as easygoing as anything.' (And truly, that's how he'd been. Not pale and dry with fear like Swede and me, but calm, with a stillness that was itself fearsome.) Except on 'easygoing' my voice slipped back into its normal range, or possibly a little higher. I discerned snickering. Again I was ridiculous before my public.

Then Elvis said gently, 'Now, Reuben. Haven't you told us how your brother sticks up for you? Protects you?'

I had.

'And now you're telling us he didn't have a thing to say after Tommy and Israel brought her home? Scared as she was by those boys, and Davy just sitting quiet?'

Posed like that, it did seem unlikely. I thought it over, sensing the court waiting. Davy *had* said something, hadn't he? Just before Ted Pullet drove in? I looked at my brother, there in the courtroom, and tried to recall.

And do you know, when Davy looked back, something was different. Something in the look itself – it was untethered somehow, loosed from Elvis and the jury and judge. He smiled at me from some planetary distance. And I thought of his way in the kitchen that night, how he'd hooked the car keys on his finger and yielded them to Dad, wordlessly, after a long and inner weighing. And I remembered.

'Why, yes, *sir*,' I told Elvis. 'He asked Dad a question. He said, How many times do you let a dog bite you, before you put him down?'

And the court did not erupt, nor the jury gasp in wonder at this revelation; only Elvis's eyebrows rose slightly, and, 'Reuben,' he said, with such gentle approval my blood gelled to a stop, 'you have been holding out on us.'

That night I agreed to break Davy out of jail. Swede knew I would. She had on her side the fact that I'd as much as damned our brother to prison and therefore death; for he would die there, or some core inside him would. We lay awake while the adults spoke in counsel long and low in the kitchen, and Swede laid our plans – desperate, slapdash, bloody plans. I was in no position to propose alternatives. I never saw her so upset or brilliant. She was like a horse let out to run.

I did make one suggestion, about guns being better than knives for the work at hand. She shook her head in regret. 'They don't have any guns. I looked everywhere. Poor Mr DeCuellar,' she added. 'Someday I'm going to buy him one.'

Yes, poor Mr DeCuellar. After my damaging performance I'd been unable to avoid his eyes, and the sorrow and disappointment they showed were as if I'd struck him in public. I tried to apologize and broke down before him, and his forgiveness was so quiet and complete I could only grieve the more.

And why, you're wondering, did I toss Elvis that line of Davy's, about putting down the dog? Well, I suppose I had to, once I'd gone and remembered it; Elvis had asked me the question, and I was tied to honesty by oath. A person can't regret honesty any more than other unavoidables – a plain face or a poor history. What I regret is how I said it: like your choice of stupid punks with something to prove. I said it with belligerence, a trait ever cultivated by fools. I said it, I tremble to admit, as Israel Finch might have. And predictably, chaos accompanied belligerence into office. For that putting-down-the-dog remark led Elvis to seek and pull from me other facts pointing to ill intent: that Davy already had his coat on to deliver vengeance when Dad stopped him; that Davy had been angry with Dad earlier, when it seemed to him the locker-room beating hadn't been nearly severe enough; that Davy, waiting on the stairs for his arrest after the shootings, had grabbed my wrist and spoken the words *I meant to*. With despair I heard myself answer Elvis's inquiries, each answer seeming horribly convicting the moment it was uttered. Oh, I was a meek enough fellow now – but it didn't matter. Elvis drew these facts from me and unfolded them to view and laid them before the court like a series of bloody hankies.

I saw it happening but could not stop it. Humility came to me too late. I'm a living proverb; learn from me.

We went to bed jittery, faking weariness. Even as Dad prayed over us for forgiveness and joy and a night of peace, Swede in her sleeping bag was clutching a box of steak knives stolen from the DeCuellars' kitchen. We shut our eyes, slurred our goodnights. The moment Dad left the room Swede bounded up and pulled jeans over her pajamas. She strapped on a belt and stuck two knives in it, right and left. Gravely she offered me the box. I chose two and with grim aspect slid them in my belt. Swede crossed her arms. She might've sailed with Francis Drake. She said, 'We are of a noble tradition, Reuben.' I buttoned up a flannel shirt and drew blood from three knuckles tucking it in.

We'd have sneaked out then, except the adults decided to have their evening coffee in the living room. This was inconsistent and very probably the work of the Lord. The front door was in the living room and we weren't likely to just waltz out through it. Trapped and mutinous, we worked our brains.

'We'll go out the window,' said Swede. But Mr DeCuellar, in his efficiency, had put his storms up right on schedule. We sat down in misery, mine counterfeit I will admit.

'I guess we'll have to wait,' I said. It was fine; outside the trees were leaning their tops around in the wind; the pane was so cold it felt wet.

But Swede was intent. 'After they're asleep, then.'

Which of course was not what I meant by *wait*. I meant the rhetorical wait, as in Wait till next year, or Just you wait and see. 'Oh, I'm sure they'll be up a long time,' I said, thinking, O Lord, let them stay up . . .

And don't you know, they did. After a while we lay down on top of our sleeping bags, just to soften the wait, and the wind tumbled stuff around outside, and a fine freezing rain began against the window. And I began to dream that a small piglet sat beside me, brown and aloof, and bit me on the hip when I rolled over. Actually, it was one of the steak knives. I sat up to feel for blood. The house was asleep, Swede too. She groused a little in a dream as I slipped the knives from her belt, but she didn't wake.

Next thing I recall is Dad kneeling between my bag and Swede's, waking us before sunup, strangely. I remember Mrs DeCuellar singing in her kitchen and the excited music of pans and perking coffee, and there was an agitation in Dad's voice that made me think, just for a moment, that we were on our way west, the car packed and pointed toward the faint cries of geese, the thrill of the cold.

Then I heard Dad say, his voice part of sleep, his voice coming off-balance into my sleep like a man feeling into a dark room, 'The sheriff was here an hour ago – wake up, kids – the sheriff has been here – kids, are you listening? Davy's broke out.'

A Boy on a Horse

The best of it, to Swede in particular, was that Davy escaped by pony. We wouldn't know this for several days, however, nor would the disturbed sheriff, Charlie Pym, who'd showed up pounding the door in the wee hours. Over breakfast Mr DeCuellar told us how he'd wrapped himself in a tartan robe and peeked between curtains before opening the door: 'Do you know who is up at four in the morning? Dairy farmers. Paperboys. Lunatics.' (Mr DeCuellar was not himself that morning; he was, in fact, grouchy. It was indecipherable to Swede and me, to whom this news was cotton candy.)

Sheriff Pym had insisted on entering. The night was wet and freezing and Pym stood dripping sleet on the rug, giving Mr DeCuellar what he called the 'onus eye.' (I am sure he meant the evil eye, the word *onus* made Swede break into such unruly giggles she had to hunt Kleenex.) The sheriff then inquired whether Mr DeCuellar had slept well.

'Thus far,' Mr DeCuellar replied.

'No visitors,' the sheriff said.

Mr DeCuellar looked at the door, then at the soaked Pym. He said, 'You can't possibly believe he would've come here.'

So all we knew, that first morning, was that Davy'd got out – maybe seven hours before. We hadn't details except that he'd taken with him a police-issue revolver and that a posse had been formed. Twelve men in six cars were out parsing the county at this moment.

'We'll have him by lunchtime,' the sheriff said – looking at Dad, who was standing in his long johns in the gloom. 'We'll try not to hurt your boy.'

It was Swede's contention, as the morning stretched on, that a posse of twelve *hundred* couldn't catch Davy. Let 'em try.

Dad said, 'Swede, if you can't talk sense, don't talk at all.'

They were the harshest words I'd ever heard him speak. I watched him sipping his coffee, his face foreign with misgiving. How I wanted to understand him! But I was eleven, and my brother had escaped from the pit where my vanity had placed him (a vain notion itself, Swede has since pointed out, yet it was certainty to me). How could my father not be joyous over such a thing? Who in this world could ask for more?

Nevertheless, the following days must've been excruciating for Dad – dreading Davy's recapture yet fearing worse. The state police were advised, and locally the posse grew exponentially; after early radio reports of the escape, fifty men appeared at the court-house, every one of them armed. Such a profusion of goose and varmint guns and beat-up World War pieces you never saw – at least such was the description given us by Deputy Walt Stockard, whose unconcealed glee over the escape must've been repugnant to Sheriff Pym. Though the very word *posse* sounds archaic, it made all sorts of sense at the time. For one thing, Davy was believed to be on foot. Since no one in Montrose County had reported a stolen vehicle – not a car, not a tractor, not so much as a Schwinn – it was assumed he was still nearby, shivering in some hidey-hole.

'Unless he got out to the highway and hitched a ride,' Dad suggested. He was trying to sell Walt on calling off the posse, something Walt hadn't the authority to do anyway. It was Davy's second day out; Walt was off duty and had come by the DeCuellars' for coffee; no doubt the sheriff thought it wise to keep an eye on Davy's family. 'He could be in Kansas City by now,' Dad said.

'Possibility,' Walt admitted. 'Though Pym believes otherwise. It was raining buckets, you know. How many folks are going to stop for some wet-muskrat-looking fellow, in a rainstorm, at that hour? Besides, he's got the best-known mug in the state right now. You think he'd try and hitch?'

It was a good point, and in fact Davy's picture was on the front page of that very afternoon's Minneapolis *Star* – a shot of him relaxed and laughing, hands folded back of his head. I still don't know where they got that photo; it was the one they'd used in their early stories, the ones extolling his bravery. Later they'd replaced it with a police mug in which his chin looked dirty and his eyes gave you not one bit of hope or information. Now the flattering picture was back, with this caption:

Bold outlaw Davy Land slips from jail, eludes manhunt. Fellow inmate: 'He up and disappeared like smoke.'

'Good grief,' Dad said. Having 'up and disappeared,' Davy'd clearly reacquired the allure that had evaporated so easily when people heard about Bubby. Now he was back to 'bold outlaw,' and while I liked the change I'd also learned a bit by now about public inconstancy. Not to mention Mighty Stinson's inconstancy. Quoted at length by reporters, Mighty told the story as one smitten by legend:

119

'And when I looked back up he was flat-out gone, I didn't hear a sound. Like he was a ghost.'

And worse:

'You know something? I knew he was going to do it. Knew it when they first brought him in.'

Pretty irresponsible of Mighty, since the truth, Walt said, was that Mighty had been sleeping like mortality itself when Davy made his move. But when else was anyone going to listen to a word Mighty said, much less put it in print?

What actually happened – and we got this from Walt, whose colleague Stube Range was on shift – was this: shortly before eleven, Stube was sitting at the night desk reading a paperback mystery. Subsequent research has revealed the book to be a Mike Hammer detective story. Stube was reading it despite Sheriff Pym's disapproval of its author, Mickey Spillane. (More research: the sheriff had met Spillane once, far back in memory, on a turboprop airliner, and Spillane had made a humorous remark about Charlie Pym's beard, which was sparse.) Suddenly Stube was distracted from the story by a polite call from Davy. The toilet in his cell wouldn't flush, he said.

Don't flush it then, Stube answered.

There's a need to, Davy replied; sorry about that, but there's a need. Davy jiggled the lever audibly. No flush.

There was apparently some back-and-forth between them, Mighty Stinson snorting in his sleep through everything because the dampness stopped his nose, but finally Stube Range put down his book, grumping good-naturedly about it I'm sure, let himself into Davy's cell, locked it behind him, and peeked in the toilet.

No suspense here. Stube awoke propped against the wall of Davy's cell. His head was sore and his memory flawed. The toilet, incidentally, worked fine; he had to use it before his replacement showed up at the stroke of twelve and released him from the cell.

Swede would point out, rightly enough, that a man reading Mickey Spillane ought to have known better, but Stube Range, as they say, had a good heart. At this crossroads in his life he would in fact leave law enforcement to begin a new career as a school janitor over in Roofing. The district was hiring, you see.

We stayed at the DeCuellars' three days after Davy's escape. Walt visited every morning, asking jokingly whether we'd seen Davy lately and bringing us news of the county's frustration. Crisscrossing the area, talking to farmers and rural deliverymen and others who might've noticed a bedraggled boy slouching hastily elsewhere, the posse had come up dry. The chase paled. Posse members began to desert, offering as excuses their wives and families and, in rare cases, their jobs. Who could blame them? Not only was the trail cold, there hadn't really been a trail to start with. By the time a bloodhound could be borrowed from a neighboring county, the great rains had blotted out Davy's scent. They gave the bloodhound a try anyway. Poor over-anticipated fellow – he couldn't smell anything but himself.

Through all this, Walt said, Sheriff Pym was losing his happy nature. Justly or unjustly, Davy had grown a higher profile than any other desperado ever to sit in the Montrose County jail. His escape only raised it higher. Pym, Walt cautioned us, felt that people were laughing at him. He'd been heard shouting blue language at the phone in his office. A Minneapolis editorialist had thrown out the combustible phrase 'hambone county rubes.'

'He's touchy what people think of him,' Walt told us – so you see, that Mickey Spillane business rings true.

By Davy's third day, Sheriff Pym had become so out of sorts Walt reported he was thinking of a house-to-house search.

'It scares me, Mr Land. Do you know how long it would take to look in every closet in Montrose?'

Mr DeCuellar said, 'The sheriff is joking, it's unconstitutional. Coffee?'

The deputy accepted. 'I'm worried about Charlie,' he said. 'He's just sure somebody's got Davy down the basement. Some young lady, he says. He keeps saying that; it bothers him awfully.' Walt Stockard was beginning to look tired. 'A lot of people like that boy, you know.'

'Yes,' said Mr DeCuellar, 'they do.' He was brisk this morning – there were times he seemed mad at Davy for getting away, or maybe he was just sick of houseguests. It had been a pretty long visit.

Walt said, 'My girls've been treating me like I'm on the wrong team.'

'They'll recover,' Mr DeCuellar said.

Walt pinched the bridge of his nose. What a kind fellow he was. He looked capable of forgetting just about anything. He said, 'Say, Rube, hand me one of those bismarcks, would you?'

That afternoon, to everyone's relief, a farmer name of Nelson Svedvig came into Montrose and filed a complaint about a stolen horse. An Arabian mare, taken from his south pasture; this would be less than two miles from Montrose.

'Taken when?' Sheriff Pym asked. Walt was standing right there, listening, is how I know.

'Not sure,' Nelson Svedvig admitted. 'I hauled a load of hay out late last week; she was there then.' He saw the sheriff looking at him and added, defensively, 'Those ponies kind of look after themselves this time of year.'

'Are your fences okay? Could be she ran off.'

Nelson replied, 'She foaled in the spring. And the

foal is still there' – adding, with rising dignity, 'and you *know* my fences, Charlie.'

That night the sheriff paid off what remained of the dispirited posse, and we took our leave of the DeCuellars. Oh, it was good to get home.

Our first night back Swede propped herself in bed, typewriter before her, listing in quilts. At first I worried she'd go back to fretting and banging the wall; but she whacked away steadily, and I soon dropped asleep in my room across the hall. Here's what I found in the morning, laid neatly on the floor beside my bed:

The moon was black as a miner's lung,
The sky was black as a shroud,
And deep in a cell that was black as a well
Two men lay moaning aloud.

And one was Rennie, who'd robbed a man,
And one was Bert, who had killed,
And the gallows outside hadn't ever been tried
But its mission would soon be fulfilled, lads,
Its mission would soon be fulfilled.

Three nooses swayed loose in a breeze like a sigh—
But who was the third who was waiting to die?

Swede came in while I was reading and perched on my bed like a satisfied cat; she saw how breathless I was, it made her pretty confident. I said, 'Is it Sunny?' But she only shrugged – she knew she had me.

He'd been awake in his room one night,
With his darling asleep by his side,
When the bold Reddick boys, hardly making a noise,
Pushed the front door open wide.

123

His bride they had threatened not once but three
*   times,*
When his travels had fetched him away.
They had followed her round as she walked through
*   the town,*
Calling names I would rather not say – no,
The names I would rather not say.

And what do you think any good man would do,
No matter what judges or laws told him to?

There was something about the poem – I almost felt
I had read it before. 'Swede,' I told her, 'this is awful
good!'

'Aw, don't,' she said.

They opened the door and they crossed the broad
*   floor*
With their minds full of evil intent.
For in town they had heard the fortuitous word
That Sundown on business was sent.

And as they approached Sunny rose to his feet,
Like a spirit he made not a sound,
And his blood rose inside as they came near his
*   bride*
And he shot the bold Reddick boys down, lads,
He shot the bold Reddick boys down.

So may a good man who has spared his wife hurt
Face death with the likes of poor Rennie and Burt.

'That's it?' I couldn't believe it; there wasn't
any more! 'He *dies*? They hang him with these two
guys?'

'Reuben, how fast do you think I can write this
stuff?'

'Oh – it's not done?'

'Reu*ben*!'

'Well, I'm sorry!' The truth was, old Sundown really tugged at me. Glad as I was that Swede was back in whatever groove made the verses click, this business of hearing half a story was insufferable. Cautiously I asked, 'What about Valdez?'

She didn't look at me. 'What about him?'

'Well, what happened to him? Who are these Rennie and Burt fellows?'

She looked at me hard. I figured she was thinking I didn't like the poem.

'Swede, it's a great poem. You know it is. I was only wondering.'

She had tears in her eyes, just that quick!

'I *love* the poem, Swede!' I was desperate, pardner.

She said, 'Sunny couldn't beat him, Reuben. Valdez. I couldn't write it.'

Now why do you suppose that made me feel so bad? A lump arose as if I were reading my own mawkish epitaph.

'So he got away?'

She didn't answer. Her silence placed or revealed a nub of fear in me – an unreasoning fear that Valdez was no invention. That he was real and coming toward us on solid earth. A preposterous idea, wouldn't you say? Yet it blazed up, so scary in its brightness that I made a wall against it in my heart, in the deepest place I owned.

The weeks wheeled along unbalanced. Swede leaned toward elation; she herself couldn't have orchestrated Davy's getaway in more fabled style. One day Walt Stockard reported to us that the Svedvig mare had come trotting home, whickering for oats but none the worse for wear. There was speculation that Davy'd ridden a dozen miles across country to the state highway and nabbed a ride. Swede also took satisfaction in the newspapers' reversal of attitude, by now so complete that a stranger reading his first Davy Land article would've finished it believing the world was improved without these Finch and Basca characters anyway and that young Land ought merely to be thanked and let go. One columnist, Aaron W. Groap at the *St Paul Pioneer Press*, was particularly susceptible to romance. I've saved a couple of his entries – here's part of one.

RIDE, DAVY, RIDE

No fretting for the past for me, folks. I'm happy in the current century. Put me in a Lincoln Continental or a turboprop leaving frozen St Paul; give me Huntley-Brinkley at six o'clock; meet me at Met Stadium for a ball game on a summer night. I'm a modern creature, friend, and I like it that way.

So how come I envy Davy Land?

He's just a kid, after all, with an outdated sense of frontier justice. A kid who went too far and landed, most deservedly, in jail. A kid who's exceeded the boundaries of our civilized lives. He ought to be locked up – isn't that right?

So how come, when I arrive at work, the first thing I do is check the AP wire to see if Davy Land's been caught? And chuckle on seeing he hasn't?

He's just a boy on a horse, after all. Just a skinny length of wire and persistence who still doesn't know he can't really escape. Such ignorance! For his face is known to every citizen. It's pasted to the dashboard of every state cop and county hack. I mentioned Chet Huntley and David Brinkley? If you saw the news last night, you know they know him too.

A boy on a horse can't outride the law. Not in 1962. The police tell us so, and perhaps they are right. America is a grown-up place, after all. It's been a long while since we loved our outlaws. Perhaps the songs we knew as kids – about Jesse James, and Billy the Kid, and the Dirty Little Coward Who Shot Mr Howard –

have no place in a world full of television and helicopters and rock and roll. Perhaps this is all for the best.

Today is 5 December. Davy Land escaped from jail twelve days ago. I've just checked the wires, and he is still free.

Excuse me while I chuckle.

You had to take Aaron Groap for what he was, of course; all but the very best columnists grab their causes with such operatic choke holds. Anyhow, as Swede said, this sort of thing beat the pants off the Bubby story.

There was no comfort in it for Dad, though. He seemed to believe he had lost his son forever, and the popular melodrama of it only made it worse. He stopped answering the telephone; he became restive and joyless. Many a night I woke to the murmur of paper and knew he was up, sitting in the kitchen with frayed King James – oh, but he worked that book; he held to it like a rope ladder. I remember creeping out once when my breathing was poor and there he was, Holy Bible on the tabletop and himself bent to it, his back cupped as a weasel's, when I tapped his arm he sat up straight, his breath seizing a moment as if the motion hurt. I told him my lungs were tight.

'All right, Reuben.' But he sat still, not rising to put water on the stove.

'What you reading?'

'Ninety-first Psalm.'

'Does it help?'

He went to the sink and held a pan under the tap. He didn't answer and I thought he wasn't hearing me. I repeated the question.

Dad lit a burner. There must've been something on the bottom of that pan, for smoke and burnt smell twined up its sides. When the water boiled he threw in

127

baking soda, which foamed and subsided. I said, 'You could read me a psalm if you want to, Dad.'

But he said, 'Not tonight, Reuben, my head hurts so.'

In early December a blizzard swept in off the plains and struck with what was measured on the flats as twenty-seven inches of snow. This was the first in what became nearly a weekly cycle of snowstorms, some of them riven by lightning, a confounding phenomenon. Dr Nokes, a medical student through much of the Great·Depression, said he recalled lightning and snow mixed only once before, during a week of examinations; he said the snow came down not in flakes but the approximate shape and size of corn kernels, and he said it preceded a spring that brought neither rain nor hope of rain, so dry were most midwestern souls.

I thought that was an awful lot to remember from something as simple as lightning in a snowstorm, but Dr Nokes laughed and said one day I too would remember hard winters in detail more voluminous than anyone would care to hear. I suppose he was right and you don't give a chipped dime for December of '62, but it was an epic season all the same, the drifts rising eventually past the kitchen window and up to the very eaves. In the afternoons Swede and I, in layers of pants, would step from the highest snowbank onto the roof of the single-story addition, then climb to the peak and go skidding down the other side to land with a *poof* in the front yard. How we missed Davy! In such snow he'd have led us into all sorts of thrilling and jeopardous traps – our backyard would've been veined with tunnels and candlelit caverns; our snowball wars would've been prolonged and ferocious. I remember one dream I had that winter, that Davy was home and climbing the roof with us, his leaps from the peak wondrously high, and in the dream the salesman Tin Lurvy was lying on his back in the snow, watching, admiration all over his face, and Lurvy was saying *Oh, my, look at him – goodness' sake, what leaping!* And here is why I remember that dream in particular: because Lurvy said – and this woke me up laughing – *I want to try that! Hey, kids, can I try that?*

We didn't go back to school, by the way. Pretty manipulative on our part: Dad hadn't the will to send us back if we truly didn't want to go, and we knew it. Preying on his depression we made ourselves useful – we washed clothes, scrubbed floors, swept cobwebs, cooked soup (it is hard to ruin soup, unless you run short of salt, and anyway Dad wasn't picky). When he approached us one day with the reluctant suggestion that we return to school after the Christmas break, Swede revealed a breathtaking bit of strategy, taking Dad into her room and displaying a stack of history and geography and arithmetic books more than a foot high. 'From the library,' she said, adding this hand-some flourish: 'I certainly don't want to lag behind my classmates.'

'Ah,' Dad said, looking at me over Swede's head – he was on to her and wanted me to know it. He didn't send us back, though, despite the fact that the school-books were but props. It wasn't as if we didn't read; while at the library, Swede had also checked out every Frank O'Rourke on the shelves, having finished *The Big Fifty* long ago. O'Rourke, she confided, wrote much better Westerns than Zane Grey.

'It's his women. They don't talk all the time, and when they ride, they ride like men.'

While interesting, I didn't see what difference this made to the story. As a reader I leaned more in the direction of pirates; *Treasure Island* simply didn't have any women, except for Long John's stanch negress, whom you never actually see.

'It makes all sorts of difference,' Swede said. She's a professor now, have I told you that? 'Every Western is a love story, you see. In Zane Grey, the hero always starts off with the wrong girl, and she has eyes that are too close together, and she has a bad attitude, like a problem horse.'

'The wrong girl is like a horse?'

'Usually a roan, a stubborn roan. The hero has had lots of horses, and this girl makes him remember that roan.'

So Westerns were love stories. Though I'd read several myself, I hadn't realized the truth of this equation. I didn't like the sound of it, either.

'Swede,' I said, 'Sunny's wife – she was the right kind of girl, wasn't she? Like one of O'Rourke's you were talking about.'

The question made her indignant. Sunny Sundown was no dummy, she said; he'd ridden some miles in his time; he would never have married a roan. I was glad to hear her say it. Last I'd read of Sunny, he had his hands full enough without that sort of problem:

Till late in the night he had fought the good fight
With his fear, and had kept it at bay;
And he dreamed of his wife, and their satisfied life,
And he woke to a wicked new day.

Then he rose in his shirt and he nodded to Bert,
Who was empty and mute as a hole,
But down on his knees Rennie wept aloud, 'Please,
Have charity on a thief's soul, Lord,
Forgive my poor dry-rotted soul.'

Three nooses swung loose as a clergyman prayed.
Three men were marched forward – and two were
    afraid.

Swede meant this to be suspenseful, of course, but even at eleven I recognized what had to happen next: somehow, a woman had to come on the scene. You don't need many Westerns under your belt to know that. And she had to be young and black-eyed and lovely, and touched by the bravery of the condemned hero.

Then up the tight street came a rider so sweet,
She was light as the dawn, and as free –
And her hair was as black as her stallion's back,
And she parted the crowd like a sea.

'Is it Sunny's wife?' I asked.

'Nope – just a woman.' She deliberated. 'You know, that's not an awful idea. But it's a different woman.' This troubled me; for I saw straight off that the beauty on the black horse was about to attempt a rescue, and also that she was deep in love with our Sunny. And him married! It was a problem.

'Why don't you change it,' I suggested, 'make this girl his wife, see – they ride away together.'

'She wasn't his wife!' Swede flared. Past tense, you notice – history, even the fictive kind, being beyond our influence.

The problem got worse when the girl actually pulled off the rescue; for then Sunny, though rushed in the moment,

Leaned down from the black and pushed her hair
  back
And kissed his deliverer twice, my lads,
He kissed his deliverer twice.

The last thing I wanted was to fight Swede, but this was terrible. 'Now he's kissing her,' I complained. 'If she was his wife, it would be okay.'

'Reuben,' Swede said, holding herself back, 'say you're about to be hanged. The rope's on your neck already! Then out of noplace this beautiful girl comes riding up and saves you – are you telling me you're not going to kiss that girl?'

131

'Well—'

'Look, Reuben. Let's say Sunny just thinks of her as a really great sister. Like me.'

I nodded, but in truth this picked at me for some little while. Hair 'as black as her stallion's back' – nuts, it would've been hard enough to think of that girl as a sister without throwing kisses into the deal at all.

By the Grace of Lurvy

Christmas 1962 looked a little meager going in.

You understand: kids of my generation grew up with stories of their parents' deprivations – tales of treeless Christmases, cold kitchens, scrawny old stockings containing naught but a polished apple. In 1962, the Great Depression was a reach back of less than thirty years – surely a millennial distance for residents of a progressive city such as Minneapolis but not so far if you lived in Roofing, on the edge of the plains.

Thus Swede and I felt certain we were about to live such a story ourselves. For Dad had found but irregular work – he repaired a furnace for the Lutheran church, mended furniture in the basement and, capitalizing on a rash of chimney fires in town, borrowed a brush and swept chimneys until he caught cold. 'I'll work through it,' he told Swede, sniffing the hot lemonade she handed him, but another day on the rooftops drove the cold lungward until he wheezed as badly as I did. I suspect he was almost grateful. I know we were – that chimney business was nasty work, the wind snapping his coat around, him up there in his janitor's boots, traipsing on icy shingles.

Still, an unemployed father meant the sort of Christmas Swede and I had always heard of, or read about in books with titles like *Days of Despair*. We pictured ourselves waking Christmas morning to bowls of oatmeal unadorned by so much as a teaspoon of white sugar. ('Porridge,' Swede said. 'Mush. Gruel.') We wondered how well we'd do in front of Dad – how grateful we could appear for a gift of, say, a navel orange. In the books, kids were unfailingly thrilled by a Christmas orange; they never felt poor at the time, it only dawned on them later. What I really wanted that year was the Spartacus model. Remember Spartacus? I never actually saw the movie, which came out I believe in 1960, but in '62 certain kids at school were still talking about its gory gladiator scenes. The dime store downtown had a model Spartacus – what a durable character he appeared, face like a badger's, sword in hand. And what a noble cause he espoused, fighting against slavery, like Abraham Lincoln. What a boy really liked about the Spartacus model was that one of the plastic pieces was a severed hand, belonging, I guess, to the fellow he'd just got done fighting. You could lay the hand anywhere around Spartacus's feet, or impale it on his sword, or paint it red and torment your sister with it.

Swede wanted something even more extravagant. 'A trip,' she said, 'out West. I want to ride west on a horse and find Davy.' She was sure he was out there, cosy under some rock, sitting on a blanket eating buffalo meat: holed up somewhere in the previous century. How great it would be to go find him! What a Christmas we'd all have!

A navel orange just seemed a little weak in comparison.

Then, ten days before Christmas, Dr Nokes stopped by. Drinking tea – our coffee was long gone – he grew alarmed at Dad's deepening cough. He set his cup down and retrieved a stethoscope from his car.

'Jeremiah,' he said warily, 'how long have you been croaking this way?'

'I actually think it's getting better,' Dad said.

'How much do you bring up?' asked Dr Nokes.

Dad cleared his throat and said he hadn't been measuring. Then, 'Swede, Reuben, is your homework done?' We hadn't any homework, of course, but we went to my room anyway. I remember noticing a strange smell right then, a heavy staleness in the air. Why hadn't I perceived it before? Air itself can rot, you know, turn lush as a forgotten peach. You want to throw open every window you see.

On the way to my room we heard Dr Nokes ask, not fooling around, 'What color?'

He's told me since – Dr Nokes has – that his main worry was not Dad's pneumonia. He was confident antibiotics and Dad's own constitution could handle that. What worried the doctor was that I might come down with it. A set of lungs like mine could turn to peat moss with very little prompting. Before leaving that night, Dr Nokes stepped me aside and spoke in confidence.

'Reuben,' he said, 'I've a hunch about your sister – that she has the makings of a doctor when she's grown. So listen: you stay out of her way, let her take care of your dad. What do you say?'

I know: I should've been far too old to fall for this sort of ruse.

'I've given her instructions, and I'll drop some medicine by. You let Swede give it to your dad. Your job is to stay out of his room. Swede should take him his meals, too.' He saw I didn't understand. Glancing around he said, 'Bedside manner. It's where she needs practice – her bedside manner is a little rough.'

'Well, what can *I* do?' Two weeks Dad was supposed to stay in bed. 'What about Christmas?'

Dr Nokes said, 'You know, I was talking to Mr Layton today. He's got a bad spine, did you know that?'

Talk about your conversational leaps. I blinked at Dr

Nokes, who went on, 'He just can't work anymore in certain ways. You're familiar with that old eyesore of a corncrib back of his house.'

I didn't understand what it had to do with Dad and said so. Dr Nokes replied, 'Mr Layton would probably hire a boy to tear that corncrib down – if the boy had a strong back, Reuben.'

A strong back? I had never imagined myself with a strong anything. Even had I guessed that the doctor only wanted to remove me from the house, put my lungs outside in healthy air, I wouldn't have cared. No words he spoke could've pleased me more.

Gerard Layton's corncrib was indeed an artifact. Tall as a boxcar, nailed up of laths spaced on oak posts, it leaned back in time. I stood in front of it, holding a crowbar, not knowing how to begin.

I mentioned the snow. This was 16 December – the birthday, Swede informed me, of Ludwig Beethoven, the great band director – and already we'd logged three or four notable snowstorms. Winter was a train crawling north. I walked all round Mr Layton's corncrib, up to my hips every step. It seemed an odd time of year for this particular job, but Mr Layton was peculiar and everyone knew it. I remember thinking the corncrib looked about ten minutes from falling over on itself, but when I poked the crowbar through its ribs and leaned down, nothing happened. The crib flatout did not notice me. I heaved to and fro. I had on Davy's chopper mitts with wool liners but felt that bar as if barehanded. At last, after extravagant effort, a nail squealed and dropped me into a drift.

Swede fretted over me appreciatively when I came in at noon. 'Oh, you're frozen! Hurry and get some dry socks on; I'll hang those on the radiator. Come *on*, Reuben, I've got soup ready!'

She squared me up at the table and set down a bowl of something white – not what you think of as soup, though dumplings bobbed on the surface. 'It's villing!' she announced.

I knew what it was. It was hot milk with a little sugar stirred in, also some butter and a shake of cinnamon.

'Dad told me how to make it. I always liked it,' Swede said. I didn't mean to hesitate, but I'd been out all morning doing a man's work. Villing was *sick* food.

'Isn't it okay?' Swede said.

'Do we have any cheese?'

She shook her head. Off in his bedroom Dad hawked something up, a dispiriting sound. I looked at the villing: if you skimmed the dumplings off you had only to pour it over toast. Presto, milk toast. More sick food.

'Well, let's eat.' By this time I felt poorly used and didn't care how gruff I sounded. To work all morning in snow to my waist, to pit my muscles and manly crowbar against an edifice as stout as Mr Layton's corncrib, to come home all dissipated and ravenous and have to sit down to a bowl of *hot milk*—

'Dad's worse,' Swede said, abruptly.

'What's the matter?'

'He's in there pounding his chest – hear him thumping? He's been doing it all morning.'

It was strange. My fingers started to tremble when she said that.

'It's his lungs, they're filling up – like yours do, Reuben. He's trying to knock it loose.'

'Be right back,' I told her.

'Wait, Reuben, you aren't to go in,' Swede said, but I was compelled by the whacking noise. Who knew constriction better than me? How many times had I thrashed my own chest – thrashed it like you would a snake, to make it slack its coils?

Dad stopped pounding when I opened the door. Sitting up in a flannel shirt, blankets over his lap and on them an aluminum pan, his face when he saw me filled with chagrin. 'I sound like a threshing crew. Ack.'

'Is it hard to breathe?'

'Reuben,' he said, 'is this what you feel like in the night?'

His breathing was like ripples on a sand beach.

'Yes, sir.'

He nodded – exhausted but watching me, it seemed, more closely than usual. 'What would you think of moving, Reuben? Dr Nokes has told me' – he paused, breathed, 'of people who have this trouble; they've gone to dry climates.' He breathed again. 'New Mexico. He says all this plumbing works better out there.' He slapped his chest.

'New Mexico?'

'High desert,' he said. And those words did sound magnificent, spoken as they were in a close, moist, ill-smelling room. *High desert.* It came to me as beautiful rolling wastes of sagebrush and grama grass and air through which you might see an antelope top a rise six miles away. Just thinking of it relaxed me. Who could not breathe in such a landscape?

Then Swede, who'd come in behind me, said: 'What if we move and then Davy comes back and we're all gone?'

Dad said, 'Well, we don't have to make our minds up right now.'

'It would be like forsaking all hope of his return,' Swede said. I know, the sentence deserved an accompanying swoon, but this was how she got some-times and by now you oughtn't to be surprised.

'He'd find us,' I argued. I was excited. I'd never seen high desert but the thought of it seemed suddenly imperative. 'Don't you think we ought to? It's out *West*, Swede.'

I watched her thinking it out: imagining Davy returning – probably on horseback, knowing Swede's turn of mind – Davy finding us gone and turning his big black into the sun and walking away; but she was also thinking of us out West, the three of us riding across prairies, siding each other, like a family invented by Frank O'Rourke, and I watched her thinking how Davy would rejoin us there and we'd become the four of us again, and possibly even the five of us, an O'Rourke woman appearing now on a strong bay mare alongside Dad.

That last was a shock, and I looked at Swede and wondered if she'd really thought it or if I'd come up with it myself.

'How about,' Dad suggested, 'if you let me get back on my feet before you both start packing?'

Then I realized I'd gone into Dad's room scared for him, but once inside hadn't even asked how he was or what I could do. Instead he'd asked, his chest filling with junk, if this was how things were for *me* in the difficult times.

I said, 'Can I get you anything, Dad?'

'Well, let's see. Yes, a glass of water.' He slapped his pillow into shape and lay back against it. 'Say, Reuben, what did you think of Swede's villing? Good, wasn't it?'

'I haven't eaten.'

'Mm.' Shallow breath. 'Well, you're going to like it.'

And it's funny, but I did. Sick food or not I had two bowls, and while I ate them Swede sat with me and agreed that the high desert was desirable and that we ought, when Dad got better, to go and at least have a good long look at it.

It was the first time I ever persuaded her to my side of anything.

Back at the corncrib I was distressed to realize all my efforts of the morning had brought down only six lengths of lath. Elementary math revealed I would be working till Easter unless I got the hang of this. I chose a junction of oak and lath and wedged the bar in.

A kid somewhere said, 'Hey!'

He was in the corncrib, crouched and peeking through laths. I had a slatted view of a boy in a corduroy coat, a fat grinning boy with plugged nostrils. You could see what was plugging them, too.

'Who're you?' I asked.

'Raymond.' He said it *Raymod*, the *n* getting detained up in nostril country.

'I'm Rube – why don't you come out of there?'

'Whatcha doig?'

'Ripping this old thing down,' I told him. 'Mr Layton hired me. Come on out of there.'

Outside the corncrib he was more of himself. The coat was unbuttoned and showed layers of shirt. His cheeks were rubbed scabby and looked like sallow Texas grapefruits glazed with effluent. Raymond was much shorter, but I'm guessing he had me by thirty pounds.

'How old are you, Raymond?'

'Six.' He twisted around and waved at a house across the alley from Mr Layton's. 'That's Gramma's, we live with her, Mob an' Dad an' me.' He looked at me fearlessly. 'Can I watch?'

'What?'

'Watch you rip her dowd?'

Raymond was a good watcher. At first I didn't want him there because I wasn't adept at the work and feared notice. But Raymond was gifted in not noticing. He sat down in the deep snow and spoke wet, unrelated sentences. 'We jus' moved here las' summer. Gramma's house idn't built good. My brudder heard a ghos' last night – *rhee*, like a horse. My dad's a buskrat trapper, got two hunderd buskrats last year.'

A lath sprang free from the crib. I managed to stay on my feet.

'I use to get beat up back hobe. There was a neighbor kid Pugger could bed his thub alla way back to here.' Poor Raymond, his passages were so obstructed he had his own dialect.

About this time I discovered a principle of physics. Mr Layton's crowbar had been broken off and resharpened and so lacked the slight angle a crowbar needs at the business end. In my ignorance I worked without fulcrum, a lousy way to pry, until finally a loose lath fell down of its own accord, wedging itself between bar and post. I shoved, and the lath I'd been worrying for ten minutes squealed loose instantly. Thereafter I worked with purchase and things accelerated. Raymond sat in the snow talking away. I never saw a boy better built for cold. His coat was open wing and wing but he was radiant with talk, and the wind blew over his big besmirched cheeks and exposed earlobes with no effect. He was like a small, hot, talkative planet.

'How strog are you?' he inquired bluntly.

I tore down a lath and flung it on the pile. 'I'm tearing down a building, aren't I?' Boy, it felt good saying that.

'You're pretty strog.' Of course, he could've outpulled me in any contest you might name, but at six he was too kind to know it.

I said, 'Well, I'm older than you.'

'Rube?'

'Yup.' I was wrestling a tough one.

'Is your brother a burderer?'

One of my mitts slipped and the crowbar dropped into the snow. Clawing it out I regarded Raymond for malice. 'Where'd you hear that?'

'Well, he shot those big kids.'

'Didn't you ever hear of self-defense?'

He shook his head. I oughtn't have been so sharp; he was only curious.

'My dad said he was a burderer.' Then, 'My dad's really strog – I bet he could tear that shed down with his bare hads. Could your dad do that?'

'Sure – not right now, though, he's got pneumonia.'

'Oh,' Raymond said. 'I had a uncle with pneumonia. He died and had a funeral, but we didn't go.'

That corncrib represented the hardest work I'd ever done; still, I suspect Swede had the tougher job back home. Not the cooking and washing and sweeping, which she'd been doing since we left school, but hearing Dad wrack and hawk and bits of his lungs hitting *whang* in the pan. When I arrived from Layton's those late afternoons, brimming with my own success and breathing deep as I ever had, Swede seemed frighteningly burdened. Of course with Swede you got used to periods of deep thought, but this was different; for she was Dad's nurse, and anyone knows a downhearted nurse signifies a sinking patient. This didn't register with me right away – by the time I got home, Dad was usually sleeping quietly, which seemed a good omen – until I crept in one evening, hoping to find him awake. I don't recall what I wanted to tell him, probably how well the corncrib was going, how much money I figured to earn off it, how generally strong and immortal I was feeling now. I stood beside him, wishing he'd awaken, a boy just wanting his dad's attention; and then standing there I had the dreamlike thought that he'd become me – his breathing something you had to listen hard to hear at all. This was more terrifying than any night I'd spent battling my own lungs; I grabbed Dad's shoulder and brought him awake.

'Reuben.' He was startled; his hands came up and took hold of my arms. 'Is everything all right?'

I was startled right back. 'Ah – you want me to boil some water and soda? Loosen you up?'

He sat upright and breathed as deeply as he could. Oh, but he was bound tight. 'Look, Reuben. I don't think steam's the thing. Maybe you'd pound my back a little.'

So I sat on the edge of his bed and he braced up best he could and I whacked him between the shoulder blades – first as hard as I dared, never having touched

142

my father in this strange way before, and then, as he nodded encouragement and his lungs began to respond, as hard as I could. How I whacked! His back was bony as a fowl's, for the pneumonia had consumed his surplus; he couldn't shore up against even my feeble thumping for more than a minute. But when he sagged back onto his pillow his breathing was discernibly easier. He smiled.

'That corncrib work is helping you, boy.'

I finished 20 December, a huge day for me; the crib had a roof of sheet tin held tight by a thousand galvanized nails, and I had to haul the ladder in and hammer upward to loosen it. Deafness threatened. When finally the tin slid away and whuffed to earth, I tilted into a snowbank to rest. I wished Raymond would show up. Nothing remained of the crib but its black upright timbers, which for frozen steadfastness seemed a jury of puritans. I wasted some minutes heaving and grunting, then shoveled to bare earth and sheared them off flush with a crosscut saw. It took all afternoon. When the last post toppled I dragged it to the stack by Mr Layton's garage, missing Raymond's six-year-old admiration for my modest strength. Had he flattered me then I'd have swallowed it whole. I stretched the day out long, picking nails and bits of lath from the snow and finally horsing the noisy sheet of tin up so the whole stack lay re-covered by its own roof. Stars were appearing, Venus in the east. I seemed to breathe buckets of air, whole arctics of it! I set the crowbar over my shoulder, thinking of the great Crockett slinging up Betsy at the end of the day.

When I got home Swede was chafed beyond reason. She clattered out the bowls for supper, poured the cornflakes, made Dad's hot water with a spoonful of lemon juice, and slapped it all on a metal tray. Recalling what Dr Nokes had said regarding her

143

bedside manner I said, 'Are you mad about something, Swede?'

She stayed clammed, entered Dad's room to lay supper across his lap and returned somewhat mellowed with his praiseful thanks. Still, she didn't speak to me. I was certain I'd done something thoughtless until she finished the dishes and sat down and began to blink. I had a stick of candy in my jacket pocket, a present from Raymond.

'Want to split a candy cane?'

She nodded and I broke it in two and gave her the crook. She stuck the long end in her mouth and in a few minutes pulled it out and pointed it at the hallway door.

'Look at 'em all,' she said.

She was talking about the Christmas cards she'd taped up, ten or twelve of them, a bumper crop. Because we hadn't much family (one uncle, no aunts, two older cousins whose wild doings we heard about secondhand), we'd never received more than six or seven Christmas cards a year. This time around there were new ones, from the DeCuellars, the Stockards, a few others.

'Don't you like them?'

''Course I do.'

'What's the matter then?' I was thinking how happy she seemed mornings – how excited she always was, pulling on her boots to head up to the post office. Dad would be sitting up with his tea by then and I'd be going out the door to Mr Layton's, and Swede would run the few blocks and rifle the PO box, a responsibility I envied, particularly now so close to Christmas.

'We haven't got nothing from Davy,' she said.

It hadn't occurred to me that Davy might send us a Christmas card, him being a fugitive from justice. Was there even precedent for such a thing? Mentally I ran down a few examples. Cole Younger? Butch Cassidy? John Wesley Hardin? Maybe these fellows were just flush with Christmas spirit, but I'd never heard about it. I mentioned these doubts to my sister.

'Wesley was illiterate,' Swede said, casually using the middle name as if on personal terms with the outlaw. 'Also, he was a skunk. He wouldn't have sent cards to anybody and he never got any either.'

'Well, what about those others?'

'Cassidy was romantic, you know that.' In fact, I did know it. The romantic quality was something he had acquired while vacationing in Bolivia. Swede had read all about the heroic Butch, how he had a fondness for the afternoon siesta, also for the words Pardon, Señorita, and other poetical phrases. It was easy to believe Cassidy would've sent off his Christmas cards, and on time too.

I was going to ask about Cole Younger, but someone stepped up on the porch and knocked. It was Mr Layton. He stood out there like a big hunched beetle and wouldn't come in.

'Boy,' he said, 'you finished her, come out here and settle up.'

This was the first I'd seen of him since he'd handed me the crowbar; he'd been sitting at his dime-store counter the whole time I tore down his crib. I had wondered how this part of the deal was to happen and now here he was, bad spine and all.

'You done a good job,' he said, when I'd slipped on my boots and stepped out.

'Thank you, sir.'

'Do you know how long that thing has needed wrecking?'

'No, sir. How long?'

He said, 'The old man who sold me the place kept horses. Percherons, great big drafters.'

I thought of Raymond and the houses across the alley. 'Where'd he keep them? Isn't the yard sort of small?'

Mr Layton chuckled. 'It was big then, boy.'

145

I hadn't anything else to ask, and Mr Layton reached for his billfold. He pulled out two ten-dollar bills and a five and said, 'You done a good job,' then patted another pocket and came out with two chocolate bars. Mr Goodbars – you know that yellow wrapper. 'One for you and one for your sister,' he said, and I accepted them and watched him go down the porch steps, needing the railing right the way down.

Two whole days I dreamed with Swede about the things $25 could buy. The bills were straight voltage, juicing all sorts of hallucinations. Could you buy a Hiawatha bicycle for twenty-five clams? Swede thought you could, and moreover figured there was room for her on the handlebars. I was also tempted by the thought of water. I knew a kid, his name is gone, who'd gotten hold of a sweet-natured canoe framed up in cedar and covered with watertight canvas. The boat smelled like a humidor and floated so light the kid claimed to have followed to its source the nameless creek adjoining the Bright River. He claimed to have paddled up through brushlands where burnt tamaracks poked from the surface of the creek and the water slowed to rest and the quiet was broken by the protruding fins of frantically spawning carp. All this magic from a wooden canoe that had been sitting disused in a barn. The kid – Alfred something, I believe, red-haired and double-jointed – had procured the boat in payment for a few days' picking rock in the spring.

'I think a canoe,' I told Swede.

'Telescope,' she replied. She'd read some poem about a farmer who so loved the stars that he arsoned his place for the insurance money and bought a glass through which the Pleiades became a scatter of diamonds on a velvet cloth.

Then again, it was almost Christmas. What about presents? Shamefully, the first person who came to mind was neither Dad nor Swede but Bethany Orchard, whom I hadn't seen in weeks. What did Bethany want for Christmas? I would've given half the money just to know.

'What're you thinking about?' Swede demanded. Such a joyous, greedy talk we'd been having, she didn't want me adrift.

'Oh, I don't know.' I faltered badly. Though you couldn't have dragged the truth from me – *Bethany Orchard* – in fact I had a sudden ache to say her name out loud.

'Reuben? You worrying about Davy?' Swede asked; and she looked so motherly and worried that I nodded and put on the gravest face I owned. To my enormous surprise and guilt she got me in a bear hug and kept me there awhile. Poor Swede, she always did think better of me than I had coming.

The next day – 23 December – Dad got out of bed. I woke from dreams of a gravel road along which I walked shoeless, picking up nuggets of gold the size of baby turtles. We had in our bathroom a hot-water tap that squeaked persistently when turned, and I heard it plainly as I stooped for nuggets. On and off it squeaked, and then I was awake and though fiscally disappointed knew Dad was up and shaving, and that the tapping I heard between squeaks was him knocking his razor against the sink to get the whiskers off. Bounding up I rapped at the bathroom door and was admitted to the sight of Dad standing at the mirror, soap on half his face and a grin showing where he'd thumbed through lather.

'Morning, Reuben.' His voice was quiet, tired, but free of the congestion that had so shortened his sentences of late.

'Are you well?' I couldn't believe it; just last night I had heard him coughing.

'Reuben, you look starved. Go off and start some oatmeal, why don't you?'

147

So off I went rejoicing, banging around the kitchen until Swede awoke and came in to issue instructions. Stirring the pot she told me it was a big day and to get the maple syrup out of the back cupboard. I looked. The syrup was gone.

'Brown sugar, then,' she said. 'Above the toaster.'

I shook my head. 'We used it up.'

'White sugar.' But that bowl too was nearly empty, and when I got out the ten-pound canister in which we kept reserves, the scoop inside rattled sorrowfully.

Swede was disgusted. 'Well, get out some apples.'

We had a bag of old apples in the refrigerator, long ignored on account of their soft flesh and wrinkly complexions. But I peeled them down and chopped them small and Swede found some Karo syrup and poured it in the oatmeal and told me to round up Dad.

He'd finished shaving and was in his bedroom. I knocked and getting no response went in. As I did he stepped from the closet where he'd been rummaging and I glimpsed him upright and as he truly was. A scream formed in my gut and emerged as a whimper. When shaving he'd worn a big T-shirt that fell below the waist of his pants, disguising his exsiccated frame just as the lather disguised his face – so obscured he might've been a healthy man, if thin. Now he came out of the closet barefaced and bare-chested. His torso was not his but someone else's – a drawn maroon's from some sea story. His face too was bereft of all extra so that suddenly I barely recognized him. How had this escaped me? Even his eyes had the transparency of incarceration, and he looked at me out of them with a mercy and pain that confused me beyond what small troubles I'd ever thought to know.

He nodded slightly, I suppose wondering what to say. 'You and Swede get that oatmeal ready?'

'Yes, sir.' I couldn't stop looking at him, at the way his khakis were belted across his hip bones.

He said, 'I'm a little surprised myself, you know.'

In retrospect it's hard to believe I didn't see instantly what to do with that money. But when it's the first you've earned by sweat you see it as special and by golly not to be spent on less than the desire of your grasping heart. The more I thought about old Alfred and his cedar canoe, the more I saw myself paddling one just like it. Convinced similar exquisite vessels lay concealed in dairy barns all over the county, I told Swede of my decision.

'We're out of food, Reuben,' she answered.

Having used great gestures describing the canoe I planned to purchase and the adventures we would enjoy thereafter, it irritated me that she would change the subject.

'Well, let's go get some then.'

'We can't.'

I really did need it spelled out for me; the truth is, I'd been wondering when Swede would take the initiative and suggest we go up to the Red Owl for groceries. We often did the shopping, the two of us, pulling our painted wagon, Dad's money in my pocket; in the winter we used a toboggan.

'If we spend any more money right now,' she said, 'we *shall* be broke.'

Her emphasis on *shall* put me in mind, as it was certainly meant to, of Pastor Reach, whose inflections left you in no doubt of his good sense. I was smitten into silence while Swede stacked dishes in the sink and ran water on them and waited for me to make myself gallant.

But I was more interested in canoes than gallantry. I was annoyed that we were out of money and Christmas almost here; also that Swede knew we were out of money before I did, and her younger than me. I was annoyed that I'd worked hard to earn $25 and now would have to give my $25 to Otto Schock, the Red Owl man. There was a lot to be annoyed about, and I could afford to grouse because Dad had eaten his small breakfast and thanked us and gone back straightaway to his bed of exhaustion. I stood festering in the kitchen. 'You don't want a canoe, then?'

I like to believe we have all said things that approach this in stupidity.

Swede didn't answer but swabbed the dishes and rinsed them and laid them up to dry. Normally I'd have taken a towel and wiped them myself, but it's difficult to do productive work and fume simultaneously – the labor dissipates your righteous steam – so I stood glaring at the back of her little blond head, which was tilted in thoughtful mien. Sensing she was going to say something sagacious, I started to leave the kitchen but was too late.

'In *Little Women*,' she said – see? – 'when Jo cut off her hair and sold it to pay for Marmee's train fare – you remember?'

Well, of course I remembered. After the shearing Jo had gone home and stunned them all with her sacrificial present, the profit from her bounteous hair, her *one beauty*, as her sisters so backhandedly put it.

'If Marmee had begged Jo to go cut off her hair and sell it,' Swede hypothesized, 'I wonder how heroic a thing it would have been.'

I didn't say anything. But I thought: Aw, crumb.

Here are some of the things we bought, Swede and I, having propped Dad in bed with a cup of beef tea: Aunt Jemima syrup in a brown bottle, twenty pounds of white Robin Hood flour, a sack of raisins and another of currants, two gallons of whole milk, a three-pound can of Hills Brothers coffee, a box of chocolates, free, Otto Schock swore, of clandestine jellies, and a Christmas turkey, purchased live from the poultryman on the edge of town, who had me hold the bird's legs as he beheaded it – how they flailed and pounded in my palms; that creature just flung me all over the yard. Strangely it was the coffee Dad seemed most happy to see and which, brewed, caused our home to feel again like a place where we might live right-side-up. Dad hummed 'God Rest You Merry, Gentlemen,' as he measured grounds into the basket and lit the gas; the pot ticked as it heated; and as it perked a smell came forth like the sunlit hill-sides of Mexico, a smell like morning camps described by Theodore Roosevelt in his days as a rancher in North Dakota. Then Dad sat at the kitchen table with a white ceramic cup all asteam and his King James before him and, seeing me, reached out to seize me at the muscle.

'That's a hero's arm,' he declared. 'Thank you, Rube, for stepping in. I'll get strong now – look here,' and he shadowboxed a moment where he sat, his hands quick again like Davy's.

'I know it,' I said, for his eyes were clear and his voice had unmuddied and found its register again.

Then somebody knocked, and when I poked my head out the kitchen Swede was admitting a man in a gray pinstripe suit. His hair was brown and flattened round his temples as if he'd just removed a fedora. He had a slick ID card in his hand and he was sniffing our newly rejuvenated air.

'Is that coffee fresh?' he asked.

It has been a defining trait of our family: the moment some simple but meaningful treat is prepared, a good fish soup or the first pot of coffee in weeks, up trots some uninvited person with an appetite.

The man in the suit was named Andreeson. He was a federal investigator and had the boldness to state that he expected to nab Davy before the turn of the year. He used that word, *nab*, and I thought Swede might kick him or perhaps lurch suddenly with the coffee, for she was serving him a cup. I hoped she would – he was smug, clearly an enemy – but she set the coffee primly before him and Andreeson picked it up and sipped without acknowledging the hospitality and said to Dad, 'He's just a kid still, after all. Gonna get pretty lonesome this time of year. He's going to make contact with you, Mr Land. You want to do the right thing when he does.'

'Which is?' Dad didn't care much for Andreeson either. Andreeson could tell it and eased his tone a little.

'I know you don't want your son hurt. So when he calls you or writes to you or however he does it, just do what's best for him.' Andreeson slipped a card from the vest pocket of his suit. 'You can reach me here.'

'I didn't know you fellows were interested,' Dad said. It wasn't impertinence, it was the truth. Until now we'd had speech with local cops, county cops, and state cops. Andreeson was our first fed. Naturally, I disliked him from the start.

'We suspect he's crossed state lines. That makes him our job.'

Dad stood and remained standing until Andreeson had to also. Dad said, 'Well, thanks for coming by.'

'When he gets in touch, Mr Land, you've got my number.'

Dad smiled at the floor a moment – so thin you could see his strength was not his own – then looked up and replied: 'Mr Andreeson, you and I will not speak again.'

That night Swede told me the story of how Cole Younger was brought in after the bank raid in Northfield – Cole and his brother James and a couple others. Twenty bullet holes they had between the three of them, eleven in Cole alone. They weren't his first, either – why, he had seven or eight others healed and aching from previous encounters. What sort of specimen do you need to be to survive carnage on that order? But in they came at last, the bloodied Youngers, and Swede told me how they were paraded in chains through the streets, and how the citizens gathered in grief and outrage to watch them pass, flinging stones and horse manure; for the Youngers as I well knew had come to town with the James boys Frank and Jesse and in result a handsome, shy, and newly married bank teller named Heywood lay cold and suited in the parlor of his mother's house. This was the question on the minds of the righteous: which of these haggard devils had done for Mr Heywood? The question was directed most pointedly to Cole, who'd been in the bank when the shots were fired.

'Night before Cole went on trial,' she said, 'the sheriff, Paxton, went in his cell. He gave Cole paper and ink, saying, "Sir, if you will name Heywood's killer, I will personally solicit for your freedom."' Swede was quiet, in the dark bedroom, and I imagined the tired and oft-perforated outlaw lying in his cell, knowing a word could condemn the guilty man and buy himself liberty at the same time. Putting myself in like position, saying it were I who'd been shot eleven times and, for example, old Raymond who'd put the lead to Heywood, I'd have broken three ink pens in my rush to impart the truth. Of course Raymond was only six, but big enough to have done the job.

And what did Mr Younger do?

'In the morning,' Swede said, with great portent, 'Paxton came for his answer. It was early – just sunrise.' She let this sink a moment so I could see what she was seeing: the sheriff standing at the cell door, his head bowed slightly, a fist at his lips. There'd be a pale-pink bar-striped window; there'd be the dawn-lit form of Cole rising to cross the cell. Yes, and I could even hear it happening: the sheriff clearing his throat, the chipping of some bird at the outset of day, the groan of the bunk as Cole heaved himself off and moved to the door with the folded paper.

'He handed it through the bars and turned his back,' Swede whispered. 'Paxton looked at the paper and it said, *Be true to your friends – though the heavens fall!*'

Dazzled, I told her it was the best thing a mortal ever did. Immediately my conscience yelped. After all, a person has to remember Colonel Travis and his line in the dirt at the Alamo; a person can't forget the pirate Lafitte, saving New Orleans in the War of 1812 when fighting for the British would've made him rich. Without such acts what good is history? But I mentioned none of this to Swede. She'd worked awfully hard to set that scene. What did it hurt me to be generous?

The good thing about our reduced circumstances, going into Christmas, was that our expectations changed. They lowered themselves to a worthy place. After walking in on my gaunt father I didn't think about Spartacus anymore; after the money was spent, I was glad it had bought coffee and flour instead of any canoe. Of course we missed the suspense associated with lumpy stockings; we missed the call of the parcels; we missed the Christmas spruce. Swede especially wanted a tree and at the last minute hung a few pathetic bulbs outside, in one visible from our kitchen window. It was an old hackberry stunted from bad soil. Even grass had a hard time in Roofing, but a hackberry's tough and knobbly as an old man.

Swede rose early and, gritting her teeth against the world, set about preparing more Christmas dinner than we could ever consume. We'd got that turkey I mentioned, him of the will to live; he went more than fifteen pounds. We had a heavy glass bowl of cranberries Dr Nokes had brought over, along with a pie from Mrs Nokes called a bob-andy pie, a creamy thing I have looked for since without success. We had sweet potatoes, though Swede in her exuberance went a little large with the brown sugar. All these things she went ahead with on Christmas Eve day because she simply could not wait for the 25th. 'I need Christmas

154

now,' she said, her hands cupped with bread crumbs disappearing into the bird.

And so during the day our appetites rose; food appeared raw on counters and was pounded and rubbed, seasoned and put to cook. Our expectations were caught and surmounted by smells – an encyclopedic warmth of poultry, potato, ovened fruit, honey, yeast, coffee. Dad slept the morning through and in the afternoon woke agitated under the weight of smells. When he walked past me I heard his stomach growl – no, it snorted, like a buck in rut, the healthiest sound he'd produced in weeks. All that long afternoon we stalked the house while Swede fussed and the smells rose up and the sun sank down; and when finally the plates were arranged and the cider poured and Swede lit a candle and pronounced a call for Christmas dinner, two things happened.

Dad laughed aloud for pure delight.

And someone climbed up on our porch and knocked.

Did you see that coming? You ought've, I would say; by now, you ought've. And yet so humble were our expectations for this Christmas – so glad were we to simply have our dad upright and able to laugh and his stomach to growl – not even uninvited guests could quench us. And Dad himself went to the door, and when he opened it in stepped our good friend Mr DeCuellar with his resplendent wife, whose hair was done up in red and silver ribbons, and in they came shouting *Merry Christmas! Merry Christmas!* and to me they handed a long box which turned out to hold a reflecting telescope of astonishing power; and to Swede they gave a pair of boots and a lariat with a ring of polished steel; and into Dad's hand they pressed a key and told him to look, look out at the street. For weeks ago, the traveling salesman Tin Lurvy had taken ill in a hotel room in Idaho; he had driven himself to a hospital in the wee hours, and though he parked safely his poor heart burst before he turned off the ignition, so that he sat there behind the wheel until dawn, his engine idling smoothly. And in his will Tin Lurvy left his house to an uncle and his car to a nephew, and to Jeremiah Land he had left his brand-new 1963 Airstream trailer, a twenty-footer with a kitchen and every necessary thing, a luxurious purchase Tin had saved toward for years. And the reason we didn't know this earlier was that our telephone service had been cut off. I'd wondered, once or twice, why nobody called.

I don't have the gift to aptly describe the rest of that evening, except to say it was a Christmas Eve beyond all gasping wishes, and that even the absence of Davy seemed somehow more temporal and bearable because of the DeCuellars' appearance and Tin Lurvy's marvelous benediction. In fact, we moved our whole dinner out to the Airstream, which Tin himself had never used; we lit the stove for heat and carried out the candle and the turkey and everything. And later, when the conversation was low and I had set up the telescope and was taking turns with Dad and Mr DeCuellar looking at the moon, I asked Dad why he kept laughing – what a sound that was, his laugh, low and confident again, like your best friend's laugh in the darkness when you've believed he was gone forever.

And Dad said, Because I was praying this morning; and I prayed, Lord, send Davy home to us; or if not, Lord, do this: send us to Davy.

The Substance of Things Hoped For

Remember August Shultz, in whose barley I made the most panicked job a boy ever did of shooting a wild goose?

At the bottom of a January cold snap we received a three-cent postcard from August:

Hello All

Old friend Speedy came by last night. I wondered if he would and By Goodness he did. Weaselly skinny but strong, sends regards, we were glad to have him, Birdie had kielbasa, it went fast!

Aug & Birdie
PS: Best to your friend Andreeson

Do you think that put Dad in an excellent humor? Swede came from the post office in high color, flagwaving that card, which confirmed what she'd been feeling for weeks – that Davy was all right; that he was gone west in the persistent fashion of outlaws; that he remained the big brother who loved us all, Christmas card or no. Wickedly satisfying to Swede was August's postscript; the hated fed must've made himself apparent to our friends in North Dakota, the louse.

Well, Swede was ready right then to step into the Airstream and ride to the western sun. Dad himself was close to ready. The day after Christmas he'd begun preparing to leave. Understand, this was done on faith alone. Keep in mind we hadn't yet heard from August Shultz; keep in mind we'd had no word at all, no hint of eye nor ear nor tingling spine as to where our boy was aimed. And yet Dad began to stock up. Cash was a difficulty, so he commenced to lay hold of unattached items around the house and sell them, doing so with an impish glee. His bedroom mirror went first, a useless piece of furniture given who owned it, and it brought $3, which turned into fifteen cans of pork and beans from the Red Owl. The beans went into the deep, mesmerizing pantry of the Airstream; a monstrous and comforting hole, you could stack food in there all morning. Dad next sold two pine dressers for $5 each – he bought a case of Dinty Moore, two canned hams, some hash. He sold a creeper long used to get under the Plymouth and change the oil – $1, eight cans of chicken noodle. Each day familiar things went away from us; each day Dad, normally lackadaisical about commerce, tallied up the take and what food it might procure. Faith brought this about. Faith, as Dad saw it, had delivered unto us the Airstream trailer, and faith would direct our travels.

'Where do you think you're going?' Dr Nokes demanded. I think he feared the sickness had touched the part of Dad's brain in charge of good sense. 'What do you have for directions?' he asked.

And Dad, eyebrows raised in delight with his forthcoming answer, said, 'I have the substance of things hoped for. I have the anticipation of things unseen.'

Dr Nokes told him point-blank he was out of his mind. Dad laughed aloud. Ten minutes later with the doctor looking on he sold his own bed, minus the putrescent mattress, to a couple who appeared stuttering on our porch. They'd just bought their first home, a neat shack with red paint faded to a newlywed's blush; impoverished by this bold purchase they'd slept on the floor until the young man, killing salamanders with a spade in the dirt basement, found a mildewed linen bag strung up in the joists. The bag contained seven Liberty dollars. They loaded Dad's bed on a creaking trailer and drove off, waving as if we were fond relatives. Dr Nokes walked away in disgust. Chuckling, Dad spread the silver dollars before us to admire. He wrote a list and told us to pull the toboggan up to Otto Shock's: noodles, tuna, bouillon, dry milk, salt, crackers, hard storage apples, chocolate bars. We elbowed and noogied all the way to the store. We were swept up, I tell you. Infected with something. Events seemed a wide water into which we'd stepped only to be yanked downstream toward some joyful end. We piled food into the trailer while Dad did the things necessary to go away for who knew how long: he drained pipes, rope-caulked windows, and otherwise buttoned down the house; while we watched from inside he dragged his mattress to a backyard snowbank and soaked it with kerosene and stood back in his canvas parka and threw on a match. It was well past dark and flames poured up showing the whole orange snowbound yard, the paintless garage, the fingery mis-shapen hackberry tree, the black straightup shape of Dad. How could we *not* believe the Lord would guide us? How could we not have faith? For the foundation had been laid in prayer and sorrow. Since that fearful night, Dad had responded with the almost impossible work of belief. He had burned with repentance as though his own hand had fired the gun. He had laid up prayer as if with a trowel. You know this is true, and if you don't it is I the witness who am to blame.

We pulled out after a frostbit sunrise, 22 January. I remember how the front end of the Plymouth heaved upward, surprised at its rearward weight. I remember how poor and strange the house looked among its neighbors as we eased away, chimney a heap of dead bricks, windows glazed with ice and dirt – already it seemed close in spirit to those weedy barns you see all gray and forgotten and sadly available to anyone who will pay the taxes. And cold, my goodness: for two weeks we'd been gripped by a cold snap which on the average night reached 30 below. Very dismaying to Swede and me, since we'd intended to ride in the plenteousness of the Airstream; how we'd planned to sprawl and stretch and scramble around! Yes, the trailer had a gas heater, but Dad couldn't be persuaded to travel 'lit.' Of course the Plymouth's own heater was a foreseeable disaster – we probably weren't much warmer in our backseat army blankets than we would've been in the trailer – or outside, for that matter, in the blistering wind.

On the way out we idled at the post office so Dad could stop the mail. Swede and I stayed in the car; she was already in a book. I remember Roofing looked different that morning – smaller, dearer. Seized by romance I wished Bethany Orchard would walk by right then and see us, hitched to the Airstream, on the very sill of a long and perilous adventure the outcome of which remained in doubt. Oh yes: here she'd come, Bethany, sent for the mail by her cheerless father; a vulnerable elfin figure wrapped against the wind. Seeing my determined profile in the window she'd fly to me: 'You're *leaving*?' And she'd look away, that I might not see the water standing in her eyes.

I'd have gotten to a good-bye kiss eventually – I could see it coming – except then a figure appeared coming up the walk: not Bethany but an old man in a ruinous corduroy barn coat. A listing bareheaded old man, undone and tattered, untrustful of his feet.

'Swede, look at that guy.'

He came on, fighting the wind. His hair was raked up and oily; his eyes were shut; his lips were moving.

160

'I think he's praying,' I told her. The old man's hands looked like suet, hanging there out of his sleeves.

'Maybe for balance,' Swede said. Sort of a cruel remark, wouldn't you say? I glanced at her; she was watching the old bum's rough go staying upright, skinny shoulders atilt, one hand swaying forward now, bumping the post office door. 'It's old Mr Finch,' she pointed out. He was much more sorrowful to look at than he had been at Davy's trial. Could he have even this day's life left in him?

'He's freezing,' I said. Swede was back in her book. But I was held tight by the old man's attempts to grip the handle, then to open that big glass door against the wind, his eyes still shut mind you and his mouth slack open – he looked dead, is what I'm telling you. Like a man so trampled of spirit he'd given over the strength of limbs. I watched his face and his futile, suety hands, and for the first time a question nipped at me: was it possible that real loss had occurred at the death of Israel Finch? That real grief had been felt?

Of course you could say old Mr Finch was a helpless and habitual drunk and whatever was lost in him was lost long ago. You could say so. I'm not suggesting you wouldn't have a strong case.

From Roofing it is some eighty miles to North Dakota. We drove without talking for a good while; after weeks of anticipation, I'll confess to feeling let down. It was so cold my limbs seemed heavy and far away. Dad drank coffee, looking at the frozen farmsteads we passed, clumped at the end of their long driveways. The Plymouth itself moaned as we drove, sounding perhaps not up to this long and heavy haul. We crossed the border late in the morning and Swede sat up blowing on her fingers and asked what that thing in the road was.

'Can't tell,' Dad said.

'It's moving.'

It was a black shape in the road far ahead that seemed to grow and shrink. So small a thing we mightn't have noticed elsewhere, but on the broad white flats of Dakota the eye goes to such specks. 'Crow?' Dad said.

'It's moving wrong,' Swede replied.

We drove on. The black object rose and dropped and assumed guessable size: about like a turtle.

'Aw, it's a piece of old trash,' Swede said – as if some hopes had been fastened to it – but getting closer we saw it was a crow after all, and dead. Struck by a car it lay all mashed to the road but for one free wing, which rose and fell by the gusts. It was a much more grievous sight than you'd think, a dead crow lying in the road out in the heart of noplace, and just before we reached it the wind brought up that wing again so it looked like a thing asking mercy.

We drove on a mile or so. 'I was just thinking,' Dad said. 'All the years I spent in North Dakota, that's the first crow I ever saw hit on the road.'

We hadn't anything to say to that.

'They're awfully smart birds,' Dad mused. 'They get out of the way.'

'What's that?' Swede pointed to something else black, farther on.

This time no one conjectured. We drove on and it was another crow, cruelly pasted and lying over at the edge, the second Dad had seen in all his years.

'Well, imagine that,' he said.

We reached August's late afternoon. Having retreated to sleep I snapped from a dream in which Swede's persistent badman Valdez had got into the Airstream and crawled into my bunk. I knew he was there but couldn't tell anyone – not that I didn't want to, I just couldn't say the right words. Time after time I got Dad's attention only to mumble some nursery rhyme instead of the evil fact. Meantime Valdez snored away in my bunk; he sounded like an Allis Chalmers, and no one could hear him but me.

'Wake up, Rube,' Dad said, as we bounced into August's yard.

Relieved, I was nonetheless unbalanced by the dream and stumbled up to the house with it still attached. Unbundling us in her hot kitchen Birdie teased, kindly, 'Somebody's too sleepy to say hello.'

But that was only part of it. In truth I was a little scared, and preoccupied about where we'd go from here. For I had asked this of Dad the previous night, asked it straight out: where do we go from August's? He didn't know. We'd simply go forth, he said, like the children of Israel when they packed up and cameled out of Egypt. He meant to encourage me. Just like us, the Israelites hadn't any idea where they'd end up! Just like us, they were traveling by faith! Indeed, it did impart a thrill, yet the trip thus far, in the frigid and torpid Plymouth, had reminded me what a hard time the chosen people actually had of it. Once traveling, it's remarkable how quickly faith erodes. It starts to look like something else – ignorance, for example. Same thing happened to the Israelites. Sure it's weak, but sometimes you'd rather just have a map.

The Last Thing He Would Do

Of course, fear and doubt must flee when such gentle
hosts as August and Birdie take charge of you, and in
fact a supper of creamed chicken and beans and sliced
nutbread can go a long way toward the Devil's
discredit. Yet for all the Shultzes' home-cooked ben-
eficence, their most nourishing offerings were details.

'He walked into the yard just before midnight,'
August said, leaning toward Swede, whom he'd
placed on his right hand. 'Ricky – ' their Walker hound
– 'barking his dumb head off, all the sudden he stops,
just his stumpy tail beating against the house. I turn on
the porch light and there's Davy sitting on the steps
and that dog shivering all over him.'

Oh, we were starved for details! After all, there'd
been but the barest crumbs since Davy's escape; we'd
no inkling of how he'd traveled – not counting a day
or two on Nelson Svedvig's mare – no whisper of
where he might've stayed, nothing from which we
might draw strength. Without a detail or two, even an
imagination as mighty as Swede's begins to atrophy.
Memory calcifies. One day you wake up and your
brother is a legend, even to you.

'Tell how he looked,' Dad said.

'Why, same as always, I guess,' August said, 'just

more grown up. He had a clean cut, right here, under his ear.' A shaving cut, it turned out; having hitched as far as Radduck, Davy'd walked into a drugstore and bought soap and a razor, employing them in the rest room of a Shell station close by. Then collaring up he stepped north into a quartering wind, meeting, as he told August, not one car on twelve miles of blacktop.

'He was dressed warm?' Dad asked.

'Why, I guess so,' August said; at which Birdie rolled her eyes and made amendment.

'He was underdressed,' she said, 'wearing an old barn coat; I sewed on some buttons. Holed pants, no hat, cotton gloves. And, Jeremiah, he was awfully thin.'

'Then he assuredly came to the right place,' Dad replied, real comfort in his voice for the first time in many days, for it was good to imagine Davy appearing on the doorstep of those who loved him. No doubt Birdie had inventoried Davy's scarcities even as she stood at the stove, reheating kielbasa; he had a glaze of dirt around his neck, she would tell Dad later, but was pink and clean on his face and ears. He ate, Birdie said, like a polite but famished baby hawk – said thank you, please, but barely chewed.

'Does he miss us?' Swede asked. 'Did he say he missed us?'

'Well, now,' August said.

'Like sunshine,' Birdie put in. 'He said it's like having no sun in the sky, Swede – he misses you that much.'

I remember thinking that was a funny thing for Davy to say, him not being generally lyrical, yet Birdie looked so sternly at August I knew she must be remembering correctly. Swede teared up and put a hand over her mouth.

'August,' Birdie suggested, after a beat, 'tell about that fellow who gave Davy the ride.'

What a tasty particular! Thumbing west, Davy'd

been picked up by a man in an Oldsmobile full of musical instruments. They lay uncased in the backseat, a button accordion, saxophone, tin whistle rolling around in the back window, and more than one trumpet haphazardly swaddled in what appeared to be tattered suit coats. The driver told Davy he was from Wisconsin heading for Los Angeles, where he would certainly get on television. He said there were actually three trumpets and they were linked together by a machined brace of his own design. By holding them just so he was able to play all three at once. The man's face was grained as an old board and he had a dark pompadour ideally groomed even at this hour. He asked Davy for money and offered to stop right there on the highway and play 'The Bugler's Holiday.' If the TV producers in Los Angeles didn't like trumpets, he also had, in the trunk, an amplifier and a brand-new Danelectro guitar on which he could play recognizable pieces of Mozart.

'Show people,' August said, in wonder.

One more gratifying detail? Sure: Davy, retiring upstairs, had twice laughed in his sleep – a strange thing to hear, said Birdie, who lay wakeful all that night, a boyish laugh drifting down those stairs again.

I can't describe the sort of peace this conversation gave me. Davy was practically in the room with us; every creak of the old house was like his footstep. I believe it was one of those rare nights Dad would've let us stay up late, but August said, 'You kids can take the west room tonight,' and that was it for us, bedtime, never mind we'd both slept on the way. I looked an appeal at Dad but got no help. Being both guests and children, Swede and I were entirely at the whim of our hosts, who meant nothing but well.

'Okay,' Swede said, very pliably it seemed to me. Why, we'd barely got started! 'I'm tired, Reuben,' she insisted, seeing my look.

Then I understood and showed it by giving out a

nice overdone stretch and a yawn. Birdie said, 'Ah, you sweeties,' August nodding along indulgently.

Only Dad was not taken in; he looked me in the eye. 'All worn out, uh?'

I couldn't just look at him and lie, so I shrugged, assuming the guilty appearance of the habitual eavesdropper. What Swede had remembered, and Dad knew it, was a swell architectural feature of that upstairs bedroom: a ventilation grate, about a foot square, set into the floor. A curious visitor tucked up in that room could slide from bed and hear every syllable spoken in the kitchen below. Of course there was the chance the adults might decide to talk off in the parlor, which had soft chairs and a davenport and a huge round-shouldered Zenith radio against the wall, also Birdie's collection of tiny spoons from all fifty states, also a set of Japanese swords August had procured while stationed in the Pacific; but the coffeepot was in the kitchen, and the action pretty much stayed there. Swede said no conversation in any room but the kitchen was worth overhearing anyway, something I'd guess is still true in much of North Dakota.

Boy, that west room was cold, though.

Minutes after Dad had tucked us in and listened to us pray and left us under fifty or so quilts, Swede said, 'Can you hear what they're saying from here?'

'No.'

We eyed the grate, some eight feet away. Light came up from it, and soft voices, and coffee smell. Heat was theoretically rising also; it was hard to tell.

'We could shove the bed over there,' I suggested.

'They'd hear.'

Laughter came up through the grate. Adults always start in with that as soon as the kids are in bed.

'Let's just tough it out,' Swede said. 'Hawkeye and Uncas wouldn't even feel this cold. Huckleberry Finn wouldn't even notice it. Come on.'

167

But I already had the covers tugged hoodlike round the top of my head. A wind had risen outside and was mourning in the eaves; the curtains were ghosting out from the wall, that's how leaky those old windows were.

'Don't tell me you want to go to sleep,' Swede said, between her teeth.

'We'll freeze solid,' I told her. 'August will come up tomorrow and we'll be down there on the floor dead – we'll be all purple.'

More laughter from below, quickly subsiding to a more serious tone.

Swede said, 'I'm going,' and slid out and crouched at the grate. I can see her still – armwrapped knees, face resolute, lit from below.

I thought I heard Davy's name. 'What is it?' I whispered. 'What'd they say?'

She waved at me to shush – you know what, I could see her breath. Finally I hopped out of bed and yanked off the two topmost quilts and heaved them over Swede like a tent and crawled in with her. She grabbed my hand. Hers was so cold it felt papery.

'—no notion at all,' August was saying, down in the kitchen. 'It was hard to know how to talk.'

'I'm sure it was,' Dad replied. 'I'm grateful to you for helping him.'

Birdie said, 'Jeremiah, he doesn't know the trouble he's in. He didn't know who Andreeson was.'

'What did you tell him?'

August said, 'We talked to him the best we could. He seemed careless about it. Said he hadn't read the papers or heard the radio.'

There was a long silence in which Birdie got up and poured coffee, and Swede leaned up to my ear and whispered *ratfink* in reference to the fed Andreeson – a word I hadn't heard before; it almost gave me the giggles. *Ratfink.* It's vulgar, I know it. One of those terms that makes it worthwhile having enemies.

'Jeremiah,' August said, 'was it like the newspaper said? The way Davy shot those boys?'

Dad said, 'Yes, pretty much as it said. He shot them down. Yes.'

At these words a thing happened I can't explain – think of some small furry animal, say a vole, going right up your spine with its cold little claws. It shook me; Swede put both arms around me or I'd have gone back to bed.

'Just so,' August said, after waiting a moment. He wanted the story, of course, and why not? Being an old friend of the family doesn't exempt you from curiosity. Though Birdie must've thought his mild pry undignified, because she said, 'August' – just that, just his name.

'He shouldn't have,' Dad said. 'It's true he shouldn't have. That jury would've had to convict him.'

'You didn't see it happen, though,' August said.

'No. Reuben saw it. I'd trade with him if I could.'

I didn't understand this right away. Trade what?

'Poor boy.'

This from Birdie – speaking of Davy, I figured, out in the weather with his collar turned up. But she meant me, for Dad said, 'You'd be surprised, Birdie. He's been real grown-up, he and Swede both. They've stood up better than I have,' he added.

It was hard talk to decipher. What was supposed to happen to you if you were present at a tragedy? Was there some sort of damage? I wasn't sure. The fact is, beyond the occasional scary dream, my chief response to the shootings was a self-centered misery that Davy'd had to go away. I just missed my brother.

They talked awhile longer, in fact a long while, but most of it went by me. Swede could crouch forever, but my knees weren't made for it. I started thinking about catchers, Earl Battey and so forth, guys who squatted that way nine innings a day. Also the cold was creeping in under those blankets, and when I tuned my ears back to the adults they were talking about wheat. The one detail I missed, which Swede told me about the next day, was that Davy had a toothache. He'd eaten his kielbasa all right but was careful about drinking the cold milk Birdie poured him; it pained a molar right down to the root. Birdie had suggested he stay long enough to see a dentist, an idea he politely turned aside. Then Birdie, her heart emboldened, pressed him to give up outlawry and return home and offer himself up for justice. In such public repentance, she said, lay his best chance for what might yet become a fruitful life. And this, Swede said, brought a great smile to Davy's face, and in that smile the Shultzes saw the truth, that turning himself in would be the very last thing Davy would do in his life, however long it lasted. After relating this, Swede said, Birdie had sounded upset and gone to bed, so I suppose wheat came up soon thereafter.

I woke next morning smelling change. No metaphors here; something was different to my actual nose. The air felt heavy, the quilts too, as blankets feel on camp-out mornings. Rising I dressed by a closet light, shutting the door mostly to keep the brightness off Swede, who was a tough one to sneak out on, not to mention unforgiving afterward. I've always liked the feeling of being the first one awake in the morning; it makes you daring somehow. I went down to the kitchen and poked around carefully – didn't turn on any lights for fear of rousting August or Dad. Lifting the coffeepot off the stove I found it half full. There were matches on the wall and I smouched one – to use a word Swede herself smouched off Mr Twain – scratched it, and lit the gas. It made a lovely blue light in the dark kitchen; in no time the pot was ticking away, and I felt self-sufficient and borderline sneaky. Then August scuffed into the kitchen in his nightshirt. He had an electric candle in his hand, one of those which comes on by itself when you pick it up in the night.

'Feel better this morning, Rube? You coughed some in your sleep.'

'Yes, sir. I didn't mean to wake you.'

'Making coffee?'

'Just heating it – is that all right?'

He opened a cupboard and reached down a box of sugar lumps. I opened another and set out two cups.

'Saucers,' August said. I got them also. He moved to the table, a strangely discordant sight in that nightshirt of his. He walked always at a slight tilt – he had poor balance, particularly in the dark, since being struck on the ear by a draft horse he'd been shoeing years before. The horse, Mike, hadn't meant harm but had swung his head round at the very moment August dropped a hoof and stood up. Mike was a Percheron of heroic dimension – his head probably weighed 120 pounds. August recovered quickly, he was no weakling himself, but it is a fact that he tipped over easily thereafter.

He said, 'You smell that, this morning?'

He meant the change I mentioned earlier. 'I don't know what it is,' I admitted. What it smelled like to me was a shovelful of earth. A wet day in spring.

'It's fog,' August said.

He put out the electric candle, and we sat there in the dark smelling the air. August was right. I recognized the smell once he'd identified it.

'It's a thing about fog,' he continued. 'Doesn't matter when it comes, it smells like April. Birdie was born April twenty-second,' he confided. 'Every time it fogs like this, I tell her, Happy birthday, love.'

On receipt of this intimate remark I suddenly understood what had been given me. Never before had I been with Dad's best and oldest friend, the beloved August Shultz, without Dad present. Nor had I been old enough to appreciate it – why, it hadn't been long since August referred to me as 'my little man.' Now

171

here we sat together, in his dark kitchen, the house asleep, talking about foggy mornings.

'Coffee hot?'

It was. August lifted the candle so I could see to pour. He showed me to tip a little coffee from cup to saucer and swirl it around to cool. We baptized a few sugar lumps. Abruptly August stood. 'I'm getting dressed. Let's take a ride.'

The fog lay rich and steamy over the barnyard. It was warm as manure; you could weigh it in a cupped hand. And it really did smell like April, though I noticed it also smelled like a wet dog; the two are not dissimilar. In the weeks previous we'd grown used to nights of 20 and 30 degrees below zero, so August's yard that morning was a decent shock. He'd switched on the yard light; it showed fog draped all over every-thing, hanging over the snow.

'Why, it's twenty-four above,' August observed; he'd tacked a thermometer to the corral. He slid the barn door open.'Good morning, Laurie. Morning, old Brit.'

Laurie and Brit, his paint mare and gelding, answered him out of the dark, stomping and chuffing. Though professing not to be the rider of the family – it's true Birdie looked more at home horseback – August loved Laurie and Brit. I have a photo of him standing between the two of them, a hand under each of their chins, little cap tilting aboard his big bald scalp. It's a good picture. Brit appears a little uninvolved, but Laurie has a look in her eye.

August bridled the horses, working in the off light from the bulb outside, whacked out the blankets and smoothed them over their backs, and hoisted up the saddles. A horse is a dusty operation and I sneezed five or six times, but my wind seemed okay, and soon August had everything cinched and squared and Laurie was reaching her nose around to poke August in the face – horse language for gladness, he told me, because she couldn't wait to get out and stretch in the warm fog.

We led the horses out. August had Brit and was already setting foot in the stirrup. 'Mount from the left,' he instructed, doing so himself. Laurie was younger and trickier than Brit, a fact that rattled me; standing under the yard light, the largeness of these animals had become plain. I had hold of Laurie's bridle and she was stepping sideways, dragging me around.

'Will she run?' Though I tried to ask this as if a running horse were my preference, August saw it for the chickeny question it was.

'Let's just walk 'em down the pasture. She'll behave. Up and grab the horn, now, there you go.'

We set off through the fog side by side. By now a deep blue had worked into the east and we rode down past the brooder house, the granary, the two fat corncribs, all these rising from blue fog at the last moment. Laurie champed and shook her head. She wanted to run, she was shivering with it, and abruptly I understood that I was scared of horses. My hands cramped on the reins. How had I not comprehended this before? Why, I could barely see the ground! Suppose Laurie stepped in a hole, she might roll over right on top of me! I'd read where cavalry soldiers had been killed, not by arrows or bullets but by their own faithful mounts who tripped at a bad time. Think about being crushed by a horse! And what if you lost your hold in a gallop, only to snag a foot in a stirrup? I'd seen that happen to fellows – sure, it was in the movies, but there was nothing fake about the dust they raised, flopping all over the place full speed ahead.

August said, 'A little restless, is she?'

'Yes, sir, I think so.'

'Just say, "Easy. Easy, Laurie." She likes your voice, I can tell.'

'Okay.' But a horse knows scared when it hears it.

My tenuous reassurances sounded anything but easy; I had to heave against those reins just to stay to a walk.

We were in the back pasture, which sloped down through spotty timber and became hummocky and ended on the bank of the George River, which we crunched down onto and headed upstream. Though nothing but ice it was good footing, for the river had frozen hard in the fall, then honeycombed and refrozen to a cindery crust. You could no more slip on this stuff than on sandpaper, and it made a satisfactory sound underhoof too. Since it was clear Laurie desired to gallop, August coerced Brit into the lead – you could tell old Brit rued leaving the barn, 24 degrees though it was. No doubt that cold fog was working on him, as it was on me. Fog inquires first at wrists and ankles. I began to wonder, as the light rose, just where we were headed, and how long till we turned back, but August ambled on while the banks of the George grew up knobby and weedy out of the fog. Though it seemed a long ride I don't suppose we'd been gone half an hour when Brit turned and shouldered up a cut bank to the left, where the clay had slid down and made a gradient off the river. We came out onto a field which, from its tufted appearance, must've lain fallow some years. August stopped and I let Laurie step up beside him.

'Sun'll be coming up,' he said.

'Yes, sir. Burn off this fog.'

'Yes, it's lifting already.' And it was – across the field I could see dark buildings, an unlit house, a small barn.

Laurie seemed to have settled, to my relief. She stood there by Brit, the two of them nodding and blowing and picking up their feet and setting them down.

'Would you guess your dad is on the mend?' August asked, which made me look at him straight on.

'Oh, he's fine – he's well,' I replied.

'I never saw him so skinny before.'

I nodded. August's concern bothered me. Why, Dad hadn't coughed in a week. Yes, he was skinny, but he'd never been thick like August. Anyone could see Dad was all right.

'Did he go to a doctor?'

'Dr Nokes is a friend of ours, a real good doctor. He's the one who delivered me,' I added, which credentialed Nokes as far as I was concerned.

August sat aboard Brit, considering this. 'Yup,' he said, 'yup.' He turned and looked at the place before us, a place that declined as the sun came up. Now we could see a boarded window, now a front step atilt, now a talus pile at the base of the chimney. But smoke did rise from its sooty mouth, and in that swayback barn a cow was asking for breakfast, and as we watched a tremendous turkey came prancing around the house, a big black tom with something on his mind.

'Do you know where we are, Rube?'

I'd been wondering that. I didn't know but felt like I should.

'Your dad grew up there.' He pointed at the upstairs window, a tall narrow one with glass in it. 'His room was in that attic. I used to ride over and spend a few days when the folks could spare me.'

I sat quiet while we watched the place. I was ashamed not to have recognized it – I'd never seen its backside before, only its face as we drove past on the county road.

August said, 'It sure looked better when your family had it. Your grandpa was quite a gardener. That shelterbelt? He had sweet plums all along the south edge. Also raspberries – your dad and I would cut out the old canes and pile them up; they made a good fire.'

The shelterbelt looked awfully sorry at present – of course, it was January. Just a strip of messy woods. But I could imagine a rich well-kept raspberry patch down there, and my grandpa, whom I remember only from photographs, stooped in his overalls doing the keeping.

The tom turkey was trotting through the yard with his head up and swiveling – looking for something to eat or scare.

'Interesting old man,' August said, 'your grandpa. Kept three or four beehives back of the plums. Arthritis in his hands, every week or so in the summer he'd go down to the hives and stir the bees up a little and poke his hands out. Take four or five stings. The poison loosened up his fingers.'

'He'd get himself stung on purpose?'

'Ask your dad about it.'

I'll admit, my knowledge of my grandparents is scattershot. Grandma was in her forties when she had Dad; Grandpa was in his fifties – late fifties. Which, since Dad married at twenty-five, made them old before my birth. A few details: Grandma was a praying woman who addressed the Lord in King James English. Grandpa preferred not to wear his teeth before photographers; they made him look horsey. It's fair to say that without them he looked surprised and dismayed, but this was probably closer to the truth.

August said, 'You getting cold?'

'No, I'm all right, it's warming up.'

'Look at that tom, what's he up to?' The turkey was stalking, circling the house. He'd come around from the front, careful as a heron, neck horizontal to keep the profile down; then he'd turn the corner and accelerate along the back of the house. Turn another corner, we'd lose him again for a minute.

Under my knees Laurie stamped and blew. I looked eastward and saw the rim of the sun. A good thing about North Dakota, it has buckets of horizon; the sun comes up and you know it is there. Also it was making heat – the sun was. I could feel it in my clothes, like March. Suddenly soaked with confidence I asked, 'Mr Shultz, how long do you think it'll take us to find Davy?'

176

Hope is like yeast, you know, rising under warmth.

August reached down to pat Brit, who'd got so still he might've been standing dead. You had to admire the strength of that horse, August was no lightweight. 'I'm sure you'll find him.'

'But how long?'

'I don't know – say, look there.'

The back door of the place had opened and a little boy stood in it, bundled in coats.

'That would be Gerald,' August informed me. 'He's five or six.'

Gerald was holding something – a big saucepan. He stood in the door, a hand on the knob, head stuck out looking around. I've seen similar poise in rabbits.

August said, 'There's a batch of kitties out in that barn – early for them, isn't it? See, he's got some oatmeal in that pan.'

Still Gerald didn't come out, though he did crane around like everything.

The tom turkey now reappeared on tiptoe upside the house. There was a low window on that side and I swear to you the turkey ducked his head passing it. I heard a quiet wheeze and it was August, chuckling.

At this time Gerald's radar relaxed. Maybe his folks got after him for holding the door open so long, or maybe he just believed the coast was clear, for out he stepped and shut the door. Of course the turkey zipped round the corner like a guided missile, gurgling with wrath and triumph; Gerald dropped the pan and lunged for safety, squeaking through the door only because the tom was diverted by the oatmeal.

Breathless I looked over at August, who was laughing with his whole body, then back at the house. The turkey danced three or four little victory circles before the door and settled in to peck at the cereal. You could watch Westerns your whole life and not see a more satisfying ambush. Then the door opened again and out slipped a little black-and-white collie. Given its size I still would've bet on the turk, but no doubt the two of them had some history, for the bird twisted itself to run and actually tripped two or three times getting away, which had to feel disgraceful, as the fall always does which cometh after pride. The collie didn't even give chase. It stood by the door, looking at August and me. Gritty little fellow – he did step up and have at the oatmeal but kept looking at us the while.

'Probably we ought to ride,' August said. 'He'll be after us next. Dog's name is Rip,' he added, as though I might get a charge out of that.

We let the horses trot the distance home – say, a trot is a jostly ride. You've seen an angry person beat his fist on a table? Imagine doing that with your tailbone for twenty minutes or so. Later Swede told me about leaning your weight up onto the stirrups and so easing the abuse on the other, but I didn't know to do that, and to be honest I don't think August was doing it either. He wasn't a smooth rider but seemed to tilt and jounce as much as me. Anyhow I didn't really mind getting knocked around some. Swede would be simmering over my sneaking off to ride. The least I could do was come back with a sore tailbone.

We got that breakfast, by the way, the one I'd been so anxious for – the toast and the hardboiled eggs and the jam. During it August winked across at me at least three times and Swede would hardly look at me; for his part, Dad took prodigious enjoyment from the fact we'd gone riding while the house was asleep, calling me Natty Bumppo as Davy had liked to do, grinning at August, even elbowing Swede out of her nettly gloom. Normally all this to-do would've thrilled me, un-Bumppolike as I was, but I got distracted watching Dad. August had this much right: Dad was skinny. Remember how shocked I was, seeing him barechested after his siege in bed? He'd lost all superfluous flesh,

178

and I saw now it had stayed lost. Skinny didn't say it. His very bones seemed loose-joined. And instead of being concerned about this, I'd simply gone and adjusted to it. Once he popped out of bed I just figured he was his old self, and if he looked a little more gristly than before, why, wasn't gristle what a man wanted anyway?

'We rode over to the farm,' I said, noting that August hadn't offered this information.

'Yes,' Dad said, 'I expected you would. Did you take the river?'

'Yes, sir. We walked over and trotted back.'

'How'd the shelterbelt look?'

I had to be honest. 'Kind of scraggly.'

Dad nodded. 'The barn?'

'It's leaning pretty good – there are cows in it, though. At least one cow. And some new kitties, I guess.'

'Uh-huh. House?'

'I saw where your room was.' I was going to say something about the boarded window, and the weathery paint, and how the chimney was coming apart, but Dad looked so skinny and thoughtful I decided not to.

He didn't ask anything else, either.

'Say, Rube,' August said, after a moment, 'tell about the turkey.'

At War with This Whole World

Across the years Swede and a whole series of horses were to wring proper use from the Mexican saddle, but for now she had to be content with riding it in the Airstream trailer. Yes, we'd brought it along. Poor Swede had begged not to leave it behind, offering Dad any number of maudlin proofs for its value: as her present from Davy it reminded her to pray for him, it would make an adequate pillow should we wind up sleeping on the prairie, it was Mexican and so longed for the West, and so forth. Nothing convincing, so when Dad at last said, Well, why not? it was purely because he was crazy for Swede and would pay any price to see her happy. The saddle granted, Swede immediately asked to bring one of the sawhorses from the garage, and thus her design began to emerge. Her final and meekest appeal was for the typewriter. She wanted to 'document our exploration.' She pointed out that Meriwether Lewis had lugged along cratefuls of pens and paper and India ink – think how tippy *that* rendered the old canoe – yet Thomas Jefferson himself had demanded it. I'm sure Dad enjoyed Swede's persuasions, but can you imagine such packing?

Would *your* father have gone along with all this?

Nevertheless, when we drove out of August and

Birdie's that morning, Swede rode ensaddled on a swaying sawhorse in the Airstream kitchen, the typewriter before her on a fold-down table. She had her coat on, though Dad had lit the heater briefly and goosed the temp to around 60, and she had paper rolled in and was observing the countryside out the louvered windows:

And so we take our leave. So we forsake the encouraging company of the last friendly outpost, riding alone into a wide cold land in pursuit of our brother. What a speck we are on this vast prospect! How small appear our chances of success!

Plainly this excerpt represents Swede at her happiest, though it made me feel bleak at the time. That part about the last friendly outpost – well, it wasn't strictly true, as you will learn, but leaving August and Birdie it sure felt so. Once we'd boarded the trailer August came coatless around the Plymouth, where he put a bear hug on Dad, a man so thin oughtn't have survived; then Dad sank behind the wheel and off we rolled, a great drop of tin glinting on the snowy plains. Swede and I hustled to the back of the trailer for a last look, saw Birdie on the front step with her hands on her hips. The hound Ricky stood beside her, wiggling his stub tail. The two of them were watching not us but August, whose face looked strangely slack; his head was tilted and he was banging on it with one hand, like a man troubled by earwater.

We are headed for the Badlands. August called it a big busted-up place and believes our Davy has gone there. However, Davy did not say so. It is a long ride west from here, but we have warm weather. There is a soft wind called the chinook, it is almost 40 outside at this writing, so warm the ditches are dark and the birds are fooled. Some miles ago a ringneck pheasant poked his head out from stubble and watched us go by.

Practically every wanted man goes to the Badlands sometime: Butch Cassidy, Mr Younger, Sam Bass. The Badlands are as good a place as any.

Swede was to write dozens of pages before we returned to Roofing, which is plenty of typing for someone using only indexes, plus thumbs for the space bar. Reading through them you will find many an allusion to distinguished outlaws of eras past and not one to the fact of motorized travel – always it is a *long ride west*, always we are *proceeding apace* through this or that settlement; Davy is surmised to be out front of us by *six days' trail*. Though I'll defend her narrative to the last, Swede's journalistic technique precluded the attendance of one or two facts – for example, not only was Davy not riding a horse any longer, he was driving a Studebaker, its floorboards rotted to mere embroidery. August for years had kept the old boat for a field car, using it to inspect fencerows, seek errant beeves, and so on. Seeing Davy's unwillingness to return home with his hands in the air, August decided the Studebaker had been more than faithful to him and needed a change of mission, also of oil. So that freezing sunup found August on his back beneath the chassis, his heart flailing with the loyal and grossly unlawful business at hand. Before Davy finished breakfast, August had affixed old license plates and obscured them with dirt and snow, filled the car up with gas from his scaffolded bulk tank, and placed bread and cheese and a sack of canned goods in the trunk. Taken together it was a good deal better than going by pony, something even Swede wouldn't have argued with, no matter its literary value.

And will we find our Davy safe,
Along this stealthy track?

And might all our implorings steal
Our outlaw brother back?

I have noticed that people who love the whole wide parade will just wing off into verse at any chance; Swede did it constantly. Taking nothing from poetry, which we all know is prized as a conduit of wisdom, these lines again suggest an inaccurate picture. What's stealthy about a green Plymouth station wagon yanking along a fat Airstream trailer? The truth is, stealth wasn't an issue. We weren't sneaking up on Davy, we were just trying to get in his vicinity. Anyway, have you ever been to North Dakota? In good sunlight you can see someone coming eight miles away.

More troubling to me was the question this verse asked – about stealing him back somehow. It seemed a reasonable proposition, and wasn't it why we were chasing after him in the first place? Yet it niggled. It put a scene before my eyes in which Davy's return depended on our persuasiveness. I tried to remember a time when I had persuaded my brother to change his mind – not just going along to humor me, which he did often, but coming indeed to believe something different. I didn't have to think long. It had never happened. It seemed unlikely Swede had done it either. Maybe Dad had, when Davy was a whole lot younger.

Determined not to descend this reasoning alone, I said, 'Swede, do you think we'll be able to talk him into coming back?'

She was quite preoccupied, midstream in something. Yet she heard the question and unstirruped her right foot and swung over to face me sidesaddle. 'Do you?'

'I don't know.'

'Seems not very likely, doesn't it?'

'Yeah.'

Swede said, 'What would you give, to get Davy home?'

The way she asked it warned me she'd been think-ing about this.

'Well, most things; I guess anything.'

'And then what if they stick him in jail?'

'Well, I don't know – knock it off, Swede.' Now that I'd started this talk, I wanted out.

'You still want him to come home if he has to be in jail?'

How's that for a rotten question?

'Come on, Reuben. You can say yes if it's true.'

But I couldn't answer. I feared the outcome of honest speech – that it might reach forward in time and arrange events to come. If I told Swede I wanted Davy back, even at the cost of his freedom, might that not happen? And if I said what I sensed was the noble thing – better not to see him at all than pale and dumb during visiting hours – might that not bring despair on this whole crusade of ours?

Then Swede, who wasn't volunteering her own answer to the question, asked another. 'How come do you suppose August gave Davy that car?'

'Help him get away.'

'Even though they tried to talk him into giving up?'

'That was Birdie,' I pointed out.

'August agreed, though, you know he did.'

I thought about August riding out front of me on the George River, he and Brit moving through the fog, a picture of freedom as good as any. August may have wanted Davy to turn himself in, yet nothing seemed more natural to me than his gift of the Studebaker. Could a person believe so strongly one way, yet take the opposite route? I wanted to ask Swede, but again, if I posed it aloud, it might become true, and then we were in for all sorts of tangles.

'Tell me what you're writing about,' I said. Writers can always be distracted this way, I was lucky to learn early in life.

'Nightshirts.'

'What, like August wears?'

'Uh-huh. What do you think of it?'

'Well, how come he wears a nightshirt anyway? A man like him.'

'He has to wear something, Reuben.'

'Well, but it seems like a lady sort of thing. Like a gown,' I persisted. 'What's the difference between a nightshirt and a night*gown*?'

'Lace,' Swede replied. She leaned forward on the saddle. 'Listen, all kinds of men used to wear them; practically everybody did in *Kidnapped*. The old awful uncle who sent David Balfour up the ruined stairs and sat waiting for him to fall? He wore one; he was wearing it at the time! Robert Louis Stevenson wore one, and you're so nuts about *him*.'

'He didn't either.' Robert Louis? Yet her declaration rang true – I could almost see the great doomed author, pale as a birch, wafting around his midnight kitchen. 'Of course everybody wore them back then,' I concurred. 'I don't suppose they had long johns yet.'

'I believe there was a general shift from nightshirts to long johns a few years after the Civil War.'

This was so much like something Mr DeCuellar would've said that I suddenly recalled the aroma of peach pie – which we'd eaten at the lawyer's own table, the morning of Davy's trial. Fresh peach pie. My eyes stung, for some reason, which made me cross. 'Well, how do you know that, anyway?'

'I just wrote it,' Swede said, picking up a sheet of typescript. 'Listen: "In the weeks before the James gang rode into Northfield, every member was wearing long johns except for Charlie Pitts." Remember Charlie Pitts, Reuben?'

'No.'

'He was the handsomest of the gang, before he got shot.'

'Oh.' I'd seen his picture in a book Swede got from the library – I suspect it's the only photo ever taken of

Charlie, the one where he's braced up dead and on display. They used to prop fellows like that in store windows for a week or two, something the Chamber of Commerce thought up to bring customers downtown, though it seems impractical in some ways.

Swede read: '"Pitts was the best dresser of the gang and vain of his appearance, enjoying the comments and company bestowed on him by ladies. He shaved regularly, carrying with him a strop razor and a sheet of tin for a mirror. He owned more stockings than most in his profession and was fastidious about changing them. He disdained"' – Reuben, listen – '"He disdained long johns, believing them to be a contrivance of the lower classes, along with mittens and pull-on boots. Charlie wore lace-ups."'

'Really?'

'Yes – and a nightshirt, to sleep in. "His genteel pretensions and particularly his preference for the nightshirt attracted rank comment from his compadres, especially from Bob Younger, whose speech was habitually impolite. When hiding in caves or deep in the woods, Bob would wait until Charlie appeared at the fire in his nightshirt, rubbing his gums with salt to keep them healthy, and would proceed to call him *Lovely Man* or *Lillian Pitts* or *Sweet Charlie O'Fairy*."'

I didn't recall this being in Swede's library book, but then she wouldn't have used it if it were. Swede has always stood against plagiarism, believing in original research.

'"At last, days before the ill-destined bank job in Northfield, Charlie Pitts walked nightshirted into a hotel room where Bob Younger sat playing cards. Bob remarked, 'Why, if it ain't the Queen of Sheba. Come sit on my lap, sweetie, I'll learn you some poker.' To which Charlie responded, 'Cole' – for the eldest Younger was playing too – 'if I teach your brother deportment, will you shoot me for it?'

'"'Have at him,' said Cole, whose cards at the moment were unpromising. At once Bob stood, clawing leather, but Charlie in early days had trained as a boxer and danced in before Robert could fire and dealt a blow to his right ear. The revolver thumped to the floor; Charlie in his nightshirt gripped Bob's hair, set his head back, and deliberately struck the exposed Adam's apple, causing Bob Younger to gag and his eyes to water and his mind to think hard, and what he thought was that perhaps the Queen of Sheba remark had been poorly timed."'

'Oh, boy,' I said.

'And that's as far as I've got.' Swede didn't explain how it connected with anything, but I suppose she'd got a glimpse of August in *his* nightshirt, and of course outlaws were heavily on her mind. Swede's journalism had a pretty wide throw.

We stopped at noon. Dad pulled over in a municipal park in Linton, this being midfield North Dakota, and stepped up into the trailer. 'Well, amigos? Shall we cook beans?'

We did, Swede ending up with the coveted knob of fat from the can; then Dad cranked the heater again, professing intent to nap. Lulled by warmth I did likewise, going sound asleep to Swede's noisome typing.

She woke me minutes later with terrible news – that stinker Andreeson was sitting in his car across the park.

'No, Swede, it can't be him. Go look again.'

'It is him, go look yourself. He saw me watching him – he waved at me, Reuben!'

That sat me up. 'Is he coming over here?'

'Wait.' Swede ran to a window, peeked edgewise. 'Nope, he's just sitting there. His car's running.'

'Is Dad awake?'

She shook no. I slipped to the window. Sure enough, there sat our self-satisfied fed in a clean beige Mercury across the city park. It was just a narrow little park; there weren't fifty yards between us and Mr Andreeson. He had a plate of something in his lap, which he kept dipping into, and a cup of coffee in his right hand.

'Look at him,' Swede said, 'chewing his french fries. He wouldn't even eat them in the cafe – afraid we'll pull out and he'll lose us.' This appeared to be true, for Andreeson kept looking our way between bites of fry. We had to keep ducking. Swede didn't want to get waved at again.

'How come he doesn't just come over and talk to us?'

I gave it some thought. 'Maybe he just wants us to see him. To make us nervous, the way the Indians are always doing.'

'We haven't done anything,' Swede said defiantly. 'All we did was go on vacation. People do it all the time.'

'Right.'

'We don't know where Davy is at all. How would we know?'

'I don't know.' I sneaked a look and got nailed. Andreeson had his eye on our window; right away, up went his dumb old hand for a wave. I waved back, like a dolt.

'Reu*ben* – now he'll come over here for sure!'

'Sorry, Swede.' I was wretched, on my haunches. 'Here, you look. Tell me if he's coming.'

But he wasn't. That must've been some plate of french fries, and the longer he ate, the more bugged Swede got. 'Smug fathead! He ought to just come over here and talk to us! Does he think we're getting all scared with him just sitting there eating? Who told him we were here, anyway?'

'Maybe we better wake up Dad.'

'Sure. Dad'll go talk things over with Mr Andreeson. Mr *Federale*,' she said, nothing expressing contempt like a timely morsel of Spanish.

'Wait a second – he's done.'

'Done what?'

'With his french fries.'

'Is he coming?'

'Nope, going.' For Andreeson had balled up his paper plate and crept the Mercury forward to a public trash can. He made his deposit, caught me watching again, saluted this time, and tooled away.

'Chicken!' Swede said. 'Shyster! Putrid fed! Gets our attention, then runs off. You know what he is? He's desperate – following us because he can't think of anything else to do.'

I admired Swede's certainty but didn't share it. For one thing, I'd had a good look at Andreeson when he was looking back. If forced I might've described that look as sharp or canny or borderline humorous. Probably not desperate, though – desperate guys don't salute.

'So where do you think he went, Swede?'

'Probably off to let us stew.'

'That shyster.'

'Probably to the public toilet.'

'Stinker.'

'We'll wake up Dad,' Swede decided, 'and get out of town. When Andreeson gets back, we'll be gone!'

'You think we should? Won't we get in trouble?'

'Did we do anything wrong?'

'No.' But it felt like we had – or were about to.

She snared my arm. 'Should we tell Dad about him, do you think?'

I nodded, ready to run do so. How often did we get to deliver Dad actual news?

But she shook her head. 'He might want to wait around and talk to Andreeson.'

'So? We're innocent. Like you said.'

'I know, but Andreeson might do . . . something unfair. He might make us go back home.'

I didn't think he could do that, even if he did work

189

for the federal government. Swede said feds often broke their own rules, a sentiment gleaned from Mr DeCuellar and one she maintains to this day.

'You think old Andreeson can tell Dad what to do?' I said. Let her answer an uncomfortable question for once.

'I'm afraid of it,' she admitted.

In the end, though, all our stratagems came to naught because Dad woke with a record headache to suggest, in a distressed whisper, that we stay parked till morning. Instantly I recollected August's apprehensions about Dad's health, but he swallowed two aspirin and promised to be better by supper, provided it was chicken and dumplings.

'He's really sick,' Swede told me, outside his shut bedroom.

But I clung to Dad's promise. 'What's in dumplings?'

'Baking powder, flour, milk.' But she wore a pout at this turn of events, and I couldn't blame her – she'd been picturing us slipping out while Andreeson sat on the toilet.

We made the dumplings with a Swanson chicken ('One Whole Chicken in a Can') and Dad as sworn emerged to eat, declaring full recovery. He didn't look much better, but then it was hard to see him; rather than use the Airstream's lamps, Dad claimed to prefer the ambient dimness thrown off by the streetlights of Linton. It was more romantic, he said – obviously cover for his light-pained eyes – but we went right along. Are you familiar with canned chicken? Romantic lighting doesn't hurt.

Someone banged on the door.

'Yes,' Dad called. It was so dark I couldn't see his expression.

'Mr Land, it's Martin Andreeson.'

Dad was silent a moment. Ever since, I've thought he believed, just for a second, that it was Davy out there, come to reconcile. He stood, struck a match, lit a mantle in the kitchen. 'Come in.'

Andreeson was hatless and smiling in a fresh hair-cut and tan knee-length topcoat. In the gaslight he glowed like hale skin. He looked younger than when we last saw him, which alongside Dad seemed monstrously unfair. He said, 'Lovely weather. I enjoy the Dakotas. Don't get out here as often as I'd like.'

Dad stood with his hands on the back of a kitchen chair, his face all pouched with headache. I couldn't help but remember the pronouncement he'd made to Andreeson that previous time: 'You and I will not talk again.' What power had flowed from him in that sentence, how prophetic and incontestable he had sounded! Dad seemed to be thinking similarly, for he gave me a wry so-much-for-pronouncements look and said, 'Do you have news for us, Mr Andreeson?'

'Why, no, I don't.'

'Then your purpose here is abstruse,' Dad said politely.

'I'm glad to explain. You departed suddenly in the middle of January. Your rent is paid through April, though you no longer draw a salary and you have no savings. Half of Roofing thinks your mind soured. They think you're out here eating locusts.'

Dad chuckled. 'How about the other half?'

'They believe you heard from your boy and are gone to meet him.'

'Which theory appeals to you?'

'I'm trying to think what else could bring you here – now.' He meant to the Great Plains in midwinter; it actually wasn't a bad question.

'We're looking for him,' Dad said.

Andreeson appeared to be waiting for explication, finally prompting, 'Did he contact you?'

'No.'

'Did he contact August and Birdie?' Notice he didn't even say *Shultz*; Andreeson's familiarity with our

191

whereabouts, finances, and friends was a type of worry I'd never encountered before.

'Yes, he did,' Dad said.

'August told me differently,' Andreeson said. 'Very loyal, though it does leave him open to accessory charges. What directions did your boy leave him?'

'None.'

Andreeson looked at Dad as though he were a slow child. 'Mr Land, it's my responsibility to find your son. At the moment it's my only responsibility. I believe we are close to him right now. If you know more than you're saying, you could save his life by coming out with it.'

'I've been honest with you, Mr Andreeson.'

'You could also save August and Birdie some grief down the line. It's a shame they lied to me.'

Dad said, 'You yourself have lied twice since stepping in here.'

That set Andreeson back a step, and he didn't contest it either. I was still wondering which two statements were false when he nodded, set his hand on the door, and said, 'Mr Land, you and I don't have to be enemies.'

'Mr Andreeson,' Dad replied, 'it appears that we do.'

So departed our putrid fed, in a gust of chinook from the door, and a few moments later in popped Swede in her overcoat – we hadn't even noticed she was gone.

'I had to run to the gas station,' she said breathlessly. There was a Phillips 66 we were using. Hanging her coat neatly in the closet she set about the kitchen in a brisk way, brewing coffee for Dad, laying things ship-shape, and finally slipping into the saddle, where she dashed off the following:

The blizzard shipped in from the west like a grin
On a darkened, malevolent face,
And the posse that sought Mr Sundown was caught
In an awfully dangerous place.

192

For their horses were sore and their chances were
   poor
Of locating warmth or repose,
When the sweet sudden sight of miraculous light
Shone dim in the dark and the snows, my lads,
A light through the dark and the snows.

And the lady who answered their knock at the door
Had answered another, an hour before.

The above was possibly four minutes' work for Swede, who remember was no typist. So fully did she own these lines, so resonant were her strokes upon the keys, that Dad said, 'My goodness, Swede, don't you know Moby Dick has already been written?' But no response. I guess she was just too elevated to hear him.

She bid them to stay, in her courteous way,
And insisted they sit by the fire,
And she poured them all brandy and sang them a song
And they slept as though lulled by a choir.

The sheriff next morning was first to awake
And he called all his men to the chase,
For a dream had suggested their quarry sought rest
In the hay in the barn on the place, lads –
He'd slept in the barn on the place.

But when they crept into the building to spy,
Gone horses, gone lady, gone outlaw, goodbye!

Dad's headache was gone in the morning – in fact, he suggested pancakes after Swede routed us from bed. The routing itself should've alerted me to something; Swede was rarely awake before Dad, whose early minutes with King James were not negotiable.

'Can't we get going?' Swede begged. It was close to

wheedling, a bad sound at that time of day. 'Let's just have cornflakes.'

Dad felt none of her urgency. No mistake, Andreeson had tossed a wet washcloth on the trip. In fact, Dad was inclined to laze around Linton awhile. After all, he'd been honest with the fed – we weren't on Davy's schedule or anyone else's. Maybe the thing to do was snuggle down and wait on the Lord. 'Anyhow, Andreeson hates North Dakota,' Dad said. 'I knew it right off. Won't he get disgusted if we just plop down for a month?'

'But Davy—' Swede began.

'Davy's in the palm of God's hand, like all of us are. A few days' wait may be the best thing for everybody.'

Normally this would've been how the discussion ended, for Dad said, 'Now, what about those pancakes?'

'I don't feel very good,' Swede said.

Dad leaned at her. 'Why, you are pale. It's early yet; why don't you go back to bed?'

Swede climbed back in her bunk. Dad turned the gas low so the trailer was dim and warm and restful. I dozed myself, hearing only the occasional turn of a page as Dad read.

Then Swede said, quietly, 'Dad?'

'Mm.'

There was a pause which brought me alert.

'I have been praying, and I believe it is the will of God that we get going.'

Dad sat back and stretched, rose up without reply and closed his Bible. 'Well, Reuben,' he said, 'get out the cornflakes. At the very least it's the will of Swede. Let's go.'

It was on this day we began to imagine ourselves truly far from home. By sunup we'd bumped into the great Missouri River and struck north along its banks. Dad had informed us that when we crossed the Missouri at

Mandan we would leave Central Time and enter Mountain Time, a concept he ought've cleared up, as it put all sorts of snowcapped expectations in our heads. Meantime it was a good drive yet to Mandan in the trailer, which was freezing. What's over as quick as a January thaw? Swede retreated to the back of the trailer to stare at the highway falling eastward behind us. 'Come on, if you're cold,' she said. That end was Dad's bedroom. She was sitting on his bed Indian-style, under a hump of quilts.

'We did it, huh?' I said. Slipped away from Andreeson, is what I meant, leaving town in the dark that way.

'Yup.'

I poked her, under the blankets. 'Think how he felt this morning, coming down to the park and us gone – think how he feels right now!'

'Pretty mad, you think?' Swede smiled, but there wasn't any winning in it, which was irritating; it seemed to me we hadn't won many rounds lately, and here was Swede refusing to enjoy a clear victory. In fact she had hollow half-moons under her eyes, like some bad old woman. She watched the empty road distrustfully.

'Maybe he doesn't know it yet,' I ran on. 'Probably he's down at the cafe, eating hardboiled eggs. He's having another cup of coffee, reading the newspaper—'

'Hating it that he's in North Dakota,' Swede added, drawn in, I figured, by my skillful use of detail.

'Yes, hating it like everything, dumb North Dakotans all over the place, and in about ten minutes he'll finish up and drive down to the city park, and we're gone! What do you think he'll do?'

But Swede's enthusiasm was momentary, for she replied, 'Well, who knows? I guess what he won't do is trot back to Minneapolis all beat and sorry. And you know what? He found us without much trouble; I suppose he can find us again.'

And that was all that was said for some time because it was cold, boy, and we seemed to gain little heat from each other, held in our own thoughts as we were, two blankety lumps watching the barren highway zip to nothing. It was a cheerless, frost-flattened world, this west edge of Central Time. The ditches that had flowed dark with runoff had refrozen in the wind. You never like it to happen, for something as hopeful and sudden as a January thaw to come to an end, but end it does, and then you want to have some quilts around.

Remember the fuel economy of the 1955 Plymouth wagon? Thirsty power under the best conditions, when pulling great weight our car became a carping slave demanding refreshment. Yes, gas was cheap, as I am constantly reminded, and yes, the Plymouth had an ample tank; still, service stations were not the frequent, well-lit, prosperous concerns they are today, and Dad had bought and filled two red five-gallon cans that might extend our range another hundred miles – generally enough to reach a gas pump, even on the Great Plains. These we cached with a case of forty-weight in a closet midships of the Airstream; shortly after leaving Roofing we'd stopped for a fill, my job being to get out the cans and have the attendant attend to them once he'd satisfied the wagon. It's funny – I'd recognize that attendant were he to appear today, for he had one ear grown all thick and proportionless beside his head, a condition described as cauliflower ear, though this looked more like a good strong burdock leaf. He looked confused when Dad handed him a $10 bill, as though thrown by the need to make change, and he admired the trailer aloud several times, admired it as though we were wealthy travelers and people beyond his reach. In return I was fascinated by the looks of his ear, the way it splayed off his skull like a bark fungus; and I recall how little meaning I gave it later when Dad told me such flagrancies were the common bane of boxers in the bare-knuckle days who routinely took ferocious hits. How comforting, those extra cans. In no way was I expecting to run out of gas; to me it only meant we were serious in this business. We would travel as far as necessary, staying gone through seasons, years if we had to, until we got what we'd come for – whatever exactly that was. Thanks to Swede I was no longer sure. But sometime in the middle of the morning, just as I was bequeathing her all my stuff should I freeze to death, Dad pulled into a Sinclair station in the midst of nowhere, and Swede and I hopped numbly down.

'Nobody here,' Dad said. It was a little white gas station with a green stripe painted all round. Emptiest spot you ever saw. All morning the wind had risen, and the Sinclair sign with its green brontosaurus rocked and groaned on high. 'I'd like to gas up,' he mused, 'but I guess we can get to Mandan – we can easily get that far. Besides, we have the reserves.'

But we didn't gas up in Mandan. We crossed the Missouri, entering Mountain Time ('The mountains must be a few miles away still,' Swede remarked), but the city of Mandan held no gas for us. First service station we came to Dad slowed way down, then changed his mind and slid by.

'Why didn't we stop?' I asked.

'Nineteen nine a gallon,' Dad replied, his eyes on the rearview. 'I believe we can do better.' An explanation I bought – why wouldn't I? – though Swede whispered there'd been a state car parked at that very station, a trooper in sunglasses inside it, watching traffic.

We cruised along into Mandan, a good-sized town on the Missouri River named for the Indian tribe Lewis and Clark wintered with. Those Mandans knew something about games, Swede told me – that's what they did with Lewis and Clark, feasted and gave presents and played games till the ice broke up.

Dad passed another gas station. 'There was one,' I told him; I thought he hadn't seen it.

'Mm, yes, there it was,' he said.

'Can we get something to eat when we stop?' I inquired.

He didn't answer and, moreover, didn't slow when we approached yet another station, by now well into town. Seeing he was about to miss this one too I opened my mouth to advise him, only to have Swede grip my coat sleeve. I yanked away; she looked scared and savage. But looking past her as we went by the station I saw a trooper in his parka and ranger hat, leaning against his car in the wind.

I'll admit the sight thrilled me. Not that I believed the trooper was looking for us, which seemed a stretch, in the dark as we were about Davy, but Swede plainly believed he was, and Dad – well, Dad wasn't stopping.

Swede signed me to keep my mouth shut.

We were all so quiet, in fact, that Mandan in my memory is a silent movie: people on the sidewalk shrugging in the hard wind and hard white useless sun, disappointingly few men in cowboy hats and those dressed wrongly in flapping bankers' topcoats, a cafe with breakfast menus posted in the window and a couple of dogs waiting at the door, an actual living long-haired Indian stepping from a barbershop, and every thing and person getting knocked around by the bossy wind except the troopers, who on that day were sitting in their state cars at every gas station in Mandan, North Dakota, looking dispassionately out their windows. And so still were these men, and so unmoved in their faces, and so flatout many were they, dispersed like hunters across a field, that I knew they were indeed looking for us, and for Davy through us. At once I took a fierce chill. A sob rippled up my throat and I couldn't do a thing about it. It sure is one thing to say you're at war with this whole world and stick your chest out believing it, but when the world shows up with its crushing numbers and its predatory knowledge, it is another thing completely. I shut my eyes and rocked.

Something Warm

It's true: the police were after us. I believe Dad knew it
in his gut when he saw the first of them. Swede knew
it too – tell you how in a minute. Later, the putrid fed
himself would confirm the fact: he'd twisted the arm
of the weak-willed chief of the North Dakota State
Patrol, a man named Muriel whose picture I've seen
since – with that name, that little dimpled chin, what
chance did he ever have? And Muriel had ordered a
disproportionate measure of his force to Mandan, plus
a few more spots along the route Andreeson had
guessed, correctly, we would choose. An easy assign-
ment, wouldn't you think? Stopping a family in a
green Plymouth wagon, pulling a twenty-foot
Airstream trailer?

They didn't get us, though; not one of them even
saw us, though we saw *them*, as I've described; we tip-
toed through that town like a fat boy through a wolf
pack. Make of it what you will. It gives me satisfaction
yet, thinking of that evening – how each trooper must
have dutifully reported to Muriel of the State Patrol
that the day had passed without event. It pleases me to
think of poor soft Muriel then garnering up courage
and laying hold of the phone and dialing Martin
Andreeson to inform him he'd misguessed.

'He's like Moses,' Swede declared of Dad, when we lay in bed that night under a hissing gas-mantle lamp. 'It was like going through the Red Sea!'

'Well, now,' I said, riffling, at her insistence, through the Old Testament. Having witnessed her very first miracle, she'd got the idea of ranking Dad among the prophets, a notion that disquieted me.

'You don't think he's up there with Moses?' Swede demanded.

I fudged. 'What about Obadiah?'

'Low.'

'Malachi?'

'Oh, come on. I don't even know what those fellows did – no disrespect.'

I saw it was going to have to be somebody famous. 'What about Jonah?'

Swede shook her head. 'Such a griper. Whine all day long. Probably God sent the whale so He could get three days of peace and quiet.'

But I was troubled. How could we place Dad, or any other living person, among these Old Testament gentlemen? These prophets who'd got up every day and heard from the Lord, regular as setting your table? These who'd struck water from dry rocks? I wished Swede had just slept through Mandan.

'It worries me,' I said.

'How come?'

I couldn't put words to it, but Swede, as usual, could.

'Afraid we're being impertinent?'

'Yes.'

'Presumptuous? Arrogant? Blasphemous?'

This still happens with Swede and me. I'll lack a word, and she'll dump out a bushel of them.

'You called Jonah a griper—'

'Well, you read about him. After the whale he goes to Nineveh and tells the pagans to repent or God'll burn them to death, and their cows too. So the pagans repent – ashes and gunnysacks from the king on down! And you know what Jonah does?'

'No,' I admitted. Actually, I thought the book ended when he got coughed up.

'He mopes! He marches off in the desert and asks God to burn those pagans anyway, and their cows.'

'Well, that wouldn't be fair,' I said.

'That's what God said too, but Jonah sat there pouting. Lip out to here! He didn't want those pagans to repent; he wanted a barbecue.'

I looked at her dumbfounded. Who would've thought? I hoped the other great prophets hadn't any such childish flaws – Elijah or Daniel. Peaceful old Daniel down in that lion hole, I just couldn't have stood it if he'd turned out to be a pouter.

'Besides, he didn't do miracles,' Swede went on. She had Jonah down now and was pounding him good.

'Well,' I said, 'he wrote a whole book and it's in the Bible.' Even Dad, much as I loved him, didn't have anything in there.

'It's a short book. Jonah didn't even want to be a prophet. He probably wanted to be a handyman.'

We left it there, thankfully. The last thing I wanted was to badmouth Jonah. As far as I was concerned, getting past the State Patrol had been miracle enough, even if nobody knew about it but us.

One thing bothered me, though: that Andreeson had gone to such exertions. Hadn't he come to talk, right in our own trailer, just the previous night? And hadn't he gone away with nothing worse from us than passive defiance? What cause had the putrid fed for hounding us?

'I was actually expecting it,' Swede said.

'Well, bully for you.' Sure, I was a little sour. 'You know, Andreeson's still looking for us. Now I guess everybody else is too.'

'Andreeson's back in Linton.'

'He wouldn't still be in Linton, you know. He'd be –
he'd be someplace else.'

'He'd of had a hard time getting out of Linton.'
Swede looked up, itching to tell me something now –
a thing she'd been saving.

'Come on, then, say it while your mouth is open.'

'I crept over there,' she declared, 'and spoiled his
car. It was an act of sabotage – don't tell Dad!'

This was so far outside what I expected, it rendered
me perfectly stupid.

'Maple syrup down his gas tank,' she explained. Oh,
how scared and proud she looked! Then the strangeness of that morning came clear. No wonder she'd
been so agitated, trying to get us out of town. No
wonder she'd rousted us out of bed!

And the previous night: remember how she entered
the trailer, just as Andreeson was leaving?

'I used the whole bottle, to make sure,' she
confessed.

Well.

No wonder she'd been against having pancakes.

Meantime, we still hadn't got gas. We'd stopped ten
miles out of Mandan and parked in the lee of a
shelterbelt, poured in our spare ten gallons, and
driven west until Dad said he had to lie down. He had
a headache: another monster, or maybe the same one
never truly gone away. His face was lined like a
Renaissance painting. He pulled off the road beside
a great empty misplaced-looking barn, no house
around it and none visible in any direction. The barn
was paintless and built of square-hewn timbers joined
at the corners in mammoth handcut dovetails. This in
a part of North Dakota where such timbers never grew
and will not grow. I don't know how that barn came to
be there but will bet you it's there still. Dad shut off the
car, saying he believed we had propane enough to
keep the Airstream tolerable until morning. Swede

asked in alarm whether we shouldn't get farther along tonight, and he replied in a tone of declining patience that if he didn't lie down his head would fall off and land in his lap.

'It's Saturday night,' Swede informed him.

'I know it,' Dad said.

'Gas stations'll be shut tomorrow.'

Dad nodded. He'd lit the heat and tucked us in – both of us in Swede's bunk; we all knew it was going to get cold. He said, 'Swede, are you going to pray tonight?'

She nodded.

'I'm going to as well. One thing I mean to ask Him is to save us some gas. Will you do the same?'

'Okay.'

'Okay. Stay warm then,' Dad said. 'Lamp out in fifteen minutes.' He didn't kiss us good night but bent near us, then pulled away – as though you could catch a headache.

'Are you tired?' Swede asked, when Dad had gone into his room and slid the door shut.

'Nope.'

'I bet it's not eight o'clock.'

'I'm awake,' I said.

'I bet it's not even seven!'

Dad's door slid open. In the amber gloom he looked scary and sunk-eyed. A man looks like that in the day-time and you'd glance around for a phone. 'Pretend it's midnight,' he said. 'Whisper.' His door slid shut.

'Wow,' Swede said – whispering.

'Are you warm enough?' I knew neither of us was; I just didn't want to talk about Dad – how awful he looked.

'No.'

We still had the lamp on and quilts piled up. My nose was running and my cheeks felt like little blocks of pine. Outside the wind had picked up; it was bumping the trailer around gently. It felt like a huge pig was out there scratching his back.

'Look, I can smoke.' Swede feigned a cigarette in the V of two fingers, raised one brow, and blew out a long strap of steam. She said, 'I am zoooo cold, dahlink,' which gave me the giggles, which made my nose run faster, which lacking a hanky led to my desperate use of a remote corner of the uppermost quilt – well, not so remote – actually a corner fairly close to Swede, a horror that goosed our giggles into full-tilt hysterics, additional nonsense being thrown in whenever one of us could find the breath to speak. You know what we did? We laughed ourselves warm.

'Reuben,' Swede said – whispering, later, when we'd turned the light out and gone quiet in a sudden spell of conscience. 'How come we even have to worry about buying gas?'

'Because we used the ten gallons already.'

'No. I mean how come we need more?'

The question didn't make sense; I lay in the dark windbumped trailer trying to figure it out.

'What I mean is,' Swede said, 'we had that thing happen today.'

'With the police.'

'Yes, that.' See, she didn't want to use the word. 'That was impossible, wasn't it? That they all missed us.'

'Sure.'

'Do you think Dad prayed for that to happen?'

'I don't know. He didn't shut his eyes that I noticed.'

'Well, you can't shut your eyes while you're driving.' Her lecturesome tone was annoying. Before today, what miracles had she ever seen?

'Well, maybe you can if you're praying for a big enough thing. If it's really something gigantic, and you're driving, maybe God just throws in that you don't get in a crash. Like at the bakery, Mrs Bushka gives you thirteen doughnuts, even though you only ask for twelve.'

'That's a disrespectful comparison, Reuben.'

'I just meant, if God hears you praying and He looks down and notices you're driving through town with your eyes shut, talking to Him, maybe He won't let you run into anything.' I gave this some thought. 'Maybe He'd take it as proof you have faith. Maybe He'd be more likely to answer your prayer.'

Swede said, 'So anytime I really want something from God I should kneel out in the street and ask Him, so He knows I'm serious.'

I hadn't a reply for that. The good thing about complete darkness is you can lie there quietly and let the other person rethink the smart-alecky thing they have just said. With any luck they'll begin to regret it, or possibly they'll believe you have a magnificent rejoinder in mind but are too well-adjusted to use it.

'I just thought,' Swede said, 'that if Dad could pray and have something like that happen, then maybe we wouldn't have to worry about finding a gas station open tomorrow.'

'You want him to pray the tank full?'

'Well – how's it so different?'

It seemed like she never asked a question to which I had an answer. 'I don't even know if he prayed, Swede. Maybe it just happened. I don't know if he ever prays for them, or if they just come.'

A brief cold moment and then she said, 'What do you mean, if they come? What other ones are you talking about?'

'Well, like when I was born. You know what happened. You don't call that a miracle?'

'Oh. Yeah.' You know how it is – you grow up with a story all your life, it can transmute into something you neither question nor particularly value. It's why we have such bad luck learning from mistakes. She said, 'I thought you meant other times.'

Of course I'd meant other times, and it now seemed like some wretched betrayal not to say so.

206

'He walked a long ways one time on nothing but air,' I told her.

It was probably the wrong place to start.

Strange, isn't it, that we'd never had such a conversation before? Strange that I could see my father step out supported on the void – and not go tell my sister? Or see him fired by his boss only to reach forth and heal the undeserving puke, or watch a pot of soup multi- plied to satisfy the most impressive of appetites, and keep all my wonderment to myself?

'Why didn't you tell me?' Swede asked.

I didn't know. Why does any witness keep shut about something? 'You could've noticed some of this yourself, don't you think? Like the saddle. I can't believe you didn't notice that.'

The saddle was a clincher of sorts for Swede. While I told the event to the best of my recall, she climbed over me out of the bunk and crossed the trailer in the dark, hands feeling out front, until she found it there aspraddle the sawhorse. There was silence while her fingers located the place high on the cantle. For a half second my mind swarmed with dread that I'd dreamed or imagined the healing of the leather – that she'd find it still torn and believe forever in my cruelty. Instead there came a hazy sigh. She whispered, 'I've been sitting on it just like normal.' Cold as it was, she stood by that saddle a long while.

It's been this part folks disbelieve – not that the saddle was made whole but that Swede had gone all this time without seeing it. Odd on the face of it, I know – I know. But we're fearful people, the best of us. We see a newborn moth unwrapping itself and announce, Look, children, a miracle! But let an irreversible wound be knit back to seamlessness? We won't even see it, though we look at it every day.

* * *

207

In the morning it was a brisk 19 degrees according to the Roofing Co-op thermometer Dad had rubberbanded to the bedrail. In case you were starting to think miracles were a convenience of mathematical dependability, we'd run out of propane during the wee hours, which also meant a cold breakfast of dry cereal and bread – the milk was a frozen cardboard cube. Outside, the wind still pushed and grieved round the trailer and we stumbled about inside it, snugging it down with an urgent quiet in our hearts, a fear strangled by cold and hurry. Dad's head still ached, but he'd regained himself enough to stretch and shadowbox and chide us toward warmth. I remember moving through a sort of stupefaction. Kneeling atop the stove, putting the coffeepot away in its high cupboard, my numb fingers hit a stack of cups and down they all came to explode around my knees. At this Swede began inexplicably to weep. I remember how slowly this appeared to happen – the detachment I felt from the descending cups, the clamor of breakage coming almost before they hit, as if sound outruns sight in the glaciated mind. I remember the noise seeming to delaminate and rearrange into a distorted assemblage of crying and bursting ice. A few moments more and I'd have cried too from pure confusion, except then Dad began to sing. Not like Caruso or anything – he was generally uncomfortable in the same room with his own raised voice – he sang lightly, almost offhandedly, and what he sang was:

Mine eyes have seen the glory of the coming of the Lord.
He is trampling out the vintage where the grapes of
   wrath are stored.
He has loosed the fateful lightning of his terrible swift
   sword.
His truth is marching on.

This lovely warlike anthem Dad sang with increasing good humor straight to its end, steadying me with his hands, picking up wicked white shards,

> *I have seen Him in the watchfires of a hundred circling
>   camps,*

dropping the shards in a paper sack,

> *They have builded Him an altar in the evening dews
>   and damps,*

sweeping up the glistening dust, my mind brightening the while and Swede's grief fading to a series of exclamatory sniffs.

> *His truth is marching on!*

Rarely have I felt such claim to a song. Certainly it was our battle hymn as much as the Republic's.

All that morning we drove cold. We drove from town to town, all of them shut to us if we'd thought to buy gas or propane: wind-sacked, immobile towns with Presbyterians and Lutherans and secure Methodists standing around their church doors. Assured laymen, all of them, with no need for fuel, while we moved slowly through, wondering moment to moment when the last spoonful of gas would drain from the tank and leave us to wait on whomever might come by. Between towns we drove west between stubbled fields, the stubble sticking up through what poor snow had blown and dried and shrunk across the plains. In no place did we see a state trooper; in no place a gas station lit from within. We drove for hours. That we didn't run dry may indeed have been the miracle Swede wanted. Nearing midday we began seeing what looked like mountains shorn off at the roots. Swede pointed them out as buttes or mesas and said it meant we were in the West for certain, a fact also evident in the presence of beef cattle and oil derricks, often in the same pasture. Swede said something about Teddy Roosevelt, her hero among all presidents, and how he'd ranched not far from here, and how the winters had been so bad in those years that ranchers sometimes lost a thousand head in a single storm. She had read a book about this, as you might expect. It was called *Ranch Life and the Hunting Trail* and was written by Mr Roosevelt himself. Swede said he was not only the best cowboy ever to live in the White House but the best writer also. He was a friend to Owen Wister, to Frederic Remington. He credited the hardness of ranching in North Dakota with his recovery from asthma and numerous other griefs. This was good information but not new to me. You couldn't be Swede's brother very long and not know the profits of the strenuous life. Just at the moment I was too cold to care. I shrugged deeper into my army woolens and watched our entrance into mesa country. Here there was barely snow at all, though leaden cloudbanks brooded overhead. The mesas followed one another down the horizon north to south. We saw fences more and more rarely; the derricks worked alone in the matted grasslands. Once I asked Dad whether we were in Montana yet, but he said no, North Dakota was a big state.

Sometime after noon the Plymouth began to miss. Not like your small cars, bless their dainty hiccups, when the Plymouth missed the whole car seized backward, cousin to a bucking horse. You had to hold your head against whiplash. Dad pulled over and Swede laid the road atlas across her knees and judged us close to a town called Grassy Butte.

'We'll stay there,' Dad said. 'Grassy Butte. I wonder if there's a garage – say, you two, let's get something warm there!' And you know, in that moment I loved the old Plymouth and its cranky ticker, for something warm was just ahead, and we were heading for it.

Already I could imagine a cafe, that rare pleasure, with cocoa in a thick white cup. And the cafe would be so warm we'd all take our coats off – honestly, Swede and I were so pleased we got giddy, poking each other as the wagon bucked along.

Before reaching Grassy Butte, though, Dad spied a farmhouse with two pumps in the drive and a red-and-white sign out front saying DALE'S OIL COMPANY. Another sign said CLOSED, but a light was on in the house and Dad pulled in, saying, 'I believe we might prevail on Dale. What do you think?'

'Prevail on Dale,' I repeated to Swede.

'To make a sale,' she added.

'And if we fail, we'll whale on Dale—'

'Till he needs braille!'

'Will you guys desist?' Dad asked.

No one answered his knock, though we could hear voices inside. He knocked again, and this time the voices got louder and the door opened and a woman was standing there with a baby goat in her arms, just a little goat suckling at a bottle she held. She looked surprised at the three of us.

'It's Sunday,' she said. 'We're shut.'

'Is Dale here?' Dad inquired.

'Sir,' the woman informed him, 'Dale has not been here since November.'

It's hard to look back and describe Roxanna to you as she was when we first saw her. Big-boned, yes, but not in the cushiony sense people often mean; tall; dirt-road blond hair in a back-swung braid; windburned in the face. She looked like some woman from a polar dogsled expedition recounted in the *Geographic*. She looked, I would say, built to last.

'My sympathies,' Dad said.

'Appreciated but gratuitous,' the woman replied – and Swede would have loved her forever for that phrase alone – 'Dale left November twenty-fifth. Every day since has been Thanksgiving.'

Well, what does a person say to that? I watched Dad look down at his feet, smiling, one hand rubbing the back of his neck. The woman stood there holding her goat, which was yanking single-mindedly at the bottle. It let go once to bleat and bump her chest with its blunt nose.

Dad looked up. 'Ma'am, I sure hope you'll sell us some gas. I know you'd rather not on a Sunday.'

At this moment a better observer than me would've seen some acquiescence in the woman's eyes, some raising of the gate. I saw nothing of the kind, but Dad must have, for when she abruptly shut the door he stayed right where he was. Swede started to talk but he shushed her. The wind snapped our coats around our legs, and now it carried a few gnats of ice. From far inside the house we heard the goat's voice. Then the door opened again and the woman came out in a parka with the fur up round her ears and walked fast ahead of us to the pumps. 'Check your oil?' she said, while the tank filled.

'It's fine,' Dad said. Swede and I had climbed back in the Plymouth, under our blankets.

'You mind if I don't do your windshield?' the woman said.

'What's your name, if I may ask?'

'Roxanna.'

The pump clicked off and she finessed it a little.

'You should change the sign to Roxanna's Oil,' Dad said.

'When it warms up, I'll do that.' Roxanna's eyelashes and her furry hood were studded with icebits, which strangely enough had a softening effect on her appearance.

'I'd think you'd do more business. It's a more attractive name, if I may say it.'

You should've seen Swede during all this – sitting straight up, head tilted – a more transfixed rubber-necker you never saw.

'Five-fifty,' Roxanna said.

Dad said, 'I don't guess you'd have any propane.'

Roxanna Cawley did have propane, in a bulk tank behind the house. We waited inside while she filled our cylinder. There was a glass counter with boxes of Butterfinger and Three Musketeers alongside some Dutch Masters cigars and a clip display of Dr Grabow's pipes. There was a gumball machine, a framed print of the Wild Bunch, the famous one where Butch sits happily on the far right, nearest the bullet holes, and there were two goats, kid and nanny, stabled in a bathroom behind the counter. Seeing us gawk Roxanna opened the door to show the satisfied mother standing on a hummock of straw, the kid curled asleep by a claw-foot tub. There was a basin of water and a crockery jar. It wasn't as dirty as you'd expect. The billy lived in the barn out back – Roxanna said he didn't deserve to be in the house, he made smells only he himself seemed to enjoy, and anyhow he'd be rejoined by his family as soon as the kid, Beth, got stronger.

'What's wrong with Beth?' Swede asked.

'Born blind. Randy kept pushing her away from Momma; he wouldn't let her eat. So I moved them in here.'

Dad said, 'Who?'

'Randy – the billy.'

'Ruffian,' Swede said. 'Thug. Miscreant.'

Roxanna smiled at Swede, who no doubt had been exerting herself toward that exact result. 'Knave,' Roxanna said.

'Scapegrace,' my sister replied – oh, she was beaming. I had to take a step back and look at her. No showoff by nature, Swede seemed actually leaning forward toward this Roxanna Cawley. I believe you could've dropped a plumbline and proved it. 'Brigand,' she sang out.

213

At which Dad in extreme befuddlement herded us out the door, saying something about finding a place for the night. Turning back to Roxanna, he asked whether Grassy Butte had a garage or a motel.

'Garage is closed; the owner's drunk. The Hi-Way Motel is right by the water tower.'

Dad held up a hand in thanks and shut the door.

We hadn't made it back to the car when we heard it open again. Roxanna Cawley was standing there looking thirstly; did I mention her knuckles before? This woman had worked.

'Or, if you'd like,' she said, 'I have a couple of rooms.'

The Skin Bag

It may surprise you, after the goats in the bathroom,
that Roxanna Cawley set a pleasant and even cultivated table. Against the grassy barrens she managed to
coax forth string beans and acorn squash and to put
them up in quantities reaching to late January –
though of course everything lasted longer with old
Dale gone. She also had sweet corn of a white variety
I'd never seen before, a strain she liked for its tender-
ness and because it froze well right on the cob. Did
you ever sit down to white cobbed corn, freshened
with butter and salt, snow meantime beating the
windows on the coldest evening of a cold new year?
Faced with such fare I couldn't even begrudge
Roxanna her advocacy of pickled beets, a bowl of
which she set down with restrained pride and
expectation. Fortunately Dad proved fond of beets.
You never know. We dined beneath a bronzed corona
in which remained but one good bulb. We ate roasted
chicken, raised out back the previous summer, and
tender potatoes brought by train from the Red River
Valley, and gravy stirred up from the cracklings. I
suppose it was a meal intended to impress, though you
don't think of a woman like Roxanna worrying about
how her hospitality comes off; she hadn't seemed at all

ashamed about the goats. But she went to a lot of trouble for us, who were after all just one small family paying a few dollars for a night's room and board. During that meal I saw Dad lean back in his chair and smile over and over again, an expression that grieved me somehow; Swede looked often at the windows, and I knew she was growing the storm in her mind, abetting it until the world should be slowed and the roads stopped and us buried at some happy length in the warmth and contentment of this house.

And what things we learned around that table, what lessons we had in the ways of independence! For Roxanna Cawley had started life on a ranch in a valley of northern Montana, a ranch like many of its neighbors given up in the Dust Bowl years and sold for the unpaid taxes. While moving into town she'd ridden with her father in the rented truck and watched a maddened ribby steer stagger across the road. The steer was blind with disease and Mr Cawley evaded it with an artful swerve, but Mrs Cawley – following in their Chevrolet – struck it broadside and was killed in that moment. Roxanna, seven and waiting in the cab, first believed it was her mother screaming, then that it was her father bellowing in grief, but actually it was the steer, which lived a few more minutes.

Thus did Roxanna grow up motherless, just as we were doing; thus by necessity did she learn from her father the principles of business. Having failed at ranching he borrowed from an uncle to purchase a clapboard theater on the main street of Lawrence, Montana. The previous owner had closed years before, having carelessly screened newsreel footage taken during the Pancho Villa troubles near the Mexican border. The jumpy newsreel displayed a line of dark-skinned peasants falling before a firing squad, citizens Mr Villa considered to be of faltering loyalty. The people of Lawrence were unprepared for such realities played out before them. Ladies swooned in their seats;

216

husbands began a commotion. A high-placed council of indignants resolved that motion pictures had no business in the community. The local newspaper called it small loss. Therefore Mr Cawley's resurrection of the movie house was viewed as a risk, even decades later. Roxanna remembered the care her father practiced in choosing films; he got most of Lawrence on his side with selections like *Tarzan the Fearless* and *Tarzan Escapes*. Johnny Weissmuller, Mr Cawley informed young Roxanna, was a man who could be counted on. Maureen O'Sullivan too, despite all the swimming she did with Tarzan; wives didn't mind their husbands watching Maureen O'Sullivan. Marlene Dietrich would've been another matter.

Swede wondered if running a theater had often put Roxanna in the proximity of movie stars. Roxanna replied not many, but once after a showing of *Kitty Foyle* her father turned up the lights and there sat Dalton Trumbo, right in the audience. I asked who Dalton Trumbo was and learned he'd written the film. You'll laugh, but I'd never known films were actually written; weren't they just actors up there talking? However, Roxanna's father, whom she called Daddy, seized the attention of the departing crowd and introduced Dalton Trumbo, the great screenwriter. It got in the paper, a superb moment for Mr Cawley, though it went hard for him later when Dalton got jailed. Had he robbed a bank or shot someone there might've been forgiveness, but he got jailed for liking communism, which was a disgrace. Mr Cawley had to take down the photo of himself and Dalton shaking hands in front of the marquee. It had hung in the lobby for years.

Swede looked disappointed at this, because after all who was Dalton Trumbo? It was only much later we learned he'd also written *Spartacus*, and by then gladiators had lost some of their shine, at least for me. But Roxanna hated to let Swede down and said that once, talking of movie stars, Lee Van Cleef had showed up. Keep in mind Van Cleef was still several years from his famous badman roles opposite Mr Eastwood – in fact, Mr Cawley almost didn't know him but had screened *The Big Combo* just a few weeks before. Van Cleef wasn't threatening in person and as he was vacationing at a mountain cabin seemed relaxed and content. He came for a showing of *Tarzan's Savage Fury*. After the movie Mr Cawley invited Van Cleef for dinner; Roxanna remembered he wore a lavender shirt and a string tie and didn't think much of Lex Barker – as Tarzans went he was no Johnny Weissmuller.

To this bit of talk Dad added nothing but leaned back in a ticking-covered chair with his hands clasped behind his neck and his legs crossed as though at home. You could see he knew zero about *Spartacus* or the great screenwriter Trumbo or, for that matter, Lee Van Cleef, and you could see that his ignorance in these matters worried him not at all. Roxanna Cawley was talking to us in a warm fashion we couldn't have guessed at when we pulled in for gas. To Dad – so long without his wife – the particular formula of meal, woman, and conversation must have seemed like a favorite hymn remembered. I'm ashamed to recall thinking it was too bad Roxanna Cawley was not lovely. I recall believing if she were only beautiful she would somehow come to spend the balance of her life entertaining us in just this way. Wrapping us in just this sort of comfort. My selfishness should no longer surprise you. Rather, the surprise might be that I thought of Dad at all; for it came to me that he was regularly alone after Swede and I went to bed at night. That he would one day be alone when we'd gone away. I watched Dad lean back shuteyed in his chair, looking tired and pleased. We were warm, finally, and I rose to the window, where hard snow was spatting against the glass.

'Reuben,' Dad said, 'how's the breathing?'

'It's okay.' Boy, I wished he hadn't mentioned it in front of Roxanna.

'Sounds a little ropy,' he said.

'I'm tired. Can I go to bed now?' I asked, aware Swede would view this as betrayal.

'Of course. I'll be up soon too. Go on, you two.'

I dreamed a devilish little man came and stole my breath. He stepped through the door with a skin bag strung limp over his shoulder and with dispassionate efficiency crouched back and slugged me in the stomach. Such an incredulous exhale! And so complete; not a wisp of air remained. In that agonized vacuum I rolled my eyes upward and beheld the stranger tying up the bag with a leather thong. He had the opening squeezed shut in one fist and was throwing half-hitches around it and yanking them tight. Now the skin bag was stretched and seamed. It was barrel-sized and taut as a blimp. Inside it was all my breath. The little man crouched again and looked at me closely. He was a pale one, a horror. Years later I would describe him to Swede and she would point him out to me, or his close cousin, in a book containing the works of Francisco Goya. When he straightened and went out the door with the taut bag on his shoulder, I saw that my breath was gone. Anyone would panic. I thrashed and lurched and arched my back. On waking I saw Dad kneeling bedside, holding my upper arms; I heard Swede crying distantly; someone I couldn't see was thumping my back. I'd never felt such thumps; they were like car wrecks. But I got a little breath back, and with each painful thump a little more. Confused, still afraid of the man with the skin bag, I tried to tear loose; in my perplexity I thought it might be he who was socking my back. You don't emerge from these episodes thinking clearly. I managed to turn enough to glimpse Roxanna Cawley in a flannel nightgown hammering my corporeal self with the strictest resolve. It was a convincing sight. In fact I felt quite rightly convinced

I would live through the night. Dad continued to hold me in place. It was a joyous bruising that bit by bit knocked glue from my lungs. I pictured it coming away in gobs. You need to understand Roxanna was hitting me with the flat of her hands, not her fists, but even so it felt like Sonny Liston was back there dealing it out. I'll bet she stayed with it twenty minutes. She was panting hard when she stopped. She sat beside me on the bed while Dad asked the usual questions. Yes I was better. Yes I was still wheezy. Yes I thought steam might help. Roxanna asked if she should go heat some water and Dad said to put some baking soda in it and a little white vinegar if she had it. Before leaving she bent and put her cheek to mine. Her hair was in a single thick braid and moist coils of it had come free – they clung to my face as she pulled away.

Next morning all geography lay snowbound. Roxanna's gas pumps stood hipdeep. The road was an untried guess. Maybe two feet of snow had fallen, or maybe six, you couldn't say. The wind had whipped it into dunes and cliffs. It was a badlands of snow.

Swede's bed was empty. I hollered for her even while realizing the whole house sounded empty. Crossing the hall into Dad's room I heard muffled scrapings and ran to the window. Sure enough, all three of them were out back. The sun was out so hard on the snow I could barely look – it was like we lived on the sun. Dad and Roxanna were clearing a wide path to the barn. They were just finishing. Now Roxanna and Swede were heaving at the big square barn door, trying to slide it open.

'Wait!' I yelled – I ran to my room, hooked my pants and shirt, ran back to the window where I could watch them while I dressed – 'Wait for me!' I banged on the glass, but they couldn't hear. I shouted again: 'Wait up!' What were they doing out there in the new snow without me? What a rotten deal! Then, surprise, I had to lean quick on the windowsill. All that yelling had used up my air. It wasn't like earlier, with the skin bag, but the truth is I had to sit down. I was sweatier than I'd ever got taking down Mr Layton's corncrib, and here I hadn't even got my pants on. Outside I heard the barn door screel open, and Swede's outcry of wonder and pleasure, and Roxanna laughing. I tell you no one ever felt sorrier for their sorry lot than I for mine there in that empty house. I crawled back in bed under the weight of the sun and joy and adventure happening outdoors, and I thought dangerous things to myself. Back to mind came every hurt I'd endured for my defect, every awaited thing I'd missed. It seemed to me such wrongs were legion in my short life. It seemed that I'd been left alone here by the callousness of my family; that should the man with the skin bag return I might not fight so hard next time; that this house was so empty even God was not inside it. He was out there with the others, having fun.

Late in the morning Swede came in red-cheeked with the news that we would stay at Roxanna's another night.

'Dad walked out on the road – there's drifts up to his chest! Roxanna says she never saw this much snow at once in her whole life. She says a couple years ago it snowed a foot and it took the county two days to plow the roads! For one foot, Reuben – and we got four or five!'

It was plain nothing could've pleased her more. Nor me under other conditions. But I'd lain the morning in a sump of self-pity, and all I could see of Swede were her blazing oxygenated cheeks, and all I could hear of her was speech gusting forth without constraint.

'We're not gonna find Davy sitting around here,' I told her.

'Well, we don't have a choice. We couldn't get out if

we tried.' Swede was wearing a hat of Roxanna's, a fur hat with a narrow brim. Snow was stuck to it and turning to water. She'd wear it all day if she could. 'Reuben, you've got to see that barn! There's the billy goat, and six sheep, one with a black nose and black ears, and a bunch of roosting chickens, we picked eggs, and there's a rope in the hayloft – I swung around like Tarzan!'

I said, 'You tell me what good it does, staying here. Tell me one way it helps Davy.'

She glared. 'You don't care about Davy, you're mad on account I went out to the barn!'

'Who cares about the barn? Tell me one way.'

Of all facial expressions, which is the worst to have aimed at you? Wouldn't you agree it's disgust?

'You fake,' she said. 'Lying there all sorry for yourself. You weren't thinking about Davy, you were thinking about poor widdow Woo-ben.'

So dead center was this that I leapt up and tackled her at the waist and landed half on top of her on the hardwood floor – a consumptive effort and strategic mistake. We scuffed around a little, she getting me twice on the jaw – fist then elbow – before the energy leaked out my muscles. She wiggled away and stood over me, and I was a gasping ruin.

'I win!' she hollered. 'Ha, look here!' She took a gigantic, wrathful, chest-filling breath. 'Look what I can do!' She blew out the breath and snatched another. She did frantic jumping jacks. She ran in place. 'See? I could do this all day! I could do it all year! All my life!'

I couldn't speak. I rolled my eyes up at her like the betrayed steer at slaughter. I could hear my heart, boy, blacksmithing away in there.

'I win!' Swede shouted. 'Come on, Rube, say uncle!'

I shut my eyes and by main strength hauled in air and said uncle.

'Uncle?' she demanded. 'What's that I hear?'

'Uncle.'

She squatted down and looked in my face. I drew back instinctively – she couldn't have known, but this was exactly what the spooky fellow in my dream had done. Anyway, I didn't want to look at Swede. It is one thing to be sick of your own infirmities and another to understand that the people you love most are sick of them also. You are very near then to being friendless in this world.

Swede said, 'Reuben?'

'Please,' I whispered.

She got hold of my shoulders and made me look at her. 'What's the matter with your lips – Reuben?'

I gathered enough air for a sentence: 'You went outside without me.' Which set her off sobbing. She wilted down on the floor next to me. It was hard to fathom after such a fight. She put her arms around my neck, too, which was gratifying, but when it is like breaking cement with a hammer just to breathe, a tight hug isn't helpful, so I had to shrug her off. We lay there quite some time, a very woebegone set of penitents. At last by lying still and thinking about a brightly lit room made entirely of ice I was able to retrieve basic respiration. I sat up and leaned against the wall. Swede pulled herself over and leaned also. She took my hand and held it while confessing all sorts of things, chiefly related to piggishness, but also the surprising fact that she actually had forgotten about Davy – just for a little while.

'I like being here,' she said, 'with Roxanna. Don't you like her, Reuben? Do you really want to leave?'

'I like her a lot.'

'We really couldn't go today. Too much snow.'

'How come Dad started the car then?' I'd heard it out there, idling poorly, sounding broke.

'We parked the trailer in the barn. Roxanna thought of it. It's just a huge barn, Reuben, you have to see.'

I didn't see it right away, but this was certainly the

work of the Lord – the work of providence, for you timid ones. It was a cup running over. Because don't you think the old state police were ever more interested in us since we'd vanished from pursuit? And wasn't it fortunate how the blizzard struck before any state cruisers happened past Dale's Oil? And where else could we have landed, I might ask, that would offer not only gas on Sunday but cheap rooms and warm meals and a hiding place for the Airstream?

'I took that baby goat for a walk this morning,' Swede said, 'all around the house. She's so smart! She followed me all around.'

'Swede?'

'You pretty soon get used to her weird eyes—'

'Where are we gonna go? I mean, when we do leave?'

She looked so blank I knew leaving was way off at the end of things for her.

I said, 'Aren't we going to get arrested as soon as we get back on the road?'

'Say, that's true! That's right,' she crowed, 'I guess we better lay low a few days! Reuben' – grabbing my arm – 'now we're fugitives too!'

She was so thrilled I feared she might tear off downstairs and tell Roxanna about it. So I hushed her and reminded her how Tom Sawyer and Huckleberry had sworn silence in the matter of Injun Joe, and how running and hiding from the law was a privilege few kids ever had, and how we ought not blow it by bragging to someone we just met.

'Don't you trust Roxanna?' Swede whispered.

'Well, sure I do. But we just got here yesterday.'

Swede nodded. 'Okay. Then let's sign in blood, like Tom and Huckleberry did. We'll cut our fingers – and swear an appalling oath.'

'Oh, for Pete's sake, Swede.' She was already up rummaging for paper, came back with a strip of brown grocery sack.

'Get out your knife.'

I had a castoff Scout of Davy's – the big blade was only knuckle-long, having been snapped off trying to pry something. I swiped it cautiously. 'Swede, it's really dull.'

'Hm – we'll use the awl.'

'The awl? No, Swede.' I'd holed innumerable leather belts with that awl; it was blunt as a baby tooth. Also corroded. 'We'll get sick,' I told her. 'We'll get lockjaw and have to go to the hospital, and then we won't be fugitives anymore.'

So we stuck with just the appalling oath. I've forgotten the exact parlance, but it was a rare and lofty oath, studded with illustrious and disused old words, such as *treachery*, and *banishment*, and *leprous*.

Roxanna was correct about the county snowplows; they weren't up to the job. Days opened and filled with work and talk and closed early. My lungs relaxed; I was allowed in the barn and taught to candle eggs. Swede climbed to the loft and pitched down hay for the sheep. Following these modest chores we cinched on scarves and went walking atop snowdrifts so hard they stayed trackless. We walked out above the road and looked down the white horizon. We were good and stuck, and dangerously happy. Late in the fifth day we saw what looked like jets of smoke spurting from the ground in the east. We put back our hoods expecting the chuffs and growls of plow trucks, but they were still too far for sound.

Next morning Roxanna and Swede cleaned out the goatpen – in the bathroom, back of the cash register – while I investigated the pictures on the office walls.

'What's this one of the town?'

Roxanna poked her head out the bathroom. 'Main street of Lawrence. That's Dad's theater on the right. The Empress, see the marquee?'

Somehow when Roxanna had told about her father's

theater, I'd pictured something more conspicuous. Hadn't it drawn notables Lee Van Cleef and Mr Trumbo? But the marquee of the Empress was nothing but a flat storefront sign across which lay CAPTAINS COURAGEOUS in tilty letters.

A toilet roared, startling the goats, yet Roxanna was wise. If you're going to stable critters inside a house, you can't do better than right by a toilet.

'How come you've got this of the Wild Bunch here?' It was Cassidy and the rest posing in new suits – you've seen it, the one with the bullet holes.

'My great-uncle spent some time with Cassidy,' Roxanna called back.

Whatever Swede had in hand dropped to the floor; it didn't make a very nice sound. 'Your uncle knew Butch Cassidy?'

'Great-uncle. They were friends,' Roxanna said. 'He's not in the picture though, so you see they weren't that close.'

A revelation of this nature might've rendered Swede paralytic until the whole story was told, but Roxanna said, 'No, you don't – you said you'd help, let's keep at it,' so Swede scraped and moiled with a renewed sense of enterprise, no doubt to grease along any emergent history.

Roxanna's great-uncle had been a gunsmith and doctor, a canny occupational blend for a young man in Casper, Wyoming, at the end of the nineteenth century. Taken to visit him by her father, Roxanna remembered a kitchen table spread always with bits of firearm: trigger assemblies, firing pins, bolts grooved silver for want of oil. She remembered his mounted vises, one large one delicate, and his magnifying lens like a jeweler's fixed to the frame of his glasses. He had a workshop in the basement but preferred the kitchen; a lifelong bachelor, he baked himself cinnamon rolls almost every morning, setting the dough to rise before going to bed. When you stepped in his door, Roxanna remembered, you smelled pastry and coffee and oil-swabbed steel.

Swede asked, a trace impatiently, how the great-uncle knew Mr Cassidy; the answer was, Same way he knew all sorts of other people. You couldn't ever visit Uncle Howard without shooing away a man in a suit. They were salesmen from the Remington and Winchester and Savage companies, or they were medical men come inquiring after his particular advice in the treatment of gunshot wounds. Running into Uncle Howard's kitchen, Roxanna had once banged into the knees of a man wearing a white shirt and black vest and a watch-fob bellyslung as if from the foregone century. The man had helped her up. Tipped his hat. He was a Pinkerton detective and offered to fingerprint Roxanna to illustrate his craft, but Howard chased him away. Howard didn't believe a person should be printed on a whim. He was an old man by this time and told his receptive great-niece that Pinkertons were honorable, as a rule, but from long habit he considered them to be on the other side of things from himself.

This was how he had met Mr Cassidy. Arriving home from church on a lovely June Sunday, Howard had been surprised to find a boy propped spraddle-legged on his front step. That's how the great-uncle described him, as a boy. The boy was leaned back on one elbow like any idler and had a piece of chalk in his hand and he was doodling with the chalk on the broad slabstone Howard used for stoop and entry. On seeing Howard the boy sprang up. He took off his hat and tucked it under his arm, coming down off the step with a warm smile and his hand out, so that Howard had the dreamlike perception of being welcomed to his own home by a stranger. The young man asked if Howard knew who he was. Nope. Disappointment rose in the young man's face. He had a parcel in his jacket and wondered if Howard might have a look.

Howard pointed out it was the Lord's day. The young man asked him just to look – if he was interested, the parcel could be left till a day the Lord hadn't claimed.

In truth, Howard wasn't in the habit of honoring the sabbath; he was more interested in honoring the pan of cinnamon rolls he'd set to rise just before leaving for church. But the young man was so engaging Howard allowed him into the kitchen, where some cattleman's hopeless carbine lay dismembered on the table. The young man sat down and unstrung his oilcloth parcel. With great sadness he lifted forth a smashed revolver. The barrel was long enough to seem ungainly and had been flattened and twisted at the base. The grips were walnut; one had been split clean and might be repaired but the other was like a pulped apple. The cylinder had been knocked free and was the lone undamaged component. Howard looked at the young man, who was swallowing repeatedly in evident grief. He said a train had struck it – that he was doing some work near the tracks and must have dropped it and a train came along and rolled right over it. Howard said it was the most heartbroken firearm he'd ever seen. No, he couldn't fix it. All the king's horses and all the king's men. The young man sat at Great-uncle Howard's table looking down at his knees. It made Howard ache.

The cinnamon rolls were just browning up and he offered one to the youngster. The roll helped. Roxanna remembered her great-uncle's rolls. His especial pride was the frosting – he ordered back East for confectioner's sugar, fifty pounds at a time, and he added melted butter and a potion of strongbrew coffee and a dried vanilla bean ground fine with mortar and pestle. After several rolls the young man's spirits lifted. He told Howard to call him Butch. He said the revolver meant a lot to him – he'd ordered it for its long barrel because he was a poor shot and wished to correct this deficiency. He had a friend Harry who could walk out

228

at dusk and spook up a dove and drill it in flight right-handed or left. It was important to Butch that Harry respect him, as the two were working together. Moved by Butch's earnestness, Great-uncle Howard assured him the revolver was an unfixable mess but offered to sell Butch a gun from his own armory. It was an 1860 Army he'd taken in trade from a retired Union captain. The captain had carried it through Antietam and a half-dozen other situations and had kept it in trim throughout. Howard had liked its action but not its dinged barrel and had refitted it with one from a brass-framed buffalo revolver circa 1855. Butch looked it over and aimed down its barrel, which similarly had that ungainly length. The modification had been cleanly done and Butch was interested but strapped. He waged negotiations upon which he was allowed to leave Howard's kitchen with the gun at half its value, the rest to be delivered upon arrival of Butch's next pay, which Butch affirmed was coming along soon.

By the time Dad stamped in – bathed in dirty oil and bits of straw – we'd learned that Butch Cassidy had indeed paid off the revolver, that Great-uncle Howard had liked the young man's company enough to close shop occasionally and dabble in outlawry, and that he'd once had the strange experience of shooting an unruly trainman in the thigh then removing the bullet four hours later at his town practice, having not even changed his clothes. I thought it was odd, the trainman not recognizing him and raising a stink, but Swede pointed out this sort of thing happened all the time. How many times did Zorro gallop magnificently out of town, everyone watching, then show up five minutes later as Diego, still breathing hard? And no one ever figured *that* out.

Dad said, 'Listen, can you hear the plows? They'll have us clear by dark.'

'Now that's auspicious,' replied Roxanna. 'I'm out of milk.'

'Also, the Plymouth is running better. Plugs were pretty much a mess.'

Swabbing noises from the bathroom.

'So we'll be able to settle up, Roxanna. We can leave tomorrow. Get out of your hair.'

I can hear him yet: *Settle up. Get out of your hair.* In that dread moment I realized some huge, imprecise, and desperate expectation had begun to form inside me. And so swiftly – I'd had no idea! *Leave tomorrow.* It left me empty and dumb. Swede too; I've talked to her about it. She wanted to run out where Dad stood picking straw off his coat and hit him in the stomach.

But clearly Roxanna was thrown for no such loop, for she emerged upbeat from the bathroom, hair kerchiefed back like Aunt Jemima's, goatmuck thumb-swiped across one cheek, forearms crossed under rolled sleeves – the word *majestic* comes to mind. She smiled brightly at Dad, saying, 'Are you in a hurry to leave, Mr Land?'

None of us, of course, was in a hurry to leave. Surely I wasn't. The truth is my short history contained no such person as Roxanna Cawley. What must she have thought when Dad, yanking me up out of nightmare, held my shoulders and instructed her to pound my back? Yet she pounded as if not just mine but both our lives were reckoned by her strength.

As for Swede, every sentence Roxanna spoke presented her with something new to admire. A movie star had eaten at her table; her great-uncle had ridden with Butch Cassidy! Also she employed words like *auspicious* while cleaning behind goats, a positive indication of dignity.

Dad's reluctance to leave, so far as I know, had little to do with Roxanna. It had more to do with Almighty God, who so far had issued no instructions about what to do next. And so we awaited some event or foretoken, a long line of which we could recount in our march toward Davy's reclamation. The divine befuddlement of the North Dakota State Patrol. August Shultz's inkling toward the Badlands. Mr Lurvy's bequest. Even Dad getting fired by the depraved Superintendent Holden – why, we'd never have left Roofing otherwise! Yet here we sat at Roxanna Cawley's in a most disturbing state of satisfaction. Every morning Dad studied the Scriptures; every afternoon we did Roxanna's chores and were repaid by revelatory tales of her adventurous and profane and torchlit forebears. Nights Swede and I dozed in the comforting far-off resonance of adult conversation. We did not eavesdrop. Sometimes we'd hear Dad deepen his inflection – he was a very good mimic, a talent he would not practice before his children – and then we'd hear Roxanna laugh. She had a low beautiful laugh, and hearing it you could only wish you'd said the thing that brought it forth. Here's a strange fact: by the time Dad declared with such candid bad timing that we could get out of Roxanna's hair, I'd begun waking in the mornings with the sensation that I'd been born in her house. That I was as native there as the painted wainscoting and the clothes tree beside my bed. In all it was as pleasant a mirage as any I'd occupied.

But eventually the plow did arrive, against all yearnings; we wrapped in coats and scarves and stood on a snowridge to watch its tortured passage. The depth of the drifts hid all but its topmost parts, so that what we observed was a headlit monster crushing through nightfall with the tip of its V-shaped scoop borne up before it like the prow of an ice-breaking ship. To make any way at all, the plow needed a running start. It would back off fifty yards or more, then clutch into low and come roaring ahead, all chains and smoke, casting up backlit clouds that made us gasp. The whole effort was so heroic Dad grabbed Swede and put her on his shoulder as if at a parade. When the plow had at last gone by, it backed up once more and the two men inside it climbed out and stood on their running boards to wave and holler, and we whooped and jumped around in reply because it was thrilling, no matter what was to happen next – it's not every day such liberators appear on your behalf, and we cheered them like Ulysses home from battle.

Then Dad said, 'Swede, Reuben, in you go. Get your things together. Go on now,' and the great moment was over. Next morning we'd have to leave – in fact, Dad seemed so determined to leave I supposed he'd received orders from the Lord at last. Upstairs I offered this idea to Swede. I only meant it as comfort.

'Did he tell you anything?' She was crying mad, firing balled-up socks in her suitcase.

Well, he hadn't, which Swede knew as well as I did.

'If God told him what to do next,' she said, 'how come nobody else heard it?'

'Come on, Swede. Nobody else heard it with Moses. Nobody else heard it with Daniel, or Paul, or Jonah.'

'*Jonah!*' she said in disgust. Then, lumping in clothes, 'If God told him what to do, how come he didn't tell us?'

'Who, Dad or God?'

'Who cares. *One* of them ought to've mentioned it.'

She stomped away to the bathroom and returned with her toothbrush and poked it in the suitcase too.

'Don't pack that yet, you'll want it in the morning,' I told her, wincing then as she spun and threw the toothbrush at me – it missed. Though tantrums were not usual for Swede, I could see there was more where this came from. I said, 'What if God told Dad where to find Davy? What if that's why we're leaving?'

This by the way was the first mention of Davy between us since the morning after the blizzard. You might remember it caused a brawl then. Not now, though. Now it just made a quiet in which Swede slitted her eyes and peeked into my heart of doubt.

'Okay, Reuben. Is that what you think happened?'

'Well, it might have.'

'Is it your true opinion God told Dad the where-abouts of Davy and we are going there in the morning?'

'No,' I had to confess.

'Then shut up about it,' she said.

Suitcases packed and rooms neatened and clothes set out for morning, we went downstairs to help with supper. It was our routine now and a busy one, Roxanna being a thorough cook. Generally I was sent to retrieve wax beans or yams or an acorn squash from the webby cellar while Swede sliced bread or laid out plates and glasses; we'd pour cider, mash potatoes, slice pickles. We did with conviction – devotion – all the things we'd done so gracelessly at home. Even as we tromped downstairs we felt the anger between us lifting, for there was something in Roxanna's kitchen that dispelled trouble.

Usually.

This time, though, she was standing at the counter with her back to us, standing in a dark wool dress pulling tight across her shoulders. The kitchen was lit by one yellow bulb above the sink. Otherwise the house was dark. The dark flowed in through every window, as if they'd all been shot out and dark and cold were coming in, and I wondered where Dad was, for we needed him here.

'Roxanna,' said Swede.

'Children,' Roxanna replied, turning to us. Though her eyes glittered she was not crying; in fact she pulled a smile from somewhere. Her hair was roped back in a French braid from which it was very winningly coming loose, and she held before her a picnic basket with a clasped lid. For heartening sights nothing beats a well-packed picnic basket. One so full it creaks. One carried by a lady you would walk on tacks for. Does all this make her sound beautiful to you? Because she was – oh, yes. Though she hadn't seemed so to me a week

before, when she turned and faced us I was confused
at her beauty and could only scratch and look down at
my shoetops, as the dumbfounded have done through
the centuries. Swede was wordless too, though later in
an epic fervor she would render into verse Roxanna's
moment of transfiguration. I like the phrase, which
hasn't been thrown around that much since the High
Renaissance, but truly I suppose that moment had
been gaining on us, secretly, like a new piece of music
played while you sleep. One day you hear it – a
strange song, yet one you know by heart.

Under the Gibbon Moon

You're maybe wondering about the picnic basket.
Though North Dakota with its wide views and
variegated grasslands is a fine place to picnic, for most
this holds only in summer. As Swede would later
report in her short, scattershot, and extremely readable
history, *The Dakota Territory as I Recall It*,

> Few westward travelers since the emergence of
> internal combustion have attempted picnics in the
> Badlands in January.

Anyone who's been there understands why.
But Roxanna Cawley was exempt from assumption.
She knew, and her neighbors knew, that when the land
lies buried in the miseries of winter, and loose boards
twist with the cold, and the air hangs glassy and
absolute over the world, that is when the merriest of
all picnics happen. Anyone can tell you these are the
times you need a picnic most, and the fact is, if you
were lucky enough to live in the North Dakota
Badlands in 1963, you could load up and have one at
will.

We didn't know where she was taking us. Dad,
driving, just followed her directions. We were a quiet

troop. Swede was curled away from me, and I couldn't have spoken if asked, for my throat ached with coming departure and with the beauty I had perceived in Roxanna. So upright and calm she appeared, there in the front seat, and so graceful, and so separate from Dad. Had the scene been mine to write she'd have scooted closer to him; she'd have reached for his hand. Were Dad's heart my tablet I'd have taken it up and erased Davy's name, so terribly did I wish to stay, and had it been whispered to me that all Roofing had burned, to the last toothpick, so that we had no home to return to, I'd have rolled down the window and shouted thanks to heaven without a thought for Dr Nokes or Bethany Orchard or anybody.

We went round a bend and Roxanna suggested we park, a difficult trick because the road was so skinny. Dad eased to the right till doors and hubcaps scraped the hard snow wall left by the plow. We piled out left. The road was a trench with sides too high to see over; we had to climb onto the Plymouth, bumper, hood, roof, which was something to laugh about and made us all more comfortable. But it was cold, up on the snow! The moon was what Swede called a gibbon moon, meaning not quite full but oval like a monkey's head, and it showed us a white hillside up which Roxanna led us, her wool dress whipping. I ran and took the basket from her and she put her mittened hand on my shoulder and so we climbed, topping the hill at last to look down at what seemed a garden of fire.

Fire, and rising steam, and specks of light – the specks pooling and runneling then blinking out to be replaced by others. The fire came from a split in the earth that had opened and zigzagged away through the hills. Smoke and heat and sporadic low flames issued from this crack and from others branching outward. It was a fearful sight for young readers of Scripture, and Swede clutched my arm even as I

236

looked at Roxanna for reassurance. No, I didn't think it was the genuine Hell; it was way too pretty. Yet Swede had read to me how the distinguished atheist Voltaire sat straight up on his deathbed, moments before aquiring the farm, and with horror in his eyes described in journalistic particulars a geography of firespouts and molten earth and dense smoke that moved in heaps along the ground – all in all, an account not far from the sight before us now. No doubt Voltaire had a moment or two of deep regret before departing into that country – I know *I* was nervous – but down we went, descending the hillside lit by orange snow, down into the lee of the hill where the wind couldn't reach. And the snow as we walked got softer and wetter, and now we could see that the specks of moving light were streams of snowmelt, and the streams pooling and grading down into the crack were what created the steam and made the air so warm and sociable the lower down we went. Roxanna told us how generations ago lightning had sliced into an aged cottonwood whose roots ran across a vein of lignite. The vein was narrow and deep and the fire settled into the coal and spread inchwise until here, a hundred years later, it lay before us, a snaky glowing web reaching away into the evening. It was only our good fortune, Roxanna said, pulling her hood back from her face, that it had happened here and not in more populous country; for then it would be a famous attraction, like Hot Springs or Lourdes, where the multitudes of rich and feeble sat around in scalding mud with cotton up their noses; as it was, we were the only folks about, and though it might be zero and blowing a gale up on the hill, down here where the ground itself seemed coming unstitched we had to undo our coat buttons and loosen our scarves.

'Mr Land, right here,' Roxanna said, and Dad took a folded blanket off his shoulder and flung it across a flat rock by the flames. The rock was bare and dry, and for radiant warmth it was like sitting on a rooftop. Before us the crack was more than a yard across and the fire pranced up out of it a foot high. Did you ever burn coal? It makes a white-gold flame with a clean cerulean core. We leaned back on the blanket and were too warm – to our joy and disbelief – even unbuttoned.

'Roxanna,' Dad said, 'it's a miraculous place. I never saw better.' He was sitting beside her. The firelight had restored his face to healthy color and she, all Frenchbraided, scarf unslung, resembled an opportunity missed by Rembrandt. I looked at Swede and saw hope showing in her face, and felt it in my own.

'Come on, Reuben,' she said, 'let's explore!' So off we went with not so much as a caution from Dad, for he was looking at Roxanna through what I fancied were new eyes, she having worked a fairy tale in bringing us to such a place. It was indeed miraculous. How else to describe a valley where in deepest winter steam plumes as if from a battlefield, where boulders crouch warm as artillery, where spreading fire wakes frozen salamanders with which to scare your sister? We ran all over that piece of ground. We forgot the picnic. We jumped over narrow places in the crack and dumped armloads of snow down it for the thrill of the hiss. Once, resting against a heated stone, we witnessed the ignition of a dead juniper, a lacy brown juniper not ten yards away – it gasped, incandesced, roared into flame and departed forever. For a moment Swede and I had the same thought, that things in this realm were subject to spontaneous combustion (try that on for an idea to give you the crawling heebies), but running over she peered down the hole where the tree had rooted itself. Below lay the vein of glowing lignite; the event we'd seen must've happened here a thousand times before.

Returning, we saw a covered pan jetting steam beside the fire, also a small Dutch oven set a bit farther back. Dad and Roxanna were talking lightly in the way adults do who've just shifted gears to accommodate children – an infuriating tone for kids attempting to sound the future. Though Swede pried skillfully, Roxanna was more than a match for her sidelong queries; we had to be content with the hearty smells from the pots and with noticing how Roxanna sat, her back against a boulder, cushioned by Dad's folded coat. Were there time for it, I'd here describe the delicacies we later spooned up: the heavily salted beef stew with pearl onions and, from the Dutch oven, a golden gingerbread sweetened with canned fruit, a caramelly mixture Roxanna called Brown Bear in a Cherry Orchard. But time was short. Dad was gazing downvalley with a flummoxed expression.

'Is that Martin Andreeson?' he inquired, pointing at a man in a coat picking his way toward us through the rocks.

Roxanna said, 'Who?'

'Martin Andreeson,' Dad replied. 'Government man. Is that him, kids? I can't quite tell.'

The fellow was wearing a kneelength coat belted at the waist and he was stepping carefully alongside the firevein. He hadn't any picnic basket and his hands were pocketed. Then out came one hand and he waved at us like some old friend.

'It's him,' I said.

Dad sighed.

'What's he want? Who is he?' Roxanna wondered.

Dad didn't answer; where was he supposed to start?

'Jeremiah?'

'Well – you'll see.'

'Hello,' said Martin Andreeson, walking up. 'Hello, Jeremiah – Reuben. Say, where's your girl?'

Dad looked round. Swede had disappeared as briskly as that juniper tree. 'Exploring, I guess. You're in time for supper, Mr Andreeson.'

'Thank you. I ate.' The putrid fed picked a boulder and sat himself down. He popped loose a cigarette and lit it from groundfire, then took a big puff and winked at me through the smoke. He always acted like he was your favorite uncle visiting from India – boy, it was aggravating.

'Roxanna, this is Martin Andreeson,' Dad said. 'Martin, Roxanna.'

'My pleasure, Mrs Cawley.'

It was quiet a moment while Andreeson smoked and looked around. You couldn't help but notice he was kind of a handsome jerk, sitting there in the glow. He looked extremely tickled, also. I figured we were in serious trouble on account of staying hid so long.

'Well?' Dad inquired.

'I'm pleased,' Andreeson replied, 'to have run across you again. Do you know, I had some car trouble back in Linton.'

'Looks like you're fixed up now.'

'I'll be honest, Mr Land. We are getting close to Davy. And the closer we get, the more dangerous for him. I'm not threatening anyone, it's just the truth.'

'Go ahead.'

'I'm asking for your help. I understand your reluctance.'

'I can't help you. If you're close, as you say, you already know more than I do,' Dad replied, adding, after a moment, 'Just for the sake of discussion, how close do you suppose you are?'

'He's in the Badlands,' Andreeson said.

'You appreciate the Badlands are fair-sized.'

Andreeson smoked a little, appeared to decide on forthrightness. 'A rancher not far from here keeps a few pigs in his barn. Last week the daughter went out to do chores and her favorite of these pigs was missing – yes, her favorite. Pen closed, barn door shut. Well, these mysteries happen sometimes. Pigs are smart, I understand. So they didn't call the sheriff till they lost a second pig the same way. Vanished from a shut pen.'

Dad said, 'Wait a minute. You think it's Davy, taking these animals – that he's here?'

'Not far from here.'

'Did somebody see him?'

Andreeson said, 'I expect he'd be taking them for food, don't you?'

'Did they *see* him?'

Andreeson seemed to feel he had offered adequate detail. 'Yes. Almost certainly.' He leaned over, dropped his cigarette into the fire, then peered down after it. 'What we'd like, Mr Land, is for you to come with us, just for a day or two. Drive around a little.'

'Drive around?' Dad said.

'We'd appreciate it.'

Through all this Roxanna had held silent. Of course I didn't know how much Dad had told her regarding Davy – nothing in our hearing. Clearly he hadn't breathed a word about old Putrid here, yet watching Roxanna you'd have guessed she not only knew my brother but had raised him herself and tutored him in evading the law. Her face was shut and latched against Andreeson, which I suppose isn't surprising, given how her great-uncle felt about Pinkertons.

'Drive around,' Dad mused. 'Mr Andreeson, do you still believe I can somehow lead you to my son?'

'Not by natural means,' answered Andreeson.

'Do you suspect the other kind are at my disposal?'

Andreeson said, 'The work I am in sometimes overlaps into other domains. You may be able to help us – I would say, calibrate our search.'

Dad stiffened. 'I'm no diviner. Don't talk to me about it.'

'No offense intended,' Andreeson said, 'but hear me out. Will you hear me out?'

Dad didn't answer.

'Two years ago there was a kidnapping, a little girl in Michigan. The kidnapper put her in a rented cabin and drove away to find a phone booth, only he went off an icy curve and smacked a barn and that was it for him. Want to guess how we found the little girl?'

'Just finish, Mr Andreeson.'

'I don't blame you. Actually, I thought my supervisor was off his nut. He'd been talking to the family and their friends. There was a sister about eleven. He came to me – this is Ray Levy, my supervisor. He thought the sister could locate the little girl.'

'You don't know what you're associating with,' Dad said.

'Well, that's the truth, and I don't pretend to. But the sister went out with us. We drove in rough circles starting from their home. Listen – it's not exactly procedure, and it doesn't make any popular sort of sense.' To his credit, Andreeson appeared less than cozy with this story he was telling. He lit another cigarette and looked at it while he talked. 'At some point she began telling us where to turn. It upset her, she cried and so forth. And we made some wrong turns, I'll not lie to you.'

We all knew the ending, though – same as you do.'

'We found her just before dark,' he said. 'The cabin was freezing. She wouldn't have made it till morning.'

The whole thing made my insides sick. Don't get me wrong, I was glad the little girl was all right. Yet it gave me a seasick clutch behind the ribs, as if my heart were bobbing loose. I wanted to bolt from there! For I found I didn't hate Andreeson anymore; I feared him, not knowing why, and can testify to you that this was worse.

'I can't do what you're asking, Mr Andreeson,' Dad said.

'You're a man of faith; everyone says it.'

'It isn't faith you're speaking of. It's something else, foolishness or spookism.'

'There's a man back in Roofing who believes you have access to – something large,' Andreeson said. 'Some unusual authority,' he clarified.

'For goodness' sake, be quiet,' said Dad.

'Your boss, Mr Holden – the fellow who fired you.'

Dad stood up. 'I thank you,' he said, 'for keeping us informed. Should anything develop, we've taken rooms with Mrs Cawley. You may reach us there.'

At which Andreeson stood up also, handing Dad a card with a phone number, stressing his sincerity and hoping Dad would reconsider. We watched him walk back down the valley, vanishing amid firelit boulders.

Now, no doubt you're asking some of the same questions I asked Swede later, back at Roxanna's. Such as, why hadn't Andreeson arrested us on the spot, complicit fugitives that he figured us to be?

'I don't know,' she answered. We were getting our pajamas on, the various thrills of the evening still working through our veins.

And why, if he was so confident about closing the net on Davy, was our Putrid willing to subscribe even to spookism to nail him down?

'Don't know,' Swede said.

'What is spookism, anyhow?' I complained. The word conjured a scary version of faith in which a person believed mostly in malicious unseen fellows who might creep up behind you and breathe on your neck hairs.

But Swede paid no mind. She was wholly taken with the ambrosial thought of staying on at Roxanna's and the turns of the past few hours. From no hint of Davy to an eyewitness sighting! From another frozen road trip to a warm reprieve – in a home that felt more like the term than Roofing ever had. I had to agree with her. It went to show that anyone could deliver good news, including a person like Martin Andreeson, even if he wasn't doing so purposefully, and even if he was the king of pukes in most respects.

The Throbbing Heart of News

I was carrying a hatful of eggs in from the barn and saw a man sitting a horse on the hillside back of Roxanna's. This was next morning before full light and he was perhaps a half-mile from the house, so what I saw was the black shape of him up there.

The rider was Davy. I knew it without question.

He sat the horse and watched me. The horse was still but for its flapping tail and as the light improved we looked at one another across the half-mile of clean blue snow. I was sure it was Davy; yet I wouldn't have been made a fool of, so I looked at the house to see who was watching. Nobody was. I waved.

The horseman didn't wave back. He turned and started working round the side of the hill. I could see the plunge and heave of the horse's chest and the Roman curve of its neck as it struggled through the deep snow. The rider urged it forward, following some upward path. Alarmed lest he leave my sight I peeled for the house, herded the eggs across the countertop where Swede was waiting to candle them, and churned back outside.

Horse and rider were gone.

'What's going on?' Swede yelled. She'd followed me and was on the back step in an apron. Roxanna had promised to teach us her great-uncle's cinnamon rolls, those he had served to young Butch Cassidy.

'There was a guy on a horse up the hill there.' I pointed. Not one to hold back, I'd certainly have claimed it was Davy, except Roxanna appeared in the door to say her neighbor Lonnie Ford pastured cattle on that hill, and on others beyond it, and kept a trail open during the winter. She had mentioned this Lonnie before – a rancher who preferred to be horseback than at home with his wife – who according to Roxanna took little joy in range beeves or the pastoral life in general.

Swede said, 'We're going to make the rolls. You coming in?'

'I'll be just a minute.'

The door shut.

I jogged to the barn, as though perhaps I'd forgot something out there, slipped in nonchalantly, then sped through to the back, dislodging hens. I vaulted into the goatpen and banged out the door into the small corral. From here I could trot off toward the hillside in question without being observed from the house.

It wasn't that I wholly believed anymore the horseman I'd seen was Davy; you can imagine how my hopes slumped when Roxanna mentioned the rancher Lonnie Ford. But it sure had looked like Davy, even if the distance was great and the light poor and the thinking wishful. If nothing else I meant to get up to where that horse trail was and follow it a little ways; it was something to do that was real and outdoors and required work. As such it was also a spontaneous adventure – I could picture how Swede would react later. 'You thought it was Davy, and you just took right off after him?' Why, it was like something Davy himself would do! Feeling lively and prideful I pressed forward. The sun was full out; the field was a glacier; I lifted my eyes to the hills.

What a hike, though. While most of the snow had blown into chalky dunes a boy could walk on, in the lee of some drifts lay soft pockets that could drop you waist-deep, and then it was a tough slog. Such travel eats time, and I imagined ways my spontaneous adventure might turn out, the better to entertain Swede. Suppose I followed the horse trail to the far side of the hill and there encountered Lonnie Ford. What would he say to a boy who'd tracked him so boldly? While Roxanna'd described him as middle-aged, I imagined Mr Ford as young (he'd looked young enough to me that morning, though anyone knows a man looks younger on horseback – it's the effect of the mount on your posture; even August Shultz shed years when he rode) and placid in nature. I imagined coming on him round the side of the hill, warming his hands over a twig fire, in fact probably brewing some coffee in a pot up there, not being welcome to do so at home, where his wife sat pining for skyscrapers. I imagined him turning to me, pleased for company, though not the sort of fellow who'd say it in so many words; asking my name, walking over to his patient horse, taking a tin cup from a saddlebag. Coffee, Reuben? Thank you, Mr Ford – yes, that'll do.

Here I was taken suddenly aback by my own poetic deficiency. Were Swede out adventuring, she'd surely concoct spunkier upshots than a cup of joe with a hen-pecked rancher. I started again. I'd come round the side of the great hill – which I was starting to climb now, to my relief – and there he'd be, the aloof and dark-browed and oftimes terrifying Ford! And stretched before him on the snow would be the corpse of the calf he had come seeking, a corpse ripped open throat to guts, eyes froze wide, tongue pushed out like the humped beef tongues at Otto Schock's Red Owl, and Ford would be kneeling there, fingers touching the perfect blood-borne tracks of a stupendous wolf. A fearful sight! And Ford would turn to me and, 'Boy,' he'd growl, 'what are you doing up here? These hills aren't for wandering on foot. Come look at these prints' – as big as my face! – 'notice, boy, he didn't even eat. He kills for sport. Probably,' Ford would conjecture, squinting about, 'probably's watching us, even now.'

Well, you can see why Swede was the writer; but I did devise several more such overbaked scenes, and they made me happy enough and killed time until I reached the horse trail; which, once reached, was nothing but the track through drifts of a single long-legged horse and not the clean footpath I'd imagined. I slumped to my haunches. Trail, my eye – it was thigh-deep in snow and all the worse for the fact that a horse had walked on it, breaking through the crust. The truth is I nearly cried at this point; for I'd worked so hard to get here, and Mr Ford had no doubt ridden home by now anyway, and Swede, of all unfairnesses, was back in Roxanna's kitchen, stirring up cinnamon rolls. I stewed in this distress till my hind end, which had rocked back in the snow, started with that cold ache that's worse for also being soaked; then, getting up, I looked back at the house and barn.

Well – they were way back there! A very decent stretch considering the terrain, and considering I was a pauper in the lung department.

It stirred me up.

I clawed snow off the back of my pants. In fact, though I badly wanted to go home and warm up, I now saw that at this height the hill tapered considerably, and that the snow up here looked generally hard-swept. It also occurred to me that cinnamon rolls are made with yeast and take a good while to rise. What would it hurt to follow the horse trail as planned? Might not Mr Ford even now be round that bend, examining the slaughtered calf?

I trotted ahead, keeping the trail on my right. From someplace a cow bawled, and the sound rattled around the frozen hills. Practically before realizing it I'd come round and was looking down at a valley beyond which rose more and steeper hills, some with barren stratified cliffsides, others with juniper and twisted scrub pine dabbing up from the snow.

Twenty yards down the trail sat Davy on a stamping bay horse.

He looked smaller and darker than my memory of him.

I tried to say – I don't know what I tried to say. I didn't say anything.

He looked me over while the horse ducked and steamed and shook its head. He had on a fur cap with ragged long flaps that fell to his chest and a green army parka so large the sleeves were rolled back. Over his jaw lay a whiskery scrub that erased the boy I might've expected; when I looked at his face I felt dizzy and fearful, for it was Davy's face and yet another's also.

But my faintness disappeared when he grinned, under the hat, and chuckled, and nodded the horse forward, saying, 'Pretty long climb, wasn't it, Natty Bumppo?'

It was hard to talk at first. He walked the horse up and offered me his hand; I took it and he lifted me up behind him. I sat back of the saddle on the horse's wide rump, a slippery arrangement; I kept tilting one way or the other while we worked down the back side of the hill. It was steeper here and the horse, name of Fry, kept skidding sideways and catching himself. I leaned forward and grabbed Davy around the ribs.

'It's all right, Rube, he's good at this.'

But to me it was like standing on a steep roof in wind, and I hung on tight. It was such a relief to hold on to my brother again; but it was strange, also. Davy's coat smelled smoky. Sulfurish. He was thinner and harder than I remembered. He seemed compressed. He spoke to the horse in quiet clipped phrases. We bumped and slid and finally angled down to a stand of juniper where the hill leveled out, and there Fry stopped.

'You all right?' Davy asked.

'Sure thing,' I said. 'Nice horse,' I added, as if I could discern any such thing.

'You freezing?'

'I'm okay.'

'Jump off, why don't you.'

'Okay.' But I monkeyed around quite a bit. The trouble came when I lay bellywise across the horse with both legs hanging down; then I froze, for once starting the downslide there'd be no stopping, and Fry seemed a tall animal.

'You're clear, Rube – slide away,' Davy encouraged.

'Yup.' But I hung tight. I couldn't see my feet, that was the difficulty. Then Fry lost patience and haunched right, and I slipped down, missed the earth and lit on my back under Fry. The horse stamped, throwing snow in my eyes. I scrambled to safety as Davy swung down, and then he did grab hold of me like I was his little brother for real, and I hugged him back, clenching all muscles so he'd notice how strong I'd become. The best thing was to hear him laugh, and his laugh was as I remembered, only deeper. Davy always had a lot of bass for his size.

'Tell the truth now,' he said. 'Did you know it was me? How'd you know?'

'Well, I could just tell! I knew right away! Even far away.' I fairly spouted; back on the ground I was a geyser of joy and vindication. 'I saw you up here and knew it was you,' I added. It *had* been my first thought, after all; he didn't have to know about Lonnie Ford.

'You didn't tell anybody, did you?'

'Why, no!' Not that I meant to portray myself as a boy of wisdom and self-restraint, but it felt fine to have Davy admire me, especially after my clumsy landing.

'Good for you, Rube. Man, I'm glad to see you.'

The great question suddenly occurred. 'But how'd you know where we were?'

'I heard you last night – you and Swede fooling around by that coal vein.' He perched back on a dead-fall pine. 'Swede doesn't sound like anybody else, you know. I tied Fry and prowled up.'

'You were watching us?'

He smiled big.

'But you didn't come out! You should've—'

'Good thing I didn't, wouldn't you say?' Davy asked, striking me silent a moment till I recalled how Martin Andreeson had showed up. He said, 'Rube, who was that guy?'

So I described the putrid fed. Though Davy had assumed being the object of pursuit, these were the first particulars he'd heard, and they fascinated him. He wanted a complete portrayal of Andreeson. He wanted to know how he spoke, what sorts of things he said, how he treated Swede and me, how he got along with Dad. He got a kick out of Andreeson spying on the Airstream in Linton, the way he waved at us, how he saluted driving away. To my great annoyance Andreeson didn't come off as badly in these recountings as I felt he deserved. But Davy didn't mind; he kept nodding and smiling and cracking his knuckles, which reminds me to mention he was still wearing those yellow farm-chore gloves he'd had on the previous fall, the day I shot the goose.

'Where do you live?' I asked abruptly; a person can't live outside in the winter with only farm gloves.

'Come on, Rube, you were saying how you shook him off in Linton.'

True enough, I'd just been getting to the good part, and when I told about Swede slinking over and emptying the Aunt Jemima down Andreeson's tank, Davy laughed so hard he tipped over onto the snow and the horse, Fry, laid back his ears and crutched about stiff-legged.

I said, 'Are you staying around here?'

He quit laughing and looked me over. 'Not far away. I'd like to show you where, but I better not. Hey, it's all right.'

I wasn't getting teary, but it surely wasn't all right.

He said, 'It's better if you don't know, Rube.'

Which sounded, I thought harshly, like he didn't trust me. 'I'm no ratfink,' I told him, with some warmth.'

''Course not,' he agreed.

We sat on the dead pine while Fry pawed the snow for browse. It might surprise you, after my longing for details, that I got few from Davy. Always one to withhold the personal, he seemed more than usually constrained, as though we were observed, or waiting for some third person to join us. He took off his fur hat and hung it from a branch to sway like an islander's removed head. For some reason I recalled old Mr Finch, freezing in the wind outside the post office. I felt awful about Mr Finch and wanted to believe Davy might have too. But I couldn't bring it up without seeming soft, maybe even disloyal; so we talked small awhile, which was satisfactory in its way, since we were at least sitting together as in more thoughtless times.

'Say,' Davy wondered. 'What is it with Dad and that lady?'

So I told how we'd met Roxanna – a little about her goats, and her dad's theater, and her great-uncle who had consorted with famous robbers. But I didn't do her justice; for example, I didn't tell how ruinous it had seemed only last night, when we'd been on the brink of departure.

'Is she liking Dad a lot?' Davy asked.

'I don't know. You saw them,' I said cautiously, 'what did you think?'

'She likes him. Boy, he looks skinny, though.'

'He had pneumonia. He's okay.'

'How about you? How're the lungs?'

When I thought about it, they were on the poor side. 'Why don't you come down to Roxanna's? I'll go down first and make sure Andreeson's not there or anything. Swede'll go crazy!'

Davy smiled at his feet. 'I guess not, Rube.'

'She's making cinnamon rolls,' I said, in the tone you employ trapping toddlers.

'Listen, I really want to. You don't know how much. I wouldn't mind meeting Dad's lady friend, either. But it sounds like this putrid fed isn't such a dope.'

'He's *kind* of a dope,' I said, loyally.

'Well, he thinks I'm here, and sure enough I am. How'd he figure that?'

It seemed to me like Davy ought've known. 'What he said was, somebody saw you. He said you took a pig out of somebody's barn. A couple of pigs.'

'Oh,' Davy said. 'Oh.' Like a gentleman, he never suggested that Andreeson had simply followed *us* out here; that had we not set out from Roofing, he'd have had no call to suspect the Badlands. Word of two stolen pigs might've reached the local sheriff, but hardly farther.

We sat a minute and he said, 'I can't come down, that's all. The truth is, Rube, I'm trying real hard to miss the penitentiary.'

I couldn't blame him. I still don't. But it put me in a hard spot. 'What am I supposed to say, then – when I get back?'

'Nothing.' He looked at me so alarmed I recognized my idiocy. 'Don't tell Dad – and especially don't tell Swede. Goodness' sakes, Reuben!'

'Okay.' But I couldn't imagine going back and not telling Swede at least. I wasn't even sure it was possible.

'Rube,' Davy said, 'honestly, I can't talk to Dad right now.'

'How come?'

Fry was champing about something and Davy stood to soothe him; at this moment a clutch of crows that had gathered overhead all decided to move on and did so, tutting and cawing. My guts went eerie. In movies this is where you'd look around for the creeping posse.

Davy said, 'You know what? I didn't steal Fry.'

It seemed an odd jump. I wouldn't have cared if he had.

'He belongs to a friend of mine. A fellow who's helped me out.'

This sounded like good news – somebody on our side. 'A rancher? Is it Lonnie Ford?'

'Nope, no rancher.' He wished to laugh here, I could see, but was held to a smile. 'This man's in some trouble. Real trouble, Reuben. He's been all right to me, though.' Davy stroked the nervous Fry, who continued to blow and push at his shoulder. The horse's fretfulness was transmissive and my brother seemed to go up on edge. He quit talking to peek here and there. He listened, not as you might listen for the bloodhound, I now suspect, but as for a distant summons – as we'd listened sometimes, roaming in the timber, expecting to be whistled down for supper. I knew our visit was about over and in panic yanked open every drawer in my brain for a way to prolong it.

Davy said, 'It's a long walk back for you – here, I'll take you partway.' He was in the saddle before I could reply, seizing my hand, hoisting me up. Fry moved out of the trees without urging and headed back up the hill.

I said, 'What's your friend's name?'

Nothing right away; then, 'Waltzer.'

'Walter what?'

'No, Waltzer. Last name's Waltzer. First is Jape – Jape Waltzer.'

'Jape? Funny name.'

He didn't reply. The horse angled up the hill, his front heaving and rearing so I had to grip Davy even tighter than previously. The whole valley was sun-struck. The day had only grown lovelier, yet I could feel brightness leeching away from me; doubt crouched in the snow all round. A horrid picture arose, in obscure colors, of Davy lying dead in a dark place, never to be discovered. It shot through me that I would not see him again – that the horse with every upward plunge bore us nearer a ruthless parting I was bound to keep secret. My breathing turned thick; a featherpillow ruptured inside. Dad came to mind, and miracles, and I shut my eyes and prayed that when we came round the hillside he would by divine leading be standing there waiting for us, his face primed with wisdom and responsibility. I believed in this picture as hard as possible, given the short time and Fry's jerky gait. Oh, if it could happen in this way, I'd run home atop the softest snow, so quick would be my feet; I'd shout the whole way there, so regenerate my lungs.

We reached the place where Davy'd picked me up and went farther round until Roxanna's place came into view. Davy said, 'Whoa, Fry. Rube, you better walk the rest.'

But I didn't let loose of him. How could I, burdened as I was?

'Rube.'

'I have to tell *somebody* about you,' I said. Boy, it sounded like whining.

He pried my arms away and turned in the saddle. 'You can't do it, Reuben. Not yet. You understand?'

But I wouldn't nod, wouldn't acknowledge this injunction. In fact I wouldn't look him in the eyes. I'd never defied Davy before and it shamed me to be doing so now. It violated the larger order – in panic I recognized that without prompt staving, I would weep.

'Then show me where you live,' I said.

'Rube, I told you – it's better you don't know.'

Under my knees Fry shifted, and I had to grab the cantle to stay aboard. I said, 'Show me or I'll tell Dad.'

So I was a ratfink, after all; no doubt this was a finklike threat. Yet who was I to bear sole knowledge of my brother's whereabouts? Did I ever claim to be Mr Atlas, or anybody close?

I hung to the cantle and watched Davy consider what I'd said, all the while with the miserable sensation of having wrecked something, but then he nodded. 'All right, Rube. Okay. Okay.'

So stunned was I to have prevailed in this that I let go my grip, and Fry took a step, and I tumbled right down in the snow.

'We have to get you some practice,' Davy muttered, as I whacked myself clean.

'Help me up,' I said. Already I was picturing Davy and this Waltzer living in some kind of wigwam or tepee, smoke coming out the top. I couldn't wait to see.

'Not now.'

'But you said!'

'Tonight.' He leaned toward me. 'I'm not taking you down there cold. I have to tell Jape you're coming.'

Something in the timber of his voice convinced me this was the proper thing.

He said, 'Can you get out of the house without rousting everybody?'

Well, of course I could. I'd read as much Twain as the next boy.

Davy studied Roxanna's place. 'Come out back of the barn. Walk straight this way. At least a couple hundred yards. I'll be close.' He turned Fry, who frisked the first few steps as though glad to be rid of me.

'Wait – what time? When should I come out?'

'When you can,' he called, without looking back. 'I'll be there. I got no other plans.'

Something was missing when I got back to Roxanna's. Coming in the back I hung my coat, unbuckled my overshoes, and tossed them in a corner to gape. 'Hello!' I yelled.

The house was quiet.

Was there ever a place you loved to go – your grandma's house, where you were a favorite child – and you arrived there once as she lay in sickness? Remember how the light seemed wrong, and the adults off-key, and the ambient and persistent joy you'd grown to expect in that place was gone, slipped off as the ghost slips the body?

Yet the feeling eased as I entered the kitchen, for the cinnamon rolls had just come out, with their beguiling aroma, and Swede was busy whisking up frosting.

'Well, where'd *you* go?' she asked.

'Just a walk. Sorry I missed breakfast.'

'You could of told somebody.'

'Boy, Swede!' I really was sorry; my dread returned; hungry as I was, the rolls didn't appeal.

'I looked in the barn and all over.'

'I just hiked around a little.' Never was I more determined to keep a secret. Should it slip, tonight was sure to fail.

She said, 'Were you looking for Dad?'

'No – isn't he here?'

'Of course not,' Swede reported. 'He went out *driving* with Mr Andreeson.'

The last thing you expected, right? Me too.

'Well, it's true. He got up before daylight and left.' She tested the frosting, picked the coffeepot off the stove, poured a splash in the bowl and began to flail.

I sat down. The truth is, my lungs felt congealed. I was so tired my hands seemed disconnected, propped on my knees way down there. I said, 'Where's Roxanna?'

'She's got a customer.'

'How come he went?'

Swede punished the frosting. No doubt she'd have been happier had an answer been available.

'How come he wants to help that guy? He *wants* them to catch Davy now?'

Of course I was hoping for some refutation here – for Swede to defend Dad's strange decision to accompany the putrid fed. That was my careful verb: *accompany*. As opposed to *join, assist, side with*.

Then I thought of something else. 'What about the spookism?' This actually shook me up the worst. 'He said it was spookism. He wouldn't go along with that, Swede!'

She still didn't reply. Out front we heard Roxanna enter the house with her customer, some happy gasbag slapping money on the counter. We heard the slide of the cash drawer, a goat bleat, the bell ding above the door, then Roxanna swept into the kitchen, her eyes bright from wind. 'Reuben!' she exclaimed. 'Where'd you go?' And she came and kissed my cheek, first time she ever did so.

'Exploring.'

'That's good. Find anything?'

She was off hanging up her coat. Swede was preparing to frost the rolls, having beaten the stuff to paste. At this moment I wanted enormously to tell them about Davy – *that* would change the color around here. Knowing I couldn't made me sore.

I yelled out, 'Roxanna, how come Dad went?'

She came out of the mudroom and took the chair next to me. I remember she was wearing a deep green sweater with a high cowl neck, and I remember how she put her elbows on her knees to look in my eyes. 'He felt he had to go, Reuben. He didn't want you to be angry about it.'

'But how come?'

She measured me for a beat or two. 'He was led to go.'

Led? This was supposed to mean the Lord was in charge and paving your way, such as letting you get fired so you'll be free to leave town, or sending you an Airstream so you can go in comfort. Dad knew something about being led, I realized, yet this I could not buy.

'Led by who? That barf Mr Andreeson?'

Roxanna turned briskly aside, as if deflecting my vulgarity. For a moment she seemed unable to look at me; when she did her eyes were so merry I was stumped indeed. She said, 'I don't think Mr Andreeson could influence your father to clear his throat.'

'But he went with him!'

'Reuben, he stayed up all night. I woke and heard him. Do you know what he was doing?'

'I suppose praying,' I answered miserably.

'Yes – not like I ever heard anybody pray.' Roxanna stopped there, still not knowing what to say about it. I noted here a deep and elegant blush accompanying her search for words. 'I got up,' she added, 'and we talked awhile – Swede, don't you think that frosting's a little thick?'

It sure was; stuck to the spoon in a fist-sized gob. Roxanna showed her to thin it with coffee and a little warm butter. How we hate waiting for things to make sense! For I can tell you now what Roxanna held back at the time: how she woke to the sound of Dad's voice raised to the pitch of argument. How she thought at first that Andreeson himself had come in the night and the two of them were having it out. Creeping from her room, she heard Dad articulating grievance against the putrid fed. She discerned adjectives, *arrogant* and *foolish* among others. Yet there was no reply. She listened to Dad pacing in his agitation. Sometimes he spoke; at intervals Roxanna heard him savagely racing through King James, as if to back up some contention. *He doesn't know You and doesn't want to*, Dad said, gasping then as though taking a blow. At this Roxanna covered her mouth, for it occurred to her with Whom he wrestled. Having long ago accepted the fact of God, Roxanna had not conceived of going toe to toe with Him over any particular concern. *Make me willing if You can*, Dad cried, a challenge it still shakes me to think of. What Roxanna heard next was a tumble like a man thrown. She'd have rushed in then, but her muscles went weak and she sat down in the hall at her bedroom door. She remembers yet the strange warmth that comforted her there; in fact, she fell asleep with her back against the wall, even as chairs tipped and Dad strove in the other room. Waking sometime later she rose without stiffness and found him at the kitchen table. He was at peace, his Bible closed, though his underwear shirt was torn across the chest. He smiled at her; he asked for coffee. When he stood he held to the back of a chair.

But Roxanna didn't tell us all this at the time. All she said was, Dad was praying in the night in great distress over the Andreeson problem, and she got up to keep him company, and their talk ranged far and wide.

'He told me how you took down that corncrib,' Roxanna said. 'He's pleased how strong you're getting.'

I figured she was trying to win my pardon for Dad. 'That wasn't so hard.'

'And then buying groceries with the money,' she added.

'I wanted a canoe.'

'He really did,' Swede affirmed.

'Well, maybe you'd reach down three plates,' said Roxanna, 'and get out the milk.' As I did she said, 'Buying those groceries, instead of the canoe? It broke your heart, I bet.'

'At first,' I admitted.

'Would you say,' she wondered, 'that you were led to do that?'

I saw what she was getting at, but it only needled me, as the honest point so often does. 'Well, sure – led by Swede,' I groused. 'That's her job, isn't it?'

Which drew Roxanna's low, beautiful laugh. 'Come on, Reuben,' she said. 'Come tell me if these rolls are as good as Mr Cassidy thought they were.'

He actually didn't die in Bolivia like everyone believed – Butch Cassidy. He died, Roxanna claimed, near the windblown hamlet of Reece, Kansas, in 1936. She knew because the outlaw had reappeared in her great-uncle's doorway in Casper around the beginning of the First World War. Howard Cawley had received an officer's commission, his skills as both gunsmith and doctor making him alluring to the U.S. Army; he was packed and sitting at the kitchen table, rolling cigarettes, when Cassidy banged on the door. Though sporting a limp and cane he retained the vitality that had so won Howard over – nope, he hadn't been shot in the famed cantina; he got the limp when an embittered horse rubbed him off on a cottonwood tree. The poor fellows in the cantina? Friends of his, God rest their souls, two boys Mark and Pugger who'd ridden down from California to be vaqueros. It had been advantageous to a Bolivian lieutenant named Jarave to believe and report he had killed the notorious American badmen when in fact the dead were mere apprentices. Butch and Harry Longabaugh weren't even in Bolivia at the time; they were riding south through Argentina to meet with an American genius, expatriate like themselves, who claimed to have con-structed a balloon in which a man could circle the world. Longabaugh had some idea of investing in the genius's proposed expedition, to what likely profit Butch never divined. Butch only went along, thinking he might get a balloon ride.

Swede during this had been perched edgewise wait-ing to jump in. 'I *knew* he didn't get shot in Bolivia. It was a lie the whole time!'

'Yes, you can imagine how it pleased Uncle Howard. He felt bad about not offering Butch better hospitality, but he'd got his commission—'

'—and the train was imminent,' said Swede.

'Yes, there was no question of his not going,'

Roxanna said, though she added how her great-uncle, when old and stove up, confided that he'd come about *one whisker* from chucking the U.S. Army and going off with Cassidy and likely would've done it had Butch just said the word.

'He should've!' said Swede.

And that was the last time Howard saw his friend. Cassidy confided he was taking a new name, Jonas Work, because he liked the honest sound of it. He told Howard to look him up when the war ended, possibly in Kansas, where he planned to enter the windmill business. Cassidy's eyes were lit: he loved windmills, loved to watch them spin. Howard believed him earnest but incapable of commencing the honest life. He said, Good luck, Butch. Jonas, Butch replied.

Well – wouldn't you agree exclusivity is the throbbing heart of news? Who else in the world knew the real ending to that story? Who knew of poor Mark and Pugger, of ambitious Jarave? We swelled up large with privileged facts. Think of standing alone on the beach when the shipwrecked survivor slogs ashore with his great tale; think of uncovering among your papers proof you are the clandestine longsought heir of something.

'But he died in 'thirty-six?' Swede inquired.

Roxanna rose smiling, went to a glass-front barrister, and brought out a scrapbook. It had burgundy covers and black pages bound with a riband, and it creaked when she laid it open.

'This came to Uncle Howard in the mail. The sender remained nameless.'

JONAS R. WORK

In Reece, Kansas, on the ninth day of October, 1936, at seven o'clock in the morning, died Jonas Robert Work, esteemed by his community and honored by his country.

Mr Work was fifty-three years of age. Providence

had bestowed on him a firm constitution and strong powers of mind. He was a veteran of the Great War and a member of the celebrated flying corps in Leon. After some dozens of missions his craft was struck by rifle fire; Mr Work landed safely but was captured and held in a Prussian stockade, bearing in his left thigh a bullet which would forever impair his stride. After some months he escaped at great peril to his life and returned alone to friendly soil.

Mr Work arrived in Reece in spring of 1918, having received an Honorable Discharge and decorations appropriate to his heroism. He entered straightway on a career in business with the Aermotor Windmill Company, for whom he was a sales representative. It may be confidently said that the majority of windmills standing in Reece as well as many in the surrounding Flint Hills were sold and installed by Mr Work. He was known as expert in locating water and in this capacity was internationally sought. Thus he traveled from Kansas to various parts of the world, returning always with a fund of adventurous tales to instruct and amuse the flock of youngsters who were welcome visitors at his veranda.

On the morning of his death he was completing repairs to a windmill at the Howell Watts ranch. Though Mr Work climbed to the mill with his usual geniality, Mrs Watts in her kitchen perceived a shout, peered from the window, and beheld Mr Work lying at the foot of the tower. She reported that though his pulse stopped within ten minutes of the fall, the muscular powers of his limbs remained in force for eight to ten hours afterward, such was the power of his constitution.

A member of Grace Baptist Church in Reece, Mr Work died in the hope and faith of his Redeemer.

We supposed over that obituary for most of the day, Swede and I – mostly Swede, whose vaulting imagination revealed mine as miserly and torpid. When I supposed it was Longabaugh himself who mailed the clipping to Uncle Howard, she said no, it was probably Longabaugh's valiant sweetheart Etta, who'd caught leprosy in Bolivia and spent her remaining years alone in a shadowy house writing sensational novels undiscovered to this day. When I credited Butch's water-witching acclaim to using a forked stick cut from a hanging tree, Swede pointed out such sticks only worked that were cut from a tree on which an innocent man had hung – all of which was beside the point anyway since Butch's yearly trips abroad were no water-locating expeditions but merry reunions with Harry Longabaugh, the two of them playing mischief with European railroads and financial institutions and bathrobed polygamous sheiks. One more? When I supposed Butch's glee at inventing a glorious military reason for his gimpy leg, Swede reversed herself and suggested it was no invention whatever – that he really had joined the army, gimp and all, piloted a frail Jenny over the German lines, and been shot down and imprisoned and escaped. 'He always did want to fly,' she said. 'Remember the expatriate balloonist?'

'What about his limbs?' I asked. That part about his limbs still being strong after he died was creepy.

'Well, it's not like he got up and was walking around,' Swede said.

'He could've – chickens do sometimes.'

'Please, Reuben,' she replied, exasperated at this disrespectful likening, 'people would've fainted.' She considered the matter. 'I suppose he just did a few sit-ups, out there by the windmill. Butch probably did sit-ups every day – he was a little vain about his physique.'

When I thought about it, a dead fellow doing sit-ups in your yard might make you faint just as handily as one strolling. I imagined Mrs Watts, running out to help poor Jonas Work – feeling in vain for his pulse – probably she was weeping at his side when he started sitting up! Probably she thought he was all right! At first, anyway.

'How many sit-ups do you suppose he did?' I wondered.

'Well, it says his muscles were in force for eight to ten hours.'

In that case, he was probably still at it when Mr Watts came in off the pasture. I imagined him coming through the front door, all tired out. 'Honey,' he'd have said, 'what do you suppose Jonas is doing out there?'

Eight to ten hours. Boy, that was an awful lot of sit-ups.

The Little Man's Country

Just past midnight that hunched bundle behind the barn was me, Reuben Land, in deep regret. Skittish, that's what I was, and unnerved about walking out into the dark. Here all day I'd imagined the glory of this act – waiting for a certain heaviness in the house, slipping on pants, ghosting down to the kitchen, pocketing gingersnaps, easing shut the door, crossing some hundreds of yards into Davy's night – just thinking of it beforehand slid me into the company of heroes. Sure, I foresaw some nerves. Dark is dark. But I remembered Tom Sawyer and Huckleberry, afraid that night in the graveyard. And David Balfour ascending the crumbly tower with his uncle downstairs listening for him to drop. And what about Odysseus, rowing down to Hell with a canteen of blood to slake the shade of Tiresius? Odysseus was scared, and look at all he'd been through. Wouldn't I, too, defeat jitters and win out for Davy's sake?

Yet I crouched against the barn. It was a moonless night and you get little light from stars, even the old familiars of which I now took stock: big Orion with his belt and slung sword, the hound Sirius at heel; the Dipper and its strayed member Arcturus. All were as bright as I'd ever seen, yet the world stood black in the void. In fact – say – no doubt it was too dark for Davy, too! How would he find his way horseback among the hills? I cupped an ear: no stamp or whicker. Relieved, I took a few steps from the barn. Even were he not waiting, I had to go some token distance to claim the attempt. I counted steps: fifteen, twenty. You mustn't think I didn't want to see Davy; I was only weak and afraid. At fifty steps I stopped. The barn was a starless hump in the night. I said, 'Davy, you here?'

Nostrils jetted at a distance, loosening my guts. Then a tiny shine bobbed and went out and appeared again and arced into a horse's liquid eyeball and Fry walked up heaving through the deep snow. He pushed his nose at my chest so hard I'd have sat down if not for grabbing his bridle. I smelled the steam from his skin, the sulfur of Davy's clothes. How dumb I'd been to doubt his coming! Then Davy laid hold and yanked me up behind him, not saying a thing, patting Fry to encourage his silence, and he reined the horse about and we walked up into the hills.

As earlier, we didn't talk right away. It was too dark and the going too lumpy. I leaned forward against my brother's back, my arms about his waist. I could feel Fry angling upslope and my own rear slipping rump-ward, a cumbrous type of riding demanding on my part a chronic forward scoot taxing muscles novel to me. In this way we continued so long I began to wonder at our direction. It had seemed at first we were following the path I'd broke earlier; now it seemed otherwise. We kept rising. I craned at the stars, think-ing to take a bearing, but the duck and plunge of Fry whisked them up and I marked only a blue disk at low declivity; were it Venus or Jupiter it would mean we were moving west. It was poor information but some-thing to think about besides slipping off the horse. Davy still seemed unwilling to speak. I could feel his attention directed frontward, a material frontward straining as though he and not Fry were carrying us and the work consumed all he could give it.

Cresting a long hill we stopped a moment while Fry blew and stooped and clipped at the snow as though for browse. I let go of Davy to sit straight. I can't describe what we saw. Here was the whole dizzying sky bowled up over us. We were inside the sky. It didn't make the stars any closer, only clearer. They burned yellow and white, and some of them changed to blue or a cold green or orange – Swede should've been there, she'd have had words. She'd have known that orange to be volcanic or forgestruck or a pinprick between our blackened world and one the color of sunsets. I thought of God making it all, picking up handfuls of whatever material, iron and other stuff, rolling it in His fingers like nubby wheat. The picture I had was of God taking these rough pellets by the handful and casting them gently, like a man planting. Look at the Milky Way. It has that pattern, doesn't it, of having been cast there by the back-and-forward sweep of His arm?

'Up, Fry,' Davy said. 'Let's go. Rube, it's pretty, isn't it?'

I was pleased – it was okay to talk. 'Do you picture God tossing them out there like that or setting them up one by one?'

We were heading downslope, a more comfortable job.

'Are you waxing poetic on me now?' Davy said.

'No – I don't think so.'

'Well, you're waxing something.'

I shut back up. Fry was rustling along downhill just as though he could see. Presently the sound changed under his hooves and the air turned cushiony. It took me a few minutes to realize we were among trees.

Davy said, 'Was it hard, not telling?'

'Nope.'

'Dad didn't ask where you'd gone?'

'Nope.' Davy hadn't any idea, of course, where Dad

had gone. I'd wondered whether to tell him and now decided to wait. Roxanna might be entirely comfortable with Dad's decision, but I wasn't up to defending it to Davy.

'You get out of there easy enough?'

'Yup.' In fact, Dad's absence, plus Swede's absorption in the revealed history of Butch Cassidy, had made my exit a piece of cake. Swede after supper had gone to her room and shut the door, seeming so pleased I knew this was no fearsome pout. Just before bedtime I called through the keyhole. I heard her bound off the bed, tearing paper; then a few sheets from her tablet slid under the door – the latest Sunny Sundown. She had it going, as you will see. 'I smouched some gingersnaps,' I told Davy.

'Yeah?' He was interested – probably hadn't had a cookie in months. He reached a hand behind his back and I set five gingersnaps in his palm. Mouth full he said, 'Got some left for you?'

'Yup.'

We rode through a treed valley where the snow seemed less and Fry eased into a smoother walk. I expected momentarily to get where we were going, to see some sign of Davy's life – the glow of a fire through canvas, say.

'Is it a tepee?' I asked.

'What?'

'You and Jape. Do you live in a tepee?'

At that he pulled Fry to a stop. He turned in the saddle. 'Rube, there's one thing; listen to me, now. Call him Mr Waltzer.'

'Well, sure.' I was taken aback. I wasn't about to be too familiar with some grown man I'd never met. What did Davy think I'd turned into since he left?

'It's a weighty thing to him, how he's addressed.'

You know something? I'd never before heard Davy speak about someone else as though that person and not he himself were in charge. Even at home, even with Dad, he seemed to obey pretty much because he wished to.

'I'll say mister.'

'Good. That's good.'

'What do *you* call him?'

Davy turned forward. 'Jape.'

Fry resumed trudging under the stars.

'And the girl is Sara,' he added.

The rest was a silent ride. Weary travel induces a kind of vacuum. Surely we climbed and descended many times, yet for me it was all a glide. My impression was of being pulled along, attracted, called. We came up finally into a saddle between two hills looking down at the same sort of fiery valley where Roxanna had taken us to picnic – a great deal less impressive, however. There was one main fissure wide as an automobile but glowing only in occasional patches with the cool radiance of a candlelit pumpkin. Flames showed from a few spotty cracks webbing away, but it wasn't a place to make anyone think of Hell or Voltaire. It looked, I would say, beyond its prime, though no doubt someone less inveterate than myself would've been impressed.

Davy said, 'Here we are.'

I saw the shape of a lighted window set well back from the glowing vein. 'You built a cabin?' I probably sounded let down. There is something about a tepee.

He clicked at Fry, who trotted down whickering and was answered by at least one horse below. I kept my eye on the window. Then beside it a door opened and a man stepped out of it and stood straight and formally in the thrown box of light. We rode to him and he clasped his hands behind his back and looked at me as though I were money.

'Little brother Reuben,' he said. 'It is my honor.'

'Hi, Mr Waltzer,' I said.

He took hold of my arm above the elbow and guided

me off the horse. Despite all I was to learn about this man, he knew how to make a boy welcome – that is, he took entire control in a way to make you feel older and soldierly. Hands on my shoulders he turned me toward himself, amended my posture, tugged at my coat, removed my stocking cap, and tucked it in my sleeve, where it lay without making a line, all this without a word; then he stood opposite me and again clasped his hands behind him. I looked round for Davy, but he was gone with Fry. Waltzer said, 'Look at me, Reuben.'

He was of unimposing height, under six feet. A practical build, big up top, one of those men you realize why it's called a chest – you had the feeling he had all the tools he needed in there and all in working order and daily use. His hair was dark and tied back in a short bob, and he had a high forehead and two rapscallion eyebrows – upswept, pointed, and mobile.

'Mm,' he muttered. Those brows of his scared me – they were like flipped goatees.

'Tired from the ride?'

'No, sir.'

'Cold?'

'No, sir, just my toes.'

'You mean to do right by your brother, I expect.'

'Yes, sir,' I replied, remembering the ratfink threat I'd made to get here in the first place. Waltzer must know about that, yet didn't seem predisposed against me.

'Hungry, are you?'

'I don't need anything, Mr Waltzer. Thank you.' But he wasn't listening. His attention was on something else. He leaned down to me.

'If I were to tell you that those hills you rode over will be shaken to dust, and that waters will rise up in their place, and that creatures like none you can think of will swim in that sea – what would you say to that, Reuben?'

He posited this as though it were imminent and as though I were alone with him in the knowledge; and so far was it from anything I'd expected, I didn't even know to be careful.

'I guess I'd want to know what day, Mr Waltzer.'

He searched my eyes, straightened, and blew out hard through his nostrils, like a horse. 'Come in and eat.'

The cabin was a clean ruin. I have since seen photos of its ancestors, which were the slave and share-cropper shacks strung beside dirt fields in southern states. It hadn't stud walls but was built up of chinked vertical boards held by stringers top and bottom – four warped walls laced together to approximate a box. It had a sooty tin roof and a floor of boards over earth, except where some had been removed for a barrel stove. The dirt under the stove was baked black. Yet for its poverty the place was livable. The stove flung heat nobly and was topped by a coffeepot and a Dutch oven that smelled of brown sugar. The Dutch oven had a lipped cover holding several fist-sized stones as if to keep in some rebellious meal. There was a tin drum of water with PERFECTION OIL, ALL ITS NAME IMPLIES painted on it. A corner of the cabin had been enclosed by means of strung ropes, from which sheets hung like laundry to the floor.

Waltzer took a stool at the table under the single window. 'Sit down.'

I didn't want to – not without Davy there. I angled against the wall and worked at my overshoes.

'He'll be in forthwith,' Waltzer said. 'A horse isn't a car. Come sit down.'

I hung my coat on a peg and sat. He leaned forward on an elbow, looking at me. 'So you found the errant brother,' he said. 'Good for you, uh?'

'I guess so.'

'Davy doesn't tell me about his family. You're a surprise.'

'I'm sorry.'

His eyes were bright as a badger's. 'Sorry doesn't matter. We should be honest with each other. I have some questions for you, and you've a few for me. Go ahead.'

He was so direct I could only doubt his meaning. He wanted me to grill him? Right now? And then he was going to grill me?

He looked at me with pity and impatience – certainly he'd expected better of Davy's brother. 'Well? What do you want to know?'

'Why you live here?' I said. It was the only thing I could think of.

His eyebrows went way up – with pleasure, I noted, to my relief. 'Sara,' he called, 'come meet Reuben, pour him some coffee.' Before the sentence ended a sheet was pulled back and she moved across to the stove, a redhead girl about fourteen in pants and a man's flannel shirt. Green plaid flannel. When she brought the coffeepot I saw she had green eyes too, though she didn't aim them at me particularly.

'Davy's brother Reuben,' Waltzer said, as she set down three enameled cups and poured. 'This is Sara. Thank you, daughter.'

She nodded to him and retired behind the sheets without revealing her voice. I'd have liked to hear it.

'I live here because it is a cheap safe place to wait for the world to change,' Waltzer declared. 'Sit straight there, Reuben. Carriage matters.'

I sat straight. 'Is it changing the way you like, Mr Waltzer?' He'd spoken, after all, of crumbling hills and rising seas; it might be a pretty long wait.

'Yes,' he said. 'I go out from time to time and have a look. It's coming around, Reuben. I take encouragement.'

Well, I didn't know what to think. It gave me a picture of Waltzer kneeling streamside taking soundings with string and lead. Yet here we sat in the frozen

272

core of winter. Entirely beyond my depth, I asked next how he knew Davy.

'Here is what happened. I went into Amidon for breakfast. It isn't far and there's a not-bad cafe there. The owner is Williams. I sat at a front table and ordered the steak and eggs and sat looking out the window. Have you been to Amidon?'

'No, Mr Waltzer.'

'The last town I know of with hitching posts. No one uses them.'

'Don't you?'

He leaned forward. 'Do I look like an eccentric to you?'

You should've seen his brows – they were pointing right at me! I shook no.

'Nor to proprietor Williams nor anyone else,' he said. 'My eccentricity can be our secret; mine, yours, and Davy's.'

I nodded with ardor.

'The telephone rang in the cafe; Williams answered. He's a good fry cook but an unpleasant man. I heard the word Studebaker. Williams hung up and approached my table. There was a car parked out front, and he asked was that my car. No, sir, it is not. Then he went back and I heard him on the phone again.

'Not long and my breakfast arrived. It's hard to do better than steak and eggs. When I looked out again a county deputy was parked down the block. Reuben,' Waltzer said confidentially, 'are you amused by trouble?'

I must've looked blank.

'You're in school, correct?'

'Not now.'

'When you were in school,' he said, lowering his voice patiently, 'how did a person most often get in trouble?'

'Talking in class.'

'Talking in class. Reuben, were boys ever sent to the principal's office for a paddling when they were caught, once too often, talking in class?'

Actually, in Roofing they got sent to the super-intendent, Mr Holden, whose paddle hung on a wall under his diplomas. Varnished to a high gloss, it had the golden demeanor of prized decor.

'Yes, sir.'

'Did you ever *see* them sent away thus?'

I nodded.

'How did you think of it, as it was happening?'

I had no answer for him.

He said, 'You were glad it was happening to that other boy. Not to you.'

I did recognize some truth here.

'Maybe you smirked a little. Happy the principal was going to thump someone else, though you had whispered in class many times yourself. Don't be offended. I can stand your unwholesomeness because in this way we are blood relatives. I sat in Williams's cafe, looking out at the deputy parked waiting for whomever owned the Studebaker. I was pleased enough to smirk, Reuben, although I didn't. A smirk looks terrible on the adult of the species. Yet I was pleased because someone was in trouble and it was not me. Don't mistake this for regret; I have none. It pleased me to think the person in trouble didn't know it yet. He was in the same cafe, having breakfast, not knowing his day was almost over. Daughter,' he called, 'Davy will be in. See about our dinner.'

She emerged from her little room again. I heard tin plates, the kettle lid, other rattles. I'd have liked to help or at least watch her work, but Waltzer talked on.

'Most pleasing to me was that no matter the deputy's charge that day, he was surely waiting for the wrong person. Do you understand that, Reuben?'

'No, sir.'

'He should've been after the bearded fellow he could

see through the front window eating steak and eggs,' Waltzer said gleefully. 'But he looked straight past me, you see. He was quite blind. In sight of wolf, he was hunting squirrel!'

At this, praise be, the door whuffed open and Davy stepped in, knocking snow off his boots. He looked at Waltzer, then at me, as if to ensure I was still myself. He asked, 'Sara, you need some help with that?'

It was hard to miss the smile she gave him.

Waltzer beamed. 'Davy, my squirrel! Your brother's curious how we met. I'm just to the moment you rose from your table at Williams's. Come finish the story!'

Davy sat, sipped the coffee Sara had poured earlier. 'I'll just listen. You tell it, Jape.'

So he finished it out: how Davy'd gone up and paid his bill, how he'd stopped beside Waltzer's table to observe the street, then returned to the counter and inquired of Williams the whereabouts of the rest room, Williams pointing to the rear of the cafe. Seeing this, Waltzer laid money beside his plate and left by the front door. He walked past the Studebaker, nodded to the deputy, rounded the corner and entered the alley where behind the cafe Davy stood hunched in calculations. Talk ensued during which Waltzer was stirred by the boy's assurance under stress. Waltzer believed in invented destiny and invented some then and there. A quarter hour later the pair of them were riding an overladen Fry into the hills above Amidon. It was too bad about the Studebaker, but a recently burst gasket had it leaking oil all over the place; perhaps it was for the best.

During this summation Sara had laid in that shack a feast of medieval plenty. She removed the stones atop the Dutch oven, setting them on the earth under the stove. The oven she carried to the table and unlidded before us, stepping back from the steam to show a knoll of sweet potatoes glazed with brown sugar encircled by sausages. She did this entirely without production, as though expecting no praise. Sure enough Waltzer talked right along. She produced half a round of black-crust bread, baked no doubt in that same oven, and broke the bread in six pieces which she laid on a checked cloth. Through all this Waltzer talked animatedly. I wondered how long she'd lived out here. What could she think of such a father? Though he wasn't without appeal – I looked at him, eyebrows rocketing now at the part where grumpy Fry carried both men into the hills – it was clear he was a difficult fellow to please. She refilled our cups and arranged our plates and tinware, receiving, I noticed, a long and thankful glance from Davy.

'Now, Reuben,' said Waltzer, reaching for the yams, 'your story. Was Davy dropping bread crumbs behind him, that you followed so efficiently?'

I lowered my head in panic. Not for a moment had I believed my narrative would be required. Also, the lateness of the hour suddenly landed on my shoulders. It had to be two in the morning. I guess I shut my eyes a moment.

'Reuben, what are you doing?'

I looked at him through twisting steam from the Dutch oven. He'd frozen as if detecting betrayal.

'Nothing,' I said.

'Are you praying over this meal I've provided?'

'No, Mr Waltzer.' I'd forgotten to pray, though you may believe I felt like doing so now.

'You are thanking God for the food,' he said, 'when He did not give it to you. I gave it to you and did so freely. Thank *me*.'

I nodded. Call me craven – you weren't there.

'Thank me then!'

I looked at Davy, who was watching his plate. I said, 'Thank you, Mr Waltzer. It looks like a good meal.'

'Absolutely it does,' Waltzer agreed. He leaned toward me, congenial again; two fingers, I noted, were missing from his left hand. 'There's no need to wet your pants, Reuben. I forgive your impolite habit. Tell us how you came here.'

'We just came,' I said. I wished he hadn't said that, about wetting my pants. I never had a predisposition toward pants-wetting, but suddenly it seemed quite possible.

'A long trip?' he prompted, ladling yams.

'Oh, yes. Real long. We got a new Airstream trailer,' I said, thinking he might find that interesting.

'Been traveling awhile, then. Looking for Davy. Gone all over the place.'

Well – 'No, we pretty much came straight here.'

He looked at Davy, who shrugged. 'Straight to us, Reuben? Tell me how you happened to do that.'

I saw he suspected Davy – that he might've given them away. I said, 'We didn't even mean to stop here. Our car broke down and we got snowed in.'

'So no one led you here,' he said.

Well, the question was dismaying. Of course we'd been led; why did everyone keep bringing this up? We'd had leading by the bushel! The breakdown and snowstorm had been leading, I could've told Waltzer; along with Mr Lurvy, and August and Birdie, and a bunch of state troopers – in fact, I thought sourly, even the putrid fed had been part of the old rod and staff employed by the Lord to goose us along.

Yet there sat Waltzer awaiting my reply, a man who bridled at the idea of God getting credit for so much as a meal on a plate.

'What kind of leading do you mean, Mr Waltzer?'

He looked at me with eyes from a dead photograph. 'What kind did you receive, young Reuben?'

I understood then that he would believe me if I told him the truth. Strangely enough it was a scarier prospect than his disbelief. What would *you* have said? Would you have spoken up undaunted, like one of Foxe's martyrs?

'I guess we had great luck,' I said – and immediately

277

there came a loathsome squeal from behind the bed-sheets, and a weighty tumbling, the sheets themselves jerking horribly about; then out sped some wild leathery being, screeching in torment, banging off walls! Waltzer roared, like the devil must at Christian cowardice! I remembered that other poor ratfink, the Apostle Peter – how he denied the Lord and heard that rooster bellowing – this squealing fiend was my rooster! Indeed it now came straight for me – I jerked my legs up to avoid it, feeling warmth just where you don't want to in times of panic – it zipped under the table and leapt up into the lap of Jape Waltzer, where it became a small dark pig atremble with terror.

'Ha,' Waltzer said, holding the pig firmly. 'Ha. Take a breath, little one. Ha-ha – calm, calm yourself, such nerves!' You could see him trying not to laugh, trying not to startle the animal. I was trembling some myself, but it was just a young pig that must've been behind the sheets where Sara lived. It had dark skin with milky pink saddlestripes and tufts of hair on its ears like a lynx, and it kept sniffing through its snotty nose while Waltzer soothed it. 'Sweet pig. Good Emil. Yes, yes, a good-natured pig. Brave pig,' he said pleasantly. 'A little bad dream? Something with big teeth and sharp claws? Yes, yes.' Without changing his tone he added, 'Daughter?'

Out came Sara. Why in the world had she stayed in there – with a pig! – instead of joining us for supper?

'Please explain this disruption,' Waltzer said. His voice was patient in a way that made me afraid. He was running his hands down the limbs of the pig, who had calmed so much as to appear dazed.

'He was sleeping out of his box, sir,' Sara replied. 'I must've stepped on his tail. I'm very sorry.'

Anyone could hear her voice was worn to the contours of apology. I looked at her meeting Waltzer's gaze and it was easy to imagine her moments ago, in her dim little room, spying the vulnerable tail. I peeked down at her shoes. Boys' boots.

'It wasn't my tail you damaged,' Waltzer said, conversationally.

'You're right, sir,' Sara replied, addressing this next to the animal. 'I'm very sorry, Emil. It *wasn't* intentional,' she added, at some risk to herself, it seemed.

Waltzer hung on to her eye a moment longer, then turned to me. I heard Sara step back and shut the curtains. Dreading to do so I looked at Waltzer, but his eyes were alive and forgiving.

'Reuben, what are your plans?' he asked.

'My plans?'

'Yes, sir. What is it you want to do?'

'Tonight, Mr Waltzer?'

He smiled, scratching Emil gently round the ears. 'In your life,' he said.

But I was so tired. I tried to think of a reply large enough for Jape Waltzer. Nothing came. My lungs had gotten shallower all through the night; and moreover I'd gone and wet my pants after all, thanks to the pig, for my lap was soaking.

'I guess breathe,' I said.

No doubt he could've taken this for impertinence, but he didn't. He spoke to the pig. 'His aspiration is respiration, Emil. He might do well to strive harder – what, Emil, are you hungry? Here is a sausage, mmm, yes. Good pig, my little cannibal.'

Davy spoke up at last. 'Jape, Reuben has some lung trouble – that's what he means.' He looked at me kindly. 'It's just once in a while. Most of the time I can't even keep up with him.'

Of course it was the sort of thing said to appease the inveterate sickly; I still would've appreciated it, except it rekindled Waltzer's interest in me. He let the pig down off his lap. 'Is that right? I've heard of this condition. Tell me, is it hard right now? To breathe?'

It sure was.

'Here. Do this.' He sat up straight and drew in the deepest breath he could, opening his eyes wide to encourage me likewise.

I straightened and inhaled. It sounded like a dozen slow leaks from an inner tube.

Waltzer leaned in. 'No, no. Make the attempt. Make up your mind and *breathe.*' And he gave me another example of a man's functioning lungs, a suck of immense force and duration. You almost expected him to explode.

I made another attempt. You have to understand this was old ground to me. More than one teacher back in Roofing had been convinced I was short of breath simply because I hadn't learned to do it properly. Or because I didn't want it enough. How many asthmatics have been told, in exasperated tones, *Just breathe*?

Waltzer shook his head in wonder. 'How do you even live, boy?'

'It's usually better,' I said. In fact, all this attention to my respiratory apparatus had made it self-conscious; it was shutting down valves all over the place. I said, 'May I please be excused, Mr Waltzer?'

He said, in evident disbelief, 'Are you strangling on me now, Reuben? Has the monster got you by the throat?'

I'll say this: I kept quiet at first. But these attacks have an exponential nature, doubling and quadrupling their hold; they push every advantage and are fearsome enough without some skeptic calling you a fake.

'Rube,' Davy said, seeing my look, 'you better lie down—'

'Here, Reuben, this is nonsense,' Waltzer said, about to try to help me again. 'Stop embarrassing yourself. Now when I count three—'

'Shut up!' I gasped. 'Shut up and let me be!' It was all the air I had. I paid for some more and added, 'Mr Waltzer.' I can't forget how the air in the cabin turned all spotty then, nor the scramble I heard, nor the broken-bat sound which was my head striking the floor, though I didn't feel that until quite a bit later.

Of all the dreams you ever had, which do you least hope to have again? For me it was the man with the skin bag – the little devilish fellow who slugged my gut, harvested my breath and bore it away on his shoulder. The moment of highest peril in that dream came when he crouched down peering at my face. His eyes were windows through which I glimpsed an awful country. I don't like telling about it. The point here is that for a long while I walked in a gray place where I felt again that little man's presence. Across a landscape of killed grass and random boulders I moved, looking for something I needed. In the dream I didn't even know it was my breath. I thought of it as a thing packed tight in a seamed bag. I knew who had it and knew I hadn't the strength to take it from him, yet there I was in his country. A sunless place – the cold from the ground came up through my shoes. The boulders lay everywhere and cast no shadows, and they were the same color as the dead grass and as the sky. I smelled decay on the wind. Had Swede contrived to be along she could've described it better. I'll say I had the sense of walking through an old battlefield upon which the wrong side had prevailed. It was the little man's country. I felt him approaching and lay down with my back against a boulder and shut my eyes to wait. He soon found me. It was colder every second and the smell of decay strengthened and mixed with sulfur as I heard his nimble steps. Even shuteyed I knew what he would do. Now he'd crouch – and I heard the creak of his boots as he did so. Now he'd lean down and look in my eyes – my lashes felt his breath.

'Reuben,' he whispered. 'Look at me.'

What choice did I have? I opened my eyes.

Jape Waltzer's face searched mine as I hope never to be searched again.

I couldn't say a thing. I was confused – wondering about the skin bag. It seemed to me Waltzer must have it and that he wanted something more besides. I wilted back from him but he leaned ever forward. I saw we were outside the cabin and that I lay against it in my coat and that Waltzer was crouched in the snow against a night of misty stars.

'Ah, you're breathing now,' he said. He smiled to reassure me, but in his eyes I saw the same dead country through which I'd just come. 'Davy's getting Fry. He'll take you back – if you can ride.'

I nodded, dreading to speak aloud lest Waltzer change his mind.

He pressed closer to me. 'You know not to tell of this place,' he said.

I said, 'Yes, Mr Waltzer.'

Then Fry cantered up out of the night. His hooves made lit whitecaps of snow and he laid back his head as though angry at bridle and bit, for Davy had interrupted his sleep.

'Come back and see us, Reuben. *I'll* teach you how to breathe,' Waltzer said quietly.

Davy lifted a leg over Fry's withers and slipped off frontwise. He gathered me up and carried me to the horse and heaved me aboard, then rocked himself up behind. I honestly had no breath. Fearing another faint I leaned back into my brother as though his were the mighty Everlasting Arms sung about, and he reached around to mind the reins and keep me upright. Fry arched his neck and chewed his bit at carrying us, but Davy ignored all complaints and we trotted up out of Waltzer's valley. Minutes gone from there, Davy asked was I feeling better. I was. In fact across parts of that homeward trip I actually slept, but it was the good kind – free of bouldered grayscapes, I mean, and robbers who had you on their ground.

Winning Her Hand

At my age Teddy Roosevelt's lungs would lock down so tight his father would gallop his fastest horse down gaslit New York boulevards with the boy astraddle before him. Mr Roosevelt was called Greatheart, and his idea was to impel air down Teddy's throat by their very speed. This fusion of hoofbeats, daring, and midnight mercy romanced Swede, but to me it spoke less of romance than of desperation. I thought of panicked Roosevelts as Teddy strove for wind. I imagined a cycle wherein his lovely mother, at the first tightness of breath, propped the boy upright and stroked his cheek and told him gentle stories of exotic pet animals, llamas and guinea fowl and allegiant shaggy knee-high ponies, or of the glorious lavender moths her brother Captain James had collected in South America, moths with phosphor wings a foot across before which natives knelt in worship. It was Mrs Roosevelt's belief such tales could turn her son's mind to pleasing things and relax his crimping passages. At times it worked, at others not. Then Greatheart, the bearded patriarch, would rise from bed and stride to the stables to saddle his fleet charger – return for his son, now bundled in wool and furs – and dash away in the night with Teddy gaping at the wind.

Did this method work for me? Maybe so. I do recall getting my breath as Fry plunged on with what seemed overconfident speed. Maybe the wind was forcing itself down in – or maybe I was just relieved to be away from Waltzer. But when we rose over the last hill and trotted down toward Roxanna's, I felt sufficiently safe from horrors to ask Davy when I could see him next. He wouldn't say. He let me off Fry a few hundred yards back of the barn. The slopes to the west were just showing blue to where you thought of calm seas; in less than two hours they'd be plain snowy hills, and I'd have to get up and candle eggs.

As it turned out, though, Swede did the candling.

I woke with a jump and a rotten fever, with Roxanna's cool hand against my forehead. You know how a room smells with fever? I squinted while she pulled the shades.

'It's still awfully bright,' I told her. The light felt like two dirty thumbs in my eyes.

She opened a wardrobe, took down a quilt, stepped up on a chair and tacked it over the window.

'Better, darling?'

'Uh-huh,' I said.

'Could you drink a little cocoa?'

I shook my head.

'Reuben?'

'No, thank you.' No doubt I sounded like some boy choking.

She came and bent over me, put her hand on my forehead again. She listened to my breathing. I squeezed my eyes shut.

'I'll get a cool cloth,' she whispered. 'We'll whip that fever.'

I nodded. To my great relief she went from the room and I wiped my eyes and settled down. The easy way she'd asked that – *Better, darling?* – I don't know why, but I could hardly answer her.

* * *

Sleep that day was a warm pool into which I dove and stayed, sporadically lifting my head to sense the world. Roxanna entered with a bowl of beef broth and later with buttered saltines. Swede stood by the bed a few times, waiting for me to open my eyes, which I didn't. Once I surfaced to the rattle of papers and found her on a chair next the bed, pretending to rub out some words on a page. Her regret at my awakening was also counterfeit. She happened to be waist-deep in a new Sundown episode.

Barely conscious, I listened like some drunken editor. You'll recall how Sunny started as ramrod lawman, then found himself compelled to questionable action and had lately grown into the best of misunderstood outlaws. This new chapter placed him in an undiscovered valley high in the mountains, a snakeless Eden and matchless hideout. Its meadows were the rippled green of the resting sea, fed by springs and by a vigorous brook twisting down to a pool with a floor of polished stones. Moreover, this valley had but one entrance, a steep slot through canyon walls which one tucked stick of dynamite could obliterate forever. Yes, Sunny owned a stick. In fact he had tucked it already, back in a crevice away from rain. Should trouble threaten he could merely strike a match and seal himself in Paradise forever.

I'll admit that even in my groggy state this seemed a lot like Lassiter's condition in *Riders of the Purple Sage*. Swede didn't mind the observation. She said other writers had told this story also and that not even Zane Grey was the first. She said it was such a true story it needed recurrent tellings so as not to fall out of circulation completely. She asked whether it would be wrong for someone to write a story about pirate gold buried under an X since Mr Stevenson had done it already. Of course not. Well, secret valleys with sealable entrances were just the same, Swede said: places and things that were so real in the world they were

285

often disbelieved. Sunny anyhow was holed up in this pretty gorge with the dynamite placed. He hadn't set it off because first he wanted his wife up there with him. I was a little bewildered about the wife business, given Sunny's undefined connections to various past ladies, but boy, I was tired; I didn't bring it up. In fact at roughly this point I drifted off again. When finally I woke of my own doing the blanket over the west-facing window was shot with orange pinpricks. The day was over, the fever whipped, and no one had come to steal my breath. I washed up and went downstairs, sticking out my chest like Horatius.

How quickly I'd come to expect Roxanna to make a big deal of me! And how kind she was not to disappoint – at my appearance she smiled, pressed her palm against my forehead, a sensation I enjoyed, remarked on my sturdy constitution to recover so fast, and introduced me to a bowl of vegetable soup. Swede ate too, while Roxanna worked in the kitchen beside us, thumping up crust for a pie. Things were close to perfect.

'When's Dad coming home?' I asked.

'This evening,' Roxanna said, checking the clock. 'He called earlier. He's sure anxious to see you both.'

'How'd it go with Mr Andreeson?'

'He didn't say much. I guess there's no big news.' She rolled out that crust in about six strokes and laid it across a metal pan.

'So they didn't find Davy.'

'Not as of this morning.'

'Well, where do you suppose he is?' It was a little mean, my persisting this way; I only asked because I knew the answer and felt smug knowing it. Maybe it was my small-hearted revenge against Dad, my way of suggesting he hadn't been *led* to go off with Putrid after all. Then Roxanna turned to me with an encouraging smile, and I saw that she was scared for Davy – scared for him though she'd never met him – and instead of smug I only felt underhanded.

'We have to be steadfast,' she said now. 'We have to have faith, you two, that's all.'

You see? She'd begun to use Dad's language. You notice something like that, and watching her I noticed too that she was wearing earrings, little gold hoops, and that while in no way impatient she seemed eager to get the pie in the oven and her hands washed and the countertop clean where she'd rolled out the crust.

Swede had been eating in unusual quiet. Out of nowhere she said, 'If Dad says we have to go back home, I'm not gonna let him.'

'Neither am I,' Roxanna replied. I looked at her quick, but she was scrubbing the counter, all business and not about to meet my eye.

We didn't even see who dropped him off. It could've been Andreeson or some underling. Who cared? What we saw was Dad standing in his overcoat between the two gas pumps. At his feet was the small cardboard suitcase he called his overnight grip, and he was whisking his hands together gazing up at the house. Roxanna was upstairs so it was only Swede and me at the living-room window – of course we were bouncing and waving like a pair of gibbons – but Dad somehow didn't see us. He stood there between the pumps looking up at the front gable. He was changed from before. We saw it straight off and quit our bouncing. His expression was curiously buoyant and alien to us. He peered up at that gable like the most hopeful yet constrained boy you ever saw – a boy on his birthday morning, scared to get out of bed for fear everybody forgot.

'What's the matter with him?' I asked Swede. 'Why isn't he coming in?'

'Ssshhh.' She grabbed my shoulder but kept her eyes on Dad. I couldn't believe it – now *she* had the buoyant expression! She'd caught it somehow.

'Good grief,' I muttered. Swede was squeezing my shoulder, transfixed by Dad, who was smoothing his hair back with his left hand. Now he looked critically at his shoes. Straightened the lapels of his overcoat. It was maddening. I started for the door but Swede had my shirt in her hard little fist. At last Dad resolved to come in. Forgetting his grip by the pumps he came up and knocked at the door, just as though he'd never seen the place before.

'Come on,' I told Swede, but still she held me back.

'Let Roxanna,' she said.

'But it's Dad.'

'Let *Roxanna*!' – hissing it at me, for now we heard Roxanna descending stairs in a tremendous rustle, shoes skidding across linoleum, then slowing into sight. And I understood. I stopped flatfoot. Roxanna was in a deep blue dress, her hair softly curled in front. Though Swede and I were certain of being her favorite people in all creation, we had the sense of being elsewhere as she glided past. I smelled perfume – that was a first, perfume in somebody's house. I'd only ever smelled it in church. Roxanna went on to the door and we shamelessly flowed along in her wake, staying back just far enough to remain unseen. Though I suspect we could've been two gibbering savants and yet accomplished that. When Dad stepped inside, still wearing that weightless expression, Roxanna reached and took his hand. I didn't hear what she said but can see their hands touching – not a passionate clasp but an easy timeless transaction as old as Scripture. Then Dad's hand let go and for just a moment encircled Roxanna's waist – he was laughing – and when he turned to us he'd never appeared stronger or more like himself or more capable of stepping up to what might be required.

That very night Dad packed up his clothes and moved out to the Airstream. I didn't fret, for it was plain now that something was forged between them and no abrupt partings were likely, but it confused me.

Following his lead I started stacking shirts in my own suitcase, but Swede came in and crouched beside me.

'We're not moving out there – only Dad,' she said.

'How come he is?'

'It's for honor,' she said.

It's a declaration you like to hear about your own father, and I was pleased by the confident way she made it. 'Oh – good.'

'He's still going to come in the house in the daytime, but he's going to sleep out there.'

There seemed to be something going unsaid here, though I didn't know how to reach whatever it was. I'd already asked the only question – How come? – and had my answer.

Swede said, 'He told me he wants to make sure the heater's working in the trailer – remember that night it got so cold?'

'Uh-huh.'

'But it's really just for honor.' She was pretty proud to have figured this out. I was proud of her, too – I would've believed the heater story for sure. It raised a question, though.

'Don't you think we should move out with him, then?'

Swede hadn't thought of that, I could tell.

'I don't think it matters,' she said.

'It matters for Dad,' I pointed out.

'Well, he's the one who loves Roxanna.'

Surprisingly, I was unembarrassed by such talk. 'Well, so do I love Roxanna. So do you, Swede.'

She gave me an oh-Reuben look. 'Well, talk to Dad about it then, if you're so determined.'

But I never did mention it to him. I feared a protracted discussion of honor, embroiled in deception as I was; honest, I came about this close to getting Dad alone and telling him the works. I never wanted to confess so badly in my life. What kept me from it wasn't my promise to Davy, either; it was my intact bewilderment over Dad's having gone off with Andreeson. Most of three days he'd been gone, and what had come of it anyhow?

'I just liked it better when Mr Andreeson was the enemy,' I complained finally.

We were in the barn, jacking up the Airstream to lie level so Dad needn't sleep at a tilt. He was kneeling at the ratchet, squinting the length of the trailer.

'I don't see what's changed,' I said.

Dad got up and leaned into the trailer, checking the bubble on a wood level he'd set inside.

'You even told him we were enemies, right to his face. Remember that?' I asked reproachfully – beyond my depth and knowing it, yet unable to shut up.

'All right,' Dad said, 'let's take stock. Why exactly is Mr Andreeson our enemy? Because he's a bad fellow?'

'He wants to stick Davy in prison.'

'And how come?' Dad said. 'No, quit that squirming. How come?'

'For what he did,' I replied eventually.

'Davy's in the wrong, then?'

'He might be.'

A moment later: 'You aren't sure, though.'

I shook no.

Dad let me stew while he reversed the ratchet and let the trailer sink an inch. He checked the bubble again and returned to the jack and brought it up a millimeter or two, and while he messed thus Tommy Basca's last moments reappeared to me, and the bafflement in his face as he scrambled bellywise over the floor.

'Okay,' I said.

'What?'

'Davy did a wrong thing.'

Dad raised his brows. 'Yet you want him to escape consequences.'

'Yes, sir.'

'Consequences represented by Mr Andreeson, who

becomes' – Dad caught my eye – 'our enemy.'

This of course was the indefensible truth. It was also incomplete; having recently become acquainted with Davy's new life and his compadre Jape Waltzer, I realized he hadn't got away from consequences by any means.

But Dad said, 'Look, Reuben. I want the same thing as you: Davy free and clear. If you like Mr Andreeson better as an enemy, then keep him one. Maybe that's your job as a boy – as a brother. My job is different.'

'How come?'

'Because I'm the dad. I have to heed the Lord's instructions.'

I hadn't any comment to this but felt myself opposite to the Lord in some way, which was worrisome.

Dad asked, 'You remember what the Lord said about enemies?'

In fact I did remember some passages about enemies. Once, sick of whiners, the Lord caused the earth to crack open like an old bun and a crowd of them fell right in. And how about the prophet Elijah, slaughtering 400 priests of Baal in one afternoon? Then there were the twisted fellows of Sodom and Gomorrah, and the time before that when God killed pretty much everyone in the world except Noah's family. The Old Testament, boy, it suited me.

'Love your enemies,' Dad said. 'Pray for those who persecute you.'

He would pick those verses.

'Rats, huh?' he said.

Davy came back that afternoon. I was on some errand and looked up to the hills; he was exactly where he'd been the first time, though he sat a different horse.

Again I didn't dare wave. I did raise my hand to my eyes as though shading off sun. At this Davy turned the horse – a paint – and started working round the side of the hill as before.

That night he was waiting for me behind the barn.

'Hey, Natty,' he started, but I shushed him. Dad was sleeping in the trailer now; we couldn't afford a whole lot of Nattying this close to home. If the nervous paint horse were even to nicker—

Davy gave me a hand and I slipped up behind him. 'Jape's gone tonight,' he whispered, when we'd gained some distance.

To call this welcome news didn't touch it. Glad as I'd been to catch sight of Davy, I dreaded seeing Mr Waltzer again. Back in the house I'd gone to my room and at suppertime told the barefaced lie that my stomach was sick. Actually it was just empty, but I couldn't go down and sit across from Dad with that man Waltzer in my proximate future. What if my pipes seized up? What if he tried teaching me to breathe again?

'He had to go pay a man,' Davy explained. 'Some debt he owed. He won't be back for a couple days.'

'Can you come home then – come home with us – since he's gone?'

This brought a silence during which I remembered a salient fact: Davy wasn't scared of Waltzer the way I was. Davy wasn't his hostage but remained by choice. He called him Jape, for goodness' sakes.

'Nope,' said my brother at last. 'Besides, what about Sara? You think I should leave her alone?'

Sara was another fact I'd forgotten about. 'Bring her along,' I suggested, hopelessly.

'That,' said Davy, grinning so I could hear it, 'might be the worst idea you had in quite awhile, Rube.'

So we rode on. The paint horse took us up at a walk, round the first hill then on as before, through treed valleys and choked washes and across flanneled hillsides, none of which a person could honestly see on account of the clouds which had got between us and moonlight. I recall the quilted jolts of that ride, the radiant warmth of the horse's rump and the sulfury odor of Davy's coat, and I recall the black remorse that flapped down and perched on me as we rode, for this time I was sneaking out on Dad. You can embark on new and steeper versions of your old sins, you know, and cry tears while doing it that are genuine as any.

What else exhausts like sustained deception? I don't know how the true outlaw does it. In the coming weeks I was to make that ride with Davy three more times. Not once did I come close to being nabbed. Not once did Swede so much as roll over when I slipped past her door. One night skirting the barn I did hear Dad praying aloud in the Airstream – talking, laughing, asking questions of the Lord as though it had been you or me or Mr DeCuellar in there – and I had to fight an ache to go straight to him and admit the weaselly nature I was fast developing. Yet even then Davy was waiting in the dark not a hundred yards away. I could hear the stamp of the paint, who seemed always a little goosey; now Davy would be leaning forward, rubbing the horse's ears, giving to the animal of his own confidence; how could I not go out to him? I told myself we might yet reach a place where Davy would agree to come home. That the things I was learning at Waltzer's table might be of value in my brother's redemption. Also I had the common weakling's fantasy, imagining myself venerated in some golden future – *Say, that's Reuben Land, who went into the Badlands at the age of eleven and found his outlaw brother*. I thought of the admiration people like Bethany Orchard would bear me, the way they would seek my company, as if I were that pilgrim Sinbad come in off the water. *Tell us about it, Reuben Land*.

And indeed I did learn some things, many of which I've had to grow into.

'We saw old man Finch,' I told Davy, as we rode

through the hills. 'It was the day we left. He was out in the wind; he could just barely stand up.'

'Well, that old souse,' Davy cheerfully replied.

But after talking with Dad, it was plain to me Davy had done a grievous wrong. Don't misunderstand, I backed my brother all the way. Yet it had come to mean something whether he felt anything like repentence. I pressed awkwardly in. 'Couldn't help but feel sorry for him.'

The paint horse stepped along at a bright pace. Davy said, 'Don't you do that, Rube. Don't you recommend regret to me – it's no help.'

'I wasn't saying anything.'

'Say I did regret it; what good does it do? I have to go on from here.' He kneed the paint to a quick trot; I grabbed his waist to stay on.

Another ride, we got talking about Sara.

'She's not really Waltzer's daughter. He got her from a fellow in Utah,' Davy said.

'Got her?' What was that supposed to mean?

'The fellow gave her to him.'

'So Mr Waltzer's like her godfather,' I said. We ourselves had godparents – August and Birdie Shultz, in fact. I'd often been comforted to think that should a boiler or something tip over on Dad at the school, we'd go live with August and Birdie instead of at some orphanage. Do you know how many times I read the Classics Illustrated version of *Oliver Twist*? Orphanages were a bad deal.

'I don't think that's it exactly,' Davy said.

'Well, fellows don't just give their kids away.'

'This was five or six years ago,' he went on. 'Sara remembers her dad.'

'Well – was he dying or something?'

We plodded ahead. This particular night was fair as you could want, not cold, the sky glutted with stars, yet all felt stained, or soon to be.

'Was he dying?' I asked again.

'Far as I know he's still alive.'

'He just gave her away?'

'Sara doesn't seem to like him much.'

That I could believe.

'All I know,' Davy said, seeming way too dis-passionate about it, 'is that she is Jape's daughter for now. When she's old enough she's supposed to marry him or something. That's what he told me: "I'm raising myself a wife."'

Raising a wife? I sat the paint's rocking haunches and sifted that idea around. It was pretty abhorrent and only got worse as Sara came more fully to mind. I remembered her now in relentless detail: her red hair bound back under a kerchief knotted at her fuzzy nape, her tired voice explaining the accident with the pig Emil, her settled grace in serving us, moving around the cabin with a woman's assurance. Now I'd gone and glimpsed her future, and it looked about as promising as Emil's. It made me scared and hot.

'That's the pukiest idea in the world,' I declared. 'Raising a wife! Why doesn't he go out and get one like everybody else does?'

Davy said, 'Why don't you ask him that yourself?'

'Did you ask him?'

'Nope.'

We walked a heavy fifty paces before I said, 'So he does scare you.'

Davy pulled the paint horse to a stop. We were alongside a hilltop and the moon was just rising out. It sure threw a lot of light for less than half a moon.

'He doesn't scare me,' Davy said. 'I don't think he scares me, Rube. I just listen close when he's around.'

'You listen?'

The horse nickered and threw his mane a little.

'What for?' I asked.

'I don't know. A sound to his voice. When he's there I listen close,' Davy replied. He seemed about 10 percent annoyed with me. 'It isn't the same thing as afraid.'

'Is Sara afraid?'

'Hard to say. Look there.' Davy pointed to our left. 'See him? An owl hunting – look at that, you can see his shadow.'

'Mm, yeah,' I said. No, I couldn't see him. Seemed like I couldn't ever see what Davy saw. Nor hear the things he heard. It was the old story. I wondered again just what he listened for when Mr Waltzer was around – Waltzer showing up in my mind just then, chewing a piece of red sausage.

'Hard to say,' Davy mused, as the paint got moving again – just in time, for the stillness was working the cold up my ankles – 'but Sara's real smart. She should be. I'd say she probably is.'

Afraid, he meant. But Davy was right, it was hard to say. You have to remember Sara had been raised these five years by Jape Waltzer and before that by a man degenerate enough to give away his little girl. She wasn't accustomed to conversation as you and I think of it.

'Did Mr Waltzer show you his fingers?' she inquired, during my second visit.

He hadn't made a point of it, but I remembered – the index and middle fingers of his left hand gone from the roots up.

'He amputated those fingers himself,' Sara declared. Her eyes were an arresting unreadable green. Suspecting I was being made foolish I looked at Davy, who was tilting his chair back, holding coffee in an enameled cup.

'He did honestly,' Sara said. 'He made me watch.'

'How come?'

'So I'd learn.'

'To cut off *fingers*?' Sure, my voice may've been a little high. It seemed radical instruction.

'No. It was my fault,' she said, apparently in explanation.

'But how come he did it?'

'They got mangled up in a chain.' Now that she'd started she seemed against continuing. She used short, reluctant declaratives. 'We were towing a car to a lake. He wanted to dump it in. He had me driving. The chain came loose. My foot slipped off the clutch while he was hooking it back up.'

Talk about abstaining from detail. Can you imagine the mileage someone like Swede would've gotten from such a grim episode? Except, as Sara'd already pointed out, her penalty for the slipped clutch was being forced to watch Jape Waltzer take a hatchet and lay the ruined fingers across a stump. Perhaps the sight depressed narrative ardor. Urged, she revealed these particulars: Jape rolled his left sleeve to above the elbow. He laid the hatchet blade first in a saucepan into which he'd uncorked whiskey. Sara he stationed with paper sack on a three-legged stool next the stump. He took the fingers separately with two clean strokes, pausing to blow after the first but not cursing or making utterance. He sweated plenty but it was only sweat, not blood, nor did his hair turn white or his mood turn permanently for the worse.

He did make Sara dispose of the fingers, though. She had to pick them up in her own and drop them in the paper sack. She didn't want to, but Jape told her to get it done before he was finished or there would be punishment. He was busy at that moment with needle and suture. She picked up the canceled digits and threw them sack and all in the crackling stove.

I woke close to noon short of breath and with reinstated fever – woke from a rolling-mutter sleep when Dad came in my room and took my hand.

'Let me hear you breathe,' he said.

I sucked up what I could.

'Pretty short, my friend. Let me get some water boiling.'

'Do I have to?' I was hot; steam would poach me alive. I could breathe well enough to smile and did so like some begging dog.

'All right, let me see if Roxanna's got an aspirin somewhere.' He smiled back and I saw he was wearing good clothes: his suntan khakis and a blue chambray button-down. He was clean-shaven and his hair was combed back and he looked better tended than usual, though at this moment he also looked anxious, leaning forward to lay a hand on my brow.

'Dad, is it Sunday?'

'Nope, Thursday.'

'You're all dressed up.'

'Oh. Well.' He looked at me as though I'd thrown him a hard one, which surprised me, as did his decision a moment later to swing away.

'Reuben, I've decided to court Roxanna. What do you think of that?'

I thought it was perfect, of course, though a foregone conclusion, even to a dull study like myself.

He seemed pleased with my approval. 'You understand, as a courting man I ought to look my best.'

'You look great,' I told him. He did, too – his shirt cuffs were rolled back smooth and his hands and forearms looked ropy and fast, even at rest.

'All right then,' he conjectured, 'what do you think of my chances?'

'Your chances?'

'Of winning her hand.'

That he would put such a question to me so directly – well, it sat me right up. I felt older, packed with consequence, and also cautious lest I say something dumb. 'How's it going so far?'

Straight-faced but with a shine back of it he said, 'I believe she regards me respectfully.'

Well, he had to gauge his chances better than that.

He had to remember how happy she'd been when he got back from his outing with Mr Andreeson. He had to remember the press of her hand when he came in the door – I sure remembered it, and it wasn't even my hand that got pressed.

'Oh, it's more than respectfully,' I said, and started to tell about the exchange we'd had when Roxanna was making the pie – how Swede said she wasn't going to let us leave no matter what, and Roxanna replied *Neither am I* – but Dad fended off this encouragement with a question.

'Did you like being here with her, while I was gone? You and Swede?'

I nodded.

'I thought you did. I'm glad.' He stood up. 'I like it myself.' He really did look good, a clean-shaven courting man with quick arms and steady eyes. He had to know that Roxanna loved him already, but he wouldn't have me pointing it out. Who could blame him? No doubt Dad had thought his pursuing days long over. Why sprint through such sweet country? How often does a man get to use phrases like 'winning her hand'? And it wasn't just talk; he truly meant to win it. He set himself toward her like an athlete. He slept in the cold trailer and spent most of each day there. He stopped entering the house casually. He knocked for admittance. Swede and I missed his constant presence, yet when he arrived the very light seemed to change – like light bouncing in off June maples. And Roxanna, always lovely now, Roxanna at his knock would look around at Swede and me as though all this were as unnecessary as it was wonderful, and she'd go to the door and there Dad would be in his best clothes, suit coat, often a hothouse carnation in hand. He assumed nothing. There was a poor nursery west of Grassy Butte, an old man's hobby, a little morgue of a Quonset greenhouse. A feeble flower is better than none, and it was my impression, for I accompanied him there more than once, that even that greenhouse became better lit and warmer for Dad's frequent visits. The old man, in baggy brown pants and suspenders, liked to tell Dad he was nuts. That romance was a detour men took from whatever work was theirs in life. Dad agreed with everything in the most cheerful fashion, and the old man sold him flowers for next to nothing.

One day we walked in from a blistering wind and there was a ruined guitar propped in a corner like a dead plant. Though scaly and fretworn, its top had a courtly arch like a violin's, with S-shaped holes each side of the strings. The old man asked was Dad a musician. No. The old man picked up the guitar in his blemished hands and turned it on its axis. He pointed out a wide crack running the length of the back, also a place where the binding at back and side had pulled apart. Dad admired the instrument, repeating he was no musician. The old man informed us the guitar had been made by a revered Spaniard late in the previous century. The top was carved from a piece of clear cedar. Rotating it again he displayed yet another crack, a hairline fault high on the neck. He'd been playing songs for his wife, the two of them picnicking the summer of 1922 on a broad rock in the middle of a stream – there'd been drought but no one knew the term *dust bowl* then or had any notion what was coming – and he'd stooped for a bottle of soda and smacked the guitar headfirst on the rock. Fearing the neck would break off entirely he'd unstrung the instrument and not played it since. A timid decision, the old man said. He regretted it. He flexed the guitar in his two hands. The neck seemed strong. Fix the back and side, he told Dad, and the guitar would play.

Dad replied for the third time that he was no musician, though now his face was alight, and he held the guitar carefully and looked at the old man as though he were some gruff uncle who couldn't be bothered to look back.

Boy Ready

Not to linger on it, but I was getting worse, a fact that seeped in the night Swede volunteered to wash dishes without me. 'Go up to bed,' she said, taking my plate and glass out of my hands. 'That wheeze is awful.'

'Thanks.'

'You want me to boil some water?'

'Sure.'

'You want Dad?'

I did, but he'd disappeared suddenly – I was too tired to wonder where.

'You want me to pound your back?'

Not right then I didn't.

'Go on up,' she said, reaching down the vinegar.

But I didn't want to go upstairs alone. I wanted to sit on the bottom step where I could see Swede. I wanted to listen to her talk. Upstairs there'd be nothing to hear but my own gaspy noises. Also, the stairs looked steep.

'Tell me about Sunny' – I took a breath – 'up in the secret valley.'

But she turned on me, not to be fooled with. I went. I recall the climb as tougher than my ascent to the hills that first time seeking Davy. Tougher by far. I leaned in the dark stairwell to rest. Down in the kitchen Swede banged and rinsed. I climbed a few

301

stairs. Of course I'd had times like this before. Of course I expected to bounce back. But four days had passed, and I knew it was bad to still be waiting. For the bounce, I mean. The stairwell now began to turn slowly as if dangling. I sat on the steps and dozed against the wall.

'Reuben?'

That was Swede's frightened whisper – there in the cold dark I had just entered a dream about freezing in the west bedroom at August Shultz's.

'Can you hear me, Rube?'

Smelling brine I opened my eyes. She was halfway up the steps, holding a steaming pan and looking at me in alarm.

'Oh,' I said.

'Are you okay?'

'Sure.'

'My gosh, Reuben – couldn't you even make it upstairs?'

I got to my feet, embarrassed and scared. 'Sure – I just got tired – see?' With Swede behind me I held to the railing and went up briskly enough the rest of the way.

'I brought you some steam; here's a towel,' she said, stuffing pillows behind me on the bed. Steam was the last thing I wanted, being already muzzy with fever, but unless I gained more air I was afraid of falling asleep again and right in front of Swede, who was pulling up a chair.

'Should I read to you now?' she asked.

She stayed a long time, reading Psalms against fear and twice rising to reboil the brine. But my lungs wouldn't loosen. I remember the room veering slowly and my eyesight tilting spotstruck around it. Swede pounded my back without result. I asked where Dad was and she said, Gone off with Roxanna she didn't know where. I wished he'd come sit by me and pray. The muscles in my legs and chest needled. Dr Nokes had described to me how oxygen is shipped round the body by arteries and capillaries, and it seemed to me these vessels were docking empty.

Meantime Dad was gone off courting Roxanna.

At this a dread realization occurred: since arriving at this house, we'd had no miracles whatever.

I shut my eyes and went back: we'd slipped through the claws of the state patrol. We'd driven hours on an empty tank. We'd taken rooms here – and then what?

You'll rightly point out plenty of subsequent wonders: Davy being encamped practically outside Roxanna's door. The alighting of Roxanna herself inside our motherless lives. But in that dark hour I thought only that it had been a long time since Dad charged me in the name of God to draw my first breath. Since he walked by grace above the earth or touched a torn saddle and healed it clean.

And I thought, without a miracle, exactly what chance do I have?

I decided then to tell Swede about Davy. I opened my eyes and she was still there reading aloud, crouched forward into a verse.

'I know where he is,' I said.

'*In the mountainous Eden unseen,*' she replied patiently. The phrase sounded familiar, and should have – she'd only just read it.

'I have a little more, if you'd like,' she said, and I realized she was risking some new Sundown on me. My lungs eased a quarter inch and I nodded to her to continue.

From a spire of stone Sunny watched for his own,
For his raven-haired intrepid bride.
For she'd sworn to seek his Arcadian peak,
Her life to spend by his side

Then a rider appeared on a day stale and seared
And approached through the undulate heat,

And her horse had the stride of a wearisome ride –
Of a horse too long on its feet.

But deep in the distance and churning up smoke,
Who are the riders come charging for broke?

Well, nuts, I knew who those riders were. They were some dirty posse been trying all this time to track Sunny down. Unable to do it honorably, they were now trailing his bride – his intrepid bride – to his hideout. And she so weary and faint.

'What's the matter?' Swede said, for at this I felt such grief I'd taken the towel and made a tent of it over my head.

'Do you hate it?' she demanded.

I shook my head, but I guess in a way I did hate it. Normally I wouldn't have – normally I'd have seen that posse as you no doubt see it, as a chance for Sunny to shine, and in front of his wife too. But my whole body mourned for air. I was hot and sick and wanted Dad to walk in.

'It's just more trouble,' I said, a great knot in my throat. 'Nothing ever goes right for Sunny. Can't you make something turn out okay once?'

'But it's going to turn out okay.' Swede paused, alarmed enough to bend principle. 'Should I tell you what's gonna happen? I haven't written it yet, but listen, Reuben – I'll tell you!' And she did, and as you'd expect Sunny rode down out of his mountain and swept his brave wife from her failing mount, and there was a wondrous gunfight among the rocks, whittling down the posse quite a bit, and the two of them worked their way under relentless fire back up the mountainside, where, yes, the stick of dynamite came into play.

'And then the whole valley's theirs for the rest of their lives, and apple trees and fish in the stream and good pasture for their animals,' Swede said. 'You see?'

You know what, though, it was no relief. In fact it was worse; for as she spoke of this perfect valley all I could see was Davy and the rotten shack he lived in, with its windy chinks and its dark pig and its frightful nutcase awaiting the world's destruction. Arcadian peak my eye. Again I was gripped with the need to spill all to Swede. I had the conviction my lungs weren't going to improve. That this time the bounce wasn't coming. Heavy with fever and unconfessed sin I said, 'Swede, will you not get mad if I tell you something?'

But she said, 'That's Dad—' hearing the door below us. Sure enough there was talk down there, a new voice, some bootstamping and up they came, Dad and a slumping fellow with a brown leather bag. He was Dr Nickles and he looked to have wrestled lately with some grievous contagion, so blue was the skin that hung about his eyes.

'What do you do for his lungs?' the doctor inquired, taking a seat on my bed. He shook down a thermometer and jabbed it under my tongue.

'Steam – water and vinegar,' Dad replied. 'Baking soda sometimes.'

'Doesn't do any good,' said Dr Nickles. 'Doesn't work. How long have you done it?' Now he was working a stethoscope's icy cup against my chest.

'Since he was little.'

'It's a worthless treatment.'

'It seems to have helped,' Dad said.

'Might as well have been crossing your fingers,' Dr Nickles muttered, moving the stethoscope an inch and listening again.

'We'd be grateful for any alternative you might suggest,' Dad said.

Dr Nickles moved the scope again. 'Breathe.'

I did my best.

'You got a flock of sparrows in there, boy. You coughing anything up?'

'No.'

305

'Feel like you need to?'

I shook my head.

'Turn around.'

He rammed the scope between my shoulder blades. You'd think it would've warmed up.

'Well, no pneumonia. Not yet. Try not to get it, young man. You're a full-blown asthmatic, has anyone told you that?'

'What would you advise, doctor?' Dad's delivery was crisp; you'll recall his laying Dr Nokes out cold, the night I was born.

'I'd advise getting him to the hospital in Fairfax till his lungs loosen up—'

'All right,' Dad said.

'—except the hospital's full of flu.' The doctor smiled, a ghastly expression. 'Influenza, the worst in years. It'd finish your boy here, I think.' Dr Nickles plucked the thermometer and read it. 'Indeed, yes. Finish him.' He enjoyed talking this way; truly, it lit him right up. Snapping open the bag he produced a handkerchief, spread it on the bed, and laid forth a brown bottle, capped syringe, alcohol and cotton. Though anxious regarding shots, the sight of these makings cheered me. Evidently Dr Nickles felt I might yet avoid being finished. He dipped up a cotton ball and asked for my arm.

'I'm going to give you a little adrenaline boost.'

'Okay.'

He had an awful time finding a vein, though – poor Nickles, when it came to poking the needle in he got shaky, his hand actually wobbled. I looked the other way, felt the point hit, then it was gone.

'Just a second,' he said.

Again the point. This time it felt hot. I looked round. He was moving it here and there under the skin.

'Don't pull like that,' he told me. I wasn't pulling but wanted to. Then he said, 'Oh!' like an exasperated aunt, and held up the syringe, which he'd broken off

306

in my arm. So it was back to the bag for more makings.
Also a tweezer. This time he took the other arm and hit
it first try. I remember the solid hot-licorice feel of the
adrenaline coming in.

Dad came back upstairs after Dr Nickles left. I'd been
sitting up in bed waiting to feel something, but except
for a certain alertness there was no change.

'I'm sorry, Reuben,' Dad said.

'That's okay – it's just a little bruise.' I thought he
was talking about the botched needle.

He sat on the bed looking slack and pale, hardly the
handsome courting man of recent days. He said, 'I
would take your place, son.'

I knew he would.

'Reuben, the water and vinegar – does it help?'

'Most times.'

'You can feel things loosen up?'

'I'm pretty sure.'

'Well,' Dad said, 'that's the treatment Dr Nokes
believes in.'

'It helps – really.'

'How about now? The adrenaline.'

'Yes,' I told him. The truth was, while we talked I'd
developed the sensation of standing up. That's my best
shot at describing it – when I looked down at my lap-
folded hands they appeared midgety and remote.

'You should try and sleep,' Dad said.

But there's little sleep for the adrenaline-charged.
You mostly dream of this or that noisome ordeal. For
me motors chugged unmuffled behind shut doors,
obscuring shouted conversations. Tin pans rang.
Trains hurled by. I was trying to ask Swede why a
person never hears of asthmatic outlaws. Finger in one
ear she replied they existed but rarely excelled. She
told a story about one who in a spectacular lapse of
judgment took up burglary and continually wheezed
so loud he woke his intended victims. In the dream I
was wrenching every muscle in the effort to breathe,

307

and waking from it the work was no less hard. Lying there I thought of Dr Nickles with his shaky hands, and how little good he'd done me, and it seemed a strange and heartbreaking comedown that Dad of all people had gone and fetched him here. And I thought too of Jape Waltzer and the way he'd removed his own mangled fingers, not one but two, and sewed up the places himself; and the idea occurred, if the great crowd of strangers were gathered who had in their ignorance told me *Just breathe*, that Waltzer would stand out as the most qualified to say it.

The bounce, and it was a good one, pulled in just before sunup. I went downstairs in the cool gloom and Dad was at the kitchen table drinking coffee with Martin Andreeson.

'Morning, Rube,' said the putrid fed. He was slouched comfortably in his chair, legs crossed, coat open. His fedora lay on the table next to Dad's King James, which was turned, I recall, to Romans.

'Morning.'

'You're improved,' Dad said, looking me over.

'A lot,' I said. I wanted to be suspicious of Andreeson, but he sat there so relaxed and unshaven and apparently appreciative of hospitality; there was an empty plate on the table and a spot of frosting at the corner of his mouth. Dad, too, seemed at ease – warm, in fact.

'I was sorry to hear about your lungs,' said Andreeson.

'I'm okay.'

He looked at Dad, who gave him a nod. 'Listen, Rube, I hope you'll think this is good news. I've been showing your brother's picture around – finally found the right man. Over in Amidon. He said he's seen Davy in town. Not just once, three or four times.'

Andreeson waited for me to answer. As if I knew what I wanted.

'Last time was day before yesterday,' Andreeson continued. 'Actually, he gave your brother a ride – dropped him off out of town.'

I have to be honest: this was kindly and quietly spoken. Andreeson seemed a different fed from he who'd shouldered into our home that first day with his talk of nabbing. Still, his nearness to Davy raised gooseflesh. I stood barefoot before him on the freezing linoleum.

'Go on, Martin,' Dad said.

Andreeson opened his mouth, shut it again, shook his head. 'I just want you folks to know we're going to be careful. Stay near the phone, Jeremiah.' He got to his feet. 'Reuben – we won't hurt Davy. That's a promise. From me to you.'

But I didn't want anything from him to me. It was suddenly important that he know my allegiance hadn't changed. 'You can't hurt what you can't find,' I replied, not looking at Dad.

But Andreeson smiled as he rose and laid a hand on my shoulder, saying, 'There you go.' He went out the door all business, setting the felt fedora on his head. My enemy.

That afternoon I went outside on every excuse. After such a scare they were all against it, but I was an exemplary weasel now and eased out the back in my coat and hood, breathing through a scarf to warm the air. I prayed, but the prayers were tangled and dissenting. I prayed the Lord would sort them out and answer as needed. Above all that He would hurry. For Andreeson was closing in. He'd told Dad to wait by the phone. I walked up and down beside the house, attempting to pray as Dad did, trying to picture God listening to me, but He remained unseeable, just the usual lit cloud, and in minutes the walking wore me out. I went inside and was rebuked by Swede for taking chances. She had no idea. We ate some gingersnaps and repaired to the living room, where I stretched myself on the couch. The idea was to feign sleep until Swede went upstairs and then pop outside, but I dropped off for real and dreamed a river of horses flowing along between banks, manes rippling, backs streaming sun. I woke inside a strange calm recognizable as defeat. Light entered the house pink and orange. I straggled outside, leaned against the house and squinted at the backlit hills. The light was expiring; already it was like looking into deep tea-colored water. I didn't, in fact, see Davy. But somewhere on the side of the darkening hill a horse lifted its voice to neigh. The sound had the clear distance of history.

I was to have one last night in the hills: another starry one, as you will hear, but with a moist hush to the air that was like something at full draw – a breath, an arrow.

Jape Waltzer was busy shoeing Fry. Whoever'd built the place had left behind an anvil and a makeshift forge. Jape had tacked new leathers to a bellows and was working up a glow that lit the shed.

'Reuben, I thank you,' he said, when Davy had ushered me in and I'd said my piece. That was it. He thanked me for the information and seemed otherwise unconcerned.

'He said they're getting close,' I reiterated, unsure whether Waltzer had understood. He stopped working the bellows. On the orange forge lay a horseshoe like a black cutout of itself. He picked it up with a set of longhandled tongs and looked it over doubtfully.

'Fry,' he said to the horse, who stood shortroped to a ring in the wall, 'let's try this on. Davy, his head.'

Davy took the bridle in both hands and whispered compliments to Fry while Waltzer leaned against the horse's left hip and picked up his foot. In the glow I could see fresh scrapes where Waltzer had filed the hoof smooth. I could see nail holes from the previous shoe.

'It's always the back left one he throws,' Waltzer said pleasantly, laying the hot shoe against the hoof. 'I don't know why.' It was plain he liked the work.

I said, 'It's just, he told Dad to stay by the phone.'

Waltzer set down the hoof and replaced the shoe in the forge. When he looked at me from under those brows I knew I'd said everything on the matter. Pumping the bellows he said, 'Reuben, look at these coals.'

They were beautiful, a breathing black-webbed orange.

'When they're like that, when they look like a jack-o'-lantern, they aren't hot enough.'

'They aren't?'

'No, sir. Not hot enough to soften that shoe.' He nodded at a stack of cut boards in the corner opposite Fry. 'If you'll feed some of those to the fire while I'm working the bellows, believe me, Reuben, we'll make some heat.'

What else could I do? Forgetting Andreeson for the moment I gave myself to the allure of the forge. It had a small steel door that Waltzer swung open. The fire-box was a mere cozy flame and I fed it full of boards. Waltzer slammed it shut and commenced pumping and shortly the wood hissed to incandescence and the wind blew in the forge until I heard voices inside it.

'Good, Reuben,' Waltzer said. He was panting. Steam came off his shirt. 'You see what you've done? Look at the coals!'

There was now only the faintest orange about them – as the afternoon sun is orange. They were white. Still they breathed. Already the edges of the horseshoe were white too.

This time it smoked when he fitted it to Fry's hoof. Fry snuffed and hopped but was well pinned. Waltzer wasted no time but laid shoe to anvil. A few strokes and he had it to size. He was dextrous for a man minus two left-hand fingers. Bent over Fry's upraised hoof he

311

reached to his mouth for a nail. He drew a small hammer from his boot top and tapped the nail till its point emerged from the hoof's clean slope an inch above the shoe. He drove a second nail, spat the rest into his palm and looked me over.

'Reuben, come finish,' Waltzer beckoned, hoof locked in his knees, wool shirt rolled to the elbows. He was sweating in the red gloom.

'Nail it home,' he said. I took the hammer. He showed me how to set the nail at the proper outward angle. Davy told Fry he was a good horse, a handsome horse. To this I would add longsuffering. Aiming carefully at the nail I tapped faintly away until Waltzer said, 'Do you do everything the same way you breathe? Whack it.' So I whacked it, grateful for Fry's resignation and at the nail's progress down and through. I set the remaining nails and Waltzer produced, again from his boot top, a set of snips and cut the nail points off flush with the hoof. He pocketed the points and set the hoof back on the ground, patting the ankle above it.

'Fry,' he said fondly; then, 'Thank you, Reuben. Well done.'

I looked at Davy, who winked. The forge was ebbing; it must've been cold in the three-walled shed, but I was warm and glad to be there.

We ate a midnight supper in the shack and still Waltzer would hear nothing of Andreeson. His disinterest was stunning. He turned the conversation to politics, astronomy, the science of well drilling, the superiority of beaver felt over wool. He claimed to have been born with no sense of smell but with extraordinary and compensatory taste buds; he never salted his food but accepted it as given, its natural flavor being satisfactory.

'For example, your meat there. I suspect you find it bland.'

It was a little lump of gray meat on a tin plate. It and

a boiled potato were supper. There they lay, all tired out.

'It's fine,' I replied. Of course it wasn't yams and sausages.

Waltzer said, 'It's bland. Pork is bland meat and people season it to their senseless palates. Take a bite, Reuben. Describe the flavor.'

I bit. The pork had been boiled a long time. Indeed it bore no trace of salt. It was like chewing a hank of old rope. Waltzer's eyes were alight and curious. Desperately I sought the elusive civil adjective.

'It's pretty good,' I told him.

'I commend your courtesy; but nonsense. I won't take offense. Nor will Emil. Do it for Emil, hm?'

You remember Emil.

I peered at the pork. Waltzer said, 'Go on. Assess the piquancy of Emil. It's all the memorial he's bound to get. Poor little Emil.' He was delighted the meat had a name; he couldn't use it enough.

And yet, surprisingly, knowing the pale lump before me was Emil was not disturbing. In fact it freed me up somehow. I chewed him up and swallowed him. 'It's – stiff,' I said cautiously. 'A little dry.'

Waltzer said, 'Go on.'

'It's dull. Blunt.'

'Yes, yes.' Waltzer liked this. A strange thing occurred: adjectives, generally standoffish around me, began tossing themselves at my feet. 'It's fibrous. Rough. Ropy.' I was faintly aware of insulting Sara's cookery, but Waltzer was nodding, smiling. His favor was better than the alternative. I basked in it; and it was fun, for a change, having the words. 'Dispirited, stagnant. Mortified. Vapid.' I wasn't sure what that last one meant, having heard it from Swede in a discussion about her second-grade teacher, but it had a ring.

'Well said,' Waltzer declared – the only time I recall that compliment being applied to myself.

'It tastes like cartilage,' I added, wanting to get that one in.

'Yes. Good. Now me.' Waltzer took a small mouthful and worked it efficiently. 'Mmm, yes.' He closed his eyes, swallowed, blew hard through his nostrils. 'I taste corn – not so much corn as I'd like. Kernels and husks. I taste beans. Bread. Pigweed, grass, earth, quite a lot of earth. Salt.'

I realized he was describing Emil's diet. He looked pained. 'Unfortunately, I also taste slops. It's a hard gift. I've encountered flavors in sausages it would be obscene to describe.'

Did I believe him? It doesn't matter. All this time my lungs had worked tolerably well. I understand now this was a period of grace. Waltzer went on treating me as though my presence honored him; wary as I was, his manner was winning and his talk beguiling. Sara stayed apart from us behind her wall of quilts. Later we stood outside the cabin, Waltzer pointing out constellations while Davy went to saddle Fry.

'There's the Great Ring,' he said. 'And there is the Totem; there's Hawk and Mouse, the Whale, Boy Ready.'

I could only nod. Having someone point out constellations is pleasant as long as they don't insist that you actually see them. Aside from the Dipper and Orion and the Teapot, constellations tend to hide in the stars.

'I never heard of Boy Ready,' I said, as though the others were familiar to me; so he aimed at its points one by one and related the myth of a child who lived in a city of wood, and how one night the city caught fire and burned so fiercely that by morning nothing remained but a field of fine ash. Only the boy escaped. One day a passing pilgrim saw him crouched at the river pursuing fish with his hands. The pilgrim took the boy on his horse to the next city, where he was fed and then celebrated as the tale of his survival spread.

The boy charmed all with his bravery and wit and was adopted by the king, and grew up trained in arms and letters; at last he became king himself and was wise and good. It was a passable story until Waltzer revealed that the boy had set the fire himself.

'He couldn't have!' I said.

'Of course he could. Calm down, Reuben; it's only a legend.'

But all Waltzer's constellations told such turned legends. There was the Bowsprit, about another rotten boy who slew his father while he slept and later became a fire-breathing pirate who devoured his victims' limbs and decorated the rail of his ship with their heads. This fellow tramped up and down the high seas challenging men and gods until a brave captain met him in battle, the two of them going sword and sword across decks for days without rest. At last the captain by superior craft cleft the other in two, at an angle, so that the pirate's head with one arm and shoulder thumped on the deck with a terminal snarl. Job done, the captain returned to his ship to wash for dinner and looked in his polished brass mirror. You see what's coming: the poor captain saw not his own face but the pirate's, and the nastiest grin all over it. Following this all his noble impulses fell away like a mail shirt, and he developed a wild controlling lust for jeweled plunder and an appetite for boiled legs and arms. 'So you can win the battle, Reuben' – Waltzer shrugged – 'but the war is lost long ago.'

'Crumb,' I reflected morosely, as Fry and Davy trotted up.

Waltzer put his altered hand on my head. 'Don't let it bother you,' he said.

But it did.

The next day Martin Andreeson called. The fellow who'd given Davy a lift, name of Robinson, had promised to show Andreeson the place he'd dropped him off. They'd been going to meet at the Amidon cafe, but Robinson never showed. There were three Robinsons in the phone book; Andreeson reached two; the third's telephone had been disconnected. Inquiring directions to the disconnected Robinson's house, Andreeson drove eight rugged miles along the edge of the Badlands. The house he found there was cold and boarded.

'The situation, Martin,' Dad said, 'requires prayer.'

I'd have given quite a bit to hear the fed's response. Whatever it was, Dad said, 'Of course – we'll expect to hear from you,' then hung up and called me over.

'Chest tight?' he asked – a rhetorical question, for he could hear what had become the usual wheeze.

'Yes, sir.'

'What can I do?'

He'd begun approaching it this way ever since Dr Nickles threw cold water on the vinegar treatment.

'Just pound a little.'

He turned me by the shoulders and I braced against the doorjamb while he worked my back. Except for the thumping it was a quiet morning, and when he stopped I could hear Roxanna humming in the next room.

'Better?'

'Yes, sir.'

He listened. 'Sounds about the same.'

'It's better.'

'Reuben,' he said out of nowhere, 'is there something you ought to be telling me?'

My insides jelled. 'I don't think so.'

'You're looking peaked,' he said. 'It wears, this whole thing, doesn't it?'

So it was only my health he was worried about.

'I'm going to the trailer and pray for your brother,' he said, such sadness in his face it was as though he knew something I didn't, instead of the reverse.

* * *

316

No word arrived from Andreeson that day. Or the next. What did arrive was a northwest wind that sang against the house. In the Dakotas it needn't snow to blizzard. The wind came low and fast, peeling the drifts. From her window upstairs Swede and I watched a cavalry charge minus the horses; wide chunks of snow tore themselves off the ground and flung forward, tumbling to white sand that coiled and rushed like Huns. It was a ground wind, a ground blizzard. Picture a storm to match any in wildness but only eight feet high. From Swede's window it was like looking down on a violent cloud. The barn protruded – its door invisible down inside the storm – and the handle of a snow shovel stuck in a drift, and Roxanna's red birdhouse on a tilting pole. Above the storm it was actually sunny; we could see the gleaming tin dome of a neighbor's silo miles away. But when we went downstairs drafts came from everywhere, and the light was gray and discouraging, and on the west wall an electrical outlet glowed with frost, a foot from a ticking radiator.

The wind lasted two days. Thinking of the cabin in the hills, with its shrunk chinking and corroded stove, I worried for Davy. Also for Sara.

'Swede,' I wondered, 'how long till you'd freeze to death in a wind like this?'

'You mean with your clothes on?'

I bridled. 'Well, what do you think? How many people are going to go out in this with nothing on?'

'Nobody *goes out* with nothing on. It's something that happens when you begin to freeze; the thermometer in your brain gets turned around. You start thinking you're hot, got too much on; you figure you'll cool off.'

I was buying none of this. Couldn't afford to. Picturing Davy all bundled up in this wind was bad enough.

'It's true, Reuben. It's like a mirage, the snow turns

to desert. Once, two college boys snowshoeing out in Wyoming – they found 'em froze solid, standing up. Snow to their waists, nothing on but boxer shorts, police couldn't fit 'em in the car so they tied 'em on top, like in deer season . . .'

Goodness knows how long Swede might've continued in this way, so I said, 'What if you were in a rotten old cabin, cracks in the walls and the wind blowing through?'

Well, that set Swede on another track even more horrific. She related a story about some troop of outcasts running out of food at the onset of a recordbook blizzard; and how hungry they all got, eating their belts and boottops, though not their lone horse, which had sensibly escaped; and how the weaker among them skidded away from reality and started gnawing their own limbs, smacking their lips yet making, you'd have to say, no nutritional gain.

As a tale of grue it was badly timed; Waltzer, too, had spoken of cannibalism, and in fact it seemed a thing he might practice without remorse. I descended to morbid reflections. Suppose the storm lasted a week? How much firewood did they have in that cabin – and how much food? With both Davy and Sara on hand, I was certain Waltzer would eat Davy first; he had other plans for Sara. I spent a vicious wish on Andreeson: if only *he* were out there with Waltzer. Then bring on a blizzard! But this bit of drama didn't satisfy as I'd supposed it might; the fed, to my puzzlement, seemed less putrid than he once had. Sitting by Swede as she read silently on the couch, I counted six of my breaths to each of hers. What I wanted was a great big inhale or, failing that, a little peace. I ventured out to the Airstream.

Dad was playing the antique guitar. Stepping into the dimness of the barn I heard its soft strings humming one lovely chord and then another. He was playing slowly yet precisely, for I heard no orphan

318

notes. I stood listening while he played any number of quiet hymns, stopping sometimes to tune a string up or down. I don't mean he was already Segovia or anything; it was only days since he'd repaired the instrument with a tube of airplane glue and a Spanish windlass tied up from long johns. Still, he had worked out many of the songs we loved in those days, 'Amazing Grace,' and 'Cast Your Eyes upon Jesus,' 'It Is Well with My Soul'; also 'Happy Trails,' and 'The Cowboy's Lament.' Sometimes Dad sang, sometimes hummed; sometimes there was a long search for this or that desired chord. I could've listened all day. When he stopped and I heard him moving about inside the trailer, I eased from the barn and shut the door.

Inside, Roxanna was stirring up bread, her latest hothouse blooms in a tin vase on the table, soup asteam in a pan just as though we were a family not perched at the edge of great loss. Even Swede seemed to have reached some sort of harbor. She sat in her room above the blizzard, fomenting joy for Sunny and his wife now that they'd obliterated the entrance to their secret valley, as well as about half that rotten posse.

The wind blew through a second night, stratifying snowbanks and encumbering roads. Then it wore out. The house fell quiet. After breakfast the others went out to shovel – I was no good for it, but Dad said someone had to stay by the phone. I did so all morning but Andreeson did not call. The afternoon idled along. I read *Last of the Mohicans* twice through – Classics Illustrated – then got out Roxanna's scrapbook and revisited Jonas Work's obit. None of this warded off agitation. None of it kept bad pictures away: pictures of Davy drawn and freezing, of snow sifting through the unchinked shack. Concentrate as I might on Hawkeye and Uncas, Jape Waltzer's tale of the cannibal pirate kept telling itself to my brain. Starring

Jape, of course – it was a part written exactly for him, with his fetching confidence and lunatic glint. Like the pirate, you could imagine Jape Waltzer winning even when he lost.

This time the county plows reached us by late afternoon. Hearing nothing from Andreeson Dad called his motel in Rathton. The owner, also desk clerk, took a message. His annoyance was audible in Roxanna's kitchen. He told Dad the federal man paid his bill readily enough but was a great deal of trouble. Sometimes he left for days, returning to his room in the small hours. It disturbed the neighbors. And always the phone calls – federal men received many phone calls and there was no telling when. The owner told Dad he was a businessman, not a secretary. From the office he had to pull on his coat and boots and go down five doors to Mr Andreeson's room; the messages were piling up; it was too cold for this.

'When did he leave?' Dad asked.

Suspending complaint the owner thought this over. Early the previous day he'd taken a call from one Mr Robinson. He was in Amidon, at the cafe. Andreeson was glad for the message – had, in fact, the owner grouchily acknowledged, tipped him a two-dollar bill for its delivery. Not long afterward, the motel lot already turning humpy with drifts, the owner had watched Andreeson's tan Mercury creeping away through the wind.

Dad hung up the phone. He stood to the window and looked west. The snow lay hard and clean-shaven and the broken hills rose up out of it – I don't guess you could find more inhospitable geography. But the wind had stopped and the cold sun put such an edge on hills and barn they might've been razored from a magazine.

'Rube,' he said, 'that Andreeson's a smart fellow, but he doesn't know one thing about winter in North Dakota.'

A thought dropped from nowhere, like a big snake.

Dad plucked his coat off the hook, heading to the trailer. I plucked mine to follow, then nearly sat down. My legs trembled, hips and kneecaps loose as dominoes.

'Something the matter?' Dad inquired.

'Yes, sir.' I didn't want to say it – the thought. Yet it coiled around me, irresistible. It squeezed, and I yielded. 'Mr Andreeson's in bad trouble.'

He looked at me, and I at his shoes.

'What is it, Reuben?'

But the snake had me so hard I could barely speak. I sagged to the floor to shiver. What I saw was Waltzer, telling of his first sight of Davy in the Amidon cafe. I saw Andreeson, encouraged – only days ago – having shown Davy's picture to the right man at last. Then Waltzer again, from my final visit: comfortable, talking easily, refusing all concern at my insistence that Andreeson was drawing near.

'Reuben,' Dad said.

It was too much to manage all at once, so I only replied, 'His name isn't Robinson, it's Jape Waltzer – and he's with Davy – and he's going to kill Mr Andreeson.'

The Ledger of Our Decisions

So I turned at last. So I betrayed my brother. Before daylight next morning we assembled horseback at Lonnie Ford's ranch. I say we. The party included Mr Ford; the young county sheriff Mike Lanz; a federal investigator, Harper Juval, who'd driven in from Bismarck; and three ad hoc local deputies. The deputies were skittish, pleased at this chance to saddle up with scabbarded Winchesters and go hunting fugitives in the snow. Mr Juval looked them over without expression. Two hours earlier a rancher had found Andreeson's Mercury parked empty on a county road – actually blocking the road, snow to its fenders. As the hilltops pinked it was briefly argued whether I had any business going.

'What are you, boy? About nine?' This was Mr Juval.

'Eleven, sir.'

'He's the only one of us who's made the trip, Harper,' said Lonnie Ford. 'At least he can tell us if we're going right.'

Of course I'd never made the trip in daylight, so my usefulness was suspect in any case. Juval examined me with distaste. 'Mr Land,' he said to Dad, 'it's your call. You comfortable with your boy going?'

Dad wanted to go himself, but Juval had nixed that the night before.

'He's up to it,' Dad said. 'I'm taking you at your word, now'; for Juval had promised that Davy would be taken quietly and without violence.

Juval nodded. Dad looked at me. I saw he was counting on me to see them quickly to the cabin. He wanted it over with – Davy safe, Andreeson alive. Perhaps he also believed that with Davy's little brother close by, the lawmen would be less apt to shoot.

'Let's go then,' Juval said, while Lonnie Ford boosted me onto a shaggy bay mare. I remember Dad, standing in the awakening barnyard, clapping softly to keep the blood in his fingers.

We rode single file into the hills, heading for what Mr Ford supposed from my description to be an old line cabin that had belonged to his ranch long before. It lay an indeterminate distance west in a valley fertile enough to offer some small pasture yet remote enough that no cattle had grazed there in a generation. Also the pasture had cracked open to lignite in the late Thirties and caught fire, which had a bewildering effect on livestock; for all Mr Ford knew, it was burning to this day.

So I felt we were heading the right direction, though you may imagine what little comfort it gave me.

Probably it won't surprise you that Swede took all this badly. That I'd kept Davy a secret from her she judged the deepest kind of lie; that I'd revealed him didn't expunge the sin but compounded it. I was both liar *and* traitor. I was an apostate. Before gaining forgiveness I was to endure any number of historical comparisons, and not just with standard traitors like Judas and Brutus and Benedict Arnold. These were a fine start but hardly enough for Swede, who remembered off the top of her head that it was little brother Ramón who'd betrayed the great *bandido* Joaquín Murieta, whose bottled head still exists in a certain tavern in Texas; you could go in this very day and pay a dollar to lift a dark curtain and see it. She knew of others, too. Any hopes I had of her rage being softened by my obvious misery proved groundless. She heard me out, then went upstairs to fling a tantrum unequaled in her history. I heard papers flying, weeping mixed with various wordless growls, and the sound of a pillow being kicked with tremendous gusto. That last, I knew, was me.

It was a longer ride than I remembered. We rode up into timbered breaks that felt familiar and along ridges of scrub pine and juniper where it seemed I'd never been. Wind had so driven the snow that in places a laden horse could walk atop it leaving only shallow tracks; but mostly they sank to their knees, shod hooves tossing up traces of sand or scoria or fine-needled ferns. There was time to roll all manner of films in my head. Bad endings prevailed. In order of riding I came second, after Mr Ford and before Mr Juval, the three deputies strung out behind.

After a time we descended a long even slope where there was room for Mr Juval to come abreast of me. He was on a bright palomino Mr Ford had been loath to saddle; I believe, in fact, that Juval paid extra for the palomino, and indeed he looked good on the animal as they came alongside.

'We going the right way then?' he asked. I feared his attention. Miserably I admitted to having no idea.

He rode at my side awhile without comment. He was older than Dad, wore a shortbrim cowboy hat, and had a clipped white beard and a web of wrinkles under his eyes. He sat straightbacked on the palomino, floating easily above the horse as it slugged through the snow.

'I consider Martin Andreeson a friend,' he said, after a time.

I nodded.

'You don't, I guess.'

'No, sir.'

We were riding through a fairly open valley I might have recognized. But the wind had erased any tracks; we could've been the first people through in years.

'Well,' he said, 'I suppose you feel like a Hall of Fame turncoat just now. Taking us to your brother.'

'Yes, sir, I do.' Why did Mr Juval want to talk about it? He knew how I felt. Arriving late, he'd stayed up much of the night talking to Dad – they'd called me down in the wee hours so Juval could ask me particulars. What weapons I'd seen in the cabin. What stocks of ammunition and food. At his request I drew a layout of the place showing windows, door, stove and chimney. He wondered whether I'd got a peek at Sara's quarters. He said the more I could tell him, the better things would be for Davy; he said this four or five times.

'You wish you'd kept quiet?' he asked.

'Davy's not the problem for your friend Andreeson,' I told him. 'It's Jape Waltzer.'

'So you mentioned.'

Last night Mr Juval had seemed, if not entirely in our corner, at least leaning toward it. When I'd told him about Waltzer – his crazy mind, his ambivalence about Andreeson's proximity, even Waltzer's own characterization of himself as a wolf to Davy's squirrel – Mr Juval had listened with evident interest. He'd made notes on a yellow pad as though each detail confirmed this Waltzer as a long-sought badman it would be an honor to catch. He'd said *yes*, *yes*.

Now he seemed much less accommodating.

Anxious for reassurance I took an ingratiating tone. 'Mr Juval, what's Jape Waltzer wanted for? What did he do?'

The slope had leveled off and his palomino was edging restlessly ahead. Juval reined back long enough to give me a look I've never forgotten – not a mean look, or disrespectful, the look perhaps of years spent in disappointment. He said, 'Son, you got to remember something. Your brother killed two boys last year, then broke jail. This Robinson, Waltzer, whatever his name is – I don't know him from Adam.' He let the reins fall against the horse's neck and trotted up to talk to Lonnie Ford.

We were getting close, riding now through country I knew for certain, yet we'd slowed. Lonnie Ford, leading, stopped to squint from time to time. The wind was getting teeth, lashing the horses' tails along their flanks and tilting Mr Juval's cowboy hat over his eyes. Under this faltering progress I had time to think it all over. To doubt what had appeared conclusive. The nearer we came to the cabin the more likely it seemed that the enigmatic Robinson really wasn't Jape Waltzer; that he was simply what Mr Andreeson had supposed, a fellow who'd given Davy a ride, then acquired cold feet about talking to a federal man. So what that Andreeson hadn't found him in the phone book – lots of people didn't have telephones. So what that Waltzer was unconcerned when I arrived all aflap about the putrid fed. It was senseless to give meaning to his reactions; the man talked about sea monsters, he steered by stars of his own invention. The idea emerged – seeming true the moment it wiggled free – that I'd betrayed my brother needlessly. That Andreeson, while he'd gone out foolishly in a dangerous storm, was in no danger from any Robinson.

I sat the bay mare, recognition of my blunder attached to my heart like a leech.

Up ahead Lonnie Ford, who'd been consulting with Mr Juval in some serious matter, turned his horse and loped back to me through the snow. Unlike the self-contained Mr Ford of my constructions, he was a nervous man with clear misery in his face. He rode up so our two horses met shoulder to shoulder; they rubbed necks, but Lonnie didn't say anything to me. Or even look at me; he kept gazing off to his left.

'Is something the matter, Mr Ford?'

He nodded. I saw he was a man for whom words were a desperate problem. I felt bad for him, though it did give me a lift somehow.

'I lease the ranch,' he said, after another hard moment. 'I never saw this cabin before. I told Mr Juval that.'

It took me a second to see where this placed us.

'Does any of this look right to you?' asked Lonnie Ford. He looked at me sideways – *anguished* is not too strong a word – then nodded at the hills around us. 'Any of it?'

My first thought was that God in my disconsolate hour had slid open a hatch. Lonnie Ford didn't know where we were! The fellow guiding us to Davy was asking *me* for directions! Suppressing dizzy yelps I took stock. We were on the west gradient of a gently beveled hill, ringed above with twisted jackpine and scrub juniper and larger trees like cedars. Ahead to the left rose exhilarating cutrock cliffs of sandstone and scoria and some schoolbrick-colored clay.

I knew where we were, all right.

Knew, moreover, if we bore to the left – behind the cliffs – we'd be steering away from Davy.

Lonnie Ford said quietly, 'I *told* Mr Juval.'

Behind us the deputies – blown clean of jocularity – had begun to mutter. Up front Juval sat the palomino, looking like a man set on winning by any means.

Someday, you know, we're going to be shown the great ledger of our recorded decisions – a dread concept you nonetheless know in your deepest soul is true.

'We have to bear left,' I told Lonnie Ford.

It was a slick climb in places, a steep one in others, and no one really wished to make it. According to my misdirection Lonnie Ford trotted forward and I saw him pointing and nodding with something like assurance. Juval reached in a saddlebag and withdrew a large pair of binoculars and trained them on the slope of rock and snowswept talus that would take us up behind the cliffs. I remember he peered through those glasses for a long time, then put them down and turned and looked at me, a trenchant gaze I couldn't return. He swung about and up we went.

We climbed strung out, so a skidding horse wouldn't panic the others. Perhaps it didn't seem as bad an ascent to me as to the rest – no natural rider, I exercised no authority over the mare, whose footing was like a guarantee. At the bottom lay a repose of burst sandstone, as though a vast slab or reef had breached from the height of land and slid rupturing down. The route then narrowed to a generous U, higher on right than left and occupied by a tribe of twisted dwarf evergreens. Only gradually did the incline become less manageable, narrowing first to a V, so it was like walking in the bow of a very small boat, then lifting before us until we leaned close over the horses' necks and felt gravity looking for a hold. Briefly I feared for my deception – that Mr Juval would throw off the climb as impossible and turn us back on course. Perhaps he would've, had the way been wide enough for a horse to turn.

Yet we gained the top. For a steep instant below the rim the mare seemed to balance upright – my heels at her haunches, arms round her neck, face in her mane – then she lurched and broke forward, coming out on level earth. There was the big cold sky moving over us. Juval and Lonnie Ford had dismounted to wait, their animals blowing and shaking their heads.

I confess to a certain exultation. My artifice had worked. The cabin lay somewhere to the right, in a valley; our way now lay clearly to the left. We were on a mesa of sorts where wind had removed all snow except a tan layer from which dead grasses poked. I slipped off the mare and stood beside her like the other men while the deputies struggled over the crest one by one. There on the mesa we enjoyed a prevalent good humor, even if my reasons were unique. Sheriff Lanz poured coffee in a thermos lid and passed it around. The deputy who'd followed me up, name of Fitger, came over and told me he was sorry to be hunting my brother. Lonnie Ford – and this ached – shook my hand. His eyes were so grateful they appeared damp, though this was probably an effect of the wind. Only Juval remained detached. While the rest of us stretched with relief, he swung back on the palomino and trotted to a small rise atop the cliffs. Profiled against sky he looked like Robert E. Lee. He had his binoculars out.

'Ford,' he called.

The rancher was sipping coffee. He sighed, handed it off and heaved aboard. He came alongside Juval, who passed him the glasses. Adjusting them to his eyes he looked over the valley. The wind snaked across the mesa. I'd been warm from the climb, but no more. The grasses hissed like wire.

Ford dismounted. Sat down cross-legged. Elbows on knees he leaned into the binoculars.

Next thing the two of them were trotting back to us, Juval looking official and stormy and Ford unreadable.

Juval coughed and spat. 'It's back down then, gentlemen,' said he, and with barely a pause rode to the rim we'd all been so pleased to master and dropped over. Nobody spoke. We were listening to the palomino's hooves sliding on rock and dirt. I felt people looking at me, but perhaps no one was. I know Lonnie Ford wasn't; for later he didn't look at me even when I wished he would, or ever again so far as I know. In a few words he told the men we'd come the wrong way. Mr Juval had discerned the cabin lying down the valley. You might expect some outburst from men so informed, but there was none. I felt instead a hush. To say I felt like a caught sneak doesn't touch it. I was a boy caught deceiving honest men.

I went over next to last, just a single deputy behind. If you've never essayed a decline like that on the back of a horse I don't know what to tell you. There's a separation from ground and a hopeless union with the animal as down you go – can't hear a thing but gravel clatter, absolutely can't steer. The mare laid her ears back, splayed her front feet, set haunches to earth, and slid. Far below I could see Juval and the sheriff standing beside their mounts. Lonnie Ford was in front of me by some yards. His horse, a big-barreled Roman-nosed quarter, began to skid sideways. I saw it happen – hindquarters bearing right, hooves scrabbling, the horse seeking balance; then its wayward back legs struck a boulder and the horse went down. Mr Ford was a man of size, but he just disappeared. The horse slid forward on its side, neck up, trying to rise. You'd have thought it would slow. It flipped once, hooves everyplace, then hit a steep drop and flipped again. All this time I was skidding along behind on the mare. At last the gradient eased and the down horse stopped. It lay in the path at an alien angle. My mare clattered to a halt beside it, the last deputy arriving behind me in a spray of broken stone.

'Where's Ford?' the deputy said, swinging down.

We couldn't see him. The way that horse had slid it wouldn't have surprised me to have to gather Ford up a limb at a time. We did locate one spurred boot sticking out from under the horse. There was nothing in the boot but a sock.

The horse was in awful shape. After that second flip it couldn't raise its head and lay trembling on the rubble. The others had joined us in mute shock except for Juval, who passed us at an angry trot, ordering, 'Don't you shoot that animal!' He headed back up the hill and stopped beside a ragged dirty clot mostly hidden by a dwarf pine. He didn't immediately get off the horse but gazed down at the clot like you would at something loathsome.

That Lonnie Ford lived at all commends the resilient design of humans, the ribcage in particular. Ford's ribcage, and it was a big one, was rolled over not once but twice by an entire American quarter horse, yet his organs remained whole. The rest of Ford was worse off. His arm lay twisted behind in such a way Sheriff Lanz diagnosed a broken collarbone. Over one shoulder a hole had been rubbed through jacket, shirt, and skin; he was down to muscle. His face on the same side was swelling purple as we watched. The only place on him that looked okay was his bare right foot. He was unconscious, which relieved us all.

The sheriff had done stints as an ambulance man and had a kit in his saddlebag. He worked on Ford where he lay, checking ribs, pasting up the shoulder, easing the arm out to the side. When with Juval's help he realigned the collarbone, Ford woke a moment to thrash, then sank as though clubbed. The sheriff directed a jury-rigged stretcher of poles and tied coats. While they moved Ford to even ground Juval put a hand on my neck and steered me to a place some yards from the others.

He asked, 'Did you misdirect me on purpose?'

When I didn't answer immediately Juval said, 'Son?'

His tone implied, if not gentleness, at least understanding.

'Yes – I did, sir.'

Juval cuffed the right side of my head so hard I spun to my knees. Next thing he gripped one shoulder and set me back on my feet, saying, 'Listen to me now.' It was difficult, as a high tone occupied my right ear, but Juval earnestly told me five or six specific things he found discouraging about my character. If you don't mind I'd rather not restate them, but they were by and large true, and seeing no advantage in disputing the more captious charges I agreed with them all, as the broken must. Concluding, he said, 'You're pretending, aren't you? To have remorse.'

If not for the belt in the ear I'd have quickly reassured him my misery was authentic, but as I said, I wasn't hearing well. I thought he was asking did I feel bad about the horse.

'Yes, sir,' I said.

He cuffed me again, same ear, and walked back to the men while I knelt in the snow.

They made Lonnie Ford as snug as possible, carrying him into a short thicket and laying him on a bed of gathered juniper. Though unconscious, the rancher had begun to twitch and mutter. When Juval was satisfied Ford wouldn't freeze solid he gathered the others, who checked cinches and spoke unhappily among themselves as they climbed aboard.

Only now did I see they were leaving me with Ford and going on to hunt Davy without me.

'Did you think we'd have you along all the way?' Juval asked. 'We'd have stationed you back with a deputy anyway. Now you'll just have to keep an eye on Ford.' The palomino wheeled about.

Lucky I was muzzy from being hit – more lucid, I might've wept for grief and outrage. As it was all I thought to do was yell, 'What should I do if he wakes up?'

'Tell him a story,' Juval called back, his voice already reduced against the Badlands.

Looking back, though, it was better to be stuck with poor Lonnie Ford than be baby-sat by a deputy. It gave me work. It kept my mind from the aches in head and soul. Every time despair came courting, Mr Ford would moan and thrash. I held his limbs when he dreamed and rebunched his juniper pillow. After a bit he started to shiver. His whole body seemed to contract and stiffen. It was spooky, a skeleton dance, and I wondered what it would be like if Mr Ford died and I had to stay who knew how long beside his body. What if it got dark? What we wanted was a fire.

Which sent me back to the horse. I'd forgotten about him – the poor downed animal lying a few yards away. He was alive though resigned, the side of his belly rising and falling, nothing else moving but his eyes. I opened the accessible saddlebag, for he was lying upon the other, and took out a can of all-purpose oil, a heavy black pouch containing harness and leather-punch and other tools more foreign, also a book called *Old American Houses* with a stained blue dust jacket. At bottom lay a small concave bottle of whiskey, wrapped against concussion in a chambray shirt. For whiskey or against whiskey, you had to admire that bottle. Battered down a hillside, bounced on by a horse – with its swaddling peeled away it lay like an amber ornament in my hand. The red paper seal was unbroken.

The horse sighed heavily. An animal that size gives off so much heat I'd snuggled against its belly. It seemed to like the company, and since Lonnie Ford wasn't making any noise I stayed awhile. I knew the horse should've been shot after the fall. The only reason he wasn't was our nearness to Davy's cabin. Juval wanted to preserve surprise. I tried to brace up. To think of anything besides the likelihood of gun-shots from the hills. We were awfully close – within a mile certainly – and the men had already been gone some time. Half an hour? How long could it take? I imagined Juval quietly issuing his orders, the men spreading out, staying low. Swede had told me how the James gang were ambushed in a farmhouse in exactly this way. My decision to tell Dad everything now lay revealed as foolishness. Swede was right. I was among the disgusting double-crossers of history. I was one of the crumbs. Cole Younger, you will recall, came out of that farmhouse with eleven gunshot wounds. I didn't think Davy could survive eleven gunshot wounds. I hoped he'd come out with his hands up when offered the chance. I hoped Mr Juval would *give* him the chance – I had doubts, despite his promise to Dad. I doubted lawmen in general. Cole Younger was sitting in a kitchen chair, Swede said, reading a newspaper, when so many rifles started popping the house shredded like papier-mâché. Among his other wounds were porcelain shards in arm and face; cup of coffee got shot right out of his hand.

Then I wondered what Davy would think, should he surrender, to see me there with Juval and the rest. Somehow this hadn't entered my thinking till now, but it made up for lost time. In this picture I saw no forgiveness for myself – not from Davy, not from Swede, not from anyone but Dad, who was so forgiving it almost didn't count.

It seemed necessary just then to touch base with the Lord. Shutting my eyes, I leaned into the horse. I prayed in words for a little while – for Davy, of course, and for Mr Ford, whom I could hear making chewing sounds in his sleep, and for my own future, which seemed a boarded-up window – and then language went away and I prayed in a soft high-pitched lament any human listener would've termed a whine. We serve a patient God. In the midst of this came the conviction I hadn't prayed for Martin Andreeson. Nor thought of him since we set out. Nor Jape Waltzer, nor Sara, who were sharing in every way Davy's hazardous morning. I'm afraid I discharged this duty quickly regarding Waltzer. Later I would wish I'd spent more on him particularly. Andreeson, whom I'd despised, now appeared to my mind as he might've to a worried brother. Talk about an unwelcome change. There in the cold, curled against Mr Ford's sighing horse, I repented of hatred in general and especially that cultivated against the putrid fed. A pain started up, as of live coals inside, and like that I knew where he was. Knew, with certainty, why he hadn't come back out of the blizzard. I began to weep. Not only for Andreeson – weeping seems to accompany repentance most times. No wonder. Could you reach deep in yourself to locate that organ containing delusions about your general size in the world – could you lay hold of this and dredge it from your chest and look it over in daylight – well, it's no wonder people would rather not. Tears seem a small enough thing. Thus I cried some, then remembered I still had to pray for Sara. It's mysterious how comfort arrives; for this too should've been full of torment, given her imminent peril. Yet thinking of her calmed my shaken spirit. I imagined her walking with friends in a sunlit park in a small town. Laughing around a supper she had not cooked. I thought of her pleasure in knowing someone like Swede, for whom all the world was an epic poem. Delivered from Waltzer and his conjugal ambitions, who knew what goodness lay in store?

'Otter!' cried Lonnie Ford, in an arid voice.

I scrambled to him – he was twisting around, mashing down the junipers. When he saw me he relaxed, panting, and looked away.

'Aunt otter,' he said. His lips were parted and thick. Between them his tongue lay dry as a toad.

'Just a second.' I ran back to the horse and returned with the whiskey. He didn't like the taste much, and it probably stung, but it restored his enunciation.

'I'm busted up,' he observed.

'Yes, sir.'

'Where'd they all go?'

'After my brother,' I replied.

He shut his eyes at this, in resentment or resignation; he shut his mouth too and tried breathing through his nose, but it was blocked and made only the merest squeal.

'How long ago?'

'An hour maybe.'

'Give me more of that.'

He couldn't use his hands. I had to pour the whiskey in his mouth by capfuls.

'Where's Billy?' he asked, at length.

His horse.

'A little ways – that way. He can't lift up his head, Mr Ford.'

'They didn't shoot him.'

'No, sir.'

He lay thinking about this. 'Those buggers.'

We sat in silence a long time. Remembering Juval's advice I asked Mr Ford if he'd like a story. He'd gone sullen and wouldn't answer. It was hard to blame him. In the end I retrieved the book from his saddlebag, *Old American Houses*, and read aloud from a chapter describing the ruinous attempts of modern citizens to update architecture better left intact. In building for themselves, the book said, many a nineteenth-century workman had indeed built well enough for the ages. It was a pretty good book, I suspect, making the case for honor, but I didn't get to read much, for soon Juval and the rest came trotting back in the blackest of moods. They'd come to the cabin, which lay open and empty with snow drifted in; they'd found no sign of any person save Andreeson, whose felt fedora sat in rumpled condition on the cold stove. In silence Juval presided over the further binding of Lonnie Ford and the construction of a travois by which he could be carried home; then we all mounted, Juval last. He shot the horse Billy through the head, and we got away from there.

The Red Farm

Dad married Roxanna on a wind-blasted Saturday in March. We were back in Roofing, Pastor Reach officiating – I wish I remembered more about it. There was a photographer, a young man with dark wavy hair and enormous energy, setting us here and there, craning through the viewfinder, then popping up to say something amusing. I have one of the photos before me now: Roxanna in lace looking lustrous as a bride ever did; Dad standing calm, his eyes enjoying the commotion; Swede laughing – that photographer was a funny fellow. At Roxanna's elbow stands her father, Mr Cawley, the theater operator. I remember thinking he seemed terribly cautious for someone in such a happy line of work. Perhaps he owned misgivings about his new son-in-law, an unemployed janitor nearly his own age. I'm in the photo also, looking like an old man. Swede, on a recent visit, saw the photo on my desk. 'Look at you,' she said, 'little Methuselah.' Indeed, she'd gotten tall as me. How could I not notice?

We came back to Roofing at the end of February, the ride into the Badlands with Juval having tipped my lungs into steep descent. I won't describe the buried and airless place I seemed to visit. Truth is it's mostly

337

gone from memory, and with my blessing. I can tell you the doctor returned – Nickles – listened with alarm, and insisted on hospitalization, never mind the chance of flu. For a few days, perhaps a week, they braced me up with pillows and adrenaline, then Nickles released me to Dad, saying, You take this boy home.

By now there was no question of Roxanna's not coming. By my release her animals were at a neighboring ranch, a classified ad was in the nearest weekly, and a sign saying CLOSED stood out by the gas pumps. We left before daylight next morning. I recall she betrayed no sadness in parting from the place. She got in the Plymouth, leaned back over the seat to plump blankets around Swede and me, then turned and flounced up beside Dad in a most girlish motion. It then occurred to me that this leaving – which to me ached with failure and despair – was for her the commencement of a gallant endeavor. Who isn't scared by as whole a redirection as that on which she now embarked? Adhering to us must've seemed a risk demanding the deepest reserves of joy and strength. Indeed you'll see shortly how deep hers reached. Glad though I was to have her along, it would be years before my gratitude approached anything like proportion. She settled into the freezing Plymouth, humming a dance tune called 'Queen Anne's Lace.' She opened a thermos of coffee, which steamed in the glow from the dash. She was all but our mother now. I shut my eyes and slept.

We came into Roofing midafternoon as school was letting out. We drove past in silence. Swede and I knew every one of those kids walking home or bunching up in front yards – knew their conversation without hearing it. We passed a parked bus and knew every kid in the windows; yet I slouched in the car, unwilling to be seen. Swede did the same. They all seemed so little changed.

The house was warm and clean, thanks to Dr and Mrs Nokes, whom Dad had telephoned long-distance the previous day. As it happened the Nokeses then boarded Roxanna for a short time – as I recall we were home one week before the wedding – by which time Mr Cawley had made the anxious drive east and Pastor Reach had met Roxanna and been assured of Dad's soundness of mind. I'll keep it quick: after the nearly guestless ceremony, Swede and I also put in a few days at the Nokeses' – Swede writing some verse it embarrassed me to listen to, all about doves in the nest and moonbeams falling on shimmering wheatfields and similar matters, as though something had happened to her mind.

The morning of our return Dad, looking like a man fed on strawberries and cream, asked about my breathing.

'It's okay.'

'Excellent,' he replied. 'You're in charge of cleaning up the Airstream.' Turned out he'd sold it to Dr Nokes, before we ever left – how else could he have paid three months' rent in advance?

'All right,' I said. 'Can Swede help?'

'Nope, I need her inside.' Dad grinned. 'Cheer up, Rube, we're moving today.'

Abruptly we crated our possessions into a borrowed trailer and pulled them seven miles north to a red farm on a hilltop. Unemployed, Dad explained, he could no longer afford town rent. The farm had belonged to Pastor Reach's great-aunt Myrtle, who, I remembered, reluctantly gave up her seat at the organ at the age of 102. Not from sickness, she just couldn't hear. In deepest January she'd given a tea for some neighboring widows, picking them up in her pristine Fairlane and dropping them off again before dark; back home she washed the dishes, read the Bible, wrote in firm script four thank-you letters and a grocery list, and died in her sleep, an end so satisfying it seems displaced in our age. The farm went to Pastor, who'd offered it to us at preposterous rent, at least until Dad found work.

It was a lovely place, the red farm. So called because house, barn, roost, and granary had been painted brick red to the furthest reaches of local memory, the farm seemed a place of order and rest, as the homes of great-aunts often do. The little house crested a meadowed hill rimmed by maple and oak. The barn was tall, with the plain angled roof of barns built farther east; in fact the whole structure lists eastward more now than in 1963, but otherwise appears the same. In coming years the red farm would prove every bit the paradise of work and exploration you might expect, but when we moved in it was a place to rest and to wait.

Because we *were* waiting – all of us, I believe, though my sense of it may have been strongest. The beast in my lungs kept me tied close. I remembered Dr Nickles's inflection when he told Dad to take me home; also the look they exchanged. Swede returned alone to school. Days passed during which I didn't leave the window seat overlooking the meadow. The infirm wait always, and know it.

We waited foremost for word of Davy. With the disappearance of Mr Andreeson, the hunt gained untold federal impetus. For months an irregular stream of investigators came knocking, asking mostly the same questions and once in a while a new one: was Davy especially strong in mathematics? Had he frequented the movies? Had we acquaintances in South America? From the first Dad treated these visitors well, answering all questions transparently, summoning Swede and me on demand and enforcing our honesty – goodness knows what Swede might've sent those fellows chasing, for behind her eyes twitched every shade of herring. From the first Roxanna offered them fragrant breads or pastries and otherwise kept her silence. It is possible to imagine some loving aunt of Butch Cassidy's doing the same. Fresh peach pie can lift a bullying reprobate into apologetic courtesy; I have watched it happen.

Andreeson, by the way, stayed missing. What happened to him is no secret, for I revealed my conviction repeatedly: Waltzer put him in the vein of burning lignite that ran past the cabin. It used to wake me sweating, the truth of it glowing inside my bones. Yet the investigators who listened to the idea seemed to give it little credit, which frustrated me until I complained about it to Swede.

'There's no proving it,' she said shortly. 'There's nothing in it for them,' she added, disappearing before I could grouse further.

Because this, you understand, was something else I was waiting for: Swede's forgiveness.

She wasn't nasty, that wasn't it. There were no more recriminations invoking Benedict Arnold or Ramón Murieta. In fact I came to miss even those. Instead it was as though she simply couldn't think of anything to say to me. Plainly the fact had dawned: as compadres go, I was neither trustworthy nor interesting.

Of course I tried to win her back, using all sorts of bait – wondering aloud whether we might get a horse, now that we lived on a farm, or asking about some adventure of Sunny's. To none of it would she rise. I grew to expect the minimal response. Dad and Roxanna noticed, but what could they do? Swede bore no indignation, called no names. She answered questions. She passed the potatoes.

One night in deep contrition I went to her room and knocked.

'Swede,' said I when she opened the door, 'can't you ever forgive me?'

'Sure,' she replied.

'Well, I wish you would. You act like I'm some old leper.'

'All right – you tell me how to act, and I'll act that way.'

Can a person be both furious and penitent at once? 'Swede, please!'

'You're forgiven,' she said, but in a voice still miles removed, and with eyes still regarding me as an abstract thing.

One thing I wasn't waiting for was a miracle.

I don't like to admit it. Shouldn't that be the last thing you release: the hope that the Lord God, touched in His heart by your particular impasse among all others, will reach down and do that work none else can accomplish – straighten the twist, clear the oozing sore, open the lungs? Who knew better than I that such holy stuff occurs? Who had more reason to hope?

And yet regarding my own wasted passages it seemed a prospect I could no longer admit.

The well appeared dry, for one thing. Though begrudging Roxanna nothing, neither could I recall a single wonder arriving through Dad's hands since we banged on her door that first Sunday. Blanketed in my window seat I puzzled it through, concluding that God, feeling overworked on our behalf, had given us Roxanna as a parting gift – a wonderful one, you understand, just what we'd always wanted, but accompanied by the end of the miraculous. Was it unjust? I'd have thought so once, and not long ago. But these activities – whining about what's fair, begging forgiveness, hoping for a miracle – these demand energy, and that was gone from me. Contentment on the other hand demands little, and I drew more and more into its circle. It seemed good to sleep. My clothes got slack and hangy. Mornings I watched the deer that came up through the hardwoods to paw the snow by the corncrib. Evenings Dad played the guitar, and the hymns and ballads and antique waltzes that emerged from the instrument seemed all the marvels I required.

342

I got a few visitors. Peter Emerson's folks brought him over one day and sat in the kitchen with Dad and Roxanna, while Peter came in with a wrapped box. He told me Superintendent Holden was mean as ever, though not as scary since his face healed up. Peter's little brother Henry had been sent to Holden's office for eating boogers during class, a habit beyond his teacher's ability to curtail. Holden sat Henry on a low chair and told him kids who did this grew into cheats unable to meet the gaze of authority. Some might evade imprisonment but none achieved meaningful rank – you could see adult booger-eaters shuffling through city dumps all over America, salvaging vegetables ignored by vermin. Henry went home weeping to confess his destiny to his brothers, of whom there were three besides Peter, two of them with strong personal resentments against Holden. This next part is like a favorite song. In mere days they located the sleepy den of a skunk family near the railroad tracks. A healthy youngster was selected. I love to imagine Josie, the eldest brother, moving through twilit Roofing toward the Holden residence, the burlapped animal yawning in his arms. Released through a basement window it curled beside the furnace, where it woke in the morning feeling anxious and vengeful. What an awful time for the super-intendent to go downstairs after a winter squash! It took the game warden three days to coax the skunk into a live trap baited with fish heads; by then Holden was living out of a suitcase in Alsop's Motel, wearing, according to Peter, the same undies every day for a week.

After that a present was almost beside the point, but I opened it anyway. It was the Spartacus model – the one with the hand.

'Look, paints,' Peter said.

* * *

In May the Orchards came with a blueberry pie. Bethany carried it in, the first I'd seen her since we made pancakes together. The memory plainly embarrassed her. She wore a dusk-blue dress and rose collar and had ripened to a supremacy that scotched conversation. It wasn't her fault. She asked how Davy was doing, and what it was like riding a horse in the Badlands. I gave it an abbreviated try; how often I'd dreamt of this girl in thrall to my adventures! But I saw that her interest was nominal and engendered by my lousy health; and anyway my voice had become a spare, unpleasant sound. Not a thing I could do about it – despite all chest-beating and operatic gestures it remained like wind through bones.

'Thanks for the pie,' I told Bethany, who fled to the kitchen and the company of grown people.

Now, it may be Swede spied on this most humble talk. Maybe she even had some notion where Bethany had stood inside my untaught thinking. I only know when evening came she slipped under my blanket on the couch, listening to Dad working up some thankful psalm. She sat beside me cross-legged, like a Sioux, and held my hand again, as though we would wait together for whatever was moving toward us through the night. At that moment there was nothing – no valiant history or hopeful future – half worth my sister's pardon. Listening to Dad's guitar, halting yet lovely in the search for phrasing, I thought: Fair is whatever God wants to do.

On a wide purple evening in June, a '41 Ford drove up to the red farm. We were all on the porch and so share this memory among us. The car was covered with pale dust and jounced slowly into the yard as though cresting surf. It came right to the house and stopped. Then Swede squealed and flew off those steps, for Davy was standing from the Ford, laughing and genuine and abruptly powerful before our eyes, scooping Swede up like some wee twerp; and as we knotted round he said, Wait, wait, and the other door opened and Sara also stood out, clearly withholding expectation, one hand atop the car as though she might duck back in. How could she foresee the warmth awaiting? How predict the radiant comfort that was Roxanna's gift? What I remember is clutching my brother's side as we walked up the porch, and Swede's feet scissoring in the air; and I remember a strange melodic sound that was Sara's laugh as she entered the house, and I hoped to hear it more.

And did – much more, as you will see. Though neither of them said Waltzer's name, what had transpired was clear enough to me. The man decided Sara had been his daughter long enough. I could shut my eyes and see him. He wanted a wife.

You think my brother Davy would've let that happen?

So they bolted one morning – just five days previous – in a car Jape had bought off a farmer in a corner of Wyoming, where they landed after fleeing the Badlands. Having no better opportunity than Jape stretching his legs they walked calmly to the Ford, scanned the foothills against detection, 'and motored on out of *that* frying pan,' Davy said, the wicked old maxim evidently not worrying him at the time.

'I thought,' he added, 'maybe Sara could stay with you.'

'Of course, and welcome,' said Roxanna.

'What about you – are *you* staying?' Swede asked Davy; having weaseled onto his lap, she wasn't about to throw him easy ones.

'I can't,' he replied, after a moment. 'You know that, Swede.' He looked, right then, for the first time in years, his age, which was seventeen.

Back home he was our leader again, however briefly. He told us how the night he broke jail he walked to and fro wearing Stube Range's jacket against the

345

freezing rain; how on the edge of town he located a one-ton Chevy with the key in the ignition; how, when he'd climbed in the cab, he glimpsed a police car moving laterally in the rearview mirror, combing a cross street. Shortly more police and county cars entered the vicinity. Davy crouched low in the truck until what seemed a ripe moment, then bobbed upright and turned the ignition, to find it dead.

Swede said, 'Reuben and I would've broke you out if you hadn't beat us to it.'

'Thanks, Swede, I knew you would,' Davy said cheerfully, putting an end to my sudden dread Swede would bring up our silliness with the DeCuellars' steak knives.

With nothing to do but put up Stube's hood and walk, Davy cut across fields, navigating by farmyard lights until a horse nickered to him out of the dark – Nelson Svedvig's mare, you may recall. Encountering barbwire he reached into Stube's front pocket and withdrew a candy bar, a Salted Nut Roll. The horse trotted up without suspicion. It led him to a fence gate. For two days Davy and that horse were best friends.

There followed on demand more details of this sort: of meanders alone or with troubled companions, meals rendered almost mannalike in hard circumstances, narrow spots departed in the nick of time. Three days after leaving August Shultz's he'd stopped at a bakery and been recognized by its grandmotherly proprietor. She gave him four loaves of bread, a bag of currants, and a fruitcake, and admonished him about shopping for groceries in plain daylight. Nights later in an alley in Mandan he fed the fruitcake to a choleric hound, then slid through the back window of a grocery store. Walking the dark aisles he pocketed tins of sardines and deviled ham until every light in the place suddenly snapped on, rendering him briefly sightless, while a door squealed open and slapping footsteps approached. Slapping, that's right; for into view walked a naked fellow, streaming wet, colossal annoyance in his eyes and a baseball bat in his knotty hands: no doubt the store owner, roused from his tub in the residence upstairs. Straight for Davy he pranced, picking up speed, while Davy went leaping away toward the window. Had the man not opted for a late soak my brother's career might've ended on the spot, but wet feet and wood floors make jeopardous allies, and the storekeeper went down in a sensational and profane tangle as Davy's shoulders were clearing the sill. Yes, he went out head first, thumping onto his chest in the alley. Backing out the Studebaker in the truest spirit of retreat he saw the storekeeper arrive at the window upright and purple; the baseball bat came twisting out, snaked over the hood and laid a long silver crack across the windshield.

In all these things Davy was expansive and good at the telling; despite the hour Roxanna served juice, brewed coffee. Yet he mostly kept quiet about Waltzer and the Badlands cabin, out of consideration, it seemed, for Sara. She'd lived with the man for years, after all. She owed him little, but not nothing.

He did allow they'd had a hard scrape getting out of the place. He and Sara had scratched a checkerboard on the dirt floor and were outwaiting a blizzard when Waltzer rode up on Fry. His nostrils were iced, his skin burnt with cold, his eyes prophetic. A vision had come to him out of the snow, a glimpse of horse soldiers. He feared staying put. Following the vein of smoking lignite he'd arrived at a capacious hole in the native sandstone. He brooked no complaint but packed the disbelieving horses and drove them toward this haven at a pace so fast it was nearly a rout. Here they all spent a whole day and more, eating bread from their pockets, sitting until the cold made them stand blanketed beside the animals. The wind died, the sky cleared. Still Waltzer would not let them return. Once they heard a rifle shot far off – a barbed sound, a long decay. Dusk of the second day Waltzer sent Davy to scout. The cabin was full of boot marks, the snow around it sacked with hoof tracks and horse manure.

Not one of us asked about Andreeson, though he lit on my heart, staying there like a guest on the porch you hope will give up and leave.

Sara was asleep in her straight-back chair. It was past eleven. When Dad went upstairs to see about her room, I tagged along.

'It's great, isn't it, Dad?' I asked. The truth is I could've wept, such sadness hung about us. I fought it back. My brother was returned; exultation was called for. Why couldn't we have the fatted calf and tambourines? A little insouciant rejoicing?

'Why, of course it is, Rube. Here, grab the corner,' he added, spreading a spare blanket on Sara's bed. It was chilly, that spare room; we'd kept the door closed until now.

'He seems real good, don't you think?'

'Yes, he does. Yes.' Dad shook up the pillow, leveled the dresser mirror on its pivot, pulled down the windowshade. He wound an old clock on the bedside stand, remarking on the hour.

'Do we have to go to bed, Dad? Can't we stay up?'

He held out his arm toward me and I went and put my head against his chest. He felt strong and thin – I could feel his pulse in my ear. He said, 'Well, of course, stay up – unless Davy wants to sleep. Then we'll let him be, right?'

I nodded. It should have been the best of nights.

Downstairs we found the others subdued as well. Roxanna sleepwalked Sara to bed and turned in also; Dad asked Davy would he rest, and Davy replied no, he'd be going shortly. Repairing to the front room we doused lights and sat in comfort while the moon rode up over the farm. Strangely, we talked little of present quandaries. There was no speculation on Davy's plans. Andreeson hovered but was not mentioned. Davy said he sure liked Roxanna, he was happy for us all. They talked about Sara, where she'd come from, her fears of this revised future; then conversation dove and resurfaced in history, picking up happenings from the great long ago like curiosities from a ruin. Therefore Davy remembered the time, in North Dakota, when a red fox came fearlessly toward us as we lay in a fencerow awaiting geese. It was full daylight and the fox performed stilted circles as it approached. Its head seemed askew. As Davy recalled I stood and would've tottered out to meet this doglike and sorrowful spook, but Dad put me behind his back and shot it. Along these lines, Dad remembered the time he was a boy and a neighboring farmer walked rabid through his yard. This fellow, name of Hensrud, got bit on the ankle by a spring skunk, quit worrying when the wound healed clean, and was taken by fits months later, after harvest. What Dad recalled was Hensrud walking between house and barn, nothing on but a union suit, an early snow curling round him. Poor Hensrud's neck cords stood forth like pump rods. Later that day, gone blind, he stumbled off a bank into the George River to drown – a merciful turn preventing some unlucky neighbor's having to shoot him.

'The Lord protects us,' Dad said.

Davy didn't reply. It was deepest night. I remember his shape in the stuffed chair next the window: clean map of chin and cheekbone, cup of coffee under drifting steam. He was watching the meadow and after some silence rose and stood close to the glass. A herd of deer had come out from a black tangle of trees. They were crossing the meadow, so shapeless at this distance seeing them was an act of faith.

'Well,' Davy said.

Then Swede, desperate to keep him and honor him, begged that he wait; off she ran, returning with her tousled binder. With remarkable bravery she turned on

349

a lamp and read aloud all there was of Sundown, beginning to end. Davy was a better listener than me – he loved it all, Sunny's doleful intervals as well as his triumphs. He wondered over plot, exclaimed at turn of phrase. He was particularly attentive to her treatment of the bandit king Valdez, who he said was exactly right: savage, random, wolflike – and also probably uncatchable, right down through time. Though, he amended quickly, if anyone living were up to the job, Sundown was that man.

We had him till dawn. By then Roxanna had got up and baked her great-uncle's rolls, which Davy ate with energy to be envied, given no sleep; and finishing up we cleared our throats and armored our hearts and stepped out into the sunrise.

Jape Waltzer was sitting beside the granary with a rifle. We didn't see him at first, though he'd not worked hard at concealment. He'd simply picked a spot – in view of the house and shaded from morning sun – and sat still. He'd even entered the barn and retrieved an old straight-back chair to ease the wait.

I am haunted yet by his patience in this business.

Davy was standing by the car, fishing for keys, when Dad fell across the hood, his forehead smacking like an echo of the shot. From the porch I spotted Waltzer sighting through smoke. He fired and the Ford's back-door windows sprayed across the gravel. As Dad skidded off the hood to flop by the front wheel, Roxanna clutched my shoulder and tugged me backward. No one screamed, though the air against my eardrums seemed beaten or flailed. As Roxanna got me to the door I heard Dad murmuring, broke her hold, and flung down off the porch.

I suppose Jape led me, like a flaring goose.

What I recall isn't pain but a sense of jarring reversal, as of all motion, sound, and light encountering their massive opposites. I felt grass and dirt against my cheek, and sorrow that Dad was shot, and confusion that I couldn't reach him.

Here my terrestial witness fails.

I shut my eyes, the old *morte* settled its grip, and the next country gathered itself under my feet.

Be Jubilant, My Feet

I waded ashore with measureless relief. Stay with me now. The bank was an even slope of waving knee-high grasses, and I came up into them and turned to look back. It was a wide river, mistakable for a lake or even an ocean unless you'd been wading and knew its current. Somehow I'd crossed it and somehow was unsurprised at having done so. Near the shore the water appeared gold as on your favorite river at sunup, but farther out it turned to sky and cobalt and finally a kind of night in which the opposite shore lay hidden.

At that moment I had no notion of identity. Nor of burden. I laughed in place of language. The meadow hummed as though thick with the nests of waking creatures, and the grasses were canyon colored, lifting their heads as I passed. Moving up from the river the humming began to swell – it was magnetic, a sound uncurling into song and light and even a scent, which was like earth, and I must've then entered the region of nests, for up scattered finches and cheeky longspurs and every sort of bunting and bobolink and piebald tanger. All these rose with sweet chaotic calls, whirling and resettling to the grass. More placid, butterflies clung everywhere to stems – some you would know, the monarchs and tailed lunas, but others of such spread and hue as to have long disappeared from the gardens of the world. The meadow was layered with flight. In fact it seemed there was nothing that couldn't take wing. Seized with conviction I spread my arms and ran for it. Nope, no liftoff – but I came close! At times my feet were only brushing the ground.

But I was drawn on. Conscious now that something needed doing, I moved ever higher on the land, here entering an orchard of immense and archaic beauty. I say orchard: the trees were dense in one place, scattered in another, as though planted by random throw, but all were heavy trunked and capaciously limbed, and they were fruit trees, every one of them. Apples, gold-skinned apricots, immaculate pears. The leaves about them were thick and cool and stirred at my approach; touched with a finger, they imparted a palpable rhythm.

It took a long while to traverse the orchard. I began to feel hungry but didn't pause; though all this fruit appeared perfectly available, I felt prodded to appear before the master. The place had a master! Realizing this, I knew he was already aware of me – comforting and fearful knowledge. Still I wanted to see him. The farther I went the more I seemed to know or remember about him – the way he'd planted this orchard, walking over the hills, casting seed from his hand. I kept moving.

And for how long? As we measure time, perhaps for weeks; but no sun shines in that sky, so days do not pass; as for the light, it seems a work of the air itself, and of all things illumined by it. Also, as many a prescient hymn suggests, a person doesn't get tired there. I walked faster, pressing ahead as if obeying a beloved command. I weaved amid curlyhorn antelope and bison browsing fruit from the lower branches; through an enormous unwary herd of horses pulling up clover and bluegrass.

Here in the orchard I had a glimmer of origin: *Adam*, I thought. Only the bare word. It suggested nothing. It was but a pair of syllables that seemed to belong to me. They seemed part of what compelled me. And now, far to my right across a valley, I saw a man afoot. His skin was dark and he wore the buckler and helm of a Spanish knight, and over his shoulder he carried a flag of arcane device. Though battered in appearance the man moved with spirit. He was like one going to his king, having served to his deepest ability. He was almost running.

And now, from beneath the audible, came a low reverberation. It came up through the soles of my feet. I stood still while it hummed upward bone by bone. There is no adequate simile. The pulse of the country worked through my body until I recognized it as music. As language. And the language ran everywhere inside me, like blood; and for feeling, it was as if through time I had been made of earth or mud or other insensate matter. Like a rhyme learned in antiquity a verse blazed to mind: *O be quick, my soul, to answer Him; be jubilant, my feet!* And sure enough my soul leapt dancing inside my chest, and my feet sprang up and sped me forward, and the sense came to me of undergoing creation, as the land and the trees and the beasts of the orchard had done some long time before. And the pulse of the country came around me, as of voices lifted at great distance, and moved through me as I ran until the words came clear, and I sang with them a beautiful and curious chant.

And now the orchard ended, and a plain reached far ahead to a range of blanched mountains. A stream coursed through this plain, of different personality and purpose than the earlier wide river. A narrow, raucous stream, it flowed upward against the gradient, and mighty fish arched and swam in it, flinging manes of spray. I meant to jump in – wherever this river went I wanted to go – and would've done so had not another figure appeared, running beside the water.

A man in pants. Flapping colorless pants and a shirt, dismal things most strange in this place. He was running upslope by the boisterous stream. Despite the clothes his face was incandescent, and when he saw me he wheeled his arms and came on ever faster. Then history entered me – my own and all the rest of it, more than I could hold, history like a heavy rain – so I knew the man coming along was my father, Jeremiah Land; and all that had happened, himself slipping down the hood of the Ford, Roxanna's hard grip on my shoulder, the air drumming in my ears like bird wings, came back like a mournful story told from ancient days.

He was beside me in moments, stretching out his hands. What cabled strength! I remember wondering what those arms were made for – no mere reward, they had design in them. They had some work to set about. Meantime Dad was laughing – at my arms, which were similarly strong! He sang out, *You're as big as me!* How had I not noticed? We were like two friends, and I saw he was proud of me, that he knew me better than he'd ever thought to and was not dismayed by the knowledge; and even as I wondered at his ageless face, so clear and at home, his eyes owned up to some small regret, for he knew a thing I didn't.

Let's run, he said. It's true both of us were wild to go on. I tell you there is no one who compels as does the master of that country – although badly as I wanted to see him, Dad must've wanted to more, for he shot ahead like a man who sees all that pleases him most stacked beside the finish. I could only be awed at his speed, which was no effort for him; indeed he held back so that we traveled together, he sometimes reaching for my hand, as he'd done a thousand times in the past; and the music and living language swept us forth across the plains until the mountains lay ahead, and up we climbed at a run.

Is it fair to say that country is more real than ours? That its stone is harder, its water more drenching – that the weather itself is alert and not just background? Can you endure a witness to its tactile presence?

We attained a pass where the stream sang louder than ever, for it swelled with depth and energy the farther it rose. Dad reached it first; I saw him mount a shelf of spraysoaked stone and stand waiting for me, backlit, silverlined, as though the sky had a sun after all and it was just beyond this mountain.

But it wasn't a sun. It was a city.

Joining Dad on the rock I saw it, at a farther distance than any yet conceived; still it threw light and warmth our sun could only covet. And unlike the sun, you could look straight into it – in fact you wished to, you *had* to – and the longer you looked, the more you saw.

Turrets! I exclaimed. I couldn't wait to get there, you see.

Then Dad pointed to the plains below, at movement I took at first to be rivers – winding, flowing, light coming off them. They came from all directions, streaming toward the city, and dust rose in places along their banks.

They're people, Dad said. And looking again, looking harder, I could see them on the march, pouring forth from vast distances: people like I'd seen everywhere and others like I'd not seen, whole tributaries of people with untamed faces you would fear as neighbors; and most were afoot, and a few were horseback, and many bore standards with emblems strange to me. And even these who were wild were singing a hymn that rose up to us on the mountain, and it was as though they marched in preparation for some imminent and joyous and sanctified war.

We listened a long time. Dad held my hand, and I felt the music growing in his fingers.

Take care of Swede, he said.

From this pass the stream threw itself over a sheer face, where mist drifted up and was struck gold by the light of the city.

Work for Roxanna, Dad told me.

Now I saw the stream regrouped below, flowing on through what might've been vineyards, pastures, orchards bigger than that described. It flowed between and alongside the rivers of people; from here it was no more than a silver wire winding toward the city, yet I made out the clean glitter of rising fish upon its surface.

I thought, Lord, can't I be among them? Can't I come in too?

Tell Davy, Dad said. He sat down on the rock and swung his feet in the stream – it was deep and swift; it would take him in a moment. I seized his arm.

Please, I said.

Soon, he replied, which makes better sense under the rules of that country than ours. *Very soon!* he added, clasping my hands; then, unable to keep from laughing, he pushed off from the rock like a boy going for the first cold swim of spring; and the current got him. The stream was singing aloud, and I heard him singing with it until he dropped away over the edge.

The Curious Music That I Hear

The excitement didn't quit while I was away: Jape Waltzer fired three more unhurried rounds at the Ford, where Davy was burrowed in the backseat. He also plugged the house a few times – five times, according to Swede's obsessive reconstructions. Four loads blew windows all over the main floor and a bed upstairs, which pretty well discouraged peeking, and one came straight through the wall into the living room, where it smacked a brass pony given Swede by a former teacher. Amid this ruin Roxanna called the sheriff, Dr Nokes, and the Lord, doubtless in the opposite order, and shouted at the girls to stay down. Later she would find Sara concealed under blankets in a cedar chest dusted with burst glass, but Swede was busy ripping Dad's closet half to shreds, hunting his shotgun. She found it, but no shells. By then all was quiet. She joined Roxanna and they opened the front door. The Ford was gone and Davy with it. Waltzer's chair lay tipped in the shade beside the barn.

Dad was propped on an elbow on the gravel, bleeding abundantly from a hole in his right side.

I was on my face in the lee of the porch.

Here's what I've been told of the next few minutes. Roxanna attended to Dad while Swede pushed me over and explored for heartbeats. Nine years old, kneeling in blood and foam, she grabbed my wrist, my neck; she felt the big dripping cave of my chest. I'm sorry still for what this must've cost her. Dad, tired but lucid, told Roxanna to quit stanching the hole in his side; when she pressed too hard he couldn't breathe. Let it flow, he told her. Let the blood wash it clean. It put Roxanna in an awful bind, for she saw the wound better than he did – its neat bird's-eye entry and gaping egress. She knew he might shortly bleed dry. She has told me how she prayed aloud while wrapping her fist in her dress and jamming it in that wound; she did her best, I know it, for a great long time, Dad coming in and out the while. Then the sound of Swede crying registered on Dad, and she went to him covered in pink froth so that he started up, thinking she was dying; but she told him it was me, I wasn't breathing, or answering, or blinking my eyes. And right about here Dr Nokes drove up; I imagine his big car bottoming out in our bumpy yard, a train of blue smoke behind.

His best turned out to be no better than Roxanna's. Ascertaining that I was gone – for my lungshot chest no longer bled, no rhythm moved anywhere, and I lay cooling under his hands – Dr Nokes turned to Dad, who looked him over without evident recognition and rolled up his eyes. By the time a county car rolled in, and a second behind it, there was, Roxanna tells me, an atmosphere of crystalline despair in which the doctor broke and sobbed. Through this scene stepped the sheriff and a speechless deputy, over their heads for certain; yet before an official word was spoken the deputy, Galen Max, yipped, 'Look there!' For I had bucked suddenly, as though kicked in the back. 'He done it again!' yelped Galen Max; and then, reports Swede, I was seized with coughing, and blood and water spouted from my mouth and nose – sorry for the detail, but it's quite glorious to me – and Dr Nokes bolted to my side and set about my recovery in a sort of delirium. It was hardly the first time I'd come awake to someone whacking my back, but it seemed a wholly new experience and one I'd come a great distance to try.

'I don't know what you were using to breathe,' Dr Nokes told me.

It was some weeks later, and he was beside my bed at the red farm.

'Not your lungs,' he declared.

At first I didn't know what he meant; my lungs felt as large and light as a May afternoon. They felt like they had in the next country, as I ran up through the orchard – except over there I hadn't given them a thought. Back here I woke each morning to the shock of perfect breathing. Had I opened my mouth and spoken Portuguese, the surprise couldn't have been more complete.

'Look,' I told Dr Nokes, inhaling an unbelievable quantity of air. It went right in!

'Yes, yes – leave some for the rest of us.'

For weeks there wasn't a day Dr Nokes didn't come by. Though professing worry over the chance of infection or of some undissolved clot cruising my arteries, he came for other reasons also. He came so we could miss Dad together, all of us, and he came because of my lungs, which posed a mystery.

One day he said, 'Your father should not have died, Reuben. Did you know that?'

I nodded, but he said, 'Not just because it's terrible to be without him, though God knows—' and here Dr Nokes seemed to slip, somewhere in his mind, then catch himself. 'I mean, injured where he was. I examined him, you know. No organs were damaged. Blood vessels, yes. But he actually shouldn't have died.'

And I, conversely, shouldn't have lived. Though I sensed this was the case, it was only years later Dr

Nokes would explain why in detail. His forebearance is to his credit. What eleven-year-old should be told that his lungs only recently lay in literal shreds inside his central cavity? Dr Nokes saw this fact with his two eyes. He felt it with his fingers. Yet mere hours later it was revealed at the hospital in Montrose that my lungs had not only endured an explosive chest wound but, in fact, seemed none the worse for wear. In fact, reported a perplexed emergency-room physician, it was as though they hadn't been touched.

Of course they had been touched; that was the very point.

Goodness, I miss Dad.

But here, let me finish quickly. Swede, who would know, says drift is the bane of epilogues. You should know that Roxanna, married to Jeremiah Land three months before he died, became as much our rock as though God Himself had placed her beneath our lives. Certainly her sacrifice was no less than Dad's. Who could've poured more courage into us? Who could've given as selflessly as she? For we were a demanding crew. Sara herself could've emptied the stores of a dozen wise parents. Oh, yes – Sara stayed with us, though at a distance she'd acquired from living with Waltzer. To begin with, it was rare to hear Sara join more than three sentences; though when she did, Swede pointed out, it was clear she would make a fine newspaper editorialist were she so inclined. For many months none but Roxanna closed the distance, and she on tiptoe; as for me, I mostly left Sara alone, admiring her strengths from across the family. A practiced eavesdropper, I'd not have listened to her talks with Roxanna for any reward; though I did overhear a visit or two with lovestruck town boys, in which she babbled with forged conviction about classmates, teachers, and popular music, so it's not as if I believed we had an angel on our hands.

Swede, whom you know reasonably well by now, quit school in frustration at seventeen to write a novel. It didn't publish, much to her later relief, but won her a sort of watchful uncle at a venerable New York publishing house. Now – after four novels, a history of the Dakota Territories, and a collection of poetry – she gets adoring letters from strangers. Her poetry book is flat-out perfect. It all rhymes! One ballad seems inspired by my own somewhat unique future. (My favorite lines: *Drat, thought dying Lazarus, / This part again.*) Others, yes, involve cowboys. Reviewers could only gape. One wrote that Swede was 'setting verse back a century,' and 'mining ground long ago found barren'; he called the book a 'blazing song of innocence.' His was not the only review of its kind, but it was the one that vexed Swede. Against writerly protocol she returned fire, writing the reviewer a long and personal critique impugning his education, prose, honor, and masculinity. *You poor man*, it started, proceeding in such readable fashion the periodical printed it whole, along with the reviewer's aghast rebuttal. There followed three or four additional exchanges, revealing my sister as the better wit, 'though flawed,' she admitted to me with a rueful spark, 'in the humility department.' Incidentally this public feud impelled Swede's poetry onto several best-seller lists – alien surroundings for rhyming verse.

You should know that Jape Waltzer proved as uncatchable as Swede's own Valdez. No doubt he went on to mischief elsewhere. Well: the farther elsewhere the better. Maybe he's dead, prancing across some pockmarked landscape trying to keep the flames off, or maybe he's just old, and a more sulfurous poison than before. Maybe he's even old and repentant. Anything is possible. I only know he is apart from us and that, as Mr Stevenson wrote of Long John, we're pleased to be quit of him.

You should know that Andreeson did indeed perish

in the Badlands, and that it was Waltzer who bludgeoned him and rolled his poor corpse into the lignite to hiss. Having this information from Davy I could hardly volunteer it officially, but there came a day when a couple in late middle age drove up to the red farm. The man came knocking, his wife stayed in the car. He had Andreeson's high forehead but none of his confidence. We sat on the porch awhile. I was twenty-five then and far too young to impart the kind of comfort these people sought. The aimlessness and sorrow in their steps would make a terribly long story, but that is another's book to write, another person's witness.

Finally, you should know this. One Thanksgiving we were all of us home, all but Davy. Swede had returned from a writing residency in Wyoming, Sara from nursing in St Paul; I was working for a carpenter in Roofing, putting up Sheetrock and a little proud of my big shoulders. We held hands round the table for a prayer of gratitude. When Roxanna reached Amen, Swede released my left hand, but Sara held on to my right.

Or maybe it was I who didn't let go.

And Davy? Listen: there's a small town in Canada, a prairie town. A place along the broad North American flyway where in autumn the geese move through by the hundreds of thousands. Since August Shultz died – following Birdie by two hard winters – I've gone north to witness that migration. The glory of a single Canada goose gliding in, trimming its angles this way and that, so close you can feel the pressure of its wing-beats – multiply this by 10,000 or 20,000 across a morning, and you too might begin creeping into frozen rockpiles before dawn. In any case, once I rose in the small hours and walked down from my rented bed to a pine-bench cafe, which in season is full of hunters sociably forking down eggs by five in the morning. Outside, leaves beat past in a wet wind. What I wanted was pancakes and sausage, so I ordered and took a clean cup and helped myself to coffee.

Davy came in the door before my short stack arrived. He wore a down jacket and new lace-up boots. At last, some decent gloves. He sat down. 'You hunting alone, Rube?'

It's not the easiest way to keep up with your brother. Some years he coasts into that town in my shadow – he's the next man in the cafe, the voice behind me at the gas station. Some years he doesn't show at all. Exile has its hollow hours. Some years I've noticed odd tilts in his speech. No doubt he has lived among accents, I hope in pleasant places, but he tells me painfully little. He asks and asks.

So I give him the news. He reads all of Swede's work; he sends regards and comments. It drives her wild that he never appears in the midst of what *she's* doing, but she knows he's crazy about her. Twice Swede has accompanied me, hoping to see him, neither time with success.

Possibly he dreads what she might ask of him.

'You got awfully big,' he told me, that first morning, in the cafe.

So I told him what happened – about my foray into the next country, and Dad catching up with me there.

Belief is a hard thing to gauge where Davy is concerned.

'And he sent you back?'

I told him Dad didn't exactly send me, but that I could go no farther. That it seemed a transaction had taken place on my behalf.

'Breathe,' Davy said. 'Let's see you breathe.'

Well, that was the easy part. Harder was describing that land itself: its upward-running river, its people on the move and ground astir with song. For just as that music stays outside the pattern I would give it, so does my telling fall pitifully short of what the place is. What mortal creations are language and memory! And so I sound like a man making the most marginal sense – as if I were describing one of those dreams that seemed so genuine at the time.

'Don't you ever doubt it?' Davy asked.

And in fact I have. And perhaps will again. But here is what happens. I look out the window at the red farm – for here we live, Sara and I, in a new house across the meadow, a house built by capable arms and open lungs and joyous sweat. Maybe I see our daughter, home from school, picking plums or apples for Roxanna; maybe one of our sons, reading on the grass or painting an upended canoe. Or maybe Sara comes into the room – my darling Sara – with Mr Cassidy's beloved rolls on a steaming plate. Then I breathe deeply, and certainty enters into me like light, like a piece of science, and curious music seems to hum inside my fingers.

Is there a single person on whom I can press belief? No, sir.

All I can do is say, Here's how it went. Here's what I saw.

I've been there and am going back.

Make of it what you will.

THE END

Acknowledgments

I'm grateful first to my parents: Don Enger, who like Teddy Roosevelt believes in the strenuous life and in vivid narration; and Wilma Enger, who read us Robert Louis Stevenson before we could talk, and who writes better letters than anyone since the Apostle Paul. Both grew up in North Dakota and built into their children a westerly tilt and a love of wide places.

Lee, my oldest brother, and my sister, Lizabeth, have bolstered me without condition and given me examples of courage, steadfastness, and the pursuit of adventure. My brother Lin has spent years with me in the trenches of writing discipline and has gently taught me more of the craft than anyone else.

Thanks are also due to my editors at Minnesota Public Radio, who sliced away my adjectives for all those years and became my friends. Rachel Reabe and Mike Edgerly read early drafts; their encouragement was salt and light.

It's my pleasure to work with Paul Cirone, who, flanked by the brilliant crew at the Aaron Priest Agency, has been tireless in bringing this book to an audience. Elisabeth Schmitz made me welcome at Grove/Atlantic from the first day; she edited these pages with surpassing insight, humor, and joy in the work.

At last, this book arose from family. My wife Robin heard every sentence aloud – openhanded with praise, she also recognized before I did when something went amiss. And without the attentive ears and irresistible ideas of our sons, Ty and John, poor Reuben would've been dull as a plank, and Sunny Sundown would've never saddled up.